Sweetfeed

SWEETFEED

BY R. AUSTIN HEALY

Marshall Jones Company
Publishers Since 1902
Manchester Center, Vermont

Marshall Jones Company
Manchester Center, Vermont
© 1996, R. Austin Healy. All rights reserved.
Library of Congress Card Catalog Number 96-75857
I.S.B.N. 0-8338-0230-5

PRINTED IN THE UNITED STATES OF AMERICA

Also By R. Austin Healy:
The Ninth Race

For my children
Richard, Jr., James, Patricia, Catherine, Maureen and Christine
And my wife, Joan
With Love.

CONTENTS

PROLOGUE

It was August 1988, on the grounds of Clearwater, the great Ostrander Estate overlooking the Hudson River at Schuylerville, New York, that a select group of music and horse lovers had gathered for a benefit concert by members of the Philadelphia Orchestra. Hostess for the evening was Meredith White Ostrander, widow of airline magnate, Houston Ostrander, a man who in his lifetime dabbled in Thoroughbred horse racing as a hobby, but whose seventy-year-old widow made it her passion when he was gone. So much so, that she built a series of elaborate barns on the five-thousand-acre estate, Clearwater, owing to the fact that it was but a few miles from the Saratoga Race Course, her favorite among race tracks.

The cream of Saratoga's August society was on hand. Mansions from Palm Beach, Florida, to Santa Barbara, California, and a dozen other rich conclaves were left to caretakers so their sparkling owners could attend Saratoga's annual racing scene. The Ostrander affair was high on the annual social calendar, attracting, along with its celebrated guest list, an army of media persons. It was a revolving door of who's who. No newspaper, magazine, or TV station of worth would dare miss Meredith Ostrander's grand party.

Old Houston Ostrander had hand picked the site for his estate some twenty years earlier. He avoided other sites nearer Saratoga proper because he wanted to distance himself from the heavy August tourist traffic yet still be within reasonable driving range of Saratoga. Besides, he was a conservative man and demanded complete privacy when times called for it. Thick lines of deep-green pine trees lined the riverbank when Houston was alive, hiding the mansion's view of the river, which elbowed just where the property line began on the north end and turned slightly eastward on the southern end. Meredith Ostrander, when asked by friends just how much river frontage they had, generally replied, "I just don't know. Someday I'll have it surveyed again." Meredith, always enraptured by rivers, had the pines cut down and replaced with lower hedges, so that now from just about anywhere near the mansion one could view the river. She felt it was especially beautiful at night when the moon reflected off its historic waters. She was fond of telling guests that part of the estate was a Revolutionary War camping grounds for some of General Schuyler's troops. Besides, her beloved Houston discovered that he had ancestral ties to the Schuyler family. Stately and youthful-looking for her age, Meredith Ostrander still had thick, curly, red hair with not a single strand of gray to be found. Her agelessness was the envy of her female peers, most of whom looked old enough to be her mother. But she had a soft socializing way that made most everyone love her. Men, young, old, and married, found her fascinating. There was a steady stream of eligible suitors following Houston's death. Meredith was encouraged by her very close friends to seriously consider marriage. However, she elected to stay single and be content with summers in Schuylerville and Saratoga and winters in Palm Beach. She'd made up her mind long ago that getting married after seventy, for the sake of getting married, was ridiculous. Besides, where would she ever find anyone as romantic and exciting as her late, beloved Houston?

This evening's musical treat featured violin concertos of Beethoven and Mendelssohn, with guest soloist, Max Freeman, known for his fiery and passionate playing. Later in the presentation the orchestra would play a short version of Bernstein's *West Side Story*. To showcase the grand musical gathering, Meredith had a series of small benches arranged in amphitheater style down on the huge, sprawling, manicured lawn near the riverbank. Twinkling lights had been strung all along the bank, through surrounding tree limbs, along the approaching driveway. And even on the mansion itself. It was a perfect background set against a star-studded sky and the ever beautiful Hudson. It would be, as Meredith Ostrander wished it, an evening to remember. Let others have their gatherings and parties. The Clearwater affair would be the benchmark of the Saratoga season, that was for sure.

It took two hours to direct all the traffic to the outer parking spaces, which were set near the horse barns on a flat stretch of pasture land. As always, Meredith provided valet parking. A college student parking cars at Clearwater on this evening could pocket $100 in tips. Not to mention that all the workers on hand got to see the celebrities while also observing the concert and post-concert festivities.

If you stood this very evening at the top of Clearwater, near the brick stairs that descended from the mansion to the outer gardens that led down to the riverbank, the sight was a flowing parade of women in lace and satin evening dresses and men in formal wear. All the gold, diamonds, and precious stones shone like the night's full array of August stars against a lavender backdrop, with the river's equally sparkling reflections adding to the pageantry.

One of the last arrivals of the evening, chauffeured in a gleaming, highly-polished Bentley, was former prima ballerina, Claire Valova, indisputably Meredith Ostrander's main Saratoga social rival, though both had learned long ago that to live and let live was a much wiser course to follow. Their battlefield, like those of many other rivals in Saratoga's August, consisted of winning over the elite crowd by tossing the biggest and best parties. Let their audiences be the judge.

The only advantage Meredith Ostrander had at this point in the racing season was that she was firing the first volley. Claire Valova's counterfire, however, would be well heard in mid-August when her first of three annual bashes got underway.

Carlos Mann, in charge of Clearwater's horse barns since they were built, rubbed his weary forehead of sixty-six years and watched, as he had done for more years than he could remember, the steady flow of cars and stellar people. He could not help but notice that Claire Valova's arrival sparked the crowd up. With heads turning in all directions, she first met Meredith Ostrander at the entrance and then gracefully made her way to the cocktail tables near the river where she wove in and out of the various groups. Yes, Carlos was admiring her too. She had such a way with people. Not that his boss, Meredith, didn't. It was just a different style. Meredith had more money, that was for sure, but Valova had that unmistakable, unrivaled charm. Carlos made sure the Bentley was parked near the far end of the pasture, near the exit, so Valova could depart without undue hesitation, as she often did at affairs like this. The fact that he had to depart from his role as master of the barns and expensive horses to administer to the parking of cars on this evening wasn't exactly to his liking. But Meredith didn't trust any other of her employees to undertake this task, so he was chosen. Meredith, however, always rewarded him handsomely for these extra duties. Carlos over the years had also observed that strong social rivals had their own code of quirky rules. You weren't supposed to upstage the hostess, especially when the hostess for the evening and the strong rival were both widows.

As early evening darkness finally fell over Clearwater, the guests were eventually seated for the evening's performance. Conversation stopped and, with the anticipation of the orchestra's appearance, a hush came over the glittering assemblage. Then Meredith Ostrander stood up and introduced Maestro Alex Field, who in turn introduced Max Freeman, and momentarily, the overture to Felix Mendelssohn's Italian Symphony filled the night, as if the music had come out of the depths of the river itself, traveled up the sprawling lawn to the mansion and was clearly heard by Carlos Mann, the lone guard to the dozens of horses stalled some two-hundred yards from the river's edge. All the elegance and charm of Mendelssohn's creative genius was heard throughout the Schuylerville hills, wrapping around each bend of the Hudson, carried on the warm August breeze that swept across Clearwater. Marvelous, magical music to soothe the soul and enlighten one's spirit. Yes, Meredith Ostrander knew how to throw a party.

It went on for half an hour, though it seemed but ten minutes to some. When it ended, they stood and clapped their approval. There was a short intermission at which time a dozen waiters, wearing white gloves, scurried through the amphitheater with magnums of champagne, filling up empty glasses. One thing for certain at any function Meredith Ostrander was involved in was that no one would go dry. Keep the party lively and keep the booze flowing. She'd have it no other way.

The presentation resumed with Ludwig van Beethoven's *Diabelli Variations,* delivered this time by a newcomer from Europe, Wallace Strauss, playing a harpsichord. The audience sat spellbound by the melodic sound. Again the music drifted on the warm air to Carlos Mann, now resting on his cot in a small cottage, most of the cars now parked, at the extreme end of the barns. Still he could hear every note as clear as a church bell.

The solitary figure who rose to her feet in the middle of Strauss' dramatic presentation and, barely noticed, made her way to the edges of the lawn where the large, neatly-cut hedges separated the manicured lawn from the scrub grass portion of Clearwater, was none other than Claire Valova. One or two who saw her leave assumed she was probably going to the ladies' room. Though one, William Squires, a Saratoga neighbor of Valova, figured she was leaving for the evening because she took her shawl with her. Or perhaps she was just going off for a cigarette.

Somewhere into the second or third movement of *Variations,* Carlos Mann, listening intently to the music, was interrupted by a crackling sound. It was a faint crackling at first, with pauses, then more crackling. It actually sounded to Carlos like kindling wood burning, the kind that snaps and crackles as it burns with more intensity. After having overseen the parking of the cars and making sure the guests were all there, he felt tired so he had undressed and gone to rest on the cot. Now he had on only his shorts and socks. He got up and looked out of the open cottage bedroom window. It was dark, save for some small lights on the fence where the last barn, No. 20, was located. He listened again. No crackling. Just Beethoven's music drifting across the pasture. He went back and lay down. Officially, he was on duty, so he couldn't dare fall asleep. But he knew from past parties that it would be a long night and his body needed the rest even if sleep wasn't possible.

He put one hand behind his head and stared up through the window at the zillion stars in the black sky. And he marveled at the beauty of it all. Beethoven's music and the wondrous stars. Could life offer a person anything more rewarding?

He closed his eyes for a moment. When he reopened them, the stars were gone and a hazy cloud blurred his sight. Then he smelled smoke. For a long minute he remained seemingly glued to his cot, unable to lift himself up to investigate the sudden change in conditions outside. His cot suddenly began to rock and he heard pounding outside. Then a flash in the sky, followed by a puff of rising white smoke. And all the time Beethoven's *Diabelli Variations* was plainly heard coming from the riverbank. More pounding about the cottage. He jerked himself up and peered out the window. In that instant, his heart sank in his chest. For as far as he could see flames were sweeping the barns. It was an inferno, with sparks and cinders shooting into the night sky and fiery balls falling everywhere. Carlos was numbed by the sight.

He ran outside, only to be met by several horses stampeding by his dwelling. He was forced back by the withering heat. Through the clouds of smoke and fire more horses, broken loose from their stalls, which had either collapsed or burned down, ran in all directions. The smell of their burning flesh was strong in his nostrils. He saw smoke one moment and then a burst of flames a second later. It was a weird assortment of small fires in one direction and large, shooting flames in the other. And then he heard a series of loud cracks, as if someone was firing a shotgun. This was followed by windows shattering. Then the loud cracks again. It was, he realized, bricks exploding. All the neatly placed rows of red brick that lined the entrance and exit to the barns were exploding under the intense heat.

Caught up in the horror of it all, Carlos had forgotten all about the guests gathered on the lawn for the concert. Fire and penetrating heat prevented him from going straight to the mansion, so he moved to the rear of the cottage, which had not yet caught fire, and proceeded on a southwesterly course, which he knew would lead him to the upper hedges and eventually to the lawn area. But as he started in that direction, a wall of cinders, carried on the strong wind that was now created by the intense heat, forced him back. So Carlos, his face red hot from the inferno about him, retreated toward the woods to the east. And all the time he could hear the screeching of the horses still trapped in some of the barns that had not yet completely burned. It was the hell on earth that Carlos remembered in a painting he had seen. Scary words from ancient scriptures that told of the earth's ending. All types of visions and thoughts raced through his mind in the unimaginable predicament.

Then the worst of all nightmares began. Flames began consuming the cars, igniting the fences and trees nearby, and pushing its intense heat toward the mansion and lawn area where the guests sat listening to the music, unaware of the horror taking place way up on the hill. Swirling clouds of thick, dark smoke were making it impossible for Carlos to breathe. He cupped his hand over his mouth and backed away in disbelief. The wind velocity picked up again and existing oxygen was depleted from the area near the barns so that the earth itself burst into flames. The flames twisted and curled skyward in long shoots of red, orange, and purple. Carlos couldn't even warn the guests. He was trapped in an area that had but one escape, and that was toward the deep woods to the rear, hopefully before the flames reached that portion of the property. As he painstakingly made his way to the woods, he suddenly saw the faint outline of a woman in a long evening dress coming in his direction. She was not running, but walking at a steady pace, as if indifferent to the pending doom that awaited anyone or anything in the fire's way. There was so much fire and smoke he couldn't tell who it was, but plainly saw her diamond necklace at a distance of some twenty yards, for the fire was reflecting off its brilliant stones. That's about all he could see in the din of the inferno.

At about ten yards from where Carlos was standing, the figure turned and walked toward the same woods that he had in mind for his escape path. He yelled out to her, but got no response. A sweep of strong wind and flames lit up the area in that moment and Carlos, for a split second, saw the mystery figure. My God, he realized, it's Claire Valova. "Stop! Stop!" He called to her. "Follow me. I'll get you out safely." Still she continued on. He ran in her direction, then stumbled over a rock. His face and upper body slammed down hard on the heated earth. When at last he was able to pick up his head, she was no longer in sight. He could only assume that she had made it to the woods safely. "Thank the Lord for that," he said aloud, his voice almost lost in the rushing wind.

Now he heard a series of explosions: starting near the point where the first cars had been parked in long lines nearest the mansion, and quickly exploding in his direction. Like giant bombs going off, one after the other the expensive carriages of the rich, engulfed in fiercely intense

heat, blew apart, doors and windows shattering and flying in all directions. Full gas tanks fueled the out-of-control flames and the noise of
each one, caught in the updraft from burning grass and hay, was deaf-
ening. One of the first vehicles to burn up was Claire Valova's Bentley.
And the terrible noise continued as dozens upon dozens of custom-built
limousines were blazed to oblivion.

Carlos was now near the tall trees of the thick woods where he could
get some rest from the piercing heat. Still, it was very hot and the air was
thick with smoke and all sorts of distasteful burning smells. He climbed
up on a limb and peered down the slope to where the orchestra had been
playing. From this vantage point he could now see the whole lower area,
all the way to the river's edge. The hundreds of string lights were still lit,
and someone apparently had turned on some of the special outside
lights that had been installed throughout the area just a year earlier. The
sight Carlos saw was one of men and women running in panic. Most of
them to the river, where he could make out several actually in the water.
He wasn't sure just how long the fire had been burning, but guessed it
must have been twenty minutes or so. The fire's speed had been swift
and deadly. By this time a neighbor had sent out an all-points alarm and
while the fire raged on, volunteer fire companies in Schuylerville and
other neighboring towns were already scrambling to their firetrucks to
respond. A half hour later the firemen were streaming into the mile-long
Clearwater estate driveway in their trucks, cars, and fire engines. A
good many of them couldn't make it down the first half mile because of
burning pasture grass whose flames leap-frogged the narrow road. The
very fence post and rails were burning and falling about the road, too.
Carlos, still perched on the limb, could see lights coming upriver. He
couldn't really see all that clearly at this point. The lawn area was like a
battlefield, with hazy smoke drifting about. But he figured rescue workers were coming by boat to help the stranded, bewildered guests from
the Hudson's cold waters. He leaned out to get a better view and suddenly the limb snapped beneath him. He twisted, tried to grasp on to an
upper branch and couldn't hold on. He reached again, but this branch
broke in his right hand and he tumbled six feet to the ground, striking
the back of his head on a hard object. His eyes glazed over. He pushed
to sit up but had no strength. A dizziness came over him. He peered up
at the sky but it was full of dark smoke clouds. He knew he was going to
pass out. He reached for the back of his head and felt the spot that had
taken the blow. He discovered a large welt on the back of his head just
above the neck. He pressed lightly to see if he was bleeding, but felt no

dampness. Just sickness in his stomach and more dizziness. He stayed conscious a few more minutes and then started to sink back to the ground. As his eyelids began to shut, he was suddenly startled by someone's presence to his right. He painfully turned his head and looked. He gulped and muttered her name, "Valova," then blacked out.

The tragic fire at Clearwater was complete and unforgiving. All barns reduced to cinders, over one hundred vehicles destroyed, some fifty more badly damaged. Part of the mansion destroyed and an untold loss of horses, equipment, and assorted items necessary to operate a going horse farm. As the *Saratoga Star* headline read the next day, "Miracle. Two-hundred Guests Survive Clearwater Fire." This was the sub-head: "Lone caretaker found near woods, suffering from amnesia, suspected of arson."

The worst tragedy of the whole affair came six days following the fire when Meredith Ostrander, bereaved over her lost horses, suffered a cardiac arrest and died after three days in the Saratoga Hospital. It was subsequently noted in a New York City social column that owing to Meredith Ostrander's death, Claire Valova alone would now reign supreme as Saratoga's most sought-after party giver and charity benefactor.

In the recesses of Carlos Mann's dimmed memory, there would always be a vision of a woman with a shining diamond necklace walking through a fiery wall of flames and smoke. He would not be able to recall the face, nor the name. Not even the time of night, or for that matter, the real details of the fire. He would be stuck away in an isolated hospital ward to be observed and probed by several doctors, all interested in what had depressed his memory in the first place. Once the hospital was done with him, Carlos would be subjected to rigorous investigation by local and state police investigators, not to mention the insurance investigators who would go over the Clearwater fire with the proverbial fine-toothed comb.

Justice would be served. Saratoga demanded it.

1. BAD NEWS

A bulletin came across the desk of city editor Frank Duffy at the *Saratoga Star* newspaper on Saturday, April 22, 1995, that drew his immediate attention and, subsequently, prompted Duffy to stop in the middle of working on the Sunday editorial page to give the bulletin further scrutiny.

The message was in two parts. First, a brief report from the *Associated Press* from the island of St. Martin N.A. in the Caribbean that the body of Ann Bifford, a 36-year-old American veterinarian and a native of Connecticut, had been found washed ashore on a stretch of beach near the plush resorts of Shoal Bay on the island of Anguilla. Secondly, that Claire Valova, 70, a former brilliant dramatic ballerina with Russia's Bolshoi Ballet who migrated to the United States in the fifties, and later became a lead dancer with George Balanchine's New York City group, died suddenly in her Fifth Avenue apartment: Cause of death not known.

Both announcements came as a shock to Duffy, and he sat at his desk stunned as his trained eyes scanned the bulletin a third time, speed-reading through the biographical portion, noticing that there were obvious inaccuracies in the AP story. Duffy could piece in the background of each of the deceased by memory alone. But this wasn't important now. He fought back tears on reading it. There was just a deep, empty feeling in the pit of his stomach, the kind one can only experience when they lose good friends. His saddened mood was doubly increased because he was the only one in the newsroom. One male sports writer and two female reporters had gone out on afternoon assignments scant minutes earlier, leaving Duffy to his editing task. In all his many years with the *Saratoga Star,* he couldn't remember when the old, high-ceilinged room seemed more deserted. Not even Maxwell, the paper's pet cat, was around to keep him company. No, this was, as it had been for all his newspaper days, a lonely vigil: a seasoned editor, working over unpolished copy against a never-ending deadline. It was different than working in his former newspaper days now that he could bang out his stories on a terminal, edit them in seconds, and change them around with equal ease.

The mechanical side of things made the job swifter, and perhaps easier, but it would always be solitary work. Duffy, like so many editors, had accustomed himself to dealing with a fair amount of boredom and repetitious newspaper work. He had also learned to take the good and bad on equal terms, reporting both with objectivity.

He was just sitting, staring straight ahead, thinking about Ann and Claire, remembering the times he had spent with them in Saratoga. Then he felt someone's presence in the room.

"You look like you've seen a ghost," the familiar voice of Duffy's long-time friend, Billy Farrell, said from the open doorway leading from the advertising department to the newsroom.

Without turning, Duffy called back, "I guess in my mind's eye I am seeing a ghost, Billy. God knows this town has plenty of them to go around. We've just added two more to the Spa's ghost roster." Then, slowly turning to face the door, he said, "I'm glad you came by. This hasn't been a good day at all."

Farrell came over and sat on the edge of Duffy's desk. He immediately saw that the old word merchant was depressed. He leaned across and took the bulletin from Duffy's folded hands and read it. When he was done, he stood up and went to the wide office windows and peered out at windswept Maple Avenue, with its curbside trees just beginning to bud in April's warmth. He could see down Maple where John Rhodes, a town character of the first order, was walking into a swift breeze and holding his hat to keep it from blowing off as he passed in front of the Metro, one of Saratoga's most popular night spots.

"Damn sad. Damn sad indeed," Farrell said to Duffy.

Duffy didn't reply.

Farrell understood why. He didn't pursue the topic. Farrell could read Duffy's mind. Both men were the same age, seventy-two. Well past their retirement date, but both glad and eager to be gainfully employed. Long-standing friends since grade school days, they attended high school together in Saratoga. Duffy, a mere five-foot-seven and weighing not a pound over 143, then went off to Dartmouth on an academic scholarship while Farrell, a stellar high school athlete weighing 215 and standing six-foot-two, took advantage of a partial scholarship to Holy Cross College. When World War II broke out, they elected to join different branches of the service. Duffy served in the army in France and Germany and came home a captain. Farrell chose the navy and landed in the Pacific. He was on two destroyers that sank in the same year. Following their post-WW II reunion, Duffy suggested they had enough medals between them to start a scrap yard. It was almost ironic that after both trying out different careers, they eventually secured jobs with the *Saratoga Star* - Duffy doing what he did best, writing and editing, and Farrell, the born salesman, opting for the highly charged advertising department.

Duffy married Martha LeRoy of Glens Falls, New York who, he later discovered, had an uncle who went to school with his father in Middlebury, Vermont. Farrell married one Meg Mara, a Saratogian who graduated from Skidmore College. They fathered two children each, a boy and girl and, as would seem appropriate, were godparents to each other's children. As Duffy used to say, "Who could keep it more local than that?"

In their Saratoga social circle of friends, both men were well acquainted with Ann and Claire.

Several minutes of silence went by. Then Farrell said, "I'm going for a drink. You care to join me?"

"Might just as well," said Duffy. "My mind's a blank right now."

"Let's do the Parting Glass," said Farrell.

"Fine by me."

Outside in the stiff, warm breeze, the sun on their faces, they strolled the half block of Lake Avenue from the paper to Saratoga's favorite Irish haunt. The Parting Glass was a bar and restaurant where someone once said men and women could drink on equal terms. Once inside they sat at the dark, familiar, mahogany bar and ordered whiskey shots with Harp's beer for a chaser.

In the background, an authentic Irish recording was playing a soft, almost mournful ballad to fit both their grieving and puzzled moods as the reality of the two untimely deaths began sinking in. And the longer Duffy and Farrell sat and drank and thought about them, the more sullen the occasion became. Three strong whiskeys already down, with three beers to complete the wash, Betty O'Connell, host barmaid for the afternoon, could plainly see that she was serving two unhappy, elder *Saratoga Star* notables. And that it would no doubt be a long afternoon into night, judging by their moods. Betty also surmised that before this day was over, she, or someone from the Parting Glass, would have to call both their wives. Certainly neither would be driving their cars home from this drinking bout. Duffy's old Ford would sit for the night in the paper's private parking lot, as would Farrell's newer Pontiac. The same scene had been played out many times before by the two, though by Betty's recollection, it was usually under happier circumstances. She couldn't remember when she had seen these two generally lively, happy-go-lucky men so depressed.

Duffy slumped on his bar stool. His small, rounded shoulders hunched forward, with his elbows on the bar supporting a beer between slender fingers. Farrell's bear-like paws held a shot glass in the right hand and a beer mug in the left, both objects hidden within his large hot-dog-sized fingers and ham-sized palms. Farrell was short in the legs and tall in the torso, so that when he sat up straight, he virtually towered over Duffy. When they talked, Duffy was staring upward all the time and Farrell downward. Duffy's voice was a low monotone while Farrell's literally barked out each word. It had been this way for all their years of friendship.

Duffy, staring at the back bar, saw himself in the mirror, Farrell's huge frame beside his. It was a sorrowful sight, he thought. This God-awful news was reminiscent of other unpleasant occasions that had prompted the two to bury their collective grief in drink from time to time.

As they were about to order their fourth round of drinks, the front door to the Parting Glass opened and Duffy turned to face Police Sergeant Dave Galea, entering.

"I thought I'd find you two here," said Galea, taking off his cap. "It's unhappy news, I know. May I have a word or two with you?"

Duffy shot him a misty-eyed look. "Why Officer Galea, you're too young to know how unhappy it is."

Galea seemed uneasy.

Their faces turned away from him.

"This is most important," Galea pleaded.

"Then out with it," said Duffy, clutching a half-empty shot glass.

Galea's eyes dropped to the floor. His voice became a mere whisper.

"Well," Duffy insisted, "if you have something to say, say it."

"I'm trying," said Galea.

"Speak up, man," Farrell piped in. "If you're that tight about it, have a drink. Loosen up."

Farrell pushed his half-empty Harp's beer into Galea's right hand. "Go ahead, no one here cares that you're on duty."

With that Galea gulped it down and set the glass on the bar.

"Now," Duffy said. "Tell us."

"I was asked by Police Chief Tom Nealy to pass along the unpleasant news that Ann Bifford and Claire Valova may have been murdered." He was about to tell them more but Duffy, spinning about on the bar stool, held up his hand with a shut-your-mouth gesture while glaring at Galea for ever having said it aloud in earshot of other Parting Glass patrons. In the same instant Farrell leaned over and, taking Galea by the shoulder, marched him toward the back dining room. Admonishing him in a deep whiskey whisper, Farrell said, "Mind who hears what you say about

14

those two lovely departed ladies, lad."

Galea, realizing the two were well on their way to tipsyville, ignored their overreaction.

"I have things to do," Galea continued. "Nealy says that Dr. Bifford was first thought to have drowned while scuba diving, but he has now been informed by a close friend on St. Martin that wasn't the case. That's all he knows on Bifford. Early reports from New York said the cause of Claire Valova's death was an aneurysm. Nealy says that's not true. The pathology reports following her autopsy claim she was poisoned, but even at that they haven't determined how." Galea paused to let them digest the message. The two men remained in petrified silence. Neither could speak. It was almost as if someone had told them that their very wives or children had been murdered.

Eventually Duffy, finding his way to a chair because his legs felt strangely weak, managed to ask Galea, "Are you certain Nealy hasn't had a few too many himself?"

"I wish it were so, Mr. Duffy. He wasn't in a very good mood when I left him to find you two. Nealy's had his belly full of murders right here in Saratoga these past few years. He's every bit as upset over this news as you."

Duffy observed Galea. He didn't look like a cop, Duffy thought. The torso was too long for the short legs. Galea's face too fat for his police cap where thick locks of salt-and-pepper hair stuck out in all directions from underneath. And yes, Duffy further observed, he had a spare tire that practically hid his gunbelt and buckle. He wasn't, by any definition, a good example of what a cop should look like. But then Duffy had been noticing for some time that Saratoga's men in blue were not up to par, at least not in his estimation. It was Duffy's opinion that every cop, at least physically, should be a certain height— no shorter that six feet—and most certainly possessing a trim, physical appearance representative of a law enforcement officer, as one might picture a state trooper to be. Duffy actually had a higher regard for the female cops in Saratoga. They kept themselves in shape in more ways than one. In the beginning, they had to fight their way onto the force, for the likes of Chief Nealy and others didn't take kindly when local Councilman Pete Farra proposed that Saratoga should have women cops. Nealy's outmoded ideas, then and now, went right along with his chauvinistic character. Galea, Duffy reckoned, was of the same bent as Nealy.

"That's the message," Galea said. "I'll keep in touch if anything else develops. Nealy said he'd keep this all quiet for now. He expects you'll do the same. He realizes you have a paper to print and that this news will make headlines. But he's hoping he can hold it back for a few days till he can put an investigation into place. If it's everything we think it is, some person or persons in Saratoga are a part of it. Nealy said he'd like to keep the suspicion of murder out of it for now, at least in print. He hopes you'll cooperate with him." Galea then started to leave, backing away slowly at first for fear they might insist he stay.

Farrell relieved Galea of this notion, saying in a voice now more tempered, "Thank you officer, we appreciate your sincerity. Tell Nealy we understand his problem. Tell him we will keep this hush, hush. At least until circumstances force us to say otherwise. Tell Nealy to keep in touch."

So there they were in the Parting Glass, feeling even worse than when they started. They were shocked and bewildered with Galea's latest revelation that both women were dead of unnatural causes. They remained in the empty, quiet, dim dining room, staring at each other. Duffy, then realizing his drink was gone, called for another round. "Make it a double," he insisted.

"Same for me," said Farrell.

Farrell noticed that familiar, inquisitive look on Duffy's face. It was the same look he had seen the old shirt-sleeve editor take on many times in the past, particularly when he didn't understand a situation or couldn't make sense of something. They were two of a kind, perhaps too much so. Old-fashioned in their thinking and manners, true, but loyal to the bone. Farrell knew that real loyalty was a rarity these days.

Duffy finished his whiskey and beer and sat back. "I want to go back to the paper now," he said.

"You'll not be doing a lick of writing after all that booze," Farrell declared.

Duffy began to rise from his chair. His thick, brushed-back white hair, in need of a trim, lapped over the suit collar. "I'm not doing any work. I just want to go back and think. Can you understand that?"

Farrell nodded his approval. "We've had our fill anyway, I'd say."

As they left the Parting Glass through the side door, a chill wind whipped at their faces. April's all-too-brief warm afternoon was beginning to turn nasty.

Back at his desk at the *Star,* Duffy, with Farrell plopped in a large swivel chair near him, flicked on the desk terminal in front of him and started pressing the keys. Duffy's crimson-flushed face glared back at Farrell.

"Mind your own business, you blockhead. I'm tapping into the paper's graveyard. Between now and tomorrow morning some young wizard in this editorial room will have to write Claire's and Ann's obituaries. It's all part of their newspaper weaning. I'll just do a little homework now on their behalf, so they get the facts right. Is that all right by you?"

"Do what you have to," Farrell said. "I'm heading home. I'm going to pretend this whole day didn't happen. I'm going to tell Meg how much I love her and the kids. In fact, I'm going to call my kids, John in Seattle, and Patty in Washington, to tell them just how much they mean to me. If today's bad news has awakened me to anything, it's just how fragile and fleeting life is. Besides, I really didn't need that last drink. It won't go over too well with Meg, I can assure you. So take care. Do your research on our two departed friends. I'll talk to you tomorrow, or soon."

Duffy's eyes were transfixed on the terminal screen as Farrell was talking and preparing to leave. He didn't bother to look up.

"Call yourself a cab, Farrell. I'll be on my way out shortly, too."

Farrell called Saratoga Cab Company and it responded within five minutes.

When Farrell was gone, Duffy again concentrated on his terminal. He punched in the search codes, all the way back to the early sixties, when he had first met Claire Valova. He'd been the interviewer when she and her first husband, a count of some means from Innsbruck, Austria, were traveling in the region. She had been dancing for some time in America for Balanchine but not in Saratoga because the Performing Arts Center was but an architect's dream at that time. Ballet was pretty much confined to New York City.

Yes, there it was, her telling Duffy at the time how much she admired the scenery in and around Saratoga. How, in her words, "This area reminds me of some small towns not far from Moscow, though their buildings and surroundings are dank by comparison." And later telling the press that it would be a marvelous place for an arts colony, perhaps even the ballet. Duffy later thinking how perceptive she was, and how startlingly beautiful, with flawless skin, short red hair, green eyes, and very sharp, delicate facial features.

They met again when she returned to Saratoga for the Performing Arts Center's grand opening in 1966, which featured the New York City Ballet in A *Midsummer Night's Dream*. By this time she was on her second husband, Clarence Davenport, a self-made multimillionaire shipping magnate from Portsmouth, England. Claire, no longer dancing, was nearing forty at the time. Her husband was in his late sixties. It would prove out in time that she would become the perennial chairwoman of New York City's, and ultimately Saratoga's, charity balls. She outlived three husbands whose collective wealth totaled $60 million. Her eventual move to Saratoga in the 1960s after marrying her third husband, David Striker, an investment banker, paralleled the revival of the old town, which had begrudgingly limped through the 1950s following the shutdown of its gambling establishments by Estes Kefauver, an overzealous and obviously ambitious United States Senator.

"I came at a time when Saratoga was beginning to gain back some of the luster and pomp it enjoyed in the late 1880s," she was quoted as saying. Duffy remembered her once expounding at a charity cocktail party that, "The ballet didn't just get into one's blood, but rather captured one's body and soul." You retire from the dance company, true. Your mind and spirit, however, never leaves the stage.

Duffy read on. Her list of accomplishments were endless. True, she had the money to do just about anything she wanted, but she didn't have to go as far as she did with her philanthropic endeavors. Many other wealthy people in the old town kept their personal and corporate pocketbooks zipped up tight. Claire Valova enjoyed helping others, supporting the arts, helping at the hospital, donating her time and energy where she thought it would benefit those less fortunate. And when it came to the ballet, she was generous to a fault. Her age may have taken her off stage, but behind the scenes she toe danced her way into every facet of the ballet's peripheral world.

After browsing for over an hour through Claire's file, Duffy switched to the more recent file on Ann Bifford. It was noticeably smaller and in no way as exciting to read; after all, a female veterinarian wasn't prone to making glitzy headlines, even in a horse town like Saratoga. But he found some surprising information, some that he vaguely recalled, some that he must have completely missed when it was fresh news.

There was a freelance piece by Todd Smith that featured Ann Bifford when she was suddenly brought in during the middle of the 1988 Saratoga season meet to take over the care of a grade 1 winning stallion, Royal Groom, who had been previously doctored by leading veterinarian Ralph Bookings. Seems there was a big controversy over Bookings' departure from Green Velvet Stable following an accusation by Green Velvet's owner, John Tower, that his Thoroughbreds were much too lame under Bookings' care. Royal Groom had been Florida's Horse of the Year with lifetime earnings of $1,800,000. Bifford later informed track officials that she found some gross errors in Bookings' medical reports as they pertained to several race horses in Tower's stables. Then, of course, Bifford had been summoned to testify at special racing hearings that were centered on a whole range of irregularities among selected stables, all the way from Kentucky to California and including the August Thoroughbreds of Saratoga.

Though Duffy didn't attend any of these proceedings, he remembered them very well. He also recalled that as quickly as the hearings had started, they were closed. Seems that pressure was exerted by powers all the way from the money circles within the racing elite to the highest offices in state government.

It always amazed Duffy how much copy was written on a particular individual. As he scanned the screen further, Bifford's file seemed to be based solely on her profession. Very little personal data was revealed. Duffy wondered why this young horse doctor had prompted so much local press. Certainly, as Duffy well knew, her talents were recognized by several prominent Thoroughbred owners. But it wasn't the high profile press generally given leading trainers or jockeys. Doctoring horses on Saratoga's backstretch stables was not, in Duffy's opinion, the hot news most young reporters went searching for.

He was growing tired of reading. Besides, his earlier nipping at the Parting Glass with Farrell was beginning to take its toll. He was about to turn the terminal off when, suddenly, his eyes fell on one last story on Ann Bifford. It had been a small feature written for one of the *Star's* Sunday editions. It centered on a rash of untimely viruses that had killed some of the country's most promising Thoroughbreds. It had all been kept pretty quiet at first in the press, but among horse owners there had been near panic. The viruses were first thought to have been imported from Europe and then contained by shipping the foreign race horses back as quickly as possible. But then it grew worse. Bifford and a handful of veterinary specialists were called upon to assess the disease for the State Racing Commission. Thus was the gist of the featured article. There were no local follow-up stories though Duffy stayed awhile longer and searched. What did catch Duffy's attention was the fact that two of the dead horses came from Claire Valova's stable. He wasn't at all aware that Claire had lost two of her best Thoroughbreds to the evasive virus. Nor that Ann Bifford had been the sole doctor in charge of them at the time. Both were chestnut colts and both had been purchased four years earlier at the Keeneland, Kentucky yearling sales. Curtain's Up was bought for $580,000 and the other, Ballet Dancer, for

$600,000. Two of the highest priced yearlings purchased that year. Fortunately, as Duffy noticed, both colts had ample insurance coverage.

It was just too much for his weary bones and mind to absorb in one day. He then decided, like Farrell, to take the safe way home by calling a cab. He shut down his terminal, checked to see that the terminals around him were turned off, flicked off the lights in the empty editorial room, and went out to wait for the taxi on Maple Avenue. The day's earlier sun and stiff spring breeze had now given way to a soft-falling rain. "Why does it always rain on sad days?" Duffy said to himself.

2. IDYLL THOUGHTS

It would be a vacation away from California, in a similar warm climate to be sure, but different in setting and temperament from his comfortable home in Palos Verdes Estates. And this time he'd be enjoying it with his new love, Sandy Blair. Mike Flint decided he'd take a leave of absence from any private investigative work to do nothing more than drift and relax for two weeks in a paradise of his choice. Flint planned to leave for New York City where they'd stay long enough to clear up some things with Harry Waite and then continue on to Anguilla. His return date would be a big question mark at this moment.

It would not be Hawaii. He'd been that route too many times. Not that Hawaii didn't offer all the things Flint treasured in a vacation. But rather, as he remembered, its beaches were getting a bit crowded these days. Its flow of tourists too noisy for his blood. He had relished vacationing in Hawaii in the early sixties, at a time when one could be more intimately connected to the islands. But that had changed now. No, he was looking for something different, something in another direction from the Pacific.

On a late evening dinner date at Southern California's Chasen's restaurant with Sandy and Monica (Flint's former movie-star lover, who was accompanied by an elderly film director who drank straight-up brandy from a snifter and looked as if he were about to cave in with each succeeding drink), it was Monica who suggested Flint and Sandy vacation on the small island of Anguilla in the Caribbean.

"You will love this place," he recalled Monica saying. "It's part of the Leeward Islands group. A few minutes by boat from St. Martin, yet so quiet and secluded you'll swear you're by yourself most of the time. I insist you try it."

Within two days of the dinner, Flint and Sandy made arrangements to fly to Anguilla. They did so with little more than a glance at a Caribbean area island map which pinpointed Anguilla, along with a string of other islands, some distance from San Juan, Puerto Rico.

So much had happened over the past year since Flint first met Sandy in Saratoga, New York, there hadn't been enough quality time to spend together. Oh, yes, he had taken her to Aspen that winter, but that turned into a harried chase after two blackmailers. So the Aspen visit, which might have given them time to sort out their Saratoga-generated whirlwind relationship, really settled nothing. Then, when they got back to Palos Verdes, Flint, who had sworn that he wouldn't take on any more assignments for at least six months, found himself embroiled in an old drug investigation that had him scurrying up and down the California coast for several weeks while Sandy sat home. This Anguilla trip would be the elixir their love life needed.

Their plan was to fly to New York, take care of a few loose ends on some prior work Flint had concluded for an insurance company and collect a handsome check. Then, he wanted to deposit a big sum of money in a trust for a little girl in Waycross, Georgia named Sara. It was a promise Flint had made to himself following last summer's so-called "Ninth Race Caper." It was the least he reasoned he could do to somehow repay Sara for the tragic loss of her mother who was murdered in Saratoga while working as an informer for Flint's friend, Harry Waite, and the elite police force at New York's Central Headquarters.

When this was done, he and Sandy would continue on to seek the peace and solitude they both craved so badly. They planned a brief visit to San Juan, a place Flint, for his worldly travels, had never seen. Perhaps they'd visit some beachfront casinos, catch a nightclub show, dine at restaurants that Monica had mentioned and, without putting too much stress on their itinerary, visit the historic district. Then they would fly by American Eagle commuter airlines to Monica's mysterious and magical island of Anguilla.

Flint and Sandy were relaxing on the veranda of his Palos Verdes cottage watching a huge, red, setting sun as it slowly disappeared on the western horizon, almost directly opposite Marina Del Rey where the sun's last rays flickered off the sails of several racing yachts making their way to their respective boat slips after a long day's sail, most probably to Catalina. The Pacific Ocean in front of them was calm, as it often was at this time of day.

"Well my love," he said, admiring her pose and realizing that this moment felt more like a dream than reality. He couldn't help doubting that his age, 47, and her youthful twenty-eight years was an attraction that could go up in smoke at any time. "Tomorrow we go to Anguilla. Are you excited?" She came to his side and buried her face in his folded arms.

"I will always be excited when I'm with you Flint. No matter where we go."

"You're really hung up on this old guy, aren't you?"

She looked at him, her dark round eyes burning into his, long strands of silken black hair flowing over her shoulders.

"I never want to hear of age again," she said. "I accept you for everything you are, including the few years difference. I was attracted to you immediately in Saratoga. I think you know that. It's my decision and I like it just the way it is."

He ran his fingers through her hair and kissed her softly. Then they remained silent for a long while, content in watching the sun go down and the darkness creep in across the still ocean surface. Inwardly, though, Flint was remembering how he and Sandy earlier that winter found themselves quite apprehensive about their trip to Boston to meet with Alice, Sandy's mother, to reveal how their Saratoga relationship ensued. And how Flint almost got cold feet just prior to the trip, feeling that having once dated and actually having been in love with Alice in the sixties, that she would probably never accept Sandy's and Flint's reasoning, no matter how convincing or persistent they were. Not to discount their age difference, either.

But it was Sandy, with her inherent talent of persuasion, who controlled that seemingly fateful meeting, winning over her mother's approval after only a few hours. The encounter, however, with Flint meeting Alice again after so many years was, as he later put it, "More nerve racking facing Alice than facing an opponent's pointed gun."

Flint, for the first time in weeks, was glad he didn't have one current assignment on the books. Perhaps, just perhaps, he'd stretch their Anguilla vacation a few days. Money was no problem and he wanted to do something special with Sandy.

Monica's director friend had sent Flint a note about a couple that owned two former America's Cup racing yachts in Simpson Bay in St. Martin. They were chartering them commercially. Flint thought that would be special. The boats, both built in Canada, had raced in the 1987 America's Cup in Perth, Australia. Flint also had another reason for wanting to visit St. Martin. His latent gambling craving could be tested at the newest casino in the sparkling complex at Port De Plaisance. Monica had boasted that the yachts moored at Port De Plaisance made the boats at Marina Del Rey appear as dinghies. Flint, intrigued with all types of boats since he was a child, couldn't wait to see them.

They went to bed shortly after midnight and awoke at 8 A.M. Sandy had packed just about everything the day before, so it was just a matter of Flint making sure the cottage's security system was activated, certain key people he dealt with were notified of his departure and tentative return date and, before going, placing a call to Harry so things in New York would be set up when they arrived.

As generally happened when he called Harry, Flint had to listen to several tales of woe about New York Central Headquarters' problems. At which Flint told Harry he couldn't care less because none of those problems interested him. In fact, Flint avoided giving Harry his exact destination in the Caribbean. Flint had been interrupted by Harry too many times in past years. This time he'd save himself, and Sandy, that all-too-familiar grief.

3. SWEETFEED

The early song birds of summer, already gathering on a chilly, misty, April morning, were chirping and flying madly about the backstretch barns of Saratoga Race Course as they trailed not far behind one of the track's most illustrious figures, 80-year-old Howard "Sweetfeed" Thompson.

Old Sweetfeed was up and at 'em promptly at 5:30 A.M. each day, doing what he had been doing for over sixty-five years feeding select Thoroughbreds his special mix of wheat, barley, oats and molasses, the feed-mix he was nicknamed after.

Like the horses, the various birds were fond of Sweetfeed's mix, and as he toted in his right arm a shiny, gold-plated, feed bucket, filled to the brim and spilling several portions of the sticky, sweet-smelling morning meal on the ground, a hundred or so birds were there to quickly devour the surplus. The bucket, the envy of every backstretch person that ever worked around Sweetfeed, was a rare and precious gift from Claire Valova, who claimed it came right from the horse farms of none other than Czar Nicholas II of Russia. The item, Valova told Sweetfeed upon giving him the treasured bucket, was retrieved from the Czar's stables shortly after the dreaded 1917 Bolshevik Revolution. Of course over a period of years, Sweetfeed embellished the story to say that the bucket was a Russian battle prize, though he couldn't ever seem to remember which year or what battle it was. It was, however, the ultimate conversation piece among his backstretch peers including those in Florida, California, and New York.

During his rounds, Sweetfeed sang a little song to the great racing stallions and mares, all now aware of his presence and stirring in their stalls.

Here's the feed to increase your speed
Go to the front and hold that lead
Remember your pal, Sweetfeed.

His ditty, sung off key in his distinct, deep, graveled voice, was also the wake-up call each day for the dozens of hot-walkers and backstretch workers at Saratoga. In a sense, you could say that Sweetfeed, because of his elder status, heralded in each day and set the track's hectic pace, all of which began long before the sun was up over Saratoga Lake to the east, or warmed the waters of the nearby Hudson River, sprayed its rays down on the artist retreat, Yaddo, and eventually beamed down on

Saratoga's sprawling array of horse barns, the track itself, and the spirals of the historic grandstands. Sweetfeed's backstretch dress code had not changed over the years. He wore high, black, rubber boots, denim overalls held up by a pair of tattered, bleached-out suspenders, a pure-wool, long-sleeved shirt and short, leather jacket. His rather long, pointed nose supported antique metal-rimmed glasses and, when he wasn't carrying the feed bucket or other objects of his trade, he was continually pulling at an Irish-made felt cap that seemed too big for his balding head. In his youth he stood six-foot, with handsome features and curly, full, blond hair, but he now walked with a deliberate limp and forward lean that made him appear not an inch over five-foot-seven. Sweetfeed, a born and bred Kentucky native, lived all his life with horses. He often said he understood them better and trusted them more than most humans.

Sweetfeed particularly enjoyed April. It was the month, he often said, "that shook off winter and welcomed summer." On the first hot day, he'd shed his leather coat and tie it about his waist, letting, so to speak, the fresh spring air finally deodorize his flannel shirt. He had an inborn adversity to bathing. Everyone who worked with him did so at a respectful distance.

"You got the goods," someone shouted out as Sweetfeed passed by Barn 13, the summer home of a two-year-old brown-bay colt, Track Baron.

"I always got the goods," Sweetfeed shouted back, immediately recognizing the voice as that of Willie "Water Man" Wilkins, who was not quite Sweetfeed's age, but certainly one of the track's veteran backstretch favorites.

"Gonna be a special day," Water Man said. "Gonna get this here Track Baron's right front leg fixed once and for all, so he can race like the wind again."

"Sounds fine," Sweetfeed said. "He's some horse. We got to pay special attention to these types. They're our bread and butter when they stay healthy and race good."

"Right you are," agreed Water Man.

In and about the barns dozens of backstretch workers now moved swiftly, grabbing feed buckets, water pails, rakes, darting in and out of the each stall with fresh straw and waiting, as they generally did each morning before sunrise, for the trainers to make their appearance. It was then that things would really begin to perk. But for the moment, it was men and women, young boys and girls, and a whole assortment of dogs and cats that stirred in the darkness. A human beehive of activity, grooming and catering to the grand Thoroughbreds that would make the *Racing*

Form headlines come August. Perhaps a potential Kentucky Derby winner was somewhere to be found amid the gray-green barns at Saratoga. If not the big one in Kentucky, then possibly a Saratoga Travers Stakes winner, a race the equine set long ago dubbed the Midsummer Derby. With some 70 horses already in stalls, and over 2,000 expected to arrive between April and August, anything was possible.

Old Sweetfeed was privileged to have served two Travers winners and one Kentucky Derby champion. Not to mention the dozens of other stakes winners he'd attended to. He had, among other things, an inert ability to also recognize telltale signs of weakness in a horse, especially the yearlings at the annual Fasig Tipton sales. While some buyers spent thousands for advice from trainers, bloodstock agents, equine reporting services, and employed the best veterinarians in making their selections at the sales, a few buyers simply trusted Sweetfeed's instincts to guide their purchases.

"You can't know what makes a horse want to win," was one of Sweetfeed's pat statements. "No one knows. I watch their eyes, that tells me a lot. I stand back and see how proudly they hold up the head. How straight the back is. How sturdy the legs. Still, it's only a guess. You don't know till they run. And you really don't know till they run with other good runners." But he had a way of picking winners, which is the reason he had lasted so long at the various tracks in spite of his age and cantankerous nature.

For all his backstretch status, though, he'd never made any serious money. In the pre-World War II days of racing, a few dollars a week was the going rate for his kind. Things improved after the war. However, he had to move around more, so the travel and incidental expenses associated with it took away any increases in salary he might have gained.

That was until he met Claire Valova. She knew nothing about horses, whereas Sweetfeed knew everything. The pretty ballerina would seek Sweetfeed's opinion long before she'd talk to her trainer. She also didn't want him working for the other owners. He knew he'd found a home with Claire Valova. Besides, she paid him double the going rate plus extras when her horses won. Inside Saratoga's oval, Sweetfeed, in Valova's mind, was sole master of her Thoroughbreds.

There was just a touch of sun beginning to beam toward the track. The Czar's bucket gleamed in the breaking dawn.

Track Baron's head leaned out of the half-open stall door as Sweetfeed lifted the bucket upward.

"Eat, big fellow. Enjoy Sweetfeed's mush."

The stallion snorted and went for the bucket, which Sweetfeed first offered and then pulled back, waiting for the Baron to swallow the first mouthful. Then he lifted the bucket again, repeating this every few seconds till he satisfied the great horse's initial hunger. Sweetfeed then fetched a water pail and set it inside the stall and watched as the Baron gulped and washed down the feed.

Then, reaching down inside his right boot, Sweetfeed removed a small plastic cylinder, quickly unscrewed the cap and, looking about to make sure no one was watching, squirted an ounce into the water pail. Track Baron finished the remainder and Sweetfeed again offered him some mix. After making sure the Baron drank two more pails, Sweetfeed patted him on the forehead and said aloud, "Now that's a winner's breakfast."

No sooner had Sweetfeed finished when he heard some commotion in an adjacent barn. He turned and walked toward the noise. Two stable boys were thickly involved in a verbal assault on each other and it appeared to Sweetfeed that it would soon lead to a fist fight. He walked right up and stepped between the two.

"You'll scare half the horses here to death with all that racket," he admonished them. "Get on with your chores. Stop this nonsense right now."

Apparently surprised by Sweetfeed's directness and tone of voice, or perhaps out of respect for his age, the two stopped and went their separate ways. He really wasn't concerned with the nature of their argument. It was his duty, as he saw it, to keep the barn area calm. After all, there was enough unnecessary noise and disturbance to go around among the horses.

Within the hour and a half that he had spent at the barns, he fed and watered seven horses, stopped for coffee and a hearty breakfast at the backstretch eatery, marked off the hot-walking schedule for four other horses, spoke to a number of workers, and made two phone calls to Tony "Let 'Em Run" Santandrea, Valova's head trainer. He then headed for an early meeting with Joe Hennesy, the track's superintendent. In earlier years he'd have walked the mile or so to the superintendent's office across Union Avenue and located near the Oklahoma Training Track, but now he rode the backstretch's electric golf cart. Sweetfeed and Hennesy were old buddies, so he always looked forward to these meetings, even if they were business related.

Hennesy, his red-Irish face not wearing the usual broad smile Sweetfeed was accustomed to seeing, met him at the office door to the modest, white, clapboard structure. He was three years Sweetfeed's junior, a foot shorter and some one hundred pounds heavier, and just now beginning to lose what had been a true crop of curly, black, Irish hair. In his hey-day Hennesy was also a dapper dresser known to attract more than one of Saratoga's social damsels, though he admitted he couldn't afford their expensive lifestyles. Sweetfeed and Hennesy greeted each other with a bear hug.

"You old rascal," Hennesy said. "You still have the strength of a lumberjack."

Sweetfeed slammed his right hand on Hennesy's back, pushing him forward in a stumbling motion. Then just as quickly he grabbed Hennesy by the waist and righted him halfway into his near fall.

Hennesy turned and eyed Sweetfeed with a disbelieving look. "Easy on this old body friend, I'm soft around the edges. You get no exercise sitting behind a desk all day."

"Get with me on the backstretch and I'll make you fit within a month."

"No, No. I'm beyond repair," Hennesy said.

They entered Hennesy's cluttered office, with its reams upon reams of yellowish paper stuffed, rolled, and piled into every corner. A grand assortment of maps, track sketches, bids on projects past and present, two wire baskets sat in the center of Hennesy's large rectangular mahogany desk, overflowing with memos and miscellaneous correspondence, a whole array of black and white framed horse photos hung randomly on knotty pine panel walls and just a faint streak of sunlight tried to force its way though a dust-coated, office picture window. Hennesy always justified this mess by telling visitors that, "This is a working man's office."

Most track people familiar with Hennesy's working habits realized he was totally disorganized, incurably set in his ways, and had fired dozens of secretaries that tried to shape up his inner sanctum. Yet to everyone's amazement, he generally got the intricate job of managing done because the people he dealt with were markedly worse organized than he was. In reality, it was a miracle that the Saratoga Thoroughbred operation ran as smoothly as it did come post time each day. Hennesy, however, didn't have to apologize to Sweetfeed, for he knew that if any one person at the track understood his unorthodox methods, Sweetfeed certainly was that person.

Hennesy moved behind his desk, plopped down in his wooden and leather swivel chair, opened a lower desk drawer, and took out a bottle of brandy. And with a sudden facial change that Sweetfeed immediately knew meant nothing good, said, "I know it's a bit early in the day for nipping, but I'm afraid you'll be needing a shot of this with the news I just received."

Sweetfeed hunched his shoulders and bent forward opposite Hennesy. "My God," he said, "I've never seen you so serious."

"It's more than that," replied Hennesy. "This is a very sad day for Saratoga and horse racing."

Old Sweetfeed was baffled. "Don't tell me, they've finally made the decision to close the Race Course and concentrate on racing down-state?"

"I wish it were that simple," said Hennesy, pouring the brandy into two paper cups with a slightly shaking right hand. "Here, drink this down."

As he drank, Sweetfeed felt the brandy hit the pit of his stomach, and he wondered how it would mix with his earlier backstretch breakfast of eggs over light and pan-fried hash. Hennesy poured Sweetfeed another and then sat back and indulged himself in another nip.

Hennesy finished his second nip and folded his hands under his chin. Though Sweetfeed had never truly seen Hennesy cry, he detected that he was about to see him shed a tear at this very moment.

Hennesy had difficulty getting the words out. Finally, with the utmost effort, he was able to speak.

"Claire Valova is dead," he said, his voice barely audible to Sweetfeed.

Sweetfeed's expression went blank. Hennesy's words literally hung in the air and Sweetfeed was fearfully made aware of the small plastic cylinder in his boot pressing against his leg. All Sweetfeed could think of in this instant was Track Baron. What would happen now? Where would he turn? He could only guess what might transpire. It took little figuring to interpret that with Claire dead, so was his gainful employ-ment. But he knew he had graver things to worry about at this time. Over and above this general employment, he had bonded himself with Claire in a much more serious secret endeavor, that was now almost impossible for him to reason out because she was dead. Hennesy was saying something else, but Sweetfeed wasn't listening. His mind was on Track Baron and the thought of what the mixer in the plastic cylinder was doing to the inside of the great stallion's stomach at this second.

"I can't tell you anymore at this time." Sweetfeed was cognizant of Hennesy's voice once more. "Except that she was found in her New York apartment yesterday."

Sweetfeed stood up. As he did, he felt the cylinder slip from his leg to his ankle, reminding him again of his early morning deed. He felt slack in his old limbs. The floor seemed to move under his feet.

Hennesy extended his hand across the desk. "That's the sad news, old friend. I must be getting on with today's training schedule, too. I know you have work to do, also. I'll keep you posted on any new developments."

"I can't believe it," said Sweetfeed, groping for something meaningful to say. "She was the best boss I ever had." Hennesy nodded in agreement, then walked Sweetfeed to the door and shook his hand once more before the backstretch sage departed.

Sweetfeed, with his mind swirling, drove the electric cart somewhat erratically, weaving back and forth and narrowly missing a passing car as he crossed over Union Avenue in the direction of his backstretch domain. John Tupper, a security guard on duty at the main gate, remarked to his fellow guard, Linda Pataki, "Looks like old Sweetfeed's had a few too many this morning."

Once back at the barns, Sweetfeed went to a pay phone and nervously dialed a number at Saratoga Lake, a number he knew well but had no idea where the dwelling was located, other than on or near the lake. It was a routine he had gone through several times in recent months, especially since getting involved with his secret work for Claire Valova. He'd simply call each time to report that a certain Thoroughbred had been properly fed. Whoever was receiving the calls for Claire Valova was none of Sweetfeed's business. Nor did he really care to know for that matter. The plastic cylinder stuck him again in the ankle, reminding him of the grave consequences that might eventually arise out of all of this. Worse yet, he felt doubly scared and alone with the knowledge of Claire's death.

He waited for the ring, his hand shaking. A voice finally answered. "You have news for me?"

Sweetfeed hesitated, then spoke. "The horse has been fed."

There was a long pause. Then the voice again. "Good work. Keep me posted on the next feeding..."

At this Sweetfeed, his own voice barely able to speak, piped in, "There's been some terrible news. I must talk to you in person. I must get some direction in all this."

"Never," replied the voice.

"But things have changed. There's been a death."

"Get control of yourself," the voice was raised an octave. "Just go about your feedings on schedule. You mustn't show any signs of being overly upset. I will handle the rest from this end. You'll get your pay as agreed to by your former employer. It's only April. We have the whole race season to think about. I'll be in touch again soon with other feeding assignments. Do you understand?"

Sweetfeed held the receiver but said nothing. In his bewildered state he was suddenly hearing Claire's soft voice and picturing her delicate face, as if her ghost had come sweeping across the great track's oval. His eyes watered and things appeared blurry for a moment.

"Sweetfeed. Sweetfeed," the voice blared once more. "Do you understand what's expected of you?"

He didn't want to answer, but was compelled to.

"Yes. Yes," he said. "I will follow your orders."

"That's fine," said the voice. "Now one other thing more: never dial this number again." It was a command, not a suggestion. "Burn it from your memory. I will give you a new number when the time is right. But that's not to say that I don't know what's taking place day and night on the backstretch. We must go about our business as usual. Everything must appear normal. I believe you fully get my message."

Sweetfeed could feel the perspiration drip the length of the flannel shirt, sticking to his back and front and beginning to itch where he tucked it into his pants. He shivered, even though the April sun was quite hot at the moment. He was weary and scared and could think of nothing more to say, so he hung up.

He then walked slowly to the far end of the barns where the woods and white fence met, and beyond that to an open patch of ground with four markers on a white post designating the resting place of four Hall of Fame Thoroughbreds; all of which he had known so well. Their owners had seen fit to give them an honored place of burial in the shadows of the historic Saratoga track, a tribute to their racing spirits.

But as he watched and thought about these four great champions, his head tilted forward in disgust at the recent events that had led four other potentially equal champions to an early demise, only to be buried without honor. He silently cursed himself for having been a part of their early deaths. Their names burned in his mind: Looking Glass II, Silent Runner, Streak and Icon, not to mention the soon-to-be dead Track Baron.

Sweetfeed knew in that instant his track life would never again be the same.

4. ANGUILLA...DEAD AHEAD

I f Mike Flint was thinking he'd finally found a place of solitude on St. Martin, other forces were in motion that would soon spoil his dream, though he was not aware of them as he and Sandy spotted the landing strip at St. Martin's Juliana Airport and watched through the plane window as the azure ocean waters, with their long strips of white-caps, headed beachward.

As they departed the plane, a warm Caribbean trade wind greeted them and Flint, savoring its intense heat, stood for a moment holding Sandy's hand, soaking it in with a deep sigh. A quick glance around told him that St. Martin was certainly not Hawaii, for it didn't have the lush green or towering mountains in the backdrop. But he knew instantly that this was his kind of climate. He smiled at Sandy who, like Flint, was seem-ingly fixed in place welcoming the same warmth and the blazing sun's rays, her long dark hair tangling about her face in the soft breeze. Then they were aware they were holding up the entire line of vacationers, all apparently as eager as he and Sandy to get to their hotels and villas. Flint was already contemplating his first dip in the blue-green waters of his soon-to-be-discovered paradise. They were to have first departed San Juan directly for Anguilla, but their flight was held up, so they opted for the flight to St. Martin. Flint then made arrangements for a boat to take them over to Anguilla. He was told the boat ride would take no more than twenty-five minutes. What he wasn't told was that the boat was an anti-quated, oversized rowboat piloted by a retired, aging U.S. Navy World War II veteran, George "Dusty" Putts, who Flint would later discover sipped a fair amount of locally produced red wine day and night, and whose ocean water savvy left much to be desired, not to mention the dubious seaworthiness of his boat.

Though Flint was content with going directly to Anguilla, Sandy begged him to stay on St. Martin for a time so she could browse through some of the shops Monica had told her about on Front Street and Back Street in the older section of Philipsburg. Flint wasn't happy about it, but he gave in and they checked their bags at the airport and took a cab to Philipsburg. While Sandy shopped, Flint seated himself at the outdoor table of a small cafe and had a double wine cooler. Though Sandy wasn't into wearing much jewelry, Flint knew she'd be combing the celebrated duty-free gold shops on Front Street.

"Buy gold in Philipsburg," Monica had told them. "No duty. No taxes. And I don't mind if you decide to bring me back a little something."

Monica was always so subtle, Flint was thinking.

When Sandy finally came back, Flint was on his third drink. This time, however, he had switched to Scotch and water.

"Close your eyes. Don't dare peek," Sandy said.

"You didn't buy me something already, did you?"

"Just shut your eyes," she insisted.

So he closed his eyes and waited. She slipped a rather heavy, cold metal object over his head and adjusted it on the outside of his short-sleeved shirt.

"Now open them," she said with a schoolgirl's excitement in her voice. He looked down. Glaring back was a solid 14K gold necklace. He was speechless for a moment. Sandy leaned over and kissed his forehead.

"That's for bringing me here," she said.

"You spent too much on this. I can tell," he said.

"Not as much as you might think," she laughed. "It's my money. I can spend it as I please. I like spending it on you."

They rode a cab back to the airport, retrieved their luggage, and then hired the same cab to take them across from the Dutch-controlled side of St. Martin to the French, northern side. Sandy had her mind set on shopping in Marigot, but Flint talked her out of it. Flint reminded her that they had reservations on Anguilla and that the boat would be waiting to take them there.

With the hot, persistent, Caribbean sun reflecting off the tops of an endless, rolling, ocean surface, and the boat pitching and rolling uncomfortably under Putts' guidance, the twenty-five minute ride seemed more like two hours. Sandy was hanging tightly to Flint's waist, as if to say he'd be her life preserver in case old Putts' boat decided to come apart midway between St. Martin and Anguilla. Flint sensed her fright and turning about, wrapped his arms around her and nestled his face into the nape of her neck.

"I know what you're thinking," he whispered to Sandy. "You'll just have to trust this guy's ability to make it to Anguilla safely, despite the shape he and the boat are in."

It was quite apparent that Putts wasn't a bit worried. Flint eyed him with a curious amusement. Putts wore a wide-brimmed, filthy, tan hat and what Flint recognized as official navy-issue white pants, with a tattered and equally dirty long-sleeve shirt. His feet were bare and callused and nearly black, either from too many years in the Caribbean sun or a combination of that and simply not bathing.

With square shoulders and a stature somewhere around five-foot-nine, Putts had a bull-legged stance which Flint figured was that of an authentic

Deck Ape in navy terms. Probably, this old swabby was off a World War II carrier, or perhaps a mine sweeper. Whatever, Putts had seen his share of saltwater duty and Flint laughed silently at the sight of him, hugging the boat's rudder as they bobbed their way toward Anguilla, the 140 horse outboard motor hissing and straining against a strong cross-channel current.

Just when Sandy felt she was about to succumb to seasickness, old Putts broke into a smile and pointed in the direction of Anguilla.

"Dead ahead folks. That's Anguilla, dead ahead."

With the boat rising and falling every second, neither of them could see Anguilla, but the fact that Putts saw it was music to their ears. The traveling of the past few days was beginning to take its toll.

Finally they were just off shore and Flint could make out a long dock with small buildings in the background. The landing site was rather flat and unimpressive at first, but once on shore, it opened up more and Flint and Sandy observed a greener surrounding.

Flint paid Putts $25 American and watched as he turned his boat around and headed back in the direction of St. Martin, his boat like a cork in the ocean.

Flint gave Sandy a reassuring kiss on the cheek. "There goes a genuine relic," he said, as Putts and his boat finally disappeared between the turbulent waves.

"The boat or Putts?" Sandy replied.

"Oh, both," Flint told her.

"He had me scared." said Sandy.

Flint kissed her again and laughed loudly. "Men like Putts always survive, my dear. They're indestructible."

Within minutes of their landing, Flint and Sandy were greeted by a male driver who welcomed them on behalf of his resort employers, Tim and Priscilla Swanton, owners of the British House, a combination of hotel with outer villas, set at the far end of a magnificent two-mile beach that faced in the direction of both St. Martin and St. Barts on one side and the open windward sweep of ocean on the other. They arrived shortly before sunset, had dinner on a long veranda with six other newly arrived guests and then promptly retired to their assigned villa for a night of uninterrupted sleep. What interested Flint most about this place when Monica mentioned it was the fact that they had no phones in any of the guests' rooms. No radios, nor televisions either.

"You'll get along much better without those things," Monica had told them. "Anguilla is an island where you don't even have much conversation. It's more for seeing and enjoying. A place to get back inside yourself."

5. TOE-DANCING ON

At precisely 9 A.M. on Saturday the resonant ringing of the bells of the Church of St. Peter, on Saratoga's lower Broadway, broke the silence of a sunny, warm, April morning. The bells were tolling for Claire Valova, soon to be wheeled on a bier in her solid bronze casket through the large double church doors where Father Tim Doyle, a much devoted admirer of her former dancing career and an equally staunch devotee of the track and Valova's great race horses, would celebrate her solemn mass of requiem. The mass would be concelebrated by a priest of the Byzantine rite, a Russian himself, Father Ivan Inovich. It would be, as everyone expected, a proper and fitting send off, replete with all the holy trimmings the universal church could offer.

All of Saratoga was aware of this particular event. So, apparently, was the world of society: from the art colonies of Paris, the race tracks of England and Ireland, California's Palm Desert Resort, along the windy shores of Newport, and most of all through the opera, ballet, and theater haunts of New York City where she had been a treasured icon to hundreds. The national press and television media had given her banner headlines, befitting her professional and social status. The *Saratoga Star* city desk was inundated with calls from points around the globe inquiring about her. For two days prior to the announced funeral, hordes of media personnel were suddenly showing up in the Spa City, quickly taking up the normally available hotel and motel vacancy space at this time of year. For local innkeepers it was as if August racing had suddenly started.

Meanwhile, at editor Frank Duffy's home, nothing had been normal since the news of Claire's and Ann's deaths. Duffy, still numb over the incidents, suffered from insomnia. So much so that he finally called his Rotary Club associate, psychiatrist Dr. Arnold Blake, asking for his advice. By this time Blake was also aware of the deaths, so he offered to see Duffy at his office in Saratoga Hospital after working hours. This was before Claire's funeral. Arrangements for Ann Bifford had not yet been announced. Duffy had learned through the wire services that Bifford's immediate family, her mother in Connecticut and one older brother in Chicago, had been notified by Anguillan authorities that the ongoing investigation of her death might delay the return of her body to the States by several days. Alarming news to her family to be sure, and most disconcerting to her friends who were anxiously awaiting detailed information on what had really happened to Ann in Anguilla, and who wanted to attend her services to pay their last respects.

Billy Farrell, though thoroughly upset at the situation, was handling it much better than Duffy and didn't suffer any problems requiring the good doctor's services. It was now time to prepare for Claire Valova's funeral. Valova had long ago left written instructions that when she died, she wanted to be buried in Saratoga on her estate.

Valova's body lay at rest in Burke's Funeral Home a half-mile or so from St. Peter's on upper Broadway. At 9:15 A.M. the heavy bronze casket was lifted to the shoulders of six impeccably dressed pallbearers and carried slowly down the steps of Burke's to a waiting eighteenth century horse-drawn cortege adding, so to speak, a touch of history and elegance not seen at a Saratoga funeral since the early 1890s.

The mourners from far and near chose their individual modes of transportation to the church, some electing to walk just to the side or directly behind the horse-drawn carriage, some riding in chauffeur-driven stretch limousines. Two jet-black, fifteen-hands-high stallions, groomed to perfection with their coats gleaming in the bright sunlight and harnessed in highly polished black rigging, pulled the carriage with the linen draped casket. The coachman was dressed in a red coat, black top hat, riding breeches and shining, black, knee-high leather boots and white gloves. He gently pulled the reins and guided the stallions down Broadway where row upon row of townsfolk were lined up to bid farewell to their beloved ballerina.

It was as touching a sight as Duffy could ever remember and, holding tightly to his wife's hand, he and Billy Farrell and his wife walked beside the carriage, nodding to the viewers. Some tossed flowers on Broadway as the cortege passed. And Duffy couldn't help but admire how Claire, though privileged in life, had touched the hearts of these people, most of them everyday working class types. She had elicited many emotions from them, mainly because she had always gone out of her way to treat them as equals, in spite of her great wealth. And they in their humble way were paying her the respect she deserved, in this tense dark hour of death. Claire's male and female peers, some having driven the four-hour trip from New York City the prior night, showing their vintage age with varying degrees of white, silver, and graying hair and rich dress, resembled a fashion house on parade. The diamond necklaces, assorted jewels, tie pins, gold watches, and other objects of apparel were the real McCoy. No rhinestones in this crowd. Down they went toward St. Peter's in the silence of the city streets, past the Firehouse Restaurant on the right where Valova was a frequent patron, singing along at the piano as Ruthie entertained. Some people were standing on the Firehouse's elevated outside patio. One little girl in a tan outfit, with a bouquet of flowers in her hands, waved as they passed. Faces were seen in the windows of the large red-brick Sheraton Inn on the left and a bit further down Broadway the steps of the courthouse were packed. John Starkweather, the court's custodian for over forty years, stood crying on the last step, his chin buried in his chest. And all the while the bells were tolling for Claire Valova, sealed in her bronze casket. A white and gold sheet held on by thin rubber bands was draped over the casket. Pinned to either side of the sheet was a pair of her toe shoes, a visible reminder to all witnessing the grand procession that the lifeless remains of Claire Valova, now encased in the box passing before them, had once glided like a gazelle over the world's ballet stages.

Surely this was the saddest of days in recent memory for many bystanders, and as the cortege approached the next block along Broadway, the crowds in front of Professor Moriarty's and Lillian's restaurants edged toward the curb to get a better glimpse of the great lady's celebrated entourage. It was, without question, a funeral to upstage all funerals. Were it not for the genuine grief and sorrow felt by all Saratogians for Valova's passing, the proceedings in front of them might have seemed theatrical in nature. As the carriage passed in front of Saratoga's two oldest thriving hotels, the Adelphi and the Rip Van Dam, Mark Spitzer, photographer for the *Star,* snapped off three quick shots, lining up the carriage just between the two ancient buildings, which Spitzer's trained eye told him would set the tempo and atmosphere for tomorrow's front-page, color picture spread. These shots, Spitzer was certain, would turn the clock back a notch to a time when the stellar hotels were among dozens of such buildings gracing the old Spa's Broadway. Claire Valova had spent many hours in the Adelphi with her ballet cohorts when the New York City Ballet was in its early summer residence and dancing at the Performing Arts Center. They used to say she raised one-hundred dollars for every glass of champagne she drank while conducting her charity gatherings. Many of the charity affairs were held on the flower-decorated courtyard of the Adelphi. The second floor balconies of the Adelphi were packed, and over the lower balcony was strung the initials CV in red and white roses.

Finally they moved by the entrance to historic Congress Park, up the slight incline past the YMCA, and came to a halt in front of the Church of St. Peter.

A large crowd was gathered on the driveway of the Holiday Inn across the street and just in front of the Inn at Saratoga, to the left of the church itself. When Claire Valova's casket was taken off the carriage and carried to the church entrance, the bells rang out once more. Seven times, with seven different chimes. The last one a long, echoing ring that chilled the hearts of all in attendance. They filed through the highly polished mahogany doors of St. Peter's, brushing against the hand-worn door knobs, and seated themselves in the rectangular interior of stiff wooden pews. It reminded Father Tim Doyle of a funeral out of the Victorian era, rather than the 1990s. The sun, shining through the luminous stained-glass church windows, shed streaks of gold, red, yellow, orange, and green down over the assemblage. When they were all seated, things quieted down and Claire Valova's casket, accompanied by the solemn-faced pallbearers, was wheeled up the side aisle, then moved to just in front of the altar where Father Doyle was standing. Frank Duffy was thinking how fitting this all was, that Claire was again in the very church that had given her so much solace in past years. The church she had often referred to as "the final retreat."

And so Father Doyle began the requiem mass after the entrance rites were given and the entrance song finished.

When it came to the homily, Doyle kept it short. Noting that, "In death a wonderful and new dimension takes place for the faithful Christian. Claire Valova is experiencing that dimension, as we all will some day, and she is with Christ."

Not a living soul at the mass doubted Father Doyle's word. Certainly in their collective minds and hearts, Claire Valova would surely ride the golden chariot through heaven's gate. Charity and goodness were her earthly trademarks.

Frank Duffy, looking rather feeble and having trouble making it to the altar's lectern, gave the first reading. Generally not intimidated speaking before a live audience, he had difficulty uttering his words of remembrance and praise for Valova. Duffy's right hand trembled as he held a small piece of paper containing his outline.

"We might not have seen Saratoga prosper as we have, had not this splendid, sweet lady stepped in when she did to help restore our own sense of history and pride. She came to us not as a magnificent dancer, which she was, but as one who walked among us daily, literally spearheading most of Saratoga's much needed charity functions. The youth of the New York City Ballet, seated here to honor Claire Valova, and all her many other friends and acquaintances have been privileged to know this vibrant, caring woman. To those older admirers who had the opportunity to see her dance, the memory no doubt will be even more vivid. Now, and in the future, when I think of Claire Valova, I will remember the great sense of community she instilled in us all. Though born in Russia, she was a true Saratogian."

His hand continued to shake and Duffy's voice began fading. He adjusted the microphone, but it did no good. He peered down at the assembly and then at his wife, Martha, seated in the front pew with Meg and Billy Farrell. He could think of nothing more to say. Duffy left the lectern slowly, whispering his long-ago altar boy's Latin invocation, "Kyrie Eleison,"—Lord have mercy on us— which only Father Doyle, nearest to him, heard.

Duffy was followed to the lectern by Heather O'Brien, a petite, dark-haired rising star of the New York City Ballet company, who spoke briefly of the positive and wonderful influence Claire Valova had on all members of the ballet during her lifetime.

"If the ballet troupe had a mother, Claire Valova was she," said the soft-spoken dancer, simultaneously brushing a tear and strand of hair from her face. "I actually only met her once. She came backstage at SPAC when we were rehearsing for Coppelia. We were very nervous all during rehearsal. She assured us we'd be fine come performance time. I can't begin to tell you what an inspiration she was to all of us that day."

When O'Brien had finished, John Ringo and Tyrone Black, two leading choreographers, came forward near the altar and, to Father Doyle's surprise, demonstrated a few steps and movements Valova was so famous for. They did not speak. It was over in a minute. The effectiveness of this tribute drew an approving response from the mourners.

It was, as everyone expected, a marvelous tribute to one tireless contributor to the arts; but especially her efforts on behalf of the ballet.

Two-thirds of the way through the requiem, the doors of the church opened and four backstretch workers, led by Sweetfeed, slipped as quietly as they could into a back pew. All were dressed in their regular daily working gear. Two were wearing the very boots that had tramped about the stalls that morning. Suddenly the church's interior was filled with the sour odor of horse manure. A smell that could be readily tolerated by the horse owners, trainers and jockeys in the church, but was very repulsive to all others. Focus was diverted temporarily from Claire Valova's requiem to the newly arrived members, as heads turned in their direction. Father Doyle, realizing what had happened, immediately lit the thurible and started incensing the altar and bier. For several suspenseful minutes the manure and incense smells fought each other for control within the church. Father Doyle smiled as the incense, so strong that its grayish, drifting smoke and aroma bordered on choking some of the faithful, virtually dissipated the sour smell.

Meanwhile, Police Chief Nealy, trying to look as inconspicuous as possible, stood near the back all during the mass, quietly observing every person. On the far side of the sanctuary, one of his trusted detectives, Bob Brownstein, did likewise. Neither police officer knew exactly what they were looking for in this widely diverse crowd. Nealy and Brownstein, and Sergeant Galea back at headquarters, aside from Duffy and Farrell, were the only people at that moment in Saratoga who knew that Claire Valova had been a victim of slow poisoning. None of them as yet knew what poison was used, nor how she had received it. Duffy had kept his promise so far and had not allowed a word to be printed that centered on foul play. It was questionable just how long he could avoid printing the whole, gruesome story. For the time being, however, the townsfolk were of the belief that their beloved Valova had died of natural causes. At least she could be honored and buried without the dark cloud smearing her send off. Ironically, in the time since her reported death, her poisoning had not yet been picked up by the major wire services nor New York City papers. Nor TV. This puzzled Nealy. Nealy, weighing the limited details of her death that were available to him, felt duty bound to come and count heads, though he and Brownstein went about it with the utmost care, trying not to make their appearance at the church look like anything more than friends saying farewell to a much admired member of the Saratoga community. If Valova's murderer, or murderers, were present, however, it would come as no surprise to them. For during their long tenure on the Saratoga police force, they had come to expect anything and prepare for everything.

At the end of the mass, there wasn't a mourner present who didn't experience the aura left by Claire Valova. After administering the final blessing, Father Doyle led the pallbearers and bier down the aisle and waited momentarily till the large church doors were again opened into a bright April sun. The fresh breeze rushed to fill the church's interior, thus avoiding any further embarrassing odors from Sweetfeed and his cohorts. Doyle glanced over at Sweetfeed for a second, noticing that he appeared bewildered and out of place in this setting. Presently the procession began edging its way toward the doors.

Outside the church Frank and Martha Duffy slowly made their way through the departing crowd, and headed toward the Inn at Saratoga,

Duffy telling her that he definitely needed a stiff drink. His color had turned ash white while sitting through the ceremony and Martha was worried. The Farrells followed.

Inside the inn, with a whiskey on the rocks to fortify his dispirited soul, Duffy sat lazily back in a padded bar chair and watched the last of the mourners leaving the church. Some walked back to Broadway while others piled into a long line of waiting vehicles. Martha, never keen on Duffy's drinking habits, noticed that the color was finally beginning to come back in his face. Martha felt relieved, so did Billy Farrell, himself having a drink along with this wife, Meg. It had been an emotional day for all, and it wasn't yet half over. In fact, it was only 11 A.M.

Martha and Meg excused themselves to go to the ladies room and Duffy, waiting till they had left, promptly ordered another whiskey. Farrell, when asked, said his drink was fine. But Duffy ordered him another anyway.

Then Duffy, looking out the barroom window at the church entrance, spotted Father Doyle and Dr. Blake having a chat.

"God knows I have to talk to the doctor," he told Farrell, pointing at them.

Farrell blinked through his whiskey glass. "I never noticed him in church."

"He came early and sat to the right," said Duffy.

Then Farrell laughed. "Unlikely he'll be giving you any consultation in the bar, Duffy."

"Never mind," Duffy barked. "I'll go out to see him. Tell Martha I'll be right back." At which he walked with apparent renewed vigor to catch Dr. Blake.

When Duffy reached the church, Father Doyle was just ending his talk with Dr. Blake. Duffy spoke to Doyle briefly, congratulating him on a fine service. Doyle was then called off to talk to someone else.

"Well," said Dr. Blake, eyeing Duffy with a smile. "How are you weathering this whole thing?"

Duffy's head dropped. "That's the problem, Doc, I'm not doing well at all. There's too many loose ends hanging out there at this time to sort it all out." He looked again at Blake, as if expecting a miracle reply, something that would ease his troubled mind in the grave moment. And Blake, reading the forlorn expression on Duffy's face, knew that he had no clear remedy for his woes. Nevertheless, he decided to make an attempt at easing Duffy's grief. Wrapping his right arm around Duffy's shoulders, Blake walked him slowly from the church in the direction of the inn. Blake did not know that Meg and the Farrells were inside the inn minding Duffy's whiskey. And Duffy didn't mention that they were there, mainly because he knew the mild valium Blake had prescribed for him two days earlier was not to be washed down with straight whiskey, or any booze for that matter. So to skirt having to go inside the inn, Duffy sat on a bench just outside and had Blake join him. Martha and the Farrells waited at the bar, Martha tapping her right foot impatiently on the barroom's newly waxed parquet floor.

"Relax," Meg admonished her. "Duffy's taking this worse than most. Maybe the doctor can do him some good."

Dr. Blake was trying to reason in his own mind why Duffy was so upset. Certainly Duffy was well acquainted with Claire Valova, but hell, Blake reasoned, so were dozens of Saratogians. Why so much remorse on Duffy's part? Blake observed the small, round face with the glasses tilting on the edge of the nose, staring back at him. Not even the rather stiff April breeze hid the fact that Duffy had a few drinks under his belt. A glance toward the large glass-enclosed bar room of the inn, with Martha and the Farrells in plain sight, confirmed his suspicions. Yes, the old editor was nipping early today, in spite of Blake's warning that mixing valium and whiskey could be lethal. Blake was inwardly glad he hadn't given Duffy a strong dose of valium. Yet Blake decided not to bring up the matter as they sat on the bench. Instead, he leaned forward and asked Duffy a direct question.

"Frank, what's the real reason you're so upset over this death?"
Blake wasn't prepared for Duffy's reaction. He then viewed the sourest of faces, almost bordering on scorn. Duffy's little round shoulders hunched up. The eyes, with a penetrating stare Blake had never seen before, were truly angry. Duffy's forehead spawned a thousand new wrinkles. Blake could feel the little man's rage. It was almost as if Duffy were about to burst. "I'm sorry, Duffy," Blake added. "I had to ask this in the manner I did." Duffy's maddening posture quietly settled back. He slumped slightly on the bench, the round face deflating somewhat.

"If you knew, Doc, you'd understand."

"If I knew what?"

Duffy hesitated, then continued. "Claire's passing was not natural. She was done in by poisoning. We haven't printed anything on it yet. Really because that's all we know. She was poisoned, but no one at this point knows how or why. So there you have it. That's why I'm so damn upset."

Blake himself now looked a trifle shocked.

"That's not all," Duffy hastily added, anxious to get the whole story off his chest. "Ann Bifford may have been murdered in the Caribbean. Can you believe such a thing? Both of them murdered. It's too much to comprehend in one week. We've been trying to keep it quiet. At least till the funeral was over."

The two men then sat silently for several minutes. After a time, Martha and the Farrells got tired of waiting in the inn and came out to join them.

Martha came over and said hello to Blake, followed by the Farrells. Duffy was so far into thought, he wasn't immediately aware of their presence. When he did look up, it was Martha he was seeing.

"I think we'd all better go home," she said softly.

Wherein Duffy grumbled a few inaudible words to himself and then stood up. He then turned to address Blake again. "It's times like these that we need your services, Doctor. When the truth is known, the whole town will no doubt be beating a path to your office."

After Duffy had spoken, Farrell was aware that Dr. Blake was now the sixth person in Saratoga to know the bad news. No, on second thought, Duffy realized there was a seventh person. The person who poisoned Valova. Or maybe even more persons. The thought of it disturbed him further. Farrell stepped between the two. "We've got some serious decisions to make in the next few hours," Farrell said. "Like Duffy here, I'd appreciate some sound advice on how to proceed."

Blake sensed in Farrell the suffering he'd seen in Duffy. Of the two, however, Blake instinctively knew that Farrell could hide his emotions better. He also understood that Martha and Meg were oblivious to the real details. And it reminded him of a saying he had read once in medical school. "Husbands and wives tell each other everything. *Almost.*"

Martha and Meg had walked off just far enough so that Blake could get in a parting remark to Duffy and Farrell.

"I haven't any momentary answer for you. If you want to come by the office in the morning, I'll set time aside to talk to you both. I do, however, have a contact that specializes in investigations of dubious nature. Depending on when the official word gets out on Claire's and Ann's deaths, and who subsequently is in charge of the investigation, would bear on his getting involved. My contact has taken on assignments in Saratoga before. But let's talk more about this tomorrow. Try your best to cope with this reality, as unpleasant and disturbing as it is. I know from experience that there can be no real peace of mind until the matter is resolved. Perhaps I can help."

Blake watched as the four strolled back down Broadway, arms locked tightly together, Farrell, with his huge bulk, seemingly holding them all up.

Later in the afternoon, at his office in Saratoga Hospital, Blake pulled out a tiny black notebook and looked at a coded phone number Mike Flint had given him one year earlier. Wondering, as he viewed the number, where and with whom Flint was at this very moment. And would Sandy Blair be with him, or waiting with longing and fear in her young heart for his return from points and dangers unknown?

6. CALL WAITING

Flint was of such a restless nature that after the initial days and nights on Anguilla, snorkeling in the morning hours, resting and reading books for most of the afternoons, and dining late into the evenings, Sandy sensed he needed a change of pace. Without waiting for him to say it, she suggested they go to St. Martin for a change of pace, but she did have one stipulation. She insisted on setting the St. Martin agenda.

They were enjoying a variety of artful Caribbean cuisine at lunch on the veranda of the British House, supplemented with a light, dry white wine that went well with the red snapper Flint was savoring, when Sandy surprised him with a neatly hand-written itinerary of their pending St. Martin visit.

"I put this together yesterday while you were in dreamland," she said. "I also made some phone calls. As you can see, we will be busy on St. Martin. You'll get your chance to play the tables at the Port De Plaisance casino, we'll have more time to browse through the gold jewelry shops in Marigot and, best of all, we'll sail on those Americas Cup racing yachts. What do you think of it?"

He finished his wine and reached for her hand. "You'll wear me out, darling."

"No," she replied, "I'll stimulate you."

There was a surge of electricity between them as their eyes met. It had been like that ever since Saratoga, continued while in California, and increased with a burning intensity with each passing day. If there hadn't been other guests within sight, he would have made love to her right on the veranda. He was thrilled that this unbelievably lovely young woman was his.

In the morning they hired a boat to St. Martin. Flint assumed that old Putts would again be their pilot, but when the boat arrived a young Anguillan, dressed in faded cut-off jeans was at the tiller.

"Where's Putts?" Flint asked.

"Gone fishing. Putts gone fishing."

Flint helped Sandy into the rocking boat. "Didn't know he was the fishing type," said Flint.

"Oh, yes. They go way out to deep water. Putts has many big fish he's caught."

What kind?" Flint asked.

"Big fish. All kinds of big fish."

Sandy smiled at Flint. "He's told you darling. Big fish."

"Sounds like some I've caught in my time." Flint added. "Big fish or big fish stories. I'm not certain which one comes first."

Sandy poked him in the stomach, then hugged him about the waist as the boat started out toward St. Martin.

The water this time across was relatively quiet. The boat went along smoothly. Flint had Sandy sit on his lap and they gazed ahead in silence. The young pilot stood straight up, feet apart, staring in the direction of St. Martin. There was only the sound of the ocean lapping at the boat's bow and the groaning of the outboard motor. It lasted like that until the boat headed into the docks at Marigot, where, once they disembarked, a cab was waiting to take them to Port De Plaisance.

Two rubber boats with outboard motors were waiting in the Port De Plaisance's protected inlet when they arrived. Several tourists were waiting near the boats. Terry, a leather-tanned Englishman, with muscular arms and hairy chest, and a completely shaven head, was handing out printed T-shirts to the tourists, some in red and some in blue. They were all to be crew members for a day on the two streamline 12 meter racing yachts moored five hundred or so yards out in Simpson Bay Lagoon.

"You must have a T-shirt," Terry was shouting to the novice crew members. "Now let me see, how many of us are here?"

"One is not arrived yet," a woman with satin blonde hair and thick dark glasses piped up.

"Well, we will be pushing off soon," Terry insisted. "If that person doesn't show, I'll make up the crew for the first boat." He started counting heads again. "We've got twenty-three on hand now. We can sail with crews of twelve. If you get sick or otherwise too tired to fulfill your assigned duty once aboard, we have staff that can take over. So don't worry. We'll sail just off the bay in tamer waters. I must remind you, we have no toilet facilities on board. So do what you have to do now. Once at sea the ocean becomes our bathroom. There was an immediate scramble for the main building's rest rooms. Ten minutes later the rubber boats, filled to capacity, were bobbing toward the waiting yachts. Flint, holding Sandy, sensed her excitement and pulse rising as the boats drew nearer the yachts.

There wasn't much time lost with instructions, as Terry introduced members of his staff drifting alongside the yachts in other rubber boats. The blue T-shirts crew boarded the first yacht and the red shirts, the second yacht. Everyone was given a position and a job. Flint was put on a rear tiller and Sandy, not keen on leaving his side, was moved forward as a grinder.

"You must do as I say when I say it," Terry barked. "We'll have the sails up in a minute and this craft will move out fast. There's a tricky crosswind today, so when I give the command to grind and so forth, don't waste any time. We don't want the other crew to win, do we?"

It was as if the racing craft was lifted suddenly off the ocean's surface. A stiff wind caught the raised sails, tilting the boat sideways and moving it swiftly ahead in a smooth cutting arc through the waves. Within seconds Terry was barking out commands to do this and that, while moving about the deck in cat-like motion to assist each crew member. The two boats raced side by side, almost even, and not barely five feet apart at first. But this changed as they came to the first buoy and had to swing sharply to make a clear turn. Sandy thought the other boat's bow was going to cut them in half they were so close. The sail swung madly across the deck to the opposite side, tilting the boat again and everyone shifted to keep their positions. Terry gave them all a broad smile and a thumbs up.

"That's good crewing. Let's show them who's best."

The racing went on for over an hour, with the boats alternating the lead and everyone becoming more adjusted to their jobs. Terry all the time encouraging them with pats on the back and thumbs up.

Flint's arms were beginning to tire with each nautical mile. Sandy ground away till her arms were numb. The tips of her fingers had no feeling. But she was enjoying it to no end. It would be, as Terry had told them earlier, a good hurt.

On the final leg of the race the boat settled into a straight run, the jib and main sail ballooning out and powering the boat forward. They were at least two lengths ahead of the rival yacht.

For all his sailing in Palos Verdes, Flint had never experienced anything like this. It was like going from a glider to an F-16 jet. The sheer power of the yacht was awesome. He looked over at Sandy, her hair wet and matted against her face, as was her T-shirt to her body. They had been wetted down a dozen times or more when the sails shifted. The raw exercise of it cleared Flint's mind of any dark thoughts he might have had from previous assignments. He found it excruciating, yet rewarding. It was just what he needed and wanted.

Then he heard a phone ringing. Or at least he thought he heard a phone ringing. He scratched at his ears. Perhaps the water was playing tricks with his hearing. Then he heard it again.

Terry moved from his command position over the crew and dropped inside the small opening at mid ship for a second. When he came back he held a wireless ship-to-shore phone in his right hand.

"Hey, It's for you Mr. Flint. Someone must talk to you."

Flint's jaw dropped open. "Who in hell's name could it be?"

He glanced over at Sandy with a look of disbelief on his face. It had to be a joke. No, on second thought, it might be Monica calling. She's be the only person to know their whereabouts. Terry handed Flint the phone.

"Flint here."

"That you Flint?"

"Yes. Yes. It's me."

The phone then squelched in his ear and the conversation was broken up by static. Then he heard the voice again. "You're not coming in too clear, Flint."

"Oh, God," Flint said aloud, as he looked again at Sandy. "I think it's Harry Waite calling from New York."

"We've got a bad connection, Flint. All I'm getting is bits and pieces between a lot of static. It's like an ocean in my ears."

"That's exactly what it is Harry. It's the ocean. We're in the middle of it at the moment on a racing yacht."

"No kidding. Well get to another phone and call me back, will ya?"

"Say what you have to say Harry, there's no other phone to be had."

"Where the hell are you anyway?" Harry asked.

"I told you. We're on the ocean off St. Martin."

"Well, we've got a big one on our hands, Flint. In fact, I'm calling you because a friend of yours called me. Haven't the slightest idea where he got my coded telephone number, but he called yesterday and asked for you. A Doctor Blake from Saratoga."

Flint held the phone away from his ear for a second. In that instant he knew his vacation in paradise was over, or about to be over. He also remembered where and when he had given Dr. Blake Harry's number. A foolish move, yes. But it was too late now. Flint had given Blake the number last summer. Without Blake's help at the time, Flint's special assignment in Saratoga would have been cut short. As distasteful as it might be, Flint knew he'd have to respond to Dr. Blake's call. Unfortunately, he'd have to get the message second-hand from Harry. Harry was long-winded and never lost for words. Someone had once told Flint that Central Headquarters' long distance telephone bills were astronomical, thanks to Harry's never-ending calls.

"Sorry, Harry," Flint said finally. "But he was the only person I could trust with that number at the time. What's happened?"

"Plenty," said Harry. "Two ladies have been rubbed out. One in New York that we have a pretty good handle on. She was poisoned. The other was drowned right there in the Caribbean. I don't know where you're staying down there, but are you anywhere near the island of Anguilla?"

Flint felt empty in the pit of his stomach. It was Saratoga *déjà vu* all over. The yacht suddenly pitched forward and bounced off some tall waves and a series of winding sounds pierced Flint's ear. Then more static. It didn't take Sandy long to realize that Flint wasn't engaged in a pleasant conversation with Harry. She was totally frightened at the prospects of what it might be.

When the static subsided, Flint resumed talking to Harry. "Look here," Flint said, "if you reached me on this boat off St. Martin, then I'm pretty sure you already know I'm staying on Anguilla. What I don't know is, how you found exactly where I'm staying and, furthermore, how you knew I was out here sailing. And don't tell me you have an operative down here keeping track of my movements. I don't need a nursemaid. How coincidental that out of dozens of islands in the Caribbean, some woman drowns on Anguilla. Now tell me, Harry, who's your spy in the Caribbean?"

"No spy," Harry said. "As always, I have friendly operatives in most places, including the Netherlands Antilles. I'm not going to give you their names. Let's say they can be trusted. Besides, you never know when you might really need their assistance. You know this game better than anyone. An ace in the hole is worth having, so they say."

"Why me?" asked Flint. Since the call, one of Terry's young staff members had taken over Flint's job at the tiller.

"What comes along, comes along," replied Harry, in what Flint took as one of his more stupid remarks. "Anyway, Dr. Blake and several of his friends in Saratoga have asked for your help. I told them it was your call. Frankly, they have no faith in the Saratoga cops to figure this one out. Believe it or not, it even gets more complicated. The poisoned lady turns out to be Claire Valova, ex-ballerina of considerable wealth. Blake says the whole town is in mourning. The drowned girl is one Ann Bifford. Apparently she was an important veterinarian among the horse racing set. She often vacations in the Caribbean, so maybe that might help you. She must have made friends down there over the years. Valova was seventy or so, Bifford only thirty-six. Blake says a newspaper editor in Saratoga name of Duffy, claims Bifford doctored Valova's stable of race horses across the country. Draw what conclusion you want from that tid-bit Flint, but I'd say someone wanted them both out of the picture in a hurry. I'll work on this New York City poisoning if you will poke around in Anguilla and see what happened to Bifford. Anguilla is an English pro-tectorate, so you won't have an easy time getting information. Besides, they've been holding her body pending completion of their investigation. The Anguillans have taken charge of the investigation, I'm told. My sources tell me they're not kind to outside meddlers. Guess her family is quite upset with not getting her back sooner. As I say, tread easy there. We don't want any altercation with the British foreign office. That's all I have for now. Watch your step, especially with Sandy there. I'll contact you tomorrow. Better yet, get to a pay phone and call me. I'll be at my health club on the East Side. Must run now."

"Thanks for the call, Harry, it's just what I needed."

"Hey, you know it was the last call I wanted to make. Blake said you were his friend. What could I do?"

"Okay, Harry. Call Blake back and tell him I'll get started. By the way, you mentioned a health club. What's a fat desk jockey like you doing going to a health club?"

Harry laughed. "I've turned over a new leaf, Flint. I'm down to two hundred pounds and dropping. They even have me running two miles a day in the gym. And what's more, I gave up smoking my favorite Havana cigars. Now is that sacrifice for you, or what?"

"I'm proud of you, Harry. Maybe we can play tennis when I get back. Sweet gymnastics."

Flint handed the phone back to Terry and sat down, forgetting as he did that he was still a member of the crew with a job to do at the tiller, at which time he realized he needed to get back at it.

"What's wrong?" shouted Terry. "You got a touch of sea sickness?"

Flint shook his head. "Might just as well,'" replied Flint. "What I've got is worse. You wouldn't want any part of it."

By this time Sandy, intuitively recognizing Flint's changed mood, came to his side. Terry took over for her at the grinder.

"It was Harry, wasn't it?"

"Who else would find me out here?"

Sandy put her arms about Flint. "Can't that man leave you alone for one week?"

Flint held her face so that their noses touched. He stared directly into her eyes. He thought he saw tears on her face but, then again, it might have been ocean spray. In any event, he knew she was on the verge of breaking into a sob or possibly losing her composure altogether in front of the sweating, hot, nearly exhausted amateur crew. None of them were remotely aware of what Sandy and Flint were going through at this dreadful moment.

Sandy whispered, "How serious is it this time. And, where is it?"

He didn't want to tell her. She waited for his reply.

"I'm afraid it's an assignment of the worst kind, dear. Your Doctor Blake and some friends in Saratoga have asked me to assist them. Part of the immediate problem is on Anguilla."

Sandy frowned and appeared puzzled. "I don't understand," she said. "What would involve Dr. Blake or anyone in Saratoga way down here?"

"I don't know, love. That's what I have to find out."

"But we made so many plans this week. Can't it wait?"

He held her tighter. "I wish it could," he said in a voice full of disgust and disappointment. "This looks like a bad one."

She drew back, stared deeply into his eyes and ran her hand across his forehead, her soft fingers coming to rest on his chin. "This was the thing Monica warned me about," she said coolly, instantly wishing she had not put it in exactly that way.

He felt hurt by her frankness, but also realized it rang of truth.

"I don't have to do this," he said. "I call the shots on these things. I can tell Blake no." He then waited for her reaction.

She was too caught up in the emotion and suddenness of it to answer. Flint waited. The yachts came within sight of Simpson Bay. The crew, engrossed in its sailing chores, was oblivious to Flint and Sandy's plight. This Anguilla trek was to provide the precious few days to recuperate and strengthen their relationship. Flint now had the feeling that it could come apart at the seams. It was the typical cat-and-mouse game that had destroyed former relationships. Danger and possible death lurked in the background of each assignment, but that was his chosen calling and he'd hadn't yet found a way to call it quits.

Conversely, he couldn't face the prospect of fracturing this thing he had going with Sandy. A rolling wave tossed the yacht to one side, sending Sandy again into his arms. She buried her head in his chest.

"I need to know you'll be there when I get back," he said quickly.

She nodded her approval. The tension slowly eased out of both their bodies.

"I believe we both owe Blake this one," he said.

Her eyes met his again. "Be careful, Mike. Don't take unnecessary risks. I know it's crazy for me to be talking like this. You've heard it all before. But I can't help being selfish when it comes to you. You're my whole world."

The crew, aware that the yacht was about to cross the final buoy first, let out a sudden, unified scream, breaking Flint and Sandy's somber mood. Terry, bullhorn in hand, blasted away at the challengers with a variety of superlatives and hearty thumbs ups to his crew. Before they could moor the yacht and break down the sails, champagne corks were flying across the deck with as much bubbly being sprayed on crew members as was drunk.

Flint and Sandy shared a bottle. Riding in the rubber transport boats back to Port De Plaisance, Flint held Sandy tight and tried to appear as natural and as happy as everyone aboard. Nevertheless, inwardly his professional self was already planning future moves, step by precarious step.

He had left Anguilla a few hours earlier as a happy-go-lucky tourist. He'd be returning as a hunter. As the boats approached the harbor a single dark, distant rain cloud hung over the bay as they slipped along. Flint was hoping it was not an ominous sign of things to come on Anguilla.

7. GRAY MOMENTS

There were a lot of worried horsemen in Saratoga this spring. Their worries were based on two prevailing facts.

Too many good horses had died too early for anyone's comfort during the winter months, not only narrowing down the field of potential stakes winners, but casting a shadow over several well-known stables, with some pretty rough things being said about the staff, handlers, trainers and veterinarians employed by those stables.

The second worry of utmost importance centered on the falling prices at the season's early yearling select sales in Kentucky. The prices paid for yearlings had soared during the eighties because a number of well healed sheiks and various other oil-rich barons tried to outbid one another. But they weren't shelling out the big bucks as the nineties arrived. Many buyers had resorted to acquiring horses privately. The back-room dealing, though fierce, was more controlled. They didn't have to cough up an extra one-hundred thousand or one million in many cases, just because the auctioneer's emotional appeals in a crowded sales pavilion coaxed the wild bidding. It was a good deal for the buyers with money to spend, but it put many consignors at a disadvantage.

Sweetfeed, walking back to the track from Claire Valova's celebrated funeral mass with this fellow backstretch hands, was deeply engrossed in thought about what to do with Track Baron. He knew Track Baron would show no signs of illness for a few days. But when the time came when the big stallion did require a veterinarian, Sweetfeed was at a loss who he would call. There would be no Ann Bifford to cover on this one. Oh, yes, The Voice had told him not worry. To proceed as normal. But he didn't put any faith or trust in The Voice now that Claire was gone. Furthermore, Sweetfeed was scared. Who was to say that The Voice would not turn on him and reveal his deep, dark secret to the police? All these unpleasant thoughts danced in his head. He had experienced severe migraines ever since he received the news of Claire's death, haunted by his past deeds and terrified of the consequences. Worst of all, there was no one to talk to about it. Not even his good friend "Water Man" Wilkins, could be told. Sweetfeed knew that he had broken his sacred trust with the horses the very first time he had agreed to participate in the outrageous scheme. At the entrance to the barns Sweetfeed left his fellow workers and went, for reasons he couldn't explain to himself, and sat outside Track Baron's stall. Along the way he couldn't help but notice the dozens of black ribbons tied around barn poles, fences and staff doors. It was the backstretch's way of acknowledging the passing of their beloved Valova. It was a bittersweet tribute for Sweetfeed, knowing in his heart the truth about her. He cringed at the thought of what would happen should the grieving horsemen and women in Saratoga on that warm spring day ever find out what Claire Valova, The Voice, and he were involved in. He theorized it would bring the racing industry to its knees.

He sat for several minutes outside the stall, listening to the great stallion shifting and rubbing against the walls inside. Then he stood up and went into the stall and drew Track Baron's head around so he could observe the stallion better. Sweetfeed was looking for signs of dizziness in the horse, but didn't detect any. Then he tossed a grooming brush to the far corner of the stall to see if the horse's hearing had yet been impaired. Track Baron's head swung up sharply. He was sure by this move the horse's hearing was not yet affected. He passed his dirt-caked hands over the stallion's eyes to check his vision. The horse's reaction was normal. He was baffled. Certainly, he thought, the poison he had given Track Baron five days earlier would be producing some symptoms by now. Sweetfeed didn't expect any major deterioration in the stallion's health at this point, however, he was expecting at least a few signs that the poison was slowly working its way through the powerful horse's body. If not, then why not? It had worked the same way on all the others. What made Track Baron so different? Outside the stall once more, he sat again and pondered this question. In the gray moments, sitting and staring across the expanse to the towering grandstands, Sweetfeed decided all was hopeless. They would find him out in time. He was certain of that. Perhaps, with his guilt so great, he felt he could eventually take the pending punishment, whatever it might be. Perhaps the rest of his few remaining years in jail, for sure. What he couldn't reconcile was Valova's reputation being smeared throughout the equine industry. He had to figure a way to keep her involvement quiet. It would serve no meaningful purpose to drag her down. After all, Sweetfeed thought, whatever her motives, she was no doubt doing it for the good of Thoroughbred horse racing. No mistaking that good horses died before their prime racing time, but Valova had a reason. She must have had a reason.

Then there was the yearling sales to think about. August was coming soon and the likes of Claire Valova were its mainstay. The wiggle of her index finger, the nod of her head, or, as was known to happen, slipping off a shoe at the critical moment of bid. She had a dozen ways of bidding, and the sales agents loved her style and often used her to beef up the sales among the buyers. It often came down to personalities bidding on a particular horse, and had nothing to do with the final bid price nor whether the hip number in the ring was really worth the dollars bid. This was the highest of highest big stakes poker. Claire Valova and her kind were masters of the game. The hundreds of thousands of dollars. . . no, the collective millions spent on yearlings by she and her friends was crucial to the sales each year. How sorely missed her presence would be. Sweetfeed fought back tears thinking about her.

After an hour or so, Sweetfeed settled down. He could hear Track Baron's heavy breathing in the stall, he listened for any signs of irregularities. He detected none. The horse apparently was much stronger than Sweetfeed had imagined. Then he began doubting if he had squirted enough liquid from the plastic tube into the water bucket. If this were so, if the exact amount wasn't mixed in with the water, then there could be even further problems on the horizon. Sweetfeed didn't know, however, that the end result culminated in a condition resembling a heart attack. The attacks were so natural that it was merely a matter of calling the resident veterinarians to pronounce the animals dead and sign the proper papers. He was concerned now that Track Baron's poison dose wasn't sufficient. Then all sorts of fearful scenarios began running through his tired brain. What if Track Baron got sick but didn't die? What if several track doctors were called to assist? What if blood samples were taken while the poison was filtering full strength through Track Baron's vessels? What of this? What of that? He couldn't help pondering all the dark possibilities that he envisioned ahead. Worst of all, this was the summer Claire Valova, Track Baron's owner, was to be inducted into the National Museum of Racing. That grand, Georgian, colonial, red-brick bastion of the Sport of Kings, situated on Union Avenue right across from the tree-lined parking lot of the famous flat track itself. Sweetfeed couldn't bear the thought that she might not take her place alongside racing's revered equine veterans. Sweetfeed knew that Claire Valova's lifelong dream, and that of all true horsemen, was to be honored for posterity by having her biographical wall plaque prominently displayed in the racing museum, right up there with Whitney and Widener. With the sour odor from his raunchy flannel shirt getting to a point that even he couldn't stand the stench, he stood up and walked over to a nearby water barrel, dipped up a pail full of the bug-infested cold water, and poured it over his head. It was the closest thing to a shampoo and a bath he'd had in weeks. It did nothing to dispense the odor, but it cooled his body and relaxed him somewhat.

With water from his soaked hair and clothing dripping into his rubber boots, Sweetfeed suddenly had an idea. He literally yelled, standing in place, at the prospects of it. It was a simple, yet profound, thought. What if he could keep Track Baron alive? Perhaps find an antidote to the poison? This would put a stop to the killings once and for all. There wouldn't be any investigation or probing by track doctors. He reasoned he could just stop doing what he had been doing and things would go back to normal. He could be the Sweetfeed of old, nurturing the horses, not poisoning them. He was delighted with the idea. But then a nightmarish second thought crossed his mind. What would The Voice do? How would he handle him? Where in all of Saratoga was The Voice? Sweetfeed was caught between the two. On the one hand he was euphoric with the idea of maybe salvaging Track Baron. On the other, he feared The Voice's certain revenge. The dilemma of opposing thoughts was driving him crazy. He sat for the longest time thinking about it. The sun was creeping down behind the clubhouse and grandstands now, and when he looked in the direction of the magnificent wooden structure with its spires silhouetted in the day's last light, the magnitude of what had taken place at the Church of St. Peter, with its chilling finality, registered in Sweetfeed's mind. For the first time in many years, the old backstretch sage felt completely alone and abandoned.

8. "MERCY ON THEIR SOULS"

Saratoga Police Chief Tom Nealy sat viewing the beautifully wood-burned carving in Dr. Arnold Blake's Victorian living room furniture at the doctor's home on upper Broadway. Nealy figured the precious pieces probably were crafted in the late 1890s either in New York City or San Francisco, and he dared not venture what they must have cost the good doctor.

The dark, highly finished, wood floors and a series of red, gold, and yellow heavy fabric drapes complemented the furniture. It was, Nealy thought, like stepping back in time.

He could also see a portion of the adjacent dining room, with its deep, rich, mahogany walls and polished silver serving trays set on an oak table which was located next to a large, smoked-glass, china closet. Truly a setting from a more genteel time. Perhaps, Nealy thought, it was a place for Saratoga's leading psychiatrist to escape from the rigors of his job. Lord knows we all need to get away from our troubles, Nealy mused.

Nealy had been invited by Dr. Blake, along with Frank Duffy and Billy Farrell, two days after Claire Valova's funeral. Nealy was dressed in a light tan suit and not his customary police uniform. He remembered with some embarrassment his first meeting one year earlier with Dr. Blake at Saratoga Hospital. Nealy had come on official business to ask some hard questions concerning a murdered girl. He left the meeting with his professional tail between his legs and his ego deflated. Hopefully, for whatever reason the doctor had called this gathering, things would go much better. Nealy had been told by the house maid who let him in that Dr. Blake would be down momentarily.

"Dr. Blake had a last-minute phone call," said the maid. "He's up in his study."

She offered to fetch Nealy a refreshment, not defining what type, but he begged off. The maid said Duffy and Farrell would be along shortly.

As Nealy sat wondering about the clever artisans who had painstakingly crafted the vintage pieces, the doorbell rang. The maid appeared again. She opened the door and Nealy heard Duffy's familiar voice echo off the parlor's hard slate floor. Farrell's booming baritone followed Duffy's.

"Ah, I see you beat us here," said Duffy.

"I'm always early," said Nealy. "It's a professional habit."

"Well," Duffy continued, "I'm generally late. Same goes for Farrell. Isn't that so, Billy?"

"If you say so, Duffy."

"I do say so."

Duffy glanced about the room and asked, "Where's Dr. Blake?"

Nealy pointed his finger skyward. "Taking a phone call upstairs."

"That's the worst thing about being a doctor," Duffy said. "Patients can't leave you alone day or night."

Duffy no sooner spoke when Dr. Blake entered the living room. "Glad you could all come," Blake said. "I thought it best to meet here and not the hospital. I sometimes think the hospital walls have ears. Not that we doctors ever get paranoid or anything. Anyway, I believe we're all still carrying this week's funeral on our collective shoulders. It's not an easy thing to cope with, nor to understand. As I often tell my patients, and no doubt have told you individually, only time can heal the pain and loss. In this case, however, we, unlike most Saratogians, have to face this death from a different perspective." Nealy shifted in his chair at the last sentence. And Duffy and Farrell appeared more than a bit uneasy. "Yes, gentlemen, I know what you know and maybe a few things more."

Nealy leaned over to Duffy and whispered, "What's he telling us?" Duffy poked the police chief in the side and didn't reply.

Farrell felt blood rush to his head, but remained motionless next to Duffy. Blake looked directly at Duffy. "I guess we might have been able to pass Claire's death off by saying she had been terminally ill for some time. But it's my understanding that a small downstate tabloid has already leaked the real reason for her death. Have you seen anything at the newsroom this morning concerning it?" Blake said flatly. Duffy realized it was a cunning way for Blake to let Nealy know that the poisoning was now common knowledge, or soon would be. It also was a subtle way for Blake to let Duffy off the hook for having told him during their talk at the church.

"Well," said Duffy. "I've been scooped by many papers in my time. These tabloids have no heart nor feeling. The answer is no. All of us, meaning the *Times, Daily News,* and *Post* have held back as we promised. Stories on Claire are set and ready to roll on a minute's notice. I can assure you that once the tabloids distribute their filthy rags, there will be an instantaneous rush by the major papers to do likewise." He held his hand on his chin as he spoke. "And no doubt I'll be besieged with local calls. Maybe we should have broken the story the day it happened." Then Duffy remembered what an editor once said when Duffy was a mere deskman on the paper. "Don't ever kill a good story. They don't come along all that often."

"If she was poisoned," Farrell added, "then she must have had some bitter enemies. At this moment I can't think of one, though. Can you?"

"No, not I," said Nealy. "She was the social stream of this town and one of the most rugged individualists I've ever known. But enemies, no. Perhaps some jealous peers, but not real enemies."

Blake moved off to the side of the large room and drew the curtains open. The furniture took on an even richer assortment of colors as the sun entered through the rounded windows and came to rest on the foursome.

"It appears we have two stories to tell," insisted Blake. "Let's not forget Ann Bifford. God only knows what happened to her in the Caribbean."

Nealy sat up. "We can't get any information from down there," he said in an awkward tone. "Governments on those islands do their own thing and cooperation with them is laughable at best. Poor Bifford's family can't even get any answers."

"I can help here," said Blake, startling his guest with his frankness.

Nealy stood up. "I don't quite understand, Doctor. What can you do?"

Blake smiled and came before Nealy, hands on hips. "I know a man who can look into such things. Let's just say he's an intelligence operative for hire." Duffy was on his feet now, as was Farrell. All three looked stunned and mystified by Blake's revelation.

Blake went on. "He's in the Caribbean now. I contacted him through a friendly intermediary. At my urging, he's on the case as I speak, though I haven't heard directly back from him either. I hope I have your support in this." Blake waited a moment for their reaction. Duffy and Farrell gave an approving nod of their heads. "He was in Saratoga just one year ago on a secret assignment, but I'm not going into the details of that visit just now. However, he has my total trust. Why Claire and Ann were murdered in equally tragic but different ways has bothered me as well as you. When the tabloids get done with their expected sensationalized versions of these deaths, at lot more people will be bothered. I can assure you that. The best thing I can think to do is to find out what really took place, if possible. Even at that, who knows where this will lead? There'll be enough summarizing and speculative analyzing to go round when all their laundry is aired. That's about all I have to say at this time. Please let me have your comments."

They couldn't reply. Blake had caught them off guard with his lightning words. Nealy was thinking silently that somewhere amid all this he was in a professional and adversarial relationship with Blake. It was nothing personal. It was Nealy's opinion that cops did their job and doctors did theirs, occasionally assisting one another when circumstances called for it. But not on a buddy, buddy basis. Nealy wasn't sure he could approve of a de facto, shadowy agent, regardless of how trustworthy, and Blake sensed Nealy's quandary. The doctor knew he had won the other two over but he also had to convince the goshawk police chief. He then decided his best approach was reason.

"I view it this way, Chief," Blake said softly. "Fact one. Our two lady friends are dead. Fact two. They both died away from Saratoga. No doubt that with all their Saratoga involvements and vested local interest, not discounting Claire Valova's extensive equine holdings, a portion of whatever investigation takes place will come under your jurisdiction. And burdened as you are now with several other unsolved murders here, would it not pay to have some outside help?"

As Blake was talking, Nealy went to the window and peered out. He observed the gardens and fountains of the doctor's backyard, admiring the enchanting rows of green shrubs and neatly cut bushes. Also the dirt beds where flowers, not yet in bloom in the cool April air, would soon fill the yard with brilliant color. Like the doctor, everything was orderly, Nealy thought. The room's furniture and the garden were an extension of the doctor's well-structured mind. The surroundings enhanced his stature. It all spoke of neatness and confidence, something Nealy knew he could never find in his hectic police work.

"You might just be right, Doc," Nealy found himself saying agreeably.

Duffy and Farrell were relieved.

Blake smiled at all three.

The maid appeared again in the room, holding a tray with four long-stemmed crystal glasses filled with white wine.

"Please join me in a drink," said Blake. "It's one of few I have on occasion."

When each had taken a glass, Blake proposed a toast. "To the memory of Claire Valova and Ann Bifford. God have mercy on their souls."

He then led them to the front door and out onto the sweeping veranda, shaking each of their hands as they departed for their cars.

Nealy slipped slowly behind the wheel of his new Chevy Impala and turned the ignition key. He made a U-turn on Broadway and headed toward downtown. Duffy and Farrell went home across town.

9. EXTRA CRISPY

Chief Nealy drove to his office on Lake Avenue where he had a pre-arranged meeting with Stuart Clayborn Witt, a gentleman Nealy had read about but had never met personally.

Witt, 72, had only recently come to Saratoga from his home in Lexington, Kentucky, where he dabbled in several profitable businesses, but really pursued his real passion, horse racing. Witt brought along with him four very promising two-year-old Thoroughbreds, one of which he figured had potential of being a contender for the year's prestigious Eclipse Award. But he kept this knowledge a secret from the horse fraternity, hoping to surprise them all come race time.

When Nealy entered his second-floor office, overlooking Lake Avenue, Witt was already there waiting. To Nealy's amusement, Witt looked like a double for the late Colonel Sanders. When Witt greeted Nealy with a big, Kentucky drawl, "How you do-in' Chief?" Nealy almost broke out in laughter. Witt's white hair stuck out at all ends, cutting off just above his shoulders, and though he was dressed in a dark suit, not white attire, the glasses and face were pure Col. Sanders. He had the girth to go with it, and to Nealy's further amusement, Witt had a broad-brimmed hat at his side.

"I'm fine, sir," said Nealy. "Please come into my inner office." Witt, apparently nursing a severe case of arthritis, struggled to his feet and went inside.

Nealy seated Witt in a large, wooden, swivel chair directly in front of his solid oak desk. "What can I do for you, Mr. Witt?"

Witt smiled back and reached into his coat pocket and presented Nealy with a yellowish-colored envelope.

"A man in Kentucky gave me this to hand to you. Said you'd understand." Nealy fingered the envelope, noticing it was sealed.

"Does this man have a name?" said Nealy, eyeing Witt with a little more curiosity.

"Yes," replied Witt. "Wainridge or Wainring. Something like that. Age is starting to creep up on me, Chief. I'm finding myself forgetting things of late." Nealy wasn't sure if Witt was joking or serious. How could he come into his office and hand out an envelope given him by some man whose name he can't remember? It made no sense at all.

"Can you venture what's in this?" Nealy asked.

"Not one iota," said Witt.

"You're sure it's for me?"

"Positive."

Nealy pulled open his desk drawer and came up with a long, silver, letter opener. "Well, let's have a look at this mysterious envelope," he said, quickly cutting it open on the short end and shaking its contents onto the desk surface.

Two small plastic cylinders appeared, followed by a folded note. Nealy unfolded the note. It was typewritten. Witt, leaning forward, almost fell out of his seat trying to peek at it. Having forgotten his reading glasses, Nealy had to draw the note closer to his face in order to read it. It was simple and to the point.

Dear Tom:

For the sake of Saratoga's reputation, please have your crime lab evaluate the enclosed plastic items. Horse racing, as we know it, may be in jeopardy, especially in Saratoga.

Best regards

Larry Wainwright

Nealy drew a bead again on Witt. "Might the man who gave you this be called Wainwright?"

Witt's face lit up. "Why, that's it. Yes, it's Wainwright. How did I forget?"

"Don't know," said Nealy letting out an exasperated sigh. "Where and when did he hand you this?"

Witt scratched his thick white hair. "He was at the sales in Kentucky. Yes, that's where. The sales. I wasn't buying that night and neither was this Wainwright. I have many clients in the racing business. So does this Wainwright. Or that's what he told me. Anyway, he knew I was coming to Saratoga and he asked me to deliver the envelope to you. Can't understand why he just didn't mail it. Would have been quicker. I've been toting it around for four weeks. Can you figure it out?"

"No," said Nealy. "I can't figure it out."

Witt began to rise slowly. "Funny thing about this Wainwright," he said. "We're competitors in a way. So I can't see why he asked me to pass it along."

Nealy was perplexed more than ever now. "Besides owning and racing horses, what exactly is your business, Mr. Witt? The local papers said you have several interests."

"Stocks and bonds. I delve into anything that produces a profit," Witt boasted with a smile. "Some interest in freight rail business. Some dealings in export and new car sales. Some I started, some inherited from my mother and daddy. Like Wainwright, though, I'm into equine insurance. I cover the ponies from birth to grave. Do a lot of life and trust stuff for rich clients, too. You very familiar with equine insurance?"

"Can't say that I am."

Witt tucked his shirt into his belt and tugged at his waistline. "Horses need insurance just like we humans," he insisted. "Better yet, owners need insurance on their expensive stock. It's a rich man's game."

Nealy turned the note face down, knowing that Witt was dying to see its content. Witt fingered his white goatee nervously and shifted in the chair. Nealy then directed some questions to Witt, asking pointedly, "You plan on making Saratoga your summer home, Mr. Witt? And if so, will you open an office up here?"

The eyes twinkled and Witt's voice lifted a pitch. "Mighty fine place, Saratoga. Could be that I will stay at least through the racing season. Not sure of conducting any business in these parts. Got more than I can handle now in Kentucky and elsewhere. But you never know. I've been known to change my mind on such matters."

"Of course to sell insurance in New York you have to be licensed. Isn't that correct?" Nealy asked.

"That's right, Chief. They got pretty strict rules in New York. But I've been up against this in other states where I do business. There's ways around it. I get myself a partner. Or just simply become the controlling investor in a local agency. Right now I'm only interested in racing my horses. Like to have you come out and see them one day."

Nealy was watching the wall clock as Witt spoke. He had other things to do, so he brought the meeting to a close by saying, "Thanks for bringing me Wainwright's note. As you're probably aware by now, it's of a private and confidential nature, so I can't tell you what's in it. Nevertheless, I would like to keep in touch with you during this season's meet. If you'd be kind enough to give me your local address, I'll contact you. And I would enjoy seeing your ponies when you have time to show me around."

Witt started to rise, then sat back down. "I'm at the Sheraton right up the street. Good service and decent food, so I'll hang in there unless something better comes along." Then he tried once more to probe Nealy about the content of the note saying, "As I say, Chief, I don't know this Wainwright except for crossing his path within the racing circles, but I'd be interested to know if the note has anything to do with our mutual business dealings."

"No, it doesn't. I can assure you that, Mr. Witt."

Witt was listening, but his eyes were trained on the plastic cylinders on Nealy's desk.

"Couldn't help but wonder what they're all about, either."

Nealy picked one up and squeezed it between his thumb and index finger. "Haven't the slightest idea, Mr. Witt. Some sort of medical container, or holder. I can tell you this, the note doesn't say. Strange, don't you think?" Witt was again making an attempt to rise from his chair. Nealy seeing that he was having difficulty, came around the desk and helped him to his feet.

"Thank ya. Thank ya," Witt said. "The old body isn't functioning exactly right. I think I'll wander over to the Sheraton bar and have a little pick-me-up. Used to take a lot of aspirin for these aching joints. Now I find that a good shot of bourbon serves just as well." He winked at Nealy. "Of course it's not my doctor's recommendation."

"If you want, I'll have someone help you downstairs."

"No. That won't be necessary," Witt insisted. "I'm fine once I'm standing. But thanks again." He moved across the inner office to the open door leading to the outside office. At the door, he lingered momentarily, turned, and called back to Nealy. "You wouldn't know a good keeper for my horses, would you?"

Nealy was in the midst of making a phone call. He hung up and came to Witt. "The best in Saratoga these days is a Sweetfeed Thompson. He's a jack of all trades on the backstretch. Feeds 'em, houses 'em and trains 'em. He's a borderline scalawag, if you know what I mean, but he knows horses inside and out. Call the track superintendent, Joe Hennesy. He'll get you in touch with Sweetfeed."

"Real fine, Chief. I'll do that," Witt said. "I had my horses shipped in a few days ago and made temporary arrangements by wire for them at the track barns, but I certainly need a more permanent arrangement. Thanks for the tip. I'll get in touch with that Sweetfeed gent."

Witt shuffled his way across the hallway to the elevator. Nealy waited till he was gone and then went back to his desk and picked up the phone again. The downstairs switchboard operator came on. "Julie," Nealy said, "can you get me the New York State Police Crime Lab in Albany? I want to talk to Inspector Steve Rosen."

Within a minute, Rosen was on the line.

"Steve," Nealy greeted him, "I'm in possession of two small plastic cylinders not much bigger than my pen. It's a transparent plastic. Came to me from an insurance guy down south. He passed along a short note but doesn't identify the cylinders. Thinking maybe you could run them by your technician for traces of whatever. And Steve, do me one more favor. See if you have a file on Larry Wainwright. He writes insurance policies on race horses. Guess he does a fair business with the breeders and owners, also."

"You sound a bit concerned, Tom."

"Call it more a precaution," Nealy said. "This Wainwright is trying to tell me something for reasons I don't understand. Somewhere, in the back of my sinking memory, that name rings a bell. I know I'll recall where and when I met him, but for now I'm lost. Anyway, I'll have these objects delivered to you personally. Thanks, Steve. I owe you one."

Nealy was unaware of how long he'd been sitting at his desk following Witt's visit and his call to Steve Rosen, until patrolman Jason Harper appeared in the office and spoke.

"Chief," Harper warned him, "They're about ready to lock up for the day. You going home or staying?"

Nealy checked the clock once more. It was 5:30 P.M.

"I'm leaving, Harper. Tell them I'm going home. And tell them no calls at home. My wife, Tilly, isn't feeling well."

Nealy sat for a few minutes longer before departing. He realized that this had been an extraordinary day, what with the surprise meeting at Dr. Blake's and all that came from it. Then the funny little visit with Witt. Finally, the strange note from Wainwright. With six or so unsolved murders weighing on his shoulders; murders that Dr. Blake so conveniently referred to, and now Claire Valova and Ann Bifford dead, the days ahead didn't appear too promising. Nealy was beginning to feel the external and inward pressures he had felt one year earlier during that "Ninth Race" thing. Pressure that became so unbearable at the time, he actually considered retiring. He was having those same thoughts as he shut off the office lights and called it a day.

10. ISLAND JUSTICE

On the cab ride over to the French side of St. Martin following their day's sailing, Flint held Sandy's hands but said very little. She understood his mood and thoughts at this time and decided that she'd just let him work out the next steps in his mind.

It was still daylight and the sun was full in a clear blue sky. The cab driver was driving with both hands on the wheel, dodging pedestrians along the narrow paved road and weaving back and forth to avoid oncoming traffic when necessary. It had Flint and Sandy alternately embracing one moment and practically falling to the floor the next. For some brief seconds they could get a glimpse of the landscape: dry, with the land noticeably water starved nearer the road, but quite lavish and green on the hill sides. Just a few hours earlier they were like kids on a trip to Disneyland, exploring the islands and making a vain attempt at exploring each other all over again. After all, wasn't this the long awaited vacation to jell everything together? As he felt the nervousness in her hands and body, he silently chided himself for putting her through this once more.

The streets in Marigot were quiet as they drove toward the docks, past the gold shops, boutiques, and bars. Off shore some one thousand yards, Flint spotted a sleek, white cruise liner. Other than that, harbor boat traffic was light. He was thinking ahead to Anguilla, Ann Bifford, the Anguillan authorities, how he was going to proceed in the investigation, who he'd have to go through to find out what really happened to Bifford, maybe find out who killed her, maybe not. Who would try and stand in his way? All the ifs that had always haunted him as he took on new assignments.

He paid the cab driver and they walked the hundred or so yards to the boat. Flint was expecting the native boy, but they were surprised to find that Dusty Putts, looking rather spiffy in a new pale blue shirt, was their pilot back to Anguilla.

"Caught a touch of sun, you did," Putts remarked as they came aboard.

"It's hotter on the other side," Flint said jokingly.

"Right you are," Putts agreed. "Funny thing, I always found the sun strongest in Simpson Bay."

Sandy didn't pick up on this statement, but Flint immediately did.

"How'd you know we were in Simpson Bay?" Flint asked.

Putts adjusted his hat and rubbed his forehead. "I make it a habit of knowing where tourists go. Find it good policy. Sometimes they get lost and we help them."

Flint and Sandy seated themselves as Putts revved up the motor and the boat spun about and headed in the direction of Anguilla.

"Can't see where one would get lost in these small islands," said Flint, continuing where Putts had left off.

Putts grinned. "That's just it, they aren't so little. We've been known to lose tourists down here. I mean lose 'em and never find 'em. Believe it or not."

"Where's the boy?" said Flint.

"Oh, I got him doing some work over at St. Barts. Good kid. Young but a good worker. Not all kids down here relish work. And that goes for the adults, too. Tourists like yourself have spoiled them."

"The boy says you like deep sea fishing," said Flint. "Said you go out quite often with friends. What do you catch?"

"Generally nothing. It's an excuse to get away from everyone. It's a paradise away from paradise. You get way out there on the sea and blend your spirit with the real ocean. The deep ocean. Once in a while we haul in a marlin or sailfish. You have to love it though. Not everyone does."

"How long you been here?" Flint asked.

"Too long," said Putts. "Spent time in Hawaii and other places before coming to the Caribbean. Kind of like parts of Florida too, but now prefer this climate. It's more even, except around October and November. That can be hurricane season in these islands, though we haven't had one recently."

Sandy was standing now, the soft, warm trade winds blowing her dark hair about her face and neck. Flint held her gently about the waist. Her earlier nervousness was gone. Putts gave her an admiring glance, which Flint noticed but elected to ignore. He also kept the boat much steadier on this trip, staying to just one side of the sharp, cutting waves by angling the boat's direction.

"We're being followed," Sandy said, pointing to port side. They all looked.

"Oh, that's my dolphin friends," Putts admitted. "They travel with me everyday. The big one I call Pete. The smaller one, Ted. Playful little guys, wouldn't you say?...Anyway, they're the two smartest fish in Anguilla. Hell, the whole Caribbean for my money. Want to see them jump for old Dusty?"

"You're kidding," said Sandy.

"Not on your life. Watch this."

Putts took out a silver whistle and blew one long note. The dolphins disappeared for a split second and when Sandy and Flint next saw them, they broke through the ocean surface like two missiles, reaching a height of ten feet or so before reentering the water. They repeated the jumps each time Putts put the whistle to his sun-parched lips.

Flint laughed. "You could make money with those two," he said, watching with a school kid's enthusiasm for the dolphins' next move.

As they drew near Anguilla's shore, Pete and Ted made one last spiraling jump and then headed off to deeper water.

"They prefer the cooler water out there," said Putts. "It's bathtub warm in the shallow coves. Not to their liking."

"It's perfect for me," said Sandy. "We love the warm water, don't we sweetheart?" pulling at Flint's arm.

Putts shoved off when they were on shore, however, Flint noticed that Putts didn't head directly back to St. Martin. Instead, he motored his boat eastward along Anguilla's coast line, about four hundred yards off shore. Perhaps he was on his way to ferry other guests, Flint thought.

Flint's mind was now preoccupied with getting to their quarters at the British House. They grabbed the lone cab that was at the dock and had the driver take them directly to their villa at the far end of the golden strip of beach on Rendezvous Bay. Sandy sensed Flint's tension now. She said nothing. He went out on the small villa patio and sat in a wicker chair and stared out across the bay. He'd been sitting there for a good twenty minutes meditating, when Sandy finally came out and sat in the chair next to him.

"You look lost," she said.

He reached for her hand and smiled. "No. I'm not lost. Not as long as I know I have you on my side. Mad. Mad is the word. Why in hell do I get myself into these things? Why can't I learn to say no?" He lifted her on his lap and brushed her shoulders with his lips. "Look, Sandy," he continued, "this isn't fair to you, I didn't bring you here to have this happen. I thought about it all the way across in Putts' boat. I'll just call Harry back and tell him I'm not up to this one."

She pressed her finger over his mouth, removed it and then kissed him softly. "I don't want you to feel guilty on my behalf. It's untimely and damn scary. You know my feelings. Still, we both know it's got to be done. My real concern is the time and place. Where will you start your investigation and who can you depend on down here to help?"

"I may have one friendly contact in St. Martin," Flint assured her.

"He's Ronnie Donato. We worked together in California twenty years ago. I haven't seen nor heard from him, but I understand he's involved in the casinos over at Simpson Bay. Not the Port De Plaisance. The larger one, Royal Tango. If he's still there, I'm certain he'll be able to give me some guidance. Ronnie was always good at getting inside local politics. I imagine he's maneuvered his way into the various politics of both the French and Dutch big wigs, and no doubt the English insiders here in Anguilla. Perhaps I can start by seeing what he knows."

Later they strolled down the deserted beach, both walking barefoot where the ocean rolled onto the golden sand, jumping back occasionally to avoid the larger breakers. It was warm with a steady breeze blowing across the narrow strip of island. This was the setting they had come to Anguilla for. Flint, however, was inwardly angry that it would soon be interrupted. They stopped about two hundred yards from the villa to watch the sunset on the water. It was a dazzling display of glimmering streaks off the rolling white caps, and it lasted until the sun finally disappeared and the ocean's surface turned black before their eyes. Then they walked back to the villa and Flint went inside while Sandy mixed two rum and Coke drinks on the patio. She expected they would at least have this evening together before he would be off doing what he had to do. She was wrong. He appeared in the doorway fully dressed in long khaki pants, short-sleeve shirt and shoes. She looked up sadly. "Going someplace?"

His face tightened. "Yes. I'm going over to see if I can find Donato. I know it's late and you don't want me to go, but I must. If you'd like, you can stay at the main house with other guests until I get back. I'll feel better knowing you're with them."

Sandy stood up and came to him. "I'm perfectly all right here, darling. I prefer you wait until morning. If you can't, you can't. I'll bury myself in a good book while you're gone." Then she quickly grabbed him about the arms, and said with a low sob, "For God's sake be careful, Flint. You're all I have now."

"I will. I will," he assured her. "Now if I can make contact with Putts again, I'll skip over to St. Martin on his boat and who knows, maybe he'll have me back by midnight." He checked his watch as he spoke. It was ten after eight. "I love you. Of course, you know that."

She couldn't speak again. She watched him go down the back path toward the British House. She finished her drink, then went inside. She felt like crying, but couldn't. She fumbled through her bags and came up with one of two novels she bought for this vacation. However, she just stared at the pages. As low key as it had all seemed with Flint, she felt otherwise. She was almost tempted to go running after him, to beg him not go to St. Martin. Even in the warm night, she shivered thinking about it. Finally she went to bed, but didn't sleep. She laid awake listening to the ocean pounding the beach and the faint sound of music coming from the British House. Most of all, she wondered about Flint. She stirred from side to side, eventually falling into a light sleep.

Flint had no luck making the boat connection with Putts, but he was able to catch a ride on a private sloop that was headed back to Marigot. On reaching Marigot he met Putts' little Anguillan pilot at the dock. Flint was tempted to ask where Putts was, but found himself answering his own questions by saying, "Oh, yes. Putts is probably out deep sea fishing."

At which the Anguillan, smiling with a pearly white-toothed grin, and apparently reading Flint's mind, motioned with his hands seaward and laughed.

"They must catch bigger fish at night," Flint told him.

Flint was conscious that the night was slipping quickly by, so he wasted no time hailing a cab to take him directly to the Royal Tango casino. Halfway there a misty rain began falling. It was the first rain Flint had encountered since his arrival in the Caribbean. The driver drove through it over the narrow road without using his wipers. Flint was amazed he could see the road. It wasn't till they had arrived at Royal Tango and Flint had paid his fare that he found out the wipers didn't work, and only one of the cab's headlights was good. Flint was tempted to ask about the car's brakes, but decided he didn't want to know if they worked or not. These were all minor dangers compared to his occupation. Flint entered the Royal Tango and found himself slipping through a crowded hallway leading to the main gambling room. It was mostly a young couples crowd, many of them doing more talking and socializing than partaking in the house's various gaming fare. As he moved along the room's periphery near the roulette and blackjack tables, he was tempted to stop and place a bet. Visions of striking it rich again crossed his mind, but he resisted. Besides, he had to find Donato whom he felt was surely in the casino. There was a burst of laughter on the crowded dance floor and Flint, for a split second, thought he saw Donato twirling a tall blonde girl to the rhythm of the casino's reggae band just under the glitter of a sparkling revolving light. He pushed his way in their direction only to discover it was a Donato look-a-like. Another twenty-minute search in the casino and a walk along the large patio and terraces on the Royal Tango's ocean side proved just as worthless. Flint stopped one of the casino's pit bosses and inquired about Donato's whereabouts. "Donato? Donato," the pit boss thought about it, then replied.

"Not familiar with him. Sure you got the right place?"

"Pretty certain," said Flint.

"I've been here five years," the man said. "No one by that name works here, I can assure you that." He held his hand to his head. "Of course you can check with the front office. They might have a handle on him."

A petite, tanned brunette at the casino's head office shook her head "no" when first asked by Flint about Donato. Flint admired her sleek black dress and off-setting pearl earrings and necklace. She was a classic stunner with a striking presence, that was for sure. But she also had the calm demeanor of a well-trained office manager and Flint recognized that she was sizing him up while they talked. Maybe even a bit of instant chemistry going on between them, he sensed.

She swung around to face him, with large round brown eyes hidden deep behind neatly curled dark eyelashes. She had a perfect symmetrical face, Flint found even a girlish appearance, but he guessed she was near thirty. Lots of well-placed makeup, but no real telling age lines. Yes, late twenties or thirty, he decided.

She smiled up at Flint from her chair and suggested he be seated so she could review her personnel files. She flicked on her computer screen and tapped a few keys. The screen immediately displayed all names beginning in D.

"Sorry," she said. "No Donato showing here."

"You sure?" he said, leaning over to glimpse the screen.

"Anyone who's ever worked here in the last eight or so years is in this file. Maybe he precedes that?"

Flint tried not to show his impatience and frustration. Nevertheless, he knew she was aware of his edginess.

She shut off the computer and stood up. In high heels, standing straight, she was exactly Flint's height. Her brown eyes widened and burned into his. He had the weird feeling that she was coming on to him, though his better judgment told him otherwise. In that very moment, he suddenly thought of Sandy back at the villa. The brunette came around and stood closer to Flint. Then, in a whisper, as if the room had ears, said, "Ronnie Donato. Yes, I do know that name. Try the Beach Trader down the street."

Austin Healy

Flint was about to say something further, but she held up her hand.
"If you're a friend, Ronnie will welcome you. If not, you're on your way
to a very unpleasant experience," she warned him. " Ronnie's a very private person these days. He doesn't take kindly to strangers. You look
like the trustworthy type, though. Good luck."

"You're a good judge of character," he kidded her. "Your help is
appreciated. Maybe I'll have an opportunity to return the favor someday.
My name is Flint."

When Flint headed for the door, she called out, "Funny that you call
yourself a friend of Ronnie's. From my brief experience with him, I did-
n't know he had any friends."

Flint found his way to the Beach Trader and went directly to the bar
and ordered a Scotch and soda. There was a decidedly different clientele
at the Trader, too. The room was filled with the smell of cheap perfume,
or as Flint preferred to call it, "inexpensive odor killer." Cigarette and
cigar smoke was thick as London fog and stunk even worse. He knew
this was no tourist hangout. Locals, mixed white and native couples and
singles, made up the heavy drinking crowd of the Beach Trader. And the
more Flint observed the more he realized that this was the atmosphere
and types that would serve Ronnie Donato.

Flint finished his drink and put a fifty dollar bill on the bar. The bartender took out for the drink and came back with the change. Flint put
his drink-free hand on the bills and shoved them toward the bartender.
"It's all yours, buddy, if you can guide me to Ronnie Donato."

The bartender reeled backward. His hands went on his hips and he
gave Flint a worried look. It was a minute that hung in space, and Flint
wasn't sure he'd be in for a fight or an answer. As always, staying out-
wardly calm, Flint was prepared for the worst. Slowly the bartender's
hands lifted from his hips and he folded his arms across his chest in a
relaxed manner.

"I'm an old friend," Flint assured him. "This is a social call. Nothing
more." At that Flint detected a soft smile on the bartender's lips. "I'll see
if he's here," he finally said, picking up a small, red, cordless, bar phone
and dialing. Flint heard the faint ring.

"Donato!"

"Man here says he's an old friend."

"What's his name?"

"Your name. He wants to know your name."

"Flint."

"The name is Flint."

Then Flint could make out Donato's reply, "No. No. Not Mike Flint?" And the bartender asked, "Mike Flint. Is that your name?"

Flint nodded.

"Yeah, That's the guy," the bartender repeated.

In the same instant, the bartender grabbed the bottle of Scotch and poured Flint another, followed with a dab of soda water. He also pushed all of Flint's bills back. "Can't take your money, Flint. You must be special. Donato says to give you anything you want. And that's on the house."

Flint jiggled his glass and the bartender filled it up again.

With two stiff drinks under his belt, Flint felt relaxed. He peered into the bar's back mirror and took in dozens of male and female faces peering back. At about mid bar he noticed the mirror's tint was a lighter shade. Perhaps it was the room's changing light that made it appear that way. But on further observation, Flint realized it was a two-way panel, and that Donato was probably seated on the other side observing everyone and every movement in the bar. It was the kind of thing Ronnie would do. Flint got off his bar stool and moved to the bar's center. Then he lifted his hand and waved at the mirror. At which a buzzer sounded behind the bar and the bartender looked up from washing some glasses, a dumfounded expression on his face, and addressed Flint, "It's the boss. He's ready to see you now."

Flint waved again and moved away from the noisy bar with its thick halo of smoke. The cheap perfume trailed after him.

The bartender pointed to a back hallway. "He's down there." Flint followed his directions.

At the hallway's end were two thick, solid wood doors. Flint waited. The door on his right opened and a man, in a two-piece, dark tan, silk suit with an open white shirt, stood in the opening. The thick, curly, grayish hair and heavy-rimmed dark glasses were not what Flint had expected. He'd known Donato as a young, muscular, slick, dark-haired, very Italian-looking Navy frogman in Vietnam. Likeable, playful, dedicated, and deadly. Well-trained in underwater demolition and equally so as an efficient killer of enemy forces. The body in the tan silk suit, however, didn't exactly fit that description. There was a pause, then Donato spoke. "Long time no see, Flint. How many years has it been?"

"Too many, I guess."

Donato stepped aside. "Come in. Excuse the mess, I wasn't expecting company."

It was a small room serving as best as Flint could tell, as an office and store room. Some cases of whiskey were stacked in the far corner near a picture window that had a view of the beach and adjacent resort hotels and marinas. Donato offered a soft lounge chair near the window while he sat on a small couch near the inner wall.

Donato took off his glasses, revealing the dark, penetrating eyes that Flint remembered. Donato's nose was slightly crooked, a casualty of a long-ago bar brawl. The right side of his face appeared larger than the left, as if he were suffering from Bell's palsy. There was none of the rawhide toughness that Flint had indelibly etched in his recollection of a younger Ronnie Donato. This killer of men, and women and children if called for, sat before him now a very changed person indeed. At least on the surface. Though Flint's instincts told him that Donato was probably yet capable of the worst ugliness if put to the test. Flint observed him closely.

"I lost track of you about 1976," Flint said. "Heard you hired out as an agent to Argentina. Tracking smugglers, wasn't it? Or was it involvement in the highjacked gold shipments they had down there?"

Donato shifted to one side and dropped his hands to a small table to fetch a cigarette and lighter. He started to light it, then stopped, set it down again. "Bad habit. I've been trying to break it for the last two months. You don't smoke, do you Flint?"

"Did at one time. You're right. It's a bad habit."

Donato went on. "As you say, I did make it to South America. Yes, it was Argentina, and later Brazil. Actually tracked an ex-Nazi general, Heinz Reuter, a holdover from the big war, who used to work for the Argentinians. He later stole that gold you mentioned. We caught up with him in Brazil just before he got rid of it. All the gold was retrieved and the Argentinians paid me well for the job. Then I ran into some bad luck. I contracted malaria."

"Damn sorry to hear that," Flint assured him, adding. "You said we caught up to the general. Who else was with you?"

Donato's head lifted up and his hands again toyed with the cigarette. Flint witnessed a sudden sadness in his eyes. Donato paused before answering. When he did speak again, his voice was labored.

"The only girl I ever loved, Marie Romero. You wouldn't know of her, of course. She worked U.S. Navy Intelligence in South and Central America. She then did six months in Nam. We met there. Her unit did all the research on the shore bases when my frogs were blowing them all to hell and screwing up what little sea power they had. When we broke with the services we decided to team up. South America was our first legit job." He paused again and stared at Flint. "She was shot and killed the night we cornered General Reuter. The general had one lousy little thug tagging along with him. He only got off one shot. Marie took it directly in the chest. It was my fault. I didn't figure he was armed." Donato rubbed his eyes. "I've been in the Caribbean for twelve years now. I run this joint and one other in St. Barts. Don't dabble in the rough stuff any more. Grew tired of its uncertainty. How about you?"

Flint was still digesting what Donato had told him. Even his hard-crusted nature could be moved by a story such a Donato's. He was going to tell Donato how much he was sorry for his troubles but, on second thought, felt it was a matter better understood between two time-tested war-horses than said. It was a canon of their risky profession to accept the good and bad times on equal terms. Though he thought of Sandy on Anguilla and silently wondered how he would react if she were suddenly killed. Would he, or could he, weather such a tragedy as well as Donato? He quickly pushed the hypothetical prospect from his conscious mind. The room was warm and Flint was ready for another drink. Donato pulled a cord on the wall and, as Flint had guessed, the two-way mirror displayed the barroom and its mixed, boozing crowd. Donato then hit a wall button and the bartender stopped in the middle of mixing a drink and turned toward the mirror. He held up two fingers, at which Donato hit the button once more. This time he held up one finger. A minute later a waitress came in and handed Flint a Scotch and soda. "I might get to like this place," Flint kidded Donato. "Especially the free drinks. But I'd enjoy it more if you'd join me."

Donato waved his hand. "I'm a teetotaler these days. It doesn't mix well with malaria medicine."

Flint took a long sip and then set his glass down, the ice cubes melting quickly in the room's oppressive temperature. Donato leaned over and flipped another switch, and instantly cool air began circulating from a wall air conditioner. Donato smiled at Flint.

"Sorry, old buddy, but I generally like it hot as hell. Got so used to the heat while in South America, anything below ninety degrees is like winter for me." Flint figured enough small talk and reminiscing had taken place. Besides, it was really getting late and he wanted to get back to Anguilla and Sandy. He polished off the balance of his drink, locked his hands together under his chin and grew serious.

"I need some help, Ronnie," he said. "I came here on vacation, but something came up and I don't know exactly how to approach it. You may have some ideas."

Donato sat forward, his dark eyes set on Flint. His face placid and his body steady. "You're chasing again. Is that it? Chasing the bad guys. Don't you ever get tired of it?"

Flint's voice grew lower in tone. "Yes, I'm tired of it. My new girl is tired of it. Everyone I know is tired of me being tired of it. But sometimes you just can't say no. Sometimes you have to go on and do the things you promised yourself a hundred and one times you'd give up. No one should know this better than you. Maybe you've found out the secret of saying no and meaning it. I haven't. That's my problem at this moment. I have a friend who wants information on a dead girl over on Anguilla and he's expecting me to come up with it. That's where I'm at. Do I tell him hell no I'm bugging out on this one? Or do I do the only honest thing I have ever known, and investigate it to its conclusion? You tell me."

The room was chilling down too much, so Donato killed the air. Standing up he went to the window and peered down at the deserted, lighted beach front. After a long pause, he spun around. "Fill me in, Mike. This girl on Anguilla, what's her name and why is her death so important to your friend? And how did she die?"

Flint related his conversation with Harry Waite, and the situation on Anguilla with Ann Bifford. Then he told Donato how he had met Sandy in Saratoga, with bits and pieces of their brief relationship, the simple innocence of their vacation plans to the Caribbean, and the suddenness of Harry's call. Then Donato asked other questions and Flint, as if going through a military debriefing, answering him, just like they had done after missions in Nam. It was a classic case of two seasoned professionals, dogmatically and pragmatically plying their trade on one another. When Flint was finished, it was like coming out of a hypnotic trance. Donato was laughing softly. "Just like the post-battlefield stuff," he told Flint. "You're a classic example of debriefed grunt."

"You got me in a weak moment," Flint admitted. "I guess I spilled my guts, didn't I?"

"It's good to spill them once in a while," said Donato, stretching his arms in the air. "That was my problem when I came back from Argentina. I had no one to talk to. Not one sympathetic shoulder to cry on. No one to tell Marie's story to. It left me a mental cripple. Few men bare the experiences we have shared. Only you and I can understand ourselves. Our past. Our damn sorry way of life. Yet we lived every hellish moment of it. You still do."

Flint was tired. "I have to go, Ronnie. I don't want to meddle with the authorities on Anguilla. I don't even have to see Ann Bifford's body. I do, however, want to know who pulled her under the day she went for a swim in Shoal Bay. I owe that much to my friend in Saratoga. Can you help?"

Donato slapped him reassuringly on the back. "I'm sure we can dig up something. Will you ever pin down the killer or killers? Probably not. The Caribbean has its own code of justice. Resort owners don't take kindly to this sort of thing. It's bad for business. Maybe their justice has already been served. We may never know, though. I do have a friendly Anguillan contact that may help. If that doesn't work out, I also know a representative of Her Majesty's Government that comes by now and then. He has ways of finding out such details. Go back to your Sandy. Enjoy the rest of your stay. I will be in touch."

It was near midnight when Flint left the Royal Tango and caught a cab to Marigot. The cab windows were open, but it was steamy hot. The cabby hummed a native tune while smoking a cigar that hung from the corner of his mouth. The cab's headlights played tag with dozens of natives walking along the pitch-dark narrow road. When they arrived at the dock, the boat with its native driver was waiting, its idling motors purring like a jungle lion. Flint was half asleep as the boat departed for Anguilla on the dark rolling ocean.

11. WITT'S END

A few days from the time Sweetfeed had given Track Baron his special bucket of feed and the added mixer from his gold-plated bucket, he was still working around the clock to keep the great horse alive. It was a dawn-to-dusk vigil, with Sweetfeed keeping Track Baron moving by a series of brisk daily walks and mild workouts, followed by doses of water and honey. The honey was an old remedy Sweetfeed had picked up from a trainer once in south Florida who claimed honey would cure anything from human mumps to the most severe case of horse colic. The secret was in administering just enough honey at a given time. Equally so, too much honey was dangerous. The trick was in getting the horse to drink along with the honey doses, even if he wasn't thirsty. Sweetfeed managed this by adding touches of salt with the regular feed. After each hot walk and workout, Sweetfeed would then spend a good half hour sponging down Track Baron with warm water, later brushing and grooming him vigorously to keep his circulation moving. He wasn't sure that anything he did would save the big fellow from his pending doom, but he had to try. Nothing was more important to Sweetfeed than saving Claire Valova's one last great horse.

He was working to that end by a lantern's light well past his bed hour, nearly 10 P.M., in Track Baron's stall, when suddenly a figure appeared out of nowhere. Sweetfeed jumped back as if confronted by one of Saratoga's fabled track ghosts. The figure said nothing. Sweetfeed cowered at the far corner of the stall, hiding, so to speak, between Track Baron and the ghost. He began to sweat so badly that water ripples dripped down the inside of his flannel shirt. His eyes watered so that the white figure now became a blur. Sweetfeed had never been so scared. Men he could face in any situation. He feared and dreaded the supernatural. Track Baron snorted and heaved to one side, thus confirming to Sweetfeed that he had indeed encountered a ghost. All his evil deeds of the past few months suddenly flashed before his eyes. The eerie figure never moved from the stall opening. It stood there in silence, menacing Sweetfeed. He was about to break down and cry of fright, his nerve endings were shattering within his shaking body. He had no place to run. Just when it seemed Sweetfeed could take it no longer, the ghost spoke.

"Did you say something?" Sweetfeed managed to ask.

The figure stepped inside the stall. "Yes. Why, yes. I'm looking for Sweetfeed. Might you be him?"

With these words, Sweetfeed felt the fright slowly seep from his limbs. "God knows, mister. You startled me all to hell."

"Oh, very sorry my good man. Didn't mean to barge in on you like this. But they said you could be found out here. That is, the man at the gate said you may be working late. Pardon my intrusion. I should have come during daylight hours."

The fact that he was a talking human being, and not a vaporized spirit of the historic oval, brought Sweetfeed back to reality. He moved from behind Track Baron and drew closer to the intruder to see who he was. In the dim light he could make out the white-bearded face. Certainly a man from the South from his distinct drawl, Sweetfeed reasoned. But why in hell was he coming to the barns at this ungodly hour of night? Sweetfeed was more than mildly surprised and puzzled by the sudden visit. In light of everything that had taken place since Claire Valova's death, he was suspicious of everything and everyone he came in contact with. It bordered on neurosis, but he couldn't help himself. He lived day to day in a state of near panic that someone would uncover what he had been up to. He viewed the stranger as no less a threat.

"Working late with Track Baron here," said Sweetfeed, trying to appear normal and calm. "Generally don't work past eight or so, but things just build up and next thing you know, the night's half gone. Is there anything particular you came for?"

The man reached out to shake Sweetfeed's hand, but quickly pulled it back again when he suddenly caught a whiff of Sweetfeed's foul odor. Not to mention the filth of his clothing and hands, both apparent in the dimmest of lighting.

"Don't let me keep you from your duties," said the stranger. "Go on about your work and I'll just be a minute. I have a business proposition you may be interested in. It involves my horses."

The very way the stranger put it sounded somewhat sinister to Sweetfeed. Was he being asked to do more dirty work, or was the stranger just probing to see where his inquiry might lead? This was a touchy situation, and Sweetfeed, realizing that the wrong answer might be incriminating, fenced it off with a rhetorical question of his own. "Is your business racing horses, or selling them?"

"A little of each," the stranger replied. "By the way, I haven't officially introduced myself. The name is Witt. Stuart Clayborn Witt, of the Lexington, Kentucky Witts. Insurance is my fame, horse racing is my game."

The word insurance sent several shivers down Sweetfeed's back. He theorized that the fatal moment was at hand. That this Stuart

Clayborn Witt was, most definitely, an insurance investigator. Sweetfeed eyed him with renewed caution as he went about grooming Track Baron. "Isn't often I talk with insurance people," said Sweetfeed. "Don't get much mixed up with complex things like insurance. In fact, I don't have any life insurance. Never really believed in it. People said I should have insurance. I say who needs it when they're dead?"

Witt let out a hearty laugh. "You got a point there, Sweetfeed."

"Hardly been sick in my life, too," Sweetfeed added. "So the sick insurance wouldn't have done me much good either."

Witt continued to be amused at Sweetfeed's rationalization about insurance.

Witt came near Track Baron and softly stroked his mane. The horse held still. Sweetfeed could tell Witt was comfortable around horses, otherwise, Track Baron would have been startled by a stranger's touch. He ran his hand down the Thoroughbred's back.

"You're right," said Witt, "insurance isn't for everyone. But take this big fellow here. He needs insurance. Could you imagine what it would cost its owner if this horse were to drop dead this very moment in this stall?"

Sweetfeed's knees went weak at the mention of it. He dropped the grooming brush and fiddled with his shirt collar. Was Witt deliberately baiting him with these remarks, or was his line of conversation simply spontaneous and innocent? Then again, what if this Witt already knew of the grand poisoning scheme?

As for Witt, he had not the least notion that Sweetfeed was harboring all these thoughts about him. His was a straightforward business deal. He wanted the best possible care for his horses while in Saratoga. If Police Chief Nealy recommended Sweetfeed, that was assurance enough for Witt that he'd come to the right man. There was no doubt in Witt's mind that Sweetfeed had the expertise he was looking for. On the other hand, Witt was appalled at Sweetfeed's general appearance and sickening stench. This old codger needs a thorough hygienic overhaul, Witt told himself. But he decided it was something he'd deal with later. For now, he was bent on convincing Sweetfeed to work for him.

All this time Sweetfeed's curiosity over Witt's real identity was reaching a fever pitch. He came around Track Baron to within three feet of Witt. "This insurance you talk about, how are you involved?"

Witt tipped his hat back and bent forward, virtually rocking on his toes and heels in a seesaw manner. "Depends on what and who's getting insured. Owner or horse. Take your choice. Maybe both. Long term, or short term. May even be a consortium getting insured, or insurance on a syndication. I do it all. Do you understand, I follow the money."

Something snapped in Sweetfeed's brain when Witt uttered, "Follow the money." He was certain now that Witt wasn't out to employ him, Sweetfeed reasoned. He was out to trap him. And with these dark images racking his brain, Sweetfeed lost all control and lunged at Witt, digging his dirty, iron-strong fingers into Witt's soft throat. Stuart Clayborn Witt, completely taken by surprise, was lifted off his feet and smashed off the stall wall several times. Grasping for breath and stifled by Sweetfeed's terrible odor, he could do nothing more than flap his arms up and down in defense of the raging backstretch elder turned madman. The lopsided struggle lasted a good five minutes. Then Sweetfeed, exhausted, let go of Witt and the lifeless body fell face down on the dust and straw stall flooring. Track Baron, as if aiding in the assault, moved two steps, and his right front leg raised up and the shoed hoof came down on Witt's head. Blood immediately spurted from Witt's mouth, followed by a long, low, suckling sound. At the same moment, a barn cat, seemingly appearing out of nowhere, scrambled across Sweetfeed's feet, scaring him so he could literally hear his heart pounding. The incident was an insane reaction that left Stuart Clayborn Witt, ex-insurance man, very dead. It took Sweetfeed a few minutes to realize what he had done. His anxiety level was so intense at this point, he found it impossible to think clearly. He was hyperventilating, gagging, and sneezing all at the same time. The horse, sensing the odd behavior, became nervous and began kicking the walls and snorting loudly. Sweetfeed, afraid the noise would wake up the other barn people, held his hand over Track Baron's nostrils and vigorously rubbed his neck and front quarters. It finally settled the horse down.

What followed was a bizarre series of moves on Sweetfeed's part that included moving Witt's canvas-covered body to a spot he believed no one would ever go looking; the venerated burial plot of the celebrated former stakes winners.

Under the pale light of an intermittent Saratoga April quarter moon, Sweetfeed dug a grave, dumped Witt into it from the cart, and proceeded to fill in the hole, all within an hour's time. Not once waking a backstretch soul. He finished by spreading a mixture of dirt and lime over the fresh grave. Then spread some more over the entire burial plot. It would not appear unnatural to anyone, because the site was generally spruced up this way each spring. With Witt disposed of, Sweetfeed had now only to worry about The Voice. Where, when and how he'd deal with The

Voice depended on many things. He'd first have to identify The Voice. The doings of this night had tired him out completely. He finally found a soft spread of hay in one of the deserted outer sheds and fell into a deep, uninterrupted sleep. He'd taken care to clean up Track Baron's stall before leaving, making sure there were no telltale signs of the struggle or any of Witt's blood stains left.

12. TRACK CADDY

On the morning following Stuart Clayborn Witt's ill-fated visit to Sweetfeed, a New York Racing Association security guard, Ed Byrnes, while on his routine patrol around the track's perimeter, discovered a white, vintage Cadillac Eldorado four-door convertible parked at a weird angle to the curb on Union Avenue. Technically, it was parked illegally. Though it wasn't Byrnes' problem, because Union Avenue parking came under the jurisdiction of the Saratoga traffic police, he wondered why it was parked there at the early hour of 6 A.M. Except for his curiosity, Byrnes would not have given the car a second thought. As it was, he merely went over and peeked inside, noticed a case of Jack Daniels and an attaché case on the back seat. It seemed somewhat unusual, but he shrugged and continued on his patrol.

Two hours later, Byrnes made his second patrol and the car was still parked in the same position. There was no heavy traffic near the track on this April day, save for a few NYRA trucks and grass mowers moving across Union Avenue, followed by a few dozen track maintenance people on their way to various duties. This time Byrnes took note of the Cadillac's Kentucky license plate "INS 1" and the shining silver horsehead hood ornament. Byrnes reckoned that the car belonged to one of the Thoroughbred owners or trainers. What he couldn't understand, is why the driver didn't park inside the track, in this case the backstretch area, which was closest to its location on Union Avenue. Cars were safer parked off the avenue, and one could avoid the inevitable parking ticket that generally befell all cars in that area sooner or later. This must be a 1950s model, Byrnes thought, and he was impressed with its mint condition. Only money kept cars like that looking this good. Whoever owned this embellished beauty certainly could afford to pay a traffic ticket, Byrnes mused. He jotted down the plate number anyway and wrote in the exact time. Later, about 2 P.M., when Byrnes got off work, he drove his car, a rickety 1975 Toyota, out onto Union Avenue and headed eastward to his home on Saratoga Lake. As he passed near the far gate, the Cadillac was still there. Perhaps he had been wrong about the car. Maybe it was disabled, not just parked. When he got home, he called the track's security office and mentioned it to George Flynn, the guard on duty. Flynn said he'd report it to the Saratoga cops. Then Byrnes, preoccupied with a fishing engagement with some friends that afternoon, never gave the matter another thought.

At precisely the same time Byrnes was speaking to Flynn, a call came into the Saratoga police headquarters from one Daisy Baker, receptionist at the downtown Sheraton Inn. Baker wanted to notify the police that Stuart Clayborn Witt, and his car, were missing. It wasn't a panic call, Baker insisted. She merely wanted the police to be aware that one of her more prominent guests had left the inn about nine o'clock the night before with word that he'd be back sometime before midnight. In the meantime, Baker said Witt had received two long distance phone calls from his home in Kentucky, both business related. The operator on duty took down Baker's information, noticing that it was the eleventh call that day on the log.

There were two missing dog reports, one lost child in the state park near SPAC, four fender-bender reports, two complaints of loud music in the Algonquin apartment building and one domestic fight in the inner city. Not a heavy call day, nor particularly alarming. The operator, Mary Astro, expected she'd get another five or so calls before her shift was up at 5 P.M. The police activity in April was generally quiet, unlike July and August when things would pick up. The men and women in blue would be going full bore in the summer months, especially when the track was in operation. The city's population would swell from fifteen to thirty thousand and, as was expected, Chief Nealy would beef up his force as well as keep a watchful eye out for the perennial jewel thieves that followed the money crowd to Saratoga each season.

So Mary Astro went on about her work, accepting Baker's call as just another daily inquiry that no doubt would take care of itself, like most of the calls that came in.

One half hour later, however, Astro got a call from the guard, Flynn, relaying what Byrnes had said about the illegally parked Cadillac on Union Avenue. Flynn asked for a license plate check. Astro complied by checking with the New York State Police data bank at the Troop G Headquarters in Loudonville, New York, just thirty miles south of Saratoga. Within minutes, Astro had her answer. She called Flynn.

"George, it's Mary. Got yourself a Southern boy with this one. The caddie's registered to a Kentucky man, Stuart Witt. Actually Stuart Clayborn Witt. Name sounds impressive, doesn't it?" She chuckled as she said it. "A bit early for a Bluegrass native to be this far north, wouldn't you say? He's probably got something to do with the horses. Owner, or trainer. You say that car's been there most of the day?"

"That's what Byrnes says," Flynn assured her.

"OK, I got a call from a Daisy Baker at the Sheraton Inn saying Witt told her he would return by midnight and didn't. Well, I'll poke around and see what we can find out about the guy. In the meantime, I'll call Dott's Towing and have it removed. Too dangerous leaving it on Union. You agree?"

"Fine by me, Mary. Likewise, we're checking with everyone on the backstretch. The guy's got to be someplace nearby. Keep me posted."

"Will do. By the way, I expect some hot tips this season. They tell me you had a good run at the windows last year."

Flynn laughed. "You know what they say about Saratoga, Mary? It's the only place going where windows clean people."

While Flynn was talking, Astro was also entering Stuart Witt's car data on an adjacent computer. She knew it would take about an hour to get back the information she desired, but by that time, Dott's would have the car in tow. She was also hoping that perhaps Witt would have been located in the interim, thus avoiding further demands on the department's already limited manpower. Chief Nealy was always harping about the PD's budget. Department heads, and the rank and file patrol officers, were instructed by Nealy to pursue nothing but the most important matters. For its size, the Saratoga Police Department was very effective, yet much slipped between the cracks because of the priority attached to it.

"Must run, George. Other calls coming in. Buzz you later."

She finished putting in Witt's data, then entered some of Flynn's remarks on a desk pad. She would later condense her log into a more formal report. For now, and for the rest of her shift, she kept busy on the computer, editing a list of donor names for the upcoming Police Horse Polo benefit, scheduled for early August. This was one of Nealy's pet projects, and every cop on the force was counted on to help make it an annual success.

When Dott's Towing arrived to take Stuart Witt's car to its garage on lower Chapel Street, Leonard Dott also noticed the unopened case of Jack Daniel's Whiskey in the back seat. He called Mary Astro and filled her in on the car's condition and mentioned the item. There was also a thin black attaché case. Strange that a man from Kentucky would leave a case of whiskey in such an easily seen position, Astro told Dott. She asked Dott to have the attaché case delivered to the PD.

"You might just as well bring along the whiskey too," she directed Dott. "God knows, in this town it might mysteriously disappear."

Shortly before her shift was done, Sergeant Galea, stopping into the headquarters on his day off to pick up his paycheck, heard her mention Witt's name. Galea had been at police headquarters the day Witt visited

Nealy. Following Witt's and Nealy's meeting, Nealy and Galea went out for a cup of coffee and Nealy, laughing about Witt's persona, told Galea that it would be an interesting summer. "If I have to listen to more characters like Witt, I'll wind up on the funny farm," Galea remembered him saying.

Galea opened the door to Astro's communications room. She spun in her chair and looked at him.

"That Witt you mentioned. Was he back here?" he asked.

She looked at him in a puzzled way. "No," she said, "they found his car on Union Avenue. It's been there all day."

"He's a big shot insurance man, or something. Guess he owns a few Thoroughbreds. I wouldn't have Dott's tow that car without first checking with Chief Nealy."

"Too late now," Mary said. "They picked it up five minutes ago. Funny though, there's no sign of this Witt. Even the Sheraton called about him. They claim he never came back last night." Then Galea thought about it. He scratched his head.

"Well, as I say, better leave a note for the chief. I'm sure he'll be interested in it. I'm not due back on duty till noon tomorrow. I'll follow up on it when I get in. Have a good day."

"As good as I can," said Astro sarcastically.

During Astro's last half hour on duty, several minor calls came in. She took them all in stride. But in the distraction of answering the last few calls, she forgot to make a note to Nealy about Witt. She finally thought about it on the way home, but later forgot again, so Nealy was never notified. Astro was confident that Galea, always a stickler for detail, would make good on his promise to follow up on it.

13. LETTERS TO THE EDITOR

Frank Duffy had anticipated a negative reaction from Saratoga residents when the news of Claire Valova's poisoning was finally published in the major papers, and eventually a front-page story in the *Saratoga Star*. What his editorial office received was a barrage of calls, the likes not seen since Senator Estes Kefauver's Spa City gambling investigations in the fifties. It was then that the ambitious Tennessee senator, heading up his special committee to investigate organized crime, turned the old town upside down. Duffy remembered the hearings and the public reaction that followed. Duffy had then sat through hours of testimony watching, as did all attending news people, the sour faces of Kefauver's colleagues, as they paraded witness after witness to talk about Saratoga's gambling. The newsroom phones rang and rang for days after the hearings. Opinions were running three to one against the paper's handling of the stories. Some thought Kefauver was given too much press.

When gambling in Saratoga was finally abolished, many readers partially blamed the paper. It was a classic no-win situation. As senior editor, Duffy took most of the heat at the time. As bad as the Kefauver affair was, the bitter Valova callers were unprecedented in their viciousness and volume. Many loyal readers of the paper called to say they were disappointed that the circumstances surrounding her death in New York City had not been reported up front. There were all types of questions for the paper. Why had the paper held back this important information? It wasn't fair to the readers. They had a right to know. Duffy, rethinking his decision to hold back the news at the time, couldn't now honestly disagree with his readers.

He realized that professional editorial ethics should have come first. The whole newspaper fraternity had an obligation to report her death factually and fully. Unfortunately they had not done so. Duffy, as well as other editors throughout the northeast, had elected to soft pedal Valova's passing. Yet that didn't make it right. Duffy's reason was simple, as far as he saw it at the time. He was protecting the reputation and integrity of a friend. The New York papers did likewise. There had been no collusion among the various editors at the time of her death. But they had all approached the story with basically the same thought in mind. Why sensationalize her death?

Now, on an extremely hot April afternoon, as Duffy sat at his desk answering many of the phone calls personally, it was akin to the worst experience he could ever remember in his newspaper career. He had just spent the better part of twenty minutes trying to explain his viewpoint to one of Saratoga's most vocal, senior dowagers and year-round residents, Sara Lee Smith, when assistant editor John Templeton tapped him on his right shoulder and pointed to another waiting phone call.

"It's very important," Templeton whispered.

"Must leave you now," Duffy told Smith. "Several calls waiting. Please drop by one day. Perhaps we can have lunch and continue this conversation more openly." He wiped his brow.

It wasn't setting too well with Sara Lee, who insisted on being heard further. Duffy finally decided to set the phone down. "So," he said aloud to everyone in the editorial room, "we lose another faithful reader. I don't have a damn choice, do I?"

All he got in return was a sympathetic stare from one young female reporter on the sports desk. Then he picked up the waiting call. "Duffy here." He was prepared for another irate caller but, to his surprise, it was Dr. Blake calling from the hospital. Blake sounded upbeat for a change.

"Our man made some progress in the Caribbean," Blake said. "No word yet on exactly where Ann Bifford's body is at this time, but we should know something shortly. He's got a contact in St. Martin that's helping. If you can pass this along to Chief Nealy and Billy Farrell, I'd appreciate it. I can also appreciate what you're going through at the paper. I can only say, hold your ground. It will take a day or two for the initial fury to subside. You know these Saratogians as well as I do. They get mad, but they don't hold a grudge. At least most of them don't."

Duffy let out a long sigh. "It's been a long day, Doc."

"I know where you're coming from. But trust me. It will pass."

"Our man in the Caribbean, what did he say exactly?"

"He was very short. Basically what I just said. He's working through an old contact to find out the details. He knows his business. We have to give him more time. Said he didn't want to talk too long on those Caribbean lines. Never know who's listening in on that network. I'll keep you posted when he calls again. He works in different ways. He might call, or we could hear through some of his operatives. Makes little difference, as long as we get results. We still have to find out about Claire Valova's poisoning. Hope Nealy can be of help here. That's about it, I must run."

"No, don't hang up," Duffy shouted. "I just talked to Nealy. He's more perplexed than ever about Valova's death. Says he got a call from New York City's chief of police saying, in effect, that they can't pinpoint the poison used. I know it sounds crazy, considering all the technical methods they have at their disposal. Nealy's not buying it, either. He thinks it's a stall for reasons he can't understand. Maybe our man can help us solve this mystery, too."

This news came as a complete surprise to Blake. He'd been of the opinion that the poison had been identified. In fact, he was sure he'd seen a faxed copy of the initial clinical report following her autopsy. At the moment, however, he couldn't remember where or who had faxed it. He wasn't even certain where it was at this time. He made a mental note to check his computer file as soon as this conversation with Duffy was terminated.

Generally every piece of information he received, be it hard copy or via e-mail, was loaded into his computer file. But if he had received a copy, why was it then that Nealy was told differently? There had been so much pressure and shuffling going on in the past several days that Blake was beginning to distrust his own memory. It was also quite apparent that Valova's and Bifford's deaths were intrinsically connected, no matter how far apart geographically the tragedies occurred. Though no one, including Nealy, had yet officially established this premise, Blake had felt it from the very outset. Blake also had the sneaking suspicion that more than one law enforcement agency was interested in their deaths. The big question was why? As for the faxed report he thought he'd received, he decided not to mention it to Duffy at this time.

"Look, Duffy," Blake continued. "I'm going to try to make contact with my man again tonight. I'll convey your information on the poison. There's probably not much he can do about it until he's finished with his investigation in Anguilla. I'll try to get him to look into it when he gets back in the States."

"Damn thing the way that island government is handling this Bifford death," Duffy complained. "I pray for the sake of her bereaved family, and everyone who knew her here, that your man can get to the bottom of it. Imagine if that were your daughter down there. I just can't understand the delay in getting her body back. What use is her body to those people?"

"I don't know," Blake answered. "We can only trust that Flint's contact will find out." It was the first time Blake had uttered Flint's name to anyone in Saratoga. He was immediately sorry he had let it slip out.

Duffy, of course, picked right up on it.

"What's his name? You said his name!"

"Forget it," Blake shouted back.

"Come on, Doc. We're on the same team, aren't we?"

"If you didn't get it the first time, I'm not about to repeat it. I told you from the beginning, his assignments are all very secretive and dangerous. Names in his business are not important. Results are. Besides, I think it's high time we all meet again to discuss where we're going with this. Don't you agree?"

Duffy acknowledged that a meeting would be in order.

"I'll call Nealy," Blake said, "Let's meet on Saturday. Don't want to make it too obvious, now that everyone in Saratoga is up in arms, so let's meet someplace outside of town. How about my uncle's place at Lake George? He's away, but I have the keys. You remember his place, don't you? It's located in Diamond Point. Say we meet at noon. Will that fit your schedule?"

Duffy was flipping through his desk calendar as Blake continued. "Fine. Noon it is. Unless, of course, Nealy can't make it."

"Oh, he'll make it," Blake insisted.

As Blake hung up the phone, his thoughts turned again to the faxed report on Valova. He turned on his computer and began searching his file. He found the report. He read it carefully, noting that it was in three parts. Blake's interest was in the last part. He was wrong. It hadn't said what poison substance was used. It did, however, hint toward low dosages of cyanide. The pathologist, Dr. Ernest E. Reynolds of New York City Hospital, figured it was administered over a long period of time; perhaps several weeks, and that it was not noticed because Valova was on a number of prescription drugs at the time. Blake wanted to pin this down as soon as possible. He instructed his secretary to contact Dr. Reynolds' office in the morning for verification of the exact toxin used. If there was any reluctance on Dr. Reynolds' part on handing out the information, Blake further told his secretary not to hesitate on going directly to the city's chief medical officer, Dr. Bennett Williams whom Blake knew personally, in fact, he had attended several medical conferences with him. There would be no pussy-footing around this issue. If all of this yielded no results, then Blake decided he'd ask Flint to come up with the answer. Of course, the most important point was to find out who had poisoned Valova. Secondly, what was the motive.

After talking with Chief Nealy, Blake called Duffy back.

"Nealy will be there on Saturday and will bring Sargeant Galea with him," he told the newsman. "Says he got some additional tidbits on Valova's death, too. Didn't want to talk about it over the phone. Wonder what he's got? There seems to be a new twist every day on this whole sordid mess."

"OK, Doc, we'll see what's next." Blake could hear the weariness in Duffy's voice. He was half tempted to give Duffy a short lecture on getting control of himself, but decided not to. Instead, he merely said, "See you Saturday."

14. PSYCHOSIS OPUS

On the day before the designated meeting in Lake George, Dr. Blake received a short communiqué from Flint which, he assumed, was transmitted from Anguilla to Harry Waite's headquarters in New York City, then by phone from Harry. There was no startling news. Flint more or less reiterated what he had reported earlier, that he was still waiting for his source on St. Martin to contact him. Also that Sandy was fine and that both were trying to squeeze in a few pleasant hours on Rendezvous Beach. Though Flint further said it wasn't easy playing at vacationing with the Bifford ordeal now hanging over his head. Flint also requested that no one, except Harry, try to make contact with him at this point, because incoming messages to Anguilla would no doubt be monitored by the local authorities. It was Flint's opinion that an island of six thousand inhabitants held few secrets anyway. Blake listened to the message on his confidential answering machine twice. When he was done, he erased it. There wasn't any doubt in Blake's mind that the first questions by Duffy and the rest at Saturday's meeting would center on what Flint had found out. Based on this message, Blake decided to tell them the truth. His answer would be terse and to the point. *Nothing.*

And Blake, knowing full well how high the group's anxiety level was running, was prepared for the barrage of redundant questions that were certain to follow. And he had to play nursemaid to Duffy, still taking a severe verbal battering from his readers, Nealy's sensitive professional pride, Billy Farrell's unwavering curiosity about every facet of the investigation, and a host of other irritating and perplexing issues. All of them, cause and effect, generated by the deaths. And Blake was thinking silently to himself how debilitating Valova's and Bifford's deaths had been to the Saratoga community on the dawn of another summer season. How the dark cloud of fear and uncertainty had permeated every corner of the town, from the pending performances of the New York City Ballet company at the Saratoga Performing Arts Center, to the pre-planned social whirl of parties on upper Broadway and, quite naturally, affecting the preparations at the great race course on Union Avenue itself. It was like a mysterious pall hanging in the air, stifling everyone's spirit and weighing into the psyche in a way that Blake had never seen before. At a time of year when everyone normally was beginning to catch cases of "Saratoga fever," Blake was witnessing a mass psychosis. He wondered, with justified trepidation, where it would all end.

15. BIG FISH

In the waning hours of a glorious, sunlit, Caribbean day, Flint and Sandy, perched on the divan of their villa, were immersed in a tantalizing and almost hypnotic spell while watching the sun's red rim dip beneath the far horizon. Save the ocean's washing on the beach, nothing seemed to move as the dark approached across the water's surface. They were only aware of their mutual soft breathing and the warmth of their bodies clinging tightly. It was long moments of silence. No words were necessary to express their reassuring, intimate feeling of oneness. For the time being, Flint's thoughts were concentrated on Sandy. He completely blocked out the Bifford girl and all the complications her drowning had aroused. The miracle of this moment was all that mattered. Sandy could read his mind. She responded to his inward peace. She wanted nothing to mar this precious time with Flint.

When the sun was gone, Flint remained motionless, his arms wrapped about her upper body as she lay back between his raised knees. He kissed her hair and the nape of her neck. He was intoxicated with the sweet smell of her shampoo. She let out a low cry as he kissed her behind one ear, twisting her head so that he kissed the other. Then they drifted into a sleep. She awoke slowly and shifted, and turned and kissed him warmly on the lips. He lifted her up, moving beneath her softness, his breathing growing stronger. She melted into his chest and buried her face in his neck. He was about to lift her in his arms and carry her inside the villa when a knock came on the villa's rear screen door.

"Not now," Flint gasped with disgust.

Sandy quickly sat up straight.

"Who is it?" Flint shouted angrily.

There was no answer.

Flint put his finger to his lips and motioned Sandy to sit still. He then sprung from his seated position to this feet and put himself between the porch door and Sandy. Moving quietly but swiftly, Flint slipped inside the villa and worked his way toward the rear door. Flint inched his way to where he could reach the rear light switch. He flicked it on, but remained a safe distance from the door, just in case the visitor, or visitors, were hostile. As it turned out, the caller was the hotel house boy who had come to deliver a message to Flint.

He handed Flint a piece of paper. It was from Ronnie Donato. Having read it, Flint crumbled it in his hand. Sandy by this time had moved inside the villa. "Flint, are you all right?"

"Yes. It was the house boy. Donato wants to see me tonight."

Sandy checked her watch. "At this hour? It's almost eleven o'clock. Where will you meet him?"

Flint turned on the inside lights and spun around to face her. The look on his face told her all she needed to know. The beauty and solitude of their earlier evening was over. Her romantic Flint, with all his softness and sweetness, was again transformed before her very eyes to the tough, rawhide Flint. She didn't like it, but she knew she had no choice.

"Donato's on the other side of the island waiting. The house boy will show me the way. Maybe we can finally get to the bottom of this nasty mess. I'd ask you to come along, but I don't think it's wise. I don't expect to be more than a few hours. Now don't worry." He kissed her on the forehead, pulling her in close as he did so. His hands were warm on her shoulders, however, she felt a sudden chill down her back. She had a bad feeling about this unexpected turn of events, yet she remained silent. She knew she had to find the inner strength to accept the unexpected, spur of the moment interruptions, no matter how distasteful or inconvenient.

While staying with Monica in California, she was reminded, ever so subtly, that these moments would come. Monica made no bones about outlining how unpleasant Flint's work could be, or how upsetting. Sandy recognized that anxious look in his eyes, the rush it gave him to know he was venturing out into the unknown world of intrigue. His whole life was one of chance and calculated risk. Like Monica, Sandy told herself that she would eventually steer him away from this life. But it would not happen this evening or any time soon. His pent-up emotions were already in high gear. He'd go off to meet Donato. Harry Waite and the people in Saratoga would get Flint's loyal, unwavering attention, no matter how dangerous, even if his life depended on it. Sandy held back tears as he kissed her once more and went out with the house boy for his rendezvous with Donato. When they had gone, she locked the doors, pulled out her yet unread romance novel, and settled in for an evening of reading. Flint had said he'd be back in a few hours, but she knew better. Who was to say? His business had no respect for time or one's feelings.

Flint decided he'd ride to his meeting with Donato by boat. He had the manager of the British House arrange for a boat. They were to meet at a small cottage resort village not far from where Ann Bifford's body had washed ashore on the white sands of Shoal Bay. At first, Flint thought it strange that Donato had picked this site. That section of the island had drawn much too much attention since her body was discovered there. It was probably still being combed over by the

Anguillan police. Flint decided not to question Donato's motives. Perhaps he had uncovered something that could not be explained elsewhere. Maybe Donato, or one of his cronies, had found a local who knew something, had seen something. Yes, it was the way Donato would work. He's always made the most use of digging up information and evidence from persons living closest to the scene of whatever it was he was investigating. Donato had made good use of this technique when they were in Vietnam. And Donato, as Flint recollected, wasn't averse to buying his information, or in some cases, using his powers of persuasion to obtain it. Donato could be intimidating to a fault. But then, that's what they had both been trained to do. And this is exactly what Flint was depending on now. He needed to come up with some facts on Ann Bifford. The boat he hired arrived a half hour later. Flint was looking for Dusty Putts or his young pilot. The boat that came for him carried neither one. It was driven by a middle-aged Anguillan who had a laughing voice, was sneaking swigs of wine from a small jug, and jumbled his words when he spoke. The thirty-minute night ride to Shoal Bay was a continuous, unrecognizable monologue by the driver at which Flint, trying his best not to embarrass the man, kept nodding his head as if he understood every gurgled utterance.

They could make out a series of house lights along the shoreline as the boat pitched along in the darkness. Aside from that, it was very dark on the ocean, though the boat did have a small bow light that shone for a distance of four or five feet. However, it was no more than a candle's light on the vast ocean surface. Like all of these boat pilots, Flint had to depend on his driver's native navigational skills and familiarity of the island's inlets and hazardous rocky points to arrive safely at his meeting. One must be trustful, he thought. Though one mustn't trust too much in his fellow man. Besides, he didn't want to become shark bait should the boat be wrecked or overturned.

They approached a wider inlet and Flint called to the pilot, "Is that Shoal Bay?"

The man tipped his jug once more to his mouth, swallowed and answered, "That be it. That be it."

It was the first words Flint understood since they had departed the British House.

Then the pilot throttled the outboard engine down to trolling speed. The boat entered the calmer waters of the bay, still some one hundred yards from shore, moving toward the beach. Flint then ordered him to kill the engine entirely.

"No can do. Engine bad. Stop engine, no start engine. No can stop engine."

"All right," Flint reconsidered. "But stay out. Go further down away from Shoal Bay. Bring us around a second time. Keep it at the same speed you're at."

When they had passed by Shoal Bay the second time, Flint noticed a red light flashing near the beach's southern end. He only saw it flash twice, but he immediately recognized what it was. It was a portable running light. He had used one in Vietnam when, in tight situations, they were needed to guide patrol boats in for night landings. Strange, Flint thought. Donato hadn't mentioned he'd use a signal in this manner. But there was no doubt about it, it was a running light. He watched closely for another flash. It never came. "Go faster," Flint shouted to the pilot. "Kick that motor and make it go." The driver did not respond to his order. Instead, he pointed the boat toward the beach again.

Flint dashed for the boat's aft. Pushing the pilot to one side, he grabbed the handle and twisted the gas lever halfway around. The boat leaped forward, its engine noisily awakening the relative calm of the bay, as they headed back toward deeper, rougher water. The wind was up and the rollers were getting much bigger. The pilot moved to the boat's center, sat down and took a few more sips of wine. Though busy maneuvering the boat, Flint kept an eye on the shoreline for the red light. If it was Donato signaling, then he'd surely use a rotating signal Flint was familiar with. If it wasn't Donato, then it could be the Anguillan police. Maybe he was wrong about the running light. It had been years since he last saw one in use. Perhaps, on second thought, it was a flashlight he had seen. Donato's message said he'd meet Flint south of Shoal Bay. Flint had difficulty keeping the boat steady in the high rollers. He motioned for the pilot to take control again.

"Go past Shoal Bay this time," Flint further ordered him. "Don't start in until we're well past the house lights."

They headed some three hundred yards down away from Shoal Bay where the beach subsided and the dark shoreline made it impossible to see a suitable landing point. Then Flint saw the red light once more. It flashed a second time, but it wasn't rotating. He knew the light could not have moved position that fast from Shoal Bay direct. He now surmised that more than one party awaited him on shore. He had only figured on Donato being there. Why would Donato include others?

"Cut the speed," he again ordered the pilot.

The pilot apparently didn't hear Flint.

"I said cut it," Flint shouted.

The boat was moving toward shore with no reduction in speed. Flint turned to admonish his driver once more but was suddenly knocked from his seat by a violent jerking motion. He hit the boat's bottom on all fours, his face actually touching the strong fish-smelling floor boards. In the same instant, the boat's motor went dead.

"Hey, you crazy bastard," Flint screamed. "You've grounded us." The pilot didn't respond. Flint sprung to his feet, realizing as he did so, that the pilot was no longer in the boat. "Where the hell did he go?" Flint couldn't estimate the boat's distance from shore. Perhaps one hundred yards. Maybe less. The stern light was no help in judging the distance. Flint, working in the dark, made an attempt to start the engine. He fumbled in the darkness for the electric start button. Finally his fingers found the button and he pressed it. No response. He slid his hands along the engine handle till he came to the ignition slot. There was no key. It didn't take him but a split second to figure out that he was a sitting duck waiting to be plucked. He could feel the rage welling up inside, at the folly of this rendezvous. He could think of only one word for himself. "Stupid." Which he said aloud, and which he knew Donato, or whomever it was waiting on shore, heard.

Then, as if lifted by a tidal wave, the boat rose from the water's surface, shook violently, twirled right, then left, and fell back down with a thunderous slapping sound, flipping Flint on his back in the process. He struggled to regain his upright position, but was jolted to the floor by another violent impact to the boat's underside. He knew he'd have to vacate the boat or it would be his coffin. If he could make it into the water, he felt he'd have a chance to swim away. Where to was not important at this moment. Flint's best survival instincts went into high gear in the harrowing split seconds of the attack. He tore off his tee shirt and pants and slid out of his sneakers. It was Flint and his boxer shorts that went over the side and dove deep down into the pitched darkness of Shoal Bay's warm waters. He had no occasion to do much free diving in recent years, except for diving for abalone in the waters off Palos Verdes Cove, so he wasn't sure how long he could hold his breath. The move was further complicated, because he had no sense of direction once submerged.

And all the time this was taking place, he was trying to determine what it was that had rocked the boat so madly. Could it have been a shark? Perhaps even a whale? All sorts of wild visions crossed his mind. He prayed otherwise, now that he was in the water. He had gone straight down from the boat, and his hands touched bottom. A good sign, for he knew he couldn't be too far from shore. He wanted to get as near to the shoreline as possible, where he could stay beneath the surface yet still be able to catch some air when needed. He also knew he'd stand a much better chance of making a run for it along the beach area, unencumbered by thick shore growth or rocky hard terrain. Especially in bare feet.

He had no way of judging the time. But his lungs were bursting when he made his first break for air. He was in five feet of water by this time, and it comforted him to know he had at least swam in the right direction. He tilted his head back and stuck his nose above the surface, sucking in one long breath of air before sinking back down. It was impossible to tell whether any one was near the area, nor could he detect any lights near the surface. With strong, measured breast strokes and equally powerful kicking, Flint edged further up the shore in the direction of Shoal Bay, so far without attracting attention. He swam quickly, however, he was beginning to feel the first signs of fatigue. His leg and arm muscles hurt, and he had to come up for air more often than he liked. At one point in the swim Flint risked putting his head above the water, glimpsing as he did so, what appeared to be the lights from the Shoal Bay Resort itself. He surfaced but for a moment, then made one last long underwater swim till he thought his limbs would fall off. At that point he decided he'd catch some more air, rest a minute, and then dash for the beach where he could then run to the resort. If anyone was waiting to intercept him, he would be near enough to the water to plunge in again. Without any weapons to defend himself, and naked save for his shorts, he knew he was highly vulnerable. He cursed himself for being so foolish. Seldom did he operate in terrain he wasn't completely familiar with. He was conscious that he had very little knowledge of Shoal Bay. And what of Donato? Hadn't he come to meet his old war time compadre? Where was Donato when Flint needed him? Or was this the worst scenario Flint could imagine, that Donato was part of it. All the ifs and whys of the moment haunted Flint in the middle of his sudden flight from whomever it was. And the laughing-voiced, wine-drinking boat pilot, what had become of him? It was a nightmarish predicament at best. He then was filled with anxiety for Sandy, alone at the British House villa. If someone was after him, he figured she'd be targeted, too. He could wait no longer. With a sudden burst of renewed energy, Flint came out of the water and hit the beach running. His heels and toes digging into the wet, sharp, granular beach sand as he ran.

Within two hundred or so yards of Shoal Bay Resort, with the lights now more pronounced on the beach and ocean, Flint spotted a figure running in his direction. The figure was about even with Flint. Then, to the right, nearer the buildings, he saw another figure running. In his concentration on these two, he was unaware of a third person closing in behind him some fifty yards off. Flint ran toward the water's edge, to a point where he was running knee-deep in the surf. The two figures adjusted their path to head him off. Then he heard the rear pursuer's pounding footsteps. Surely they were armed, Flint thought. The ocean would be his only hope of escape. He plunged once again into the rolling surf and started swimming out. The all-too-familiar sound of bullets hit the water around him, with a dull impact. He heard no shots, figuring they were using silencers. He took one more agonizing swoop of air into his burning lungs, and returned to the black Caribbean depths, bullets dancing about his head and shoulders as he went under.

Not being able to hold his breath any longer, he came up. He got twisted around in his rush to dive, and now was within thirty yards of the beach. He heard a man's voice, then another. A third and fourth person came running along the beach. Flint knew he couldn't tread water much longer, and he certainly couldn't dive again. It was either drown like Ann Bifford had drowned, or take his chances fighting his way on the beach. He didn't like either choice. But if he had to cash in his career this dark evening, it might as well be on the beach. He started forward.

When he was just about waist deep and coming as fast as he could beachward, one of the four figures, the one nearest the water, suddenly fell face down in the sand. Flint heard no shot. Then, in swift succession, the second, third and fourth figures fell where they stood near the beach front. Flint, staggering in the surf, was dumfounded. He waited, then proceeded cautiously. He came out of the surf and slowly moved toward the motionless bodies. Aside from the bodies, no one was outside the resort buildings. He knelt down and rolled one of the bodies over. His eyes were still open and his tongue was stuck between his teeth. Flint couldn't tell if he was an Anguillan or a Jamaican. He inspected the others. They were all islanders, that's for sure.

"Damn sorry lot, the whole rotten bunch of them," the voice of Dusty Putts said from his seated position twenty yards from Flint, taking him by complete surprise.

"Putts! What in hell are you doing here?"

Putts stood up and ambled over to Flint. He tossed him a cotton shirt. "Oh, I like to play nursemaid. Sorry I don't have a pair of pants or shoes for you, Flint. You look a little water logged. But I came by on the spur of the moment. Seems these scoundrels had planned a different reception for you. Well, they won't be greeting anyone else real soon, will they?"

Flint pulled the shirt over his shivering body. "Putts," he said frankly, "I don't know what happened here. I didn't hear any shooting."

Putts smiled, "Wouldn't waste a bullet on the likes of these. Besides, it might disturb the tourists. That would be bad for Anguilla's resort business." While he was speaking, he drew from under his white shirt three pieces of round wood, each about two feet long and approximately two inches in diameter.

"Let's just say I blew them away," Putts said. "Look closer, Flint. They ain't dead. They've been tranquilized. Notice how they're all biting their tongues. Reminds you of a bunch of sleeping monkeys, don't it?"

"Sandy's at the villa. I've got to go, " Flint said.

"Relax," Putts insisted. "She's fine. Besides, she's not at the villa now. She's with my people. She's safe."

Flint stood up. "Your people?" he asked. "And who may that be?"

Putts was still toying with the pieces of wood. He hooked them together, then put one end to his lips and blew hard. Flint heard a faint whizzing sound. Putts came closer. "Check out that beach chair over there." Flint saw the chair some fifteen yards away.

"I don't get it, Putts. What's the chair got to do with all this?"

"Come, I'll show you," Putts grinned.

He went over with Flint and inspected the chair. Reaching down he plucked a small dart from one chair leg. Then another. He also pulled a dart out of the back of the chair. "That's what it's all about," he said, handing Flint the assembled wooden piece. "Haven't you ever see a blow gun?" he continued. "Got this one from a Semang native while I was in Malaya several years ago. Took it home and hung it on the wall. Years later I learned to use it. Damn nasty silent weapon, isn't it?"

Flint handed it back to him. "Nasty but not final," Flint said. "What will you do with them when they wake up?"

"Don't even care," Putts said. "We will be long gone. No need to kill them. They'd only be replaced. These goons can be hired for a song and dance. The islands are full of 'em."

101

"So I take it that your little act as a boat pilot between St. Martin and Anguilla, is a cover?" Flint asked, his eyes trained on Putts in the semi-darkness of the beach.

Putts thought for a moment, then answered. "Yes. I play the clandestine game. Sound familiar to you, Flint? Also, like yourself, I'm one of the good guys. Might just as well tell you up front I'm CIA. Understand you once worked with us."

"The CIA and several others," Flint shot back. "Can't say that my stay with the agency was a happy one. I say I resigned. They say they ousted me. Take your pick."

"Oh, it doesn't matter to me," Putts reassured him. "We all get caught up in our jobs at some point along the way. You and I do the dirty work the guys in the ivory tower can only theorize about. They plan, but we carry them out. It's a far cry from the swivel chairs at headquarters to situations like this."

Flint detected a tinge of disgust in Putts' tone. He knew the feeling. He'd been down the road with the CIA in earlier days, so he could sympathize with Putts. Flint had taken all the silly games he could play from the CIA bosses. Still he was thankful for what they had taught him. In spite of their covert operations and, at times, the CIA's self-inflicted ineptness, the basis for what Flint did later, was rooted in many CIA fundamentals. It seemed to Flint, that Putts might have hung on too long with the agency. Nevertheless, Flint was thankful for Putts' presence this eventful night.

"Let's clear out of here," Putts barked. At which four or five other men appeared on the beach from nowhere, carrying an inflated rubber boat. "Jump aboard," shouted Putts to Flint. "We're taking a little ride."

"In that thing?" Flint groaned.

"It'll float just fine," Putts insisted. "Besides, we don't have far to go. Sandy is waiting for you."

The nylon seat and boat's rubber bottom was cold on Flint bare legs and feet. It was a warm night, but Flint was cold. The shirt helped, but a strong breeze, and the water lapping over the sides of the boat, added to his discomfort. Wherever it was Putts was taking him, he was anxious to get there as soon as possible. When they were out a ways, Putts turned on the running lights, also a stern light that covered quite a distance. "I apologize for the abruptness of all this," Putts said leaning toward him. "But these situations call for quick action. By the way, I know you were on your way to meet your old Nam buddy, Donato. Actually he had no intention of meeting you. We found him over on Rendezvous Bay beach making a move toward your villa. I guess we spoiled his plan to snatch Sandy. Sneaky fellow, Donato. We've been tailing him for over a year now. Shame, in a way, a man with all that talent and potential. Dope, smuggling, extortion, prostitution, money laundering, even spying. That's why we got on his case. Unfortunately the CIA couldn't do much about his dealings. Not while he was jumping from one island to the other. Too many damn foreign governments to contend with. Washington cringes every time we suggest something from the field. He peddled a lot of classified navy data to Cuba. They say he even had meetings with Castro. I think it was all bullshit, but one never knows in the Caribbean. Donato had some tricky domestic schemes going, too. Used to run into Ocala, Florida, they say, where he engineered the death of some pricey race horses. Profited off some insurance scam with each pony he knocked off."

Flint sat up straight. "You did say Ocala?"

"Quite right," Putts shot back.

"Was Saratoga ever mentioned?"

Putts looked at him. "Yeah. I heard Saratoga mentioned."

"Where is Donato now?" Flint probed.

"Right where he doesn't want to be," Putts laughed. "He's probably squirming in his five-by-eight-foot compartment and sweating his brains out on the *Big Fish*."

"You lost me," Flint insisted. "Explain."

"Be patient," Putts said. "We're almost there."

Then Putts pulled the small whistle from his pocket and pressed it to his lips. Ted and Pete, his two trained dolphins, came shooting out of the ocean, making parallel dives through the stern light's strong beam. Putts blew once more, and they appeared again, this time jumping across one another. They completed six more stunts and then disappeared.

"You showed me this before," said Flint.

"Yes. I remember," Putts answered. "But that was in daylight. They perform equally well at night."

Flint, suddenly realized what Putts was trying to convey to him, began laughing and laughed so hard, he almost couldn't catch his breath. "My boat wreckers," said Flint. "I couldn't imagine what rocked us so hard."

"Not much else I could do," Putts said. "If you had gone ashore at that moment, they would've surely cut you down. I figured you'd be safer in the water. Old wine-drinking Freddy, your pilot, jumped ship some three hundred yards from shore. He's one of Donato's boys. Didn't get far though. Ted and Pete gave him a bump he won't soon forget. Guess he panicked at first, thinking they were sharks. That sobered him up in a hurry."

At a point on the ocean, some five miles from Anguilla, Putts had the boat's motor cut. The ocean was calm and they just drifted for several minutes. Flint was really puzzled.

"What's up?" he asked.

Putts didn't answer right off. He went to the stern and had one of his men raise the stern light so that it shot skyward. Then he had it lowered again. Then Flint felt the ocean stir, and bubbles began appearing all around the boat. There was a great swish-swish sound, followed by a rush of water as a massive, black, whale-like form sprang from the depths about one hundred yards to the boat's port side.

"There's my *Big Fish*," Putts said proudly.

Flint strained his eyes to focus on the giant object.

"Come on," said Putts. "Don't you recognize a nuclear sub when you see one?"

Putts waited until the sub had surfaced fully and the water settled down. Then he ordered the motors started again and they proceeded forward. Halfway there, the sub deck lights came on. Then a blinding search light shown in their faces. Finally they heard muffled voices coming from the sub. Eventually they came close enough to make out the words.

"Bring the boat mid ship," a voice blared from the loud speaker.

Putts took control of the boat and cut back its speed. They came alongside the sub and touched its huge hulk with a dull, deep metallic sound. Several crew members then appeared on the wet deck and began assisting them aboard. They were directed to an open hatch and climbed down a steep ladder to the sub's inner compartments, actually one room short of the sub's control room. Then a gray-haired naval officer appeared from the control room, smiling. He extended his right hand to Flint and Putts. "Welcome aboard *Big Fish*, Mr. Flint. I'm Captain Bob Flew. Old Dusty here, he's a regular on this ship. Glad you made it safely."

Putts was wiping his face dry of salt water with a towel. "Had a slight problem at Shoal Bay. It was solved in a hurry. I'm sure my friend here is more interested in meeting someone else right at the moment. Wouldn't you say, Flint?"

"She's waiting for you three bulkheads away," replied Flew.

The intensity with which Flint and Sandy embraced each other moments later in the privacy of her compartment, lasted for five minutes. Neither said anything. It suddenly hit Flint just how defenseless he had left her at the villa. If it hadn't been for Putts, she may very well have been dead at this moment. He held her tight. She pressed her face into his chest. The fragrance of her hair was intoxicating. It had been like that ever since Saratoga. Each touch, the very slightest motion on either's part, sparked this immediate passion. It was now intensified and deepened, knowing that only for the sake of Putts' quick action at the villa and at Shoal Bay, both their lives might have been snuffed out by Donato and his thugs. They were still tightly embraced when Putts knocked on the compartment door.

"Sorry for the interruption," he apologized, "but we'll be getting underway shortly. Besides, I figured you'd want a word with Donato, Flint. We're taking him, and you two, as far as Florida. We've got all your baggage on board. Hopefully my men got everything. As you can understand, we were in a slight rush at the villa, circumstances being what they were."

Flint looked at Putts and shook his head. "I always thought I was the one that kept up a whirlwind pace. You've outdone me, Dusty." As he spoke, he kept one arm around Sandy's shoulders. "I'm used to taking chances, you know that. I didn't expect to have Sandy caught up in all this. And I especially didn't expect if from Donato. I can't tell you how I'm burning inside with this whole thing. Perhaps I shouldn't talk with him, lest I kill him on the spot."

Putts could see the fire in Flint's eyes. "Personally I'd like to stick him in a torpedo tube and deep-six him. Unfortunately, I will be turning him over to the FBI in Florida. He's got a rap sheet a mile long, not counting this little Anguilla episode. We know he's murdered before. We just don't know how many times. You might just as well take the opportunity to ask him anything you want now. He'll be lost in the FBI scuffle once we park him in Florida."

Flint thought it over and decided he would talk to Donato.

They walked to the sub's control room and then went down to the third level crew's berthing quarters where Donato was being held. Donato, his face drawn tight and apparently fatigued from lack of sleep, was looking downward while handcuffed to a bunk in a sitting position when Flint entered the narrow passageway to the sleeping section.

The room was deadly silent, save for the faint sounds of the sub's engines. They had left Sandy in the control room and Putts, after leading

Flint to Donato, stayed in an outer room, but within earshot. Two of the sub's junior officers accompanied Putts.

The small compartment was hot and stuffy. Made even stuffier by the tension between the two men.

Flint finally broke the silence. "I'm not sure I'm talking to the Ronnie Donato I once knew in Vietnam, or the sleazy lowlife he's become? Maybe you can clarify this for me?" He stared at the disheveled figure on the bunk, then continued. " You're in deep trouble I'd say. Wouldn't you agree?" The long hair was thrown back with a flick of the head and the dark, tired eyes looked up at Flint.

"Oh, you're so quick to judge, Flint."

At which Flint had all he could do to hold back smashing him before catching control of his anger, and replying. "Yeah, I'm a pretty good judge. When someone comes to kill me, and my lady, I get real judgmental. When it comes from someone I trusted, it gets even worse. I guess you've slipped so far beneath the slime you can't distinguish right from wrong. But that doesn't excuse your actions by one iota, as far as I'm concerned."

There was a threatening tone to Flint's voice that Donato hadn't heard before. He realized the direct confrontation approach wasn't going to work, so he veered into another line of conversation.

"I want to make a deal," he suddenly said.

"Not with me," answered Flint.

"You or anyone you can influence," he suggested.

Flint pressed his sweating hands together and pondered it. "I don't think you have much bargaining power. At least not in your present predicament. But let's hear what your deal is."

He watched Donato squirm back and forth near the bunk. His eyes were squinting and his hands shook slightly. Flint waited for his answer, but Donato hesitated, prepared to stand up and then sat back down again. It was a sight Flint never thought he'd ever witness from this battle-scared veteran.

"Well," insisted Flint, "I'm waiting."

Donato finally stood up, lifted his head and directed his eyes at Flint. The squinting had ceased.

"I can fill you in on Ann Bifford."

"I bet you can," Flint said.

"Do you want to hear it or not?"

"Only if it's the truth," Flint rebuked him. "I'm in no mood for a cock 'n bull story. Besides, we haven't all night to discuss this. Tell it straight and tell it fast. As I said, I don't make deals. To me, deals are a cop-out. Whichever group winds up trying you, be they the feds, civilian authorities or even the military, I can only pass along my recommendations based on the information you come across with. Providing it's factual and helpful to the ongoing multiple investigations surrounding you, it may have some bearing on sentencing, whatever that may be. Now let's not waste anymore time. Get on with it."

Donato cleared his throat and began. "I had a feeling someone from the States would come to the Caribbean to investigate Bifford's death. Though honestly, I never expected it would be you. Maybe some cops from Connecticut or New York, doing the routine check to pacify the family, or something along those lines. When you showed up I knew I was in deep cotton. I acted out of defense. Anyone in my racket would do the same. As for Bifford, it was a simple contract. I was offered the standard ten thousand bucks to kill her. Then they insisted it had to look like an accident, so I upped the ante to fifteen thousand. I had help. We caught her swimming late in the afternoon at Shoal Bay. I personally didn't pull her under. I'll swear on a Bible to that. But I did plan the drowning."

"You said they," Flint interrupted him. "Who are they?"

"I'll get to that," Donato assured him. "Let me finish first."

"Continue," Flint said.

"There's been others in the past few years. Not all drownings. We shot them, knifed them, strangled them, and even poisoned a couple. I've contracted for sundry people, too many to fully remember. As you well know, we don't exactly keep records in this dirty business of ours. Bifford's case was a little tougher. She was part of a three-contract deal. One old socialite in New York and some bloodstock agent in Keeneland, Kentucky."

He stopped to eye Flint. Then went on. "My deal is this. I can identify what these killings were all about. Maybe even give you a solid lead to the funding source of the contracts. But I want to bargain before I give anyone this extended information. Can you blame me?"

"I can only remember when I dealt with a guy called Ronnie Donato who had some character and scruples, and now has turned into a pathetic mess. Yeah, I can blame you. I can blame you for flipping over. I can blame you for killing innocent people. I can blame you for undermining the country and flag you once swore to defend. Don't ask me a stupid question like that, especially when you already know the answer." Flint stopped and gave Donato a stare that went right through him. Donato then went on with his sordid story of murder for contract.

"Anyway, I don't recall the New York dame's name. I gave that contract to a guy in New Jersey who specializes in poisoning his victims. I don't know what he used to kill her. I know it took some time because again we were asked to make both deaths look natural. I know it took about three months. Reason is, I only got half the money up front and the rest when she was dead."

"What's his name?"

"Ben the Chem," they call him. "He's a rummy chemist that got fired from Sterling Winthrop or one of those drug companies some time ago. Had a thing for young girls and gambling, too. He is great at latching on to elderly women with almost hypnotic, Rasputin-like attachment. He gains their complete confidence assuring them he can treat any illness better than any doctor. They believe him. That's what happened in this case. He got on that dame's good side and she let him see her every day and give her the so-called medicine thinking she'd get well from whatever it was she was really suffering from. From what I understand, you have to give small doses orally every day for quite a while. It's too telltale to do this stuff by a daily injection. He's done Mafia contracts in the past, but the mob didn't trust him. On the contrary, I found him quite good. If we can work something out, that is work something on my behalf, I'll include his address with some others. What do you say?"

"You know what I say. No deal, no matter what you come up with." Donato gave Flint a sneer. "Maybe I'll just clam up. Perhaps the feds will be more receptive to a deal."

Flint grabbed him by the neck and pressed his index finger to Donato's jugular. "We talk now. You tell me everything you know, or maybe there won't be a rap session with the feds. Remember, Ronnie, that was my Sandy you tried to snuff out. That's provocation enough for me to kill you on the spot. Understand me?"

True fear returned to Donato's eyes. He didn't doubt Flint for a moment. He had been with Flint on one or two occasions in Nam when all the hell and fury Flint could muster was displayed. He decided not to hold anything back. "Ben has extensive experience with all types of sophisticated chemicals. Hell, he knows more about chemicals than a rocket scientist. . . ." He paused to catch his breath in the rather stuffy confines of the crew's berth. Then, clearing his throat, he continued, "As I say, I wasn't privy to everything that went down in New York with the old dame. But I did hear later that Ben's 'medicine' was cyanide. Divers down here use cynaide to slowly stun rare tropical fish which they in

108

turn ship off to Japan and other markets. Deadly stuff. I hear the cyanide is killing off the coral as well. So I guess it's just as lethal on humans. Ben did a thorough job. It finally stopped her heart. The pathologist must have the full report out by now, don't they?"

"I wouldn't know," answered Flint, growing more angry with Donato as the whole sordid story was drawn out. "Just keep talking, we don't have much time."

"Not much else to tell. Ben killed her, we took care of Bifford here. I'm not going to tell you about the others. None of them were related to these two, anyway. Of course we killed a few four-legged fillies as well as some promising stallions. But that was mostly in the late eighties when insurance companies were paying out big cash sums without much inquiry into the various horse deaths. Funny how easy it was to get away with things like that during the go-go years. It's pretty tight right now. I don't have to tell you that. If it weren't, you'd probably not be here on this case."

Flint pushed closer and pressed the fingers of his right hand into Donato's chest. "Cut the small talk, Ronnie. I want details. Specific details. Get me?"

"Okay. Okay. But I can't exactly recall everything," he said, shifting back on the bunk now. "I got a contact in Keeneland, Kentucky, who specializes in hauling horses to sales auctions. He generally hauls between the Fasig Tipton Kentucky sales and the Fasig Tipton sales in Saratoga in August. He backhauls other horses for a variety of owners and trainers to many places in the south. His name is Max Steiner. I have never been to Keeneland or Saratoga sales, but I have met Steiner in Ocala once or twice. We got soused on gin and tonic one hot humid night, and the guy later introduced me to a trainer, Bernie Price, who later contracted me to kill a few horses. Mind you, we did it in a way that appeared like a natural death. The same way Ben the Chem made it appear with the New York dame. It was the easiest money I ever made, while it lasted. I split when I heard other charges pending with the feds. It ain't true, but they're trying to pin a spying charge on me. You understand how serious that can be?"

"If it's true, I hope they hang you," Flint shot back.

"I'm a peg below a scum bag, that's true. But I'm not a spy. Not in a hundred years. Believe me or not."

Flint checked his watch. "Sorry, Ronnie. Time's up. You better jar that memory of yours a little better if you want a deal with the feds. So far your information is weak at best, and questionable, I'd say."

Donato then reached out. There was pure panic in his face. "Give me a few more minutes. It'll come out."

It was a sensitive moment in the conversation, and Flint knew it. Donato was in deep, inner turmoil, uncertain, scared and a bit confused on the surface, though Flint also knew from past experience that Donato could put on a good act when times called for it. Flint also knew Donato was no coward. Flint came back. "Straight and fast, Ronnie. No padding. Facts. Just facts."

"I'll tie it together. Bernie Price, Max Steiner, and a guy called Wainwright. He's the inside insurance guy. He cut the checks when the horses were officially declared dead of natural causes. The call I got on the Bifford hit came from Florida, but I didn't recognize the voice. I assumed, however, it was the same order of command. It's been going on for ten years. There could be other players. That's all I can tell you. The goons I hire here are mostly floaters. We got all types of bad eggs drifting in from Jamaica and other points in the Caribbean. They'd kill their mother for a dime. I'm not sure where I'll end up when this is all done. Probably Leavenworth. Who knows? I know one thing. We had a damn good bunch back in Nam in the sixties. A lot of close calls, too. As bad as it was, I'd give my right arm to be back there now."

There was a pathetic sadness to his voice. Flint knew he was talking to a fallen, broken hero. It pained him inside to witness it. He left Ronnie Donato slumped on the bunk, his chin pressed against his chest, staring at the floor.

16. TROUT BAIT

The whole mixed-up mess about Stuart Clayborn Witt's disappearance had generated several phone calls to Tom Nealy's office, and the resident manager of the Sheraton had made two personal visits concerning Witt's sudden absence. Just about everyone at police headquarters was involved in the search, yet Nealy himself, wasn't really aware of the situation. As strange as it may seem, he was so preoccupied with the deaths of Valova and Bifford, plus a hundred sundry other police duties, his subordinates failed to bring him in on the disappearance. It finally dawned on Sergeant Galea that Nealy, having been one of the last people to talk to Witt, should be told. So when Nealy received word from Galea about Witt, he was more than a little disturbed.

"Why wasn't I brought in on this immediately?" he shouted, his angry baritone voice resonating off the marble-lined hallways of the court house. Shortly afterward, the hotel called again, and Nealy went into another rage. It took him a few moments to settle down before taking the call. "Yes. Yes." Nealy was heard saying. "Yes. We're all working on this. That is to say, we're working on this like we're working on two or three other missing persons inquiries. It's an ongoing thing. Most of them turn up within twenty-four to forty-eight hours. I grant you, Mr. Witt's disappearance is beyond the norm. But I'm sure he'll surface somewhere in the next day or so. Yes. Yes. He stopped by my office and we chatted. He said he was holed up at the hotel. If I remember right, he was concerned about his horses. He asked me for a reference. I suggested he talk to Sweetfeed. Yes. Sweetfeed. He's a trainer. Can't believe you haven't heard of him. He's been a fixture at Saratoga for more years than I can remember. Anyway, I gave Witt directions. Oh, you say Witt's car was found out near the race course? Well then, that makes sense. That's where I sent him. I've been busy. I just got word of his disappearance. My staff has been handling it. I can assure you, I'll get personally involved from here on. Yes. Yes. Thank you for calling. That's what I'm here for. Thank you. I'll keep you informed. You do likewise. Let me know if he checks back in. Good day, sir."

Nealy's face was bright red. Sergeant Galea was the only staff person willing to face him after the call. Nealy's receptionist and the others, made a beeline for the exits.

Nealy spun to face Galea. "I'm sick and tired of these calls. Sick and tired of the way things are going around here. Can't anyone get it right?"

Galea shrugged his shoulders. "Don't know how to tell you this Chief, but Witt has disappeared off the face of this earth. I've been out to the race course and also checked the car after it was towed in. No one has seen nor heard from him since the other evening."

The chief dug his chin into his hands and shook his head from side to side. Then he stared up at Galea. "What's Sweetfeed got to say about it?"

"We obviously didn't know you had sent Witt to see him, so we haven't talked to him yet," Galea responded.

Galea's lips pressed together, the way Nealy had often seen him do when caught in a perplexing situation. The hands moved nervously about his belt buckle.

Nealy stood up. "Get your tail out to that backstretch and don't dare come back till you find out what's happened to Witt. You understand where I'm coming from?"

"Right Chief. I'll get to it immediately. Might even check again with that NYRA guard who first noticed Witt's car. Byrnes, I think his name was Byrnes."

"It doesn't matter to me who you check with," Nealy snorted, then he hesitated. "On second thought, it does matter. Obviously, Sweetfeed. Then, how about dropping in on Joe Hennesy. Hennesy's got the ears and nose for anything that happens on Union Avenue. It's worth a try."

"I'll do what I can," Galea reassured him. "But we've dragnetted that whole area already."

Nealy's blood pressure went up three points. "Dragnet. Dragnet. I'm not talking about playing Joe Friday, here. I'm talking about plowing up the entire area if need be. Start with the stable boys. Interview every hot walker and trainer. Even owners if you must. Check with Yaddo. Perhaps the old goat walked off into the woods there. It's a big place. They've been known to lose horses on site. Stuart Witt could easily get lost in the maze of grounds and buildings at night. Just find him."

Galea left headquarters with Nealy's voice ringing in his ears. It wasn't quite 3 P.M., but for some reason it seemed darker than normal at that hour, even though the day had been sunny and clear. On his way on Union Avenue Galea observed the large well kept homes. Pre-summer landscaping and gardening work was underway at some of them, with the small array of pickup trucks and equipment Galea was familiar with. He knew most of the landscape contractors by first name. They, in themselves, were a hearty bunch, all now glad to see the cold, icy days of Saratoga's long winter gone. Winter actually brought on hardship for many of them not able to find suitable seasonal employment once their summer and fall work was over. Though many switched to snow removal and inside maintenance work, winter never provided enough jobs to go around, and the work that was available didn't pay very well. Like the geese from Canada, however, a few of the smart contractors went south for the winter months, some tagging along with the wealthy set to care for their estates in Florida and Kentucky. Galea recalled that one gardener, Randy Scott, survived winter by baby-sitting vacated Saratoga winter mansions. It was Randy's easily recognizable red pickup with the double rear wheels that Galea spotted as he turned the corner at Eastern and Union Avenues just opposite the Reading Room, where a multitude of seasonal racing and charitable functions were conducted. Though nearly fifty, Randy Scott could pass for a man in his late thirties. With slick, neatly combed black hair, a year-round tropical tan, broad shoulders and standing six-foot-three in bare feet, Scott appeared a cut above the rest of his peers. In the words of his buddies, he always got the best "yard jobs" in Saratoga each season. What most of his competitors never realized, was that Scott, who held a degree in sociology from New York University, obtained many jobs because he could worm his way into the owners world by talking to them on their level. He used his intelligence and formal training to the utmost. Better yard jobs translated into bigger profits. For the last two years, Scott had been hired by Joe Hennesy to oversee landscaping at the track. So he was familiar with the track's workings and a familiar figure on the backstretch in season.

Galea pulled his white and blue squad car up behind Scott's truck and got out.

"Out early this year," Galea said, as Scott, a shovel in hand, ceased turning over a garden to shake Galea's hand.

"We'll have a great crop of flowers this year," Scott assured him. "Not much snow this past winter. Oh, some of the ground might have gotten too frozen, but we'll fix that up. What can I do for you, Sergeant?"

Galea smiled. "You're reading my mind, Scott."

"Not exactly," Scott replied. "But you have that inquisitive look about you today, Sarge."

"Well," said Galea, "we seem to have lost one of our horse owners. Man shows up one day at Chief Nealy's office, has a chat and then goes off not to be seen again. Found his car a short distance down Union there, near the backstretch gate. Supposedly on his way to see Sweetfeed. Not a soul saw him come or go. Strange, isn't it?"

"Who's the owner?" asked Scott.

113

"Guy called Witt. Stuart Clayborn Witt. Insurance man from Lexington. Owns a few ponies. Came here early looking for someone to care for his race horses. No fly-by-night. Real money, though I wouldn't put him into the Vanderbilt league."

"We've been working this street for a week now," Scott said. "To be honest with you, traffic has been light. Mostly us guys and some painters doing a job mid-block. What was he driving?"

"Big white Caddy convertible. Big as they come. Older. You couldn't miss it."

"Guess not," Scott said, setting the shovel down and wiping his brow with a large red handkerchief he drew from his hip pocket. "Maybe someone picked him up. Does he have friends in Saratoga?"

Galea frowned. "I'm not sure of that. The Sheraton people are nervous. He's been staying there since he arrived. It'll probably hit the *Star* headlines by tomorrow. They don't need publicity of this nature right now. Well, Nealy's looking for all the help he can get. Put the word out among the contractors, will ya?"

Galea jumped back into the patrol car and rolled down the driver's side window. "On second thought, Witt apparently came this way after working hours. So unless there was someone around after dark, we'll be hard pressed to find witnesses. Damn frustrating thing, ain't it?"

Scott, still perspiring about his face, leaned on the car with both hands. "I've been in Saratoga just long enough to know that it can be both frustrating and mysterious. I'm sure he'll show up someplace though. I'll tell the boys and girls to watch out for him. Of course I'd like a description."

Galea laughed. "Find a guy who looks like Colonel Sanders except he wears dark suits, and you've found Witt. I'm serious."

"There's a dozen of them each season," Scott joked. "Saratoga is characters row in summer."

"One will do for now and it's not summer yet," said Galea as he put the car in drive and sped off down East Avenue toward the practice track at Clare's Court, where he hoped to find Sweetfeed. In the back of his mind he filed away that it was strange that Randy Scott hadn't noticed Witt's car. If anyone would have seen it, certainly Scott would be the one.

Galea was tempted to go back and see if he couldn't jar Scott's memory a tad more. But time was short and he wanted to get to Sweetfeed. Galea knew that Sweetfeed spent many of the early mornings and afternoons at Clare's Court working the horses under his care. No galloping like they did at the nearby race course because Clare's Court was too small and too narrow. But a chance to watch and observe the makeup of a Thoroughbred, get a feel of his pace and timing and, eventually, fit the horse to the right jockey. Sweetfeed was known for his excellent pairing of horse to rider. His suggestions were taken seriously by most owners and trainers. Not many track devotees had Sweetfeed's pure instincts for such things.

As it so turned out, Galea found Sweetfeed at the Court, talking to Tony Santandrea. Sweetfeed was easy to spot in his woolen shirt. Galea parked the squad car and came in the Court to greet the two. Both were leaning on the white railed fence, deep in conversation. Santandrea, dressed in jeans, fedora and plaid, long-sleeve shirt, was doing most of the talking while constantly adjusting his hat from one side of his head to the other. Galea had seen him perform this apparently unconscious twitch many times in the past. On race days, hyper and anxious as a trainer can get, he'd virtually twist the hat from front to back and back again, not realizing what he was doing. When told about it by others, he'd laugh and respond that at least it was his hat he was playing with and not his bushy black hair, admitting he'd be bald were it the latter.

Galea waited a few minutes till they were through with their talk.

Santandrea then turned to Galea. "The bulls are after us."

Galea smiled. "No. Not today. Just a digging expedition. List it under the missing persons file."

"What's that you say?" Sweetfeed jumped in.

"Got us a missing owner," Galea said.

"Can't say that I have seen anyone except a few of Sweetfeed's boys," Santandrea reassured him.

Galea came over to the fence. "A gentleman came to town a few days ago. Nice old fellow from Kentucky. Damn thing was, he visited with Chief Nealy just before he disappeared. So the chief is hell bent on finding him in a hurry."

Sweetfeed shifted from the fence to stand straight up facing Galea. "How long this fella been missing?"

"Too long," Galea said. "Actually about thirty-six hours. We found his old Cadillac convertible parked on Union Avenue, so we know he was out here someplace following his meeting with Nealy." Then he eyed Sweetfeed and continued, "in fact, Nealy said he sent Witt to see you."

"Don't know any Witt. Which Witt would that be?" Sweetfeed asked, his voice dropping as he spoke.

"Called himself Stuart Clayborn Witt. As I said, of the Kentucky Witts. I don't know if that means anything. Perhaps he came from a rich titled Southern clan. I just don't know. But he has money. Insurance business and other interests, that's for sure. All I know is that I have to find him. If he didn't make it to you, Sweetfeed, where in God's creation did he make it to?"

Tony Santandrea spun around, tipping his fedora to one side in predictable fashion. Galea was amused by the action.

"Look," Santandrea insisted. "I've been at the track for five days. Not every minute, but early morning to sometimes ten at night. I know everyone that works around here, especially at this time of year. Were it in August, I might not notice an extra body floating about the backstretch. But not in April. We're a tight-knit family this time of year." Then Santandrea grabbed Sweetfeed's iron-hard right arm and held it up. "This man knows everyone and then some. If he says this Witt character wasn't out here, I'm sure he wasn't. Who knows? He might have been taken right out of his car on Union Avenue and hauled away. Though I can't imagine that happening in Saratoga, certainly not in April. Sorry we can't help you, Officer. Sorry we can't help the chief either. I like Nealy. He's done a good job with this community, in spite of what his detractors say."

Galea had the look of a man lost for words. The three stood for a long while in silence. Two horses came by, running a slow gate. Sweetfeed pressed on the fence as they passed. Galea watched the old horse merchant's eyes observing the horses and riders. Galea understood that he had arrived at a time when these horsemen were actually working. He still had some questions on his mind, but figured it was no use pursuing them. So he was really in a dilemma. He couldn't face the prospect of going back to Nealy and telling him he'd come to a dead end. He wasn't up to that right now.

"Well, gentlemen," Galea said in a voice that more than belied his disappointment. "I'll have to talk to a few more workers. Maybe, just maybe, someone saw something unusual the other night on Union Avenue. If not, then I have my work cut out for me. The whole damn Saratoga police force has its work cut out for it. Don't know how well you know Nealy, but he's one miserable guy when on the warpath."

Galea left the two to their previous private conversation and to their horse training. As much as Galea loved going to the race course in season, he never could understand how the backstretch breed could spend so many working hours and days at the track without eventually tiring of its repetitive routine. "It must be in their blood," he said softly to himself as he drove away in the direction of the outer backstretch, where he hoped to talk to some of the newly arrived workers. Then he had Joe Hennesy as his next call. If the race course manager couldn't shed any light on Witt's disappearance, Galea knew he'd be putting in some very long days and nights on this investigation. Nealy would see to that.

Five minutes later on the far backstretch, Galea parked the patrol car fifty yards from Track Baron's barn. When he slid from behind the wheel and stood in the dusty, sand-filled tracks where carts, feed trucks and graders made their daily rounds, he saw no one. In the distance then, he saw one of the workers watering a garden. He walked in that direction, noticing as he went that large mounds of fill were piled in various locations on the race course track. Beyond that he observed a giant earth grader and off to his right, a large yellow front-loader machine. Early season track grooming, he reasoned. Still the only worker in sight was the one man doing the watering. When he reached him, the man, or as Galea now saw, a boy perhaps in his late teens, was just beginning to shut the hose off. Dressed in a jeans outfit, with the short coat looking as if it were two sizes too small, the boy was wearing knee-high rubber boots, a dark pull-over cap, with bright red kerchief tied about his neck. His face had a ruddy brown complexion and Galea noticed that his head was much too big for his slender body.

"Doing your gardening early this season?" Galea said as he drew near the boy who, upon seeing Galea in uniform, looked startled.

"Oh, this here is no garden, sir. Well, in a way it's a garden. It's a burial garden. Some real fancy horses buried under the soil, I'd say."

"Horses you say?" Galea inquired, peering down at the ground where the watering had taken place.

The boy, still holding the hose, gestured with one free hand. "Yep. These were great stakes winners. Owners decided to bury them right here. Not a bad place, so close to the track. Kind of like they belong near the track." Then he pointed to the other side of the plot to four metal plaques mounted on foot-tall round stones. "Tells all about the four Thoroughbreds buried here. All great runners in their time. Take Silent Runner over there, he won the Travers. Next to him is Streak. One of the first owned by a sheik. They say he was bought right at the Tipton Sales and trained in England. Came back and won the Jim Dandy. My favorite was Looking Glass. Small horse, under fifteen hands high, but he outran everyone when he won the Test Stakes. The last one buried here is a filly, Icon. That was one of Miss Valova's best runners. Icon won the Whitney. Now they're all part of Saratoga's history, wouldn't you say?"

Galea nodded in approval, adding. "It's a fine resting place. By the way son, what's your name?"

"Luke Clinton. Most of the help here just call me Clinton. Most don't know my first name."

Clinton turned the hose on again and a soft, vapor spray shot out. He shifted his position from the front of the plot to the rear, and Galea, anxious to ask him if he'd seen anything of Witt, followed him.

"Funny damn thing," Clinton suddenly said. "The ground is like a sponge. Last year it was hard as rock. Now it's soft. Someone's raked it over. Don't know who. Maybe one of the owners came by and decided to spruce it up. Still can't understand why it soaks up so much water. Strange, isn't it?"

"Well," said Galea, "we've had a screwy winter. Actually pretty warm and dry. We need rain."

"Same down south," Clinton agreed. "Dry as a bone. Grass turned to straw before it could be cut. Bad time for fires, too. My boss, Mr. Wilkes, he's got a place in Dade County and he had two barns burn down this winter. Two wells went dry and, if I remember right, so did some wells on nearby farms. Worst thing in the world, drought. Nothing goes on without water. Not on a horse farm, anyway."

"How long have you been coming to Saratoga?" Galea asked.

"Let's see. This will be my fourth year. Yes, four years. I started with Mr. Wilkes and stayed with him. Pretty good boss. Pays well, too."

Galea sized him up again, figuring that he had probably been hired by Wilkes when he was no older than fourteen or fifteen. It was a typical backstretch scenario. Kids from the hill country working for peanuts, for owners who could well afford to pay them a decent wage. Galea was aware that child labor laws were blatantly ignored in the horse business. But that wasn't his concern now. All he had on his mind was Stuart Witt. Find Stuart Witt. Make Nealy happy. He then spent the next five minutes filling the boy in on Witt's mysterious disappearance hoping, upon hope, that maybe he'd seen Witt in his movements on the backstretch. To his disappointment, Galea got only a blank stare from Clinton. Galea's frustration level was maxing out. He thanked Clinton for his time and went back to his patrol car. He hadn't yet reached the vehicle when his digital beeper went off. It was headquarters calling. He jumped in the car and called the main switchboard. Wanda Gable, a new trainee, answered.

"Galea checking in."

"One moment," said Wanda.

Galea waited a full minute but she didn't get back to him. He hung up and called again.

"Saratoga Police. Where can I direct your call?"

"Wherever it was you were going to direct me when I called the first time," Galea said, with deliberate sarcasm.

"Sorry, Sargeant. Still trying to master this computer board. Had you, then lost you. Anyway, Chief Nealy wants to talk to you. I'll put you right through."

Galea heard Nealy pick up the line. He also heard a female voice talking very loudly in the background to Nealy. It went on for several moments. Finally, Nealy spoke. "Got a guest here," he said. "She's not really happy with the way I'm handling things down here. Millie Perkins from the Sheraton. While she's sitting in front of me, I'm in hopes that you can give me some good news on Witt. Like you have found him, or at least know his whereabouts. Might that be asking too much?" Galea held the phone away from his right ear. He wasn't about to impair his hearing once Nealy got his answer.

"Zero, Chief. Absolute zero. Not a soul at that track knows where he is." He could hear Nealy's breathing rise, then a long, silent pause. He waited for the inevitable tongue lashing. He was surprised when Nealy's voice came back in a whispered tone, almost as if he had suddenly developed an acute case of laryngitis.

"You say Witt can't be found? That's what you said, right Sargeant? The man is gone. No one knows where? Am I hearing you right? Is that what you're telling me?" Galea felt the fire over the phone and understood that if Millie Perkins hadn't been sitting in that office, at this very moment, Nealy would be filling the air waves with a dozen nasty expletives. He was happy to be spared this exercise.

"We've got a tough one, Chief. Don't know if you're up to suggestions right now, but I'd be prone to calling the state police for help on this one."

"Hell we will," Nealy finally found his upper octaves. "Don't want them. Don't need them. What's this coming to? Crying wolf to the NYSP everytime we have a minor problem?"

"It's a matter of degree," Galea answered. "Question. Is this a minor problem or a big one?"

Nealy ratcheted his voice up two pitches. "Only big if we make it big. Understand me?" Then Galea heard him address Millie Perkins, telling her he had an important, confidential call and would she mind terminating their meeting at this point? The reception was so clear, Galea heard the door close as Millie departed Nealy's office. Galea braced himself for the real barrage. It came in a repetitive, staccato, incoherent diatribe run of sentences which had Galea wondering if Nealy hadn't completely lost all his marbles. Nealy went on for five minutes, finally reaching the point where he talked himself out. Galea was used to this. Letting Nealy blow out the frustration was equal to defusing a bomb. You had to have patience.

When he deemed it safe to reply, Galea did so, saying. "Perhaps you're right, Chief. Let's give it another twenty-four hours before we even think of bringing in the state police. I have a few more sources I'd like to check out in the meantime. I'll touch base with you tomorrow afternoon. How's that?"

"I don't like the smell of this whole thing," Nealy said, his voice choked with exhaustion. "Do what you can, Tom. Scour this damn town from top to bottom. I'm depending on you. You're the only one I can trust with this hot potato."

Galea couldn't remember when Nealy last had addressed him by his first name. Could it be the chief was mellowing under the pressures of the job?

Galea didn't accept that premise. In fact, he liked the iron-fisted Nealy better. Nealy said goodbye and hung up. Galea sat for several minutes thinking out his next move. Suddenly it dawned on him that he hadn't inquired about current whereabouts in Saratoga of Witt's horses. Witt had told Nealy he shipped a few from Kentucky, so they had to be nearby. With this thought in mind, he went to see Joe Hennesy.

A light rain was falling when Galea drove across Union Avenue and pulled into the long road near the Oklahoma Track to Hennesy's office. He spotted Hennesy's familiar station wagon with its Track 1 license plate. There were no other cars parked in the area. Galea entered the small office but found it empty. He went outside and looked over to the track. One pickup truck was passing by the entrance gate to the practice track. Galea ran out and hailed it down. He recognized the driver, a guy from town, known as Sawdust. Seems everyone on the backstretch had a nickname. Sawdust, when asked, said Hennesy was over in the far barn area caring for some abandoned horses. Didn't know whose exactly. Galea got back in the patrol car and drove the two-hundred yard distance to the barns. Sure enough Hennesy, pacing up and down outside one stall, hands on hips with a look that said he wasn't a bit happy with what he was seeing inside the stall, greeted Galea with a nod. Then Hennesy blurted out, "How in hell's name can anyone leave four Thoroughbreds in this condition? You tell me that?"

Galea peeked inside the nearest stall. A horse was on its side, breathing heavily and letting out deep guttural noises as it tried to right itself. The stall had not been cleaned out either and the stench was vile. He could readily understand Hennesy's position.

"Where's the owners?" Galea asked.

"You tell me," Hennesy remarked.

"Terrible way to treat animals," Galea insisted.

"I've seen people shot for less," said Hennesy. "Christ, man brings four healthy horses up here from Kentucky and deserts them. Doesn't make any sense? You have any idea how much money he had invested in these ponies? Must be $600,000 tied up here. Who would throw away that kind of money? Not to mention the inhumane aspect of it. A sorry sight. Can't remember when I've seen anyone treat horses in this manner."

Galea, holding his nose as he backed away from the stall, took a look at the other stalls. All the horses were in the same sordid condition, as were their stalls. The magnitude of the mistreatment shocked him. He was in complete sympathy with Hennesy.

"Who rented this barn?" Galea finally asked.

"Don't know," said Hennesy. "I was away for two days. One of my assistants, Ron Farley, must have booked them in my absence. Farley is off today, but I'll have someone in my office check the log book." Hennesy, not wanting to see more, walked away in disgust. Galea did likewise, going back to the patrol car and spinning sharply around in the soft dust of the barn area, followed Hennesy's station wagon to his office. Hennesy's secretary had already left for the day, so Hennesy took out the large, leather-bound log book and ran his finger down the entries of the last few days. He flipped the page and continued to check. His finger stopped on the last line of the second page.

"Here it is. All four horses registered to Stuart Clayton Witt of Lexington, Kentucky. Brought them in a few days ago. According to this, he wasn't present when they arrived in Saratoga. The delivery slip is signed by the truck driver. Let me see. Stanford Wright, Fleetway Horse Transportation, Keeneland, Kentucky. This Witt handled it all by fax to this office. Even the financial arrangements."

"Witt. You said Witt?" Galea grabbed the log book.

"That's right. Stuart Witt. You know him?"

"Not personally," said Galea. "Wish I did, and I wish I knew where he was this very moment. Chief Nealy would like to know the same thing."

"How's that?"

"That mess in the barns tells it all," said Galea, moving around the desk to the phone. "Mind if I use this?"

"I don't get it," said Hennesy. "What kind of trouble is this Witt in?"

"He's missing," replied Galea while continuing to dial Nealy's office. It rang twice, then went dead. He dialed again. Still couldn't get through. He then dialed the operator. She confirmed that there was trouble on the lines into police headquarters, and recommended he call on the backup system, which was located in Ballston Spa. Galea decided he'd wait and call later. He then told Hennesy, "The neglected horses and Witt's sudden disappearance. It all adds up. He wouldn't leave these horses intentionally. His car was found on Union Avenue. He was out here looking for Sweetfeed. Nealy suggested it. He was trying to hire Sweetfeed or someone to take care of his stock. Probably made some temporary arrangements for feeding, but he didn't check to see if it had been done. You say the horses had already arrived. Witt apparently got here following their arrival. He came to Nealy's office after that. Horses had to have something to eat and drink when they arrived, wouldn't you say?"

"Oh, the trucker might have fed and watered them on the way up. But feeding was not included in Witt's contract. At least according to what I see here. That was his obligation, or whoever he entrusted his horses with." Galea sat down in the vintage swivel chair at the desk. He tipped back his cap and fingered his temples in silence. Hennesy was still turning the pages of the log book. "Better go completely through this damn thing," said Hennesy. "Always used to check it daily before we got too busy around here. Don't want to discover any more sad situations out there like this one. Word like this gets out and we'd be out of business in thirty days. I cringe at the thought of it."

Galea couldn't sit still. He rocked from side to side, his feet hitting the inner sides of the desk each time he rocked. After a time he rose and stretched his arms above his head. Hennesy, who was sitting on the corner of the desk, quickly moved to the swivel chair, letting out one big exhausted yawn as he plopped down.

"I have to talk to Farley," Galea then said. "Maybe he knows something. When's he due back at the track?"

Hennesy took out the schedule book and opened it. "Not for two days. He's working a split shift here for the balance of the month. But you can try his home. That's if he's not off trout fishing. Farley's found a home for himself over on the Battenkill near Arlington, Vermont.

Goes there every free moment. Doesn't catch much, but says it doesn't matter. He's always been a nature lover."

Hennesy handed Galea the phone and dialed Farley's number. As expected they got no answer.

"It's not my day for telephones," quipped Galea.

"Wait one minute," Hennesy said. "He may have his mobile working. I'll try."

Galea heard a faint ring this time.

"Give him some time," said Hennesy. "Who knows, he may be landing a big brown trout this very second."

He no sooner spoke when Farley, his voice barely audible, came on the line. Hennesy then hit the desk-top speaker button and they commenced a three-way conversation.

Galea spoke first. "Ron, this is Sergeant Galea. Talking here with Joe Hennesy in his office. We've got a mess on our hands and thought you might help us clear it up."

As faint as the mobile phone transmission was, Galea could hear the Battenkill in the background. No denying that Farley was fishing, and probably with hip boots on.

"Do all I can," said Farley.

"Man named Witt. Do you recall signing his horses in?"

"Not exactly," answered Farley.

"Try again," insisted Galea. "Witt. Stuart Clayborn Witt. A name you don't come across every day."

He could hear Farley sloshing about.

"You in midstream?" inquired Galea.

"No," said Farley, "I'm right near the stream bank. But wouldn't you know it, my right foot is stuck in mud."

"Well, I'll hang on till you're free," Galea assured him. "On second thought, I can't hardly hear you. any chance of you getting to another phone in the area?"

"There's a bait shack down the road. I'll give it a try."

"OK. OK. Call us right back."

As they sat and waited for Farley's return call, Galea engaged in small talk. Trivial questions about the track and its operations, some of which Hennesy found amusing. Hennesy ultimately realized that Galea had less than a layman's knowledge of the track. In Hennesy's opinion, cops that spent as much time around the track as Galea did should be better versed. Yet without showing his surprise, Hennesy answered each mundane question. While Galea talked, Hennesy was anxiously watching the wall clock. Fifteen minutes had slipped by but no return call from Farley. When a half hour passed, both men looked puzzled. It was then forty-five minutes and eventually one hour without a call.

"Where in hell is that bait shop he talked about?" Galea said.

Hennesy shifted around in the chair. He looked worried. "I know that little place," Hennesy admitted. "It's right over the Vermont line. Purchased some trout flies there myself one season. The name escapes me. Some guy from Cambridge owns it."

"Hand me the phone again," Galea said. "I'll call the Cambridge police. They'll know it."

He got through to a Cambridge patrolman just coming off road duty. He knew the shop, also its owner. "Terry's." Even gave Galea the phone number and exact location.

Hennesy smiled. "Had it right on the tip of my tongue."

Galea dialed Terry's and a man, his voice full of excitement and with labored breathing answered.

Galea told him who they were waiting to hear from.

The breathing on the other end of the line continued, but the man's word choked off.

"Is Ron Farley there?" Galea shouted.

"Are you a relative?"

"Not exactly."

"We're trying to locate his next of kin."

Galea rose up straight. The hairs on his head going just as straight. "What's this kin stuff? Who am I speaking to?"

"This is Terry Ford. I own the bait shop."

"Where's Ron Farley?" Galea found himself asking again.

"There's been a terrible accident." said Ford. "The Vermont State Troopers are with him now. He's still at the Battenkill."

"Can't be so," Galea said. "He was on his way to your place to call us. We've been waiting more than an hour for his call."

"I'm so sorry," Ford said, "Ron Farley drowned in the Battenkill just about an hour ago. One of my regular customers found him. Nothing could be done. They said water filled his boots and dragged him under."

Hennesy, listening on the speaker phone, swore three times and buried his face in his hands.

17. AGENT WHITE

The Saturday meeting at Lake George took place as scheduled. Yet it was not a pleasant day weatherwise. Long, low clouds of rain hung over the deep green Adirondack Mountains, letting out periodic sprays over the lake, which was rippled with foot-high waves. A cool westerly wind was blowing. It was not the day Dr. Blake had hoped for. He'd anticipated sunny weather, perhaps a bit cold, but clear, then while driving to the lake from his home in Saratoga, he heard the weather reports. That's the way Lake George was. Conditions could change in a matter of hours. So as Blake pulled his Lincoln four-door sedan into the winding driveway of his uncle's estate just north of the village near Diamond Point, he did so with the car lights on. Even with the nasty weather, the old castle-like edifice with its commanding view of the lake looked imposing. It had been the place where Blake, as a boy, had spent many happy hours. Built at the turn of the century by a rich railroad family, Blake's great-uncle, upon acquiring the property, modernized the estate. He planted many new shrubs and trees, re-wired the main house and adjacent buildings, installed new docks and repaired the original wooden boathouse. He then did the lawns over, personally directing the re-sodding of five acres and attending to all the details when it came to repaving the driveway and a half dozen smaller roads on the property. Castle Rock, as it was called, was unique. One of only three castled structures on the thirty-two-mile long blue glacier lake, upkeep and general maintenance was expensive, but that didn't matter to a man who had amassed between sixty and seventy million dollars through a series of wise investments. One included buying stock in General Electric in the thirties when it was considered a risk.

So a castle in Lake George, a beach house in Palm Springs, Florida, a hunting lodge in Montana and a penthouse in New York City were but a few of his uncle's earthly possessions. And all of them dutifully paid for. Fine that a man had achieved so much in life. Blake had always admired his uncle's business sense. Like the castle, however, his uncle was growing old. Too old at 86 to fully enjoy or appreciate the rewards of his life's work. And with no heir apparent, save for Blake, his uncle's death one day would bring an end to this opulent era. For Blake, the very thought of becoming beneficiary of Castle Rock conjured up visions of conflict. With all that new money, he wondered if he'd ever be able to keep up his practice within reasonable perspective.

Regardless of money, Blake knew that Castle Rock was a dwelling well past its prime and practical usefulness.

He climbed the concrete steps to the wide veranda where he was protected from the rain and waited for the others to arrive. Five minutes later he saw headlights appear at the driveway's entrance. It was Billy Farrell and Frank Duffy, driving in Duffy's Ford. They approached Castle Rock cautiously, creeping the car up the drive. Blake, realized that their ages were showing, also. You don't drive at 70 like you did at 20, Blake was thinking. He watched as the two old duffers scrambled out of the car in the driving rain and made their way to where he was standing. Duffy's glasses were dripping water when he reached the veranda level. Farrell, still able to negotiate without glasses, guided Duffy to a wicker chair and sat him down.

"Cold as hell up here," Farrell said, rubbing his hands together.

"'Tis April, Farrell. April's not summer. Not yet anyway."

Duffy adjusted the collar on his tan trench coat and tucked his hands into the pockets. Both men were wearing fedoras and they dripped water as well.

"Let's get inside and wait for Nealy and Galea," Blake offered.

"Fine by me," said Duffy. "Hope you got the heat on."

"It's always on this time of year," Blake assured him. "Uncle keeps the place heated all winter. If not, the walls would crack and the plumbing would burst. Of course there's no one here in winter. Still, a place like old Castle Rock needs some attention. Man up the lake drops in and checks on things. Also plows the place and keeps the heavy snow off the roofs. Ice and snow built up so bad one day they had to hire a crew of five to chip it off the drains. We've got the original slate tiles on this place. Ice has been known to split them, too."

Duffy, once inside the warmth of the castle's huge living room, took off his coat. Farrell did likewise. Now they were standing in front of a large window that gave them a view of the castle's sprawling front lawn and the boathouse some one-hundred yards down the slope. With the rain, there was not any of the lake to be seen.

Duffy ran his hand across the top of a dark, solid mahogany table in front of the window and peered out. "You know, Blake, I did a story on Castle Rock a bunch of years ago, before your uncle purchased it. It was in damn sorry shape at that time. If I remember right, it was built by Ronald Williston, the great-grandson of Fredrick Williston, the railroad tycoon. Is that right?"

Blake had to think a moment.

"Can't say, Duffy. I know it was the Williston family who built Castle Rock, but I don't remember which one. As you say, it was sadly in need of repairs when Uncle bought it. My parents brought me here often in summers past. By then it was fixed up. Story I have heard over the years was that Williston was a close friend of Spencer Trask, and when Trask decided to build Yaddo in Saratoga, he also built a near twin to Castle Rock just up the Lake. Williston then built this place."

"Sounds right," Duffy agreed. "My research at the time surfaced some strange goings on with the Williston clan."

"How's that?" Blake inquired.

"Oh, they say the senior Williston, the original railroad baron, was always looking for ghosts. Used to hold seances right here in the castle. Things that also play right up your alley, Doctor. Williston toyed with occult wisdom and was very interested in Eastern religions. I found that later he was into some sort of mind control. I believe that's what did him in at the end. Williston's penchant for the weird and mysterious got him into big trouble with the local gentry. He became enraptured with a local girl in Lake George and tried to woo her with gifts and money. She was a simple type, actually in love with some farm boy from Ticonderoga at the time. Anyway, Williston tried to draw her into spiritualism and paranormal activity, and when that failed, he tried to control her mind. Told her he'd make her the female spirit guide of his loyal following. None of it impressed her. He was then forty-six and she was eighteen. Besides, he had no following. Maybe one or two nuts who might have believed in his eccentric ways, but no real following. Funny you haven't heard this story before, Doctor."

Blake moved to the center of the room. He folded his arms and stared at the editor. "Duffy, you amaze me. I bet you've forgotten more things than we will ever learn in two lifetimes. I'm stumped on this one. Uncle's had the place a long time. Never once did I hear him mention anything of this nature. When we get back in Saratoga see if your fancy computer can dig out that piece. I have to read it."

"Sure," Duffy said. "We'll have it."

Then Duffy added, "Strange. Your uncle made lots of money on General Electric stock, didn't he?"

"So they say," agreed Blake.

"Well," said Duffy, "Williston was one of the earliest members of the Theosophical Society. Do you know who they were?"

"Yes," Blake admitted. "I have read about them. Actually studied some of their early teachings and beliefs when I was doing post graduate work. What makes you bring them up?"

"Just a point of interest," said Duffy. "I'm a great one for drawing parallels. In this case, Williston fussed with the Theosophical bunch and, wouldn't you know, they say Thomas Edison was a member. Now that may mean nothing at all. But as I say, I like to draw parallels, be it situations or among people." Duffy smiled over at Blake. "Your uncle into any of these weird things?" he asked quizzically.

"Not that I know of," Blake said. "Money has been Uncle's only God. I think he made up his mind long ago to have his heaven right here on earth."

Billy Farrell let out a deep belly laugh.

Just then a car entered the driveway, followed by a second vehicle. "Finally, they're here," Blake said.

As pre-arranged, only the five principal figures were to be at this meeting. It was to include Blake, Duffy, Farrell, Nealy and Galea. As the big oak double doors to Castle Rock opened for the latecomers, Blake, Duffy and Farrell were startled when a sixth man came through the entrance. Nealy stepped forward to introduce him. "Meet FBI agent Ken White," Nealy said, immediately relieving any apprehensions the three had. "I thought it best to include him at this gathering. He'll shed new light on this mess."

White, a six-foot-two stoutly built man in his mid thirties, with jet black hair and intelligent dark eyes, stepped up and shook their hands. It would take a few minutes for them to adjust to White's sudden appearance, and Duffy, though not objecting to his presence, felt a little uneasy having a federal agent involved, knowing what he and the others already knew about the murders. Duffy's reasoning being: what if he started to question each about the first few days? About why the paper had held back information on Claire Valova's death. Or Ann Bifford's death for that matter. Not that there was any criminal aspect to what they had decided but rather, was it not likely that White might question the propriety of it? That in itself could be embarrassing to a seasoned newsman like himself. Duffy just didn't want too many players involved. The whole thing was ticklish enough.

Blake broke the ice by saying, "Glad you could come, Agent White. We need your professional input."

This said, they all marched through the castle's tall-ceilinged halls to a spacious drawing room, or smoking room as Blake called it. Like the living room, this room offered an equally beautiful view of the south front lawn, docks below and the lake, though it was still shrouded in a gray mist. Blake turned on some brass table lamps. He went to a cabinet and drew out a tray holding a variety of bottles.

"Take your pick," he said. "I recommend Uncle's brandy." Then he looked over at Duffy. "Yes. We've got some Irish whiskey for you and Farrell. Chasers and ice are in the other cabinet. Maybe this will take away the day's chill." He saw Duffy's face light up at the mention of it. Farrell, skipping the chaser and ice, belted down a stiff double whiskey and let out a relieved sigh.

Duffy sipped his water-and-whiskey mix slowly, smelling the aroma of the drink with each sip. Galea was the only one not drinking. Blake had rose wine, Agent White a Scotch and soda and Nealy opted for straight gin over ice.

"It's too bad we're here on such serious business," Farrell added, "Otherwise we could play poker."

"Another time," insisted Blake. "I promise."

Nealy glanced out the window and caught some movement out of the corner of his eye. "Say, Dr. Blake, who's that fellow?"

Blake squinted. "Oh, that's old Mr. Butcher. Robert Butcher, our nearest neighbor. He has to be in his eighties. He's not here very often. Don't worry about him."

Drinks taken, they settled into the subject at hand.

Nealy spoke first. "I brought Agent White with me to explain some vital things the FBI is investigating that in part involves some of the area we've been looking into. But first I have some more bad news. Word has been received from the Vermont State Police that Ron Farley, a race track worker Sargeant Galea was trying to connect with while the guy was fishing in Arlington, was found dead and now they figure it was foul play. Seems another fisherman saw someone struggling with Farley on the river bank just before he went under. This witness, however, was quite a ways downstream and couldn't do anything about it. Didn't even get a good description of the assailant. The other trout fisherman that did finally come to assist Farley never saw the assailant. As first reported, he thought Farley accidentally slipped and his waders filled with water dragging him under in the strong current. If he was forced under, we can only assume this nasty business is going to get worse." The reaction to Nealy's statement was one of shaking heads and bewildered looks. Duffy's face turned a pale white. Nealy continued. "Now for Agent White. He can't give you all the details of the bureau's involvement at this time. He can, I believe, give us some background on certain things taking place in the horse industry that the government has uncovered in the past few months. From what he has already told me on the way up here, the implications are far reaching and have totally changed thinking within Thoroughbred racing circles. Nealy then asked White to explain.

White moved to the edge of the soft leather divan he was seated on. He loosened his tie and took off his dark blue suit jacket.

"I'm here both officially and unofficially. What we say in this room today will not go further than that front door. Officially I will tell you things that only a few members of the FBI know at this time. As Nealy said, not everything. I can't reveal all details. So I want you to feel at ease and trust me. I came up from Washington months ago to look into some insurance fraud cases in New York. They involved several incidents of payoffs among horse people. I can tell you that what we found was not nice. Believe me when I say there are dozens of murdered Thoroughbreds along this trail we've been following." He watched the shocked expression on their faces as he spoke. "Trainers, veterinarians, insurance brokers and prominent owners have been implicated in many of these deaths. The list is long and unbelievable. It will, in time, all come out. When it does, you'll be shocked by the number of people charged with these crimes. Furthermore, and probably the most difficult to comprehend, are some of the people in high places that have participated in these insurance schemes. I'm not naming names at this point. I'm not allowed to. I can assure you, it touches the most untouchables." He hesitated. "Shall I go on, or do you want a refill first?"

Duffy waved his hands. "Continue. Continue. The drinks can wait."

White went on. "As you may know, they changed the insurance game in 1986. If you owned a race horse in the early eighties, you could sell it and still continue to reap money from that horse if it continued to win races. They legislated that perk to encourage people to buy into the game. It was a get-rich deal for many buyers and sellers. As I say, the Tax Reform Act of 1986 took away the perk. So many owners found out that their performance horses were worth more dead than alive. The criminal elements that always follow the money people around saw an opportunity. They'd kill the horses for a piece of the insurance payoff. It seemed just that simple. But it wasn't. You just don't shoot a fifteen-hundred-pound animal. That's too obvious. No insurance company is going to pay off on a horse that has been shot. They had to make it look natural. It could be done. They knew it. But sooner or later along the way the ones doing the killing would have to have the cooperation of some of the horse people. This includes everyone from hot walkers, groomers, veterinarians and trainers to owners. I say every one of the above, without question. Anyway, the people that kill horses have become very sophisti-cated in their methods. When they're finished most deaths look very nat-ural. Even seasoned veterinarians are fooled."

At this point he was abruptly cut off by Duffy. His Irish face puffed up and Duffy, still holding his drink suggested, "I find that a crock. How can anyone kill a horse and make it appear anything but what it is, murder?"

White waited a second, then answered, "I'll give you methods. You can draw your own conclusions, but these methods were ones we inves-tigated and verified through our labs in D.C. So far no one has disputed our findings." White then drew from his pocket two small white balls and quickly tossed them at Duffy who, on seeing them coming, ducked at first. He took out a few more balls and tossed them to the others. "Can't hurt you fellows. They're too light. After all, they're only ping pong balls. The kind you'd buy in any retail sporting goods store. Squeeze two of these up a horses nostrils and the beast will suffocate within ten minutes. Most doctors will say the horse died of a heart attack. Reason being, who'd expect foul play? And the symptoms are about the same. Or they may electrocute their prey. Two or three stiff jolts of 220 watts will do the job. Again, many diagnosed as heart failure or death by colic. To date, we're investigating over fifty cases. Some insurance payoffs top three million. Lastly, the killers are using a whole variety of chemicals. This is our most difficult area. Doctors claiming a horse died of a common cold or virus, only to have our lab technicians find out it was some sort of poison. You name it, they use it. Who are we looking for at this time? Probably more people than we'd like to admit. It gets stickier as we go up society's ladder. Stickier yet when we uncover race officials and politicians that are involved in the payoffs. Then, of course, we have to collect the facts and eventually pursue prosecution. That's the hard part. You can pinpoint a suspect, but you can't always tie him directly to the killings. Even the insurance money is often laundered as clean as a fresh sheet."

White stopped again and gave his comments a chance to sink in. Everyone in the room, including Nealy, looked baffled by what they had heard. He was laying bare facts they didn't want to hear. Most of them had dealt with crooks and chiselers in the past. Every race track had its share of them, even New York City and Canadian mob types. But this was different. Wholesale killing of fine Thoroughbreds. Worst yet, Thoroughbreds killed by their owners.

It was a tense delivery, with White closing by saying, "We're . . . that is the bureau, is coming at this from a different direction than local and state police. This must be understood. Nealy says you have your own investigation of sorts underway. I'm not going to ask who or where this is taking place. I do want to assure you that the FBI's goal is the same as yours. We're out to find the killers and the persons behind the insurance frauds who have hired the killers. If you can help us in that pursuit, we'd appreciate it. If I can help you, then I will. Claire Valova and Doctor Ann Bifford, somehow got caught up in this mess. We don't know why they were killed. It could be for any number of reasons. Perhaps they were privy to information that proved too dangerous. Like yourselves, I can only speculate in Ann Bifford's case, we can't prove she was killed, or mysteriously drowned, as the situation calls for. As you know, she was a veterinary toxicologist. Word did come today that Anguillan authorities are planning to release her body to the family by early next week. No one knows why they've had a change of heart. We did get skimpy reports that there had been an incident on Anguilla last evening that may have prompted them to act. That whole area of the Caribbean is tourist driven. Adverse publicity they don't need. Her body will be flown to Florida, then home. The bureau will be interested in the autopsy findings. As you may understand, we're treating this as an international case. Other government agencies may be included in the investigation. Certainly in the Caribbean region."

When White finished talking, he poured himself a whiskey over ice and sat down. Everyone was deep in thought. Only the tinkling of the ice in White's drink broke the somber silence in the smoking room. It was as if someone had dropped a bomb and they were all waiting for the dust to settle.

Farrell and Duffy made their way to the tray once again and fortified their drinks, Duffy pouring a double shot this time and spared the water. And then the meeting reached a paradox. All had questions they wanted answered, but all were fully cognizant that these very questions could not, in fact would not, be answered at this time. So they all sat waiting for the next guy to pick up where Agent White had left off.

Nealy took over the floor once more.

"We thank Agent White for coming today. He has to get back to The City tonight, so we won't keep him any longer. I have his card if you feel he's to be contacted in the future."

The rain had stopped and, for a brief period the lake was visible half way across. Nealy walked White to his car.

18. CAT NAP

S ergeant Galea's visit to Clare's Court sent renewed fears through Sweetfeed's mind that someone would eventually uncover the insurance scheme, which ultimately might direct the investigation his way. This thought, coupled with the fear that Witt's body, now planted among the revered, deceased Thoroughbreds on the backstretch, might also be discovered, tripled his anxiety. Two days had passed since Galea's visit, and Sweetfeed, giving it much thought, decided that he'd take two courses of action. First of all, he would remove Witt's corpse. Where to move it was a big question, but Witt had to be moved. Secondly, he would make a concerted effort to find out who The Voice was, not knowing in the least how he'd go about accomplishing this, either. Both tasks presented formidable obstacles. Witt wasn't a monstrous problem. It was just a matter of timing. He'd have to dig him up in a hurry at a time when the backstretch was deserted. But with May quickly approaching, and more workers arriving each day, even this would take some dedicated planning. Thinking back on the night he did Witt in, Sweetfeed amazed himself at the speed with which it all took place. He didn't know his own strength that eventful evening. Witt's unlikely grave was dug in record time, not more than twenty minutes, using only a barn spade. In his troubled mind, Sweetfeed went through the steps he had taken.

The raw power he had killed Witt with, followed by lifting the lifeless body into the barn cart and subsequently pulling it to the grave site, and then digging furiously while sweat poured from his own forehead, was as real to him now as on the night it happened. He had dug so hard, the handle of the shovel burned his hands, so much so that he still bore two burn marks on the inner right thumb. Both hands were highly callused from the exercise. Sweetfeed rubbed his rough hands together and looked at the burn marks. One problem he'd have to solve up front was Clinton who was in charge of watering that area of the backstretch barns, including the burial site. Sweetfeed knew he'd have to come up with a rational reason for digging inside the plot, one that would satisfy Clinton's curiosity, should he inquire.

Facing up to the second task, that of tracking down The Voice, would be a pure game of Blindman's Bluff. The prospect of even attempting it shook Sweetfeed from head to toe. He'd seen the meanness dealt out to horses. He could only imagine worse things were The Voice to discover what he was thinking at this moment. Nevertheless, Sweetfeed had a plan and he envisioned it would go something like this: On The Voice's next phone call, Sweetfeed would tell him that something very serious had come up and that he wanted a private meeting to discuss it. He'd insist that they meet on the backstretch, but not in or around the barns. Sweetfeed was familiar with all the area surrounding the backstretch. Certainly, with a little coaching, he could draw The Voice off toward Yaddo where the woods and underbrush afforded an ideal setting for surprise. Then he'd devise a first-strike strategy and do away with The Voice once and for all. He's get rid of him as he had Witt. Quick and without hesitation. Yes, he'd put an end to all these secret calls and all the fear he'd felt ever since being involved with The Voice. Yes, that's the way it would come off. It would void out all traceable ties to past murders. With Valova and Bifford gone, plus the snooping insurance man, Witt, cold beneath the ground with the horses, The Voice was Sweetfeed's only barrier to a clean break. He knew he had no other choice but to kill The Voice.

Sweetfeed was hedging against the clock now. It was just about time for The Voice to contact him again. Subconsciously his mind was rehearsing what he was going to say, how he'd tell him that they had to meet. That a serious problem had come up that could not be discussed by phone. And for the sake of privacy and secrecy, the meeting would have to be at the designated site. Sweetfeed was sure he could pull it off.

This accomplished, Sweetfeed's focus now centered on removing Witt, preferably this very evening when the backstretch had gone to sleep.

After inspecting Track Baron in his stall, Sweetfeed went to bed at nine P.M. He shut his eyes, but didn't sleep. The sounds of the backstretch came through the thin walls of his bunk house. The horses kicking and rubbing against stall walls. The cry of a barn cat seeking shelter from the cool evening. The small talk and laughter of workers before they retired to await an early morning rising. The animal sounds he was all too familiar with. He could go long hours without sleep. It was a trait all backstretch people acquired early on. Much like circus hands, their lives pivoted within their surroundings. This night he was awake for another reason. Apprehension built within him as he contemplated going out to dig up Witt. Just how far down was Witt? Sweetfeed couldn't remember. In his haste that frightful evening to get rid of Witt's body, Sweetfeed's recollection of just how deep he dug the grave was a blur. Was it four feet? Perhaps five? Certainly not more than six or seven feet? How fast could he dig him out? Would the plot belie his dirty work when he was done? Where would he go with Witt?

That was the biggest dilemma. There was an old drainage pipe on the far end of the track seldom cared for by ground crews. Sweetfeed had discovered it several years ago while driving a tractor in the area. Witt's body would fit nicely into the pipe. Then a chilling prospect crossed Sweetfeed's mind: How badly decomposed would Witt be? Would he fall apart during transfer? God, that would be terrible, Sweetfeed thought, as he twisted several times in his bed. He wrestled with the pros and cons of his night's work until 11 P.M. when he rose and pulled on his boots. There was dead silence outside his bunk house. The waning April night's air hung heavy, damp and cold as he stepped outside. He reached for a shovel, tucked it under one arm and proceeded to the burial site. Only two small night lights were burning in the barn area, so that the plot itself was quite dark. He carried a flashlight in his hip pocket, but he dared not turn it on. He moved slowly to the center of the plot, careful not to trip over the memorial markers. Once feeling that he was in the right spot, he began to dig. The shovel hit immediate resistance. He put the full weight of his right boot on the shovel and pushed. It sprung back at him. He reached down and felt the ground, not being able to see anything in the pitch darkness. It was then he discovered a circular piece of hard metal. Taking a calculated chance that he may be seen by someone, he covered the end of his flashlight and shined it on the object for a moment.

"Damn. Damn," he whispered in disgust. It was an engraved metal piece, some four feet in diameter, one inch thick. He hadn't time to read the inscriptions. He was not aware it had been put there following the night he had put Witt to his final rest. Not only was it on the exact spot, but Sweetfeed, after several tries, found he couldn't move the piece. Trying to pry it up with the shovel also proved fruitless. He stood shivering in the cold for several minutes thinking of a way to proceed. In the end, he could think of nothing. This evening's venture would have to be called off. He was just leaving the plot when a light shown in his face. His hands went up to his eyes and he arched his neck. "Who in hell is that?" he called out.

"That you, Sweetfeed?" Water Man's squeaky voice said.

"No, it's someone else. You know darn well it's me, Water Man. What you doing out here at this hour?"

Water Man turned off the flashlight. "My cat done stray. Sometimes he comes here. Don't know why he likes this graveyard, but he does. You seen him?"

"Can't say that I have," replied Sweetfeed.

"He's black and white with an all-white tail. If you do see him, let me know."

Water Man started away then stopped. "Hey, Sweetfeed, what you doing out here anyway. You lost a cat, too?"

"No. I lost my shovel. Did some work out here earlier. Forgot it."

"Strange," said Water Man, "thought you always went to sleep by nine or so."

"Always do, except for tonight. This shovel cost twenty bucks. Couldn't leave it here overnight. Not in this damp night air."

"Guess you're right," said Water Man. "Well, I'm going back. Look out for my cat, will ya?"

"I'll do that," said Sweetfeed.

He waited for Water Man to leave. "You'll have to stay down there another day, you old buzzard," Sweetfeed mumbled softly. "But don't worry, I'll get you up. You'll be put where they won't be apt to find you." On his way back he saw a black and white cat scurry from out of Track Baron's stall. It ran full speed down along the barns and disappeared in the direction of the plot.

"Go on, cat," said Sweetfeed. "Keep Witt company."

19. PAUPER'S PLOT

While the crew of *Big Fish* guided the sleek, dark cylinder silent and deep through ocean depths, Flint, Sandy and Captain Flew dined in the main mess on a special gourmet fare of fillet of sole, New York strip steak, pan-fried shrimp and choice California chardonnay wine. Putts did not join them. He decided he'd spend some time drilling Donato before they had to turn him over to the FBI in Florida. He was under no illusion that Donato would confess anything more than he had confessed to Flint, but Putts planned to use a softer approach. He would appeal to reason, knowing that Donato's fear of Flint at this point, plus his irrational state of mind, had forced him to suppress the truth. Putts would not go as far as to suggest clemency for information, but he'd tell Donato that things would go a lot easier with the feds were he to cooperate. In short, Putts was suggesting the makings of a deal, whereas Flint, in his rage, said no deal was possible. If Donato insisted on clamming up, then Putts would take what information they had and pass it along to the FBI. It was all a matter of degree. In reality, Putts' first obligation was to the CIA. If he had to share information with the FBI, he'd do so only when it was appropriate. Otherwise, he'd do what he had always done when both government agencies were investigating the same person or situation, he'd be ambiguous and vague.

Halfway into dessert, Putts appeared. Flint noticed the familiar smile was missing and he appeared fatigued.

"Sit and have something to eat," Flint offered.

"Maybe a cup of coffee," Putts said.

Flint pushed a cup in front of Putts as he sat down between Sandy and Captain Flew. "If you're like the rest of these navy types, I bet you drink it black?"

"The darker the better," Putts agreed.

"I'm an exception to that," Flew added. "I take cream in mine."

"So much for my assumptions," laughed Flint.

Sandy, having finished her dessert and coffee, yawned and put her head on Flint's shoulder. "I think I've had it. Too much excitement for me in too short a time. Hope you don't mind if I leave you gentlemen?"

She had no sooner said it when Flew hit a nearby button and the compartment door to the mess area opened and in stepped a marine guard.

"Escort Miss Blair to her quarters," Flew ordered.

Flint smiled. "Rank has its privileges," he said. "I'll be with you soon, darling." He kissed her on the forehead. After she had gone, they moved from the mess table to some softer chairs.

Flint turned to Putts. "You didn't look too happy following your talk with Donato. Did he give in at all?"

"Yes and no," said Putts. "Depends on what we say on his behalf to the bureau boys in Florida. I know you're not interested in cutting a deal for him. I also can appreciate your reasons. On the other hand, I can cut a deal. No clemency. That's out. But he's got certain information both the CIA and the FBI need to further the investigation, especially the Cuban connection. I don't for a minute think he's a spy. What little he knew from our Caribbean operations would be of no use to Castro and his cronies. There would, however, be plenty Donato could give us on the drug running and money laundering. So without getting you further involved with Donato and his problems, here's some information he gave me that will help you when we reach Florida. For the record, though, you didn't get these from me."

Putts handed Flint a piece of paper. On it was some background information on Steiner and Ben the Chem, with three addresses. Two of the addresses were for Steiner, one in West Palm Beach and one in Fort Myers.

"Donato swears it's the last known addresses of Max Steiner and Ben the Chem," said Putts. "You can tackle those two because, as I said earlier, the CIA is not interested, nor do we have any authority to go after two murders in the States. I'm sure you can dispose of this matter in good style." He winked at Flint.

"Yes," agreed Flint, "an old friend of yours in New York will be happy to get Ben the Chem's address. Harry Waite, remember him?"

"Is that cantankerous rascal still operating Central Headquarters in the Big Apple?"

"They can't get rid of him," Flint smiled. "He's the driving force. Besides, I need someone I can fight with from time to time. Waite makes my job interesting. Yes, he's still at the Central's helm. In fact, I'm going to call him. While I go after Max Steiner, Harry can do some leg work on this Ben the Chem character. I'm sure we can teach him a few tricks about chemistry he hasn't seen. Assuming Harry's dislike for men who poison elderly ladies, I wouldn't be surprised he doesn't stuff Ben the Chem in a giant test tube when we catch up to him."

Flew broke out in laughter. "Who the hell is Ben the Chem?"

"Would you believe, he's a chemist who delights in mixing little drinks for his victims with all sorts of toxic substances. Kills them slowly. According to Donato, he killed Claire Valova, stringing her death out over three months with daily dollops of cyanide. Can you imagine how awful that must have been? And all the time she was getting sicker, her doctors were treating her for an acute heart condition. I guess he killed a dozen or more Thoroughbred horses in the same manner. It's all tied together in the horse insurance fraud investigation going on from Florida to New York. I got involved on behalf of some close friends in Saratoga. They expect the worst up there this racing season. They've already discovered several suspicious horse deaths and, to make matters worse, Ann Bifford's drowning and Valova's poisoning. My contacts in Saratoga say the FBI is investigating over fifty cases right now. We're just now learning how widespread this racket is. Probably would have gone undetected for some time if they had stuck to killing just horses. But when they started knocking off doctors and socialites, they blew the lid off a very lucrative scam." Flint stopped for a moment to finish his brandy, then continued. "Where will we be putting in at Florida?"

"About a third of the crew will be going ashore for a few days' leave at Fort Lauderdale. We plan on boating you and Sandy into the Intracoastal Waterway from about three miles off shore. We've made arrangements for you to stay with a former ship's captain in Lauderdale for as long as you like. We'll have your luggage delivered to his place. Putts will give you a phone code just in case you want to reach us. We will be heading for South America in ten days, but the phone call will get through."

They had one last drink before retiring. Flint figured he'd call Harry Waite right away about Ben the Chem. Then, catching up to Max Steiner in Florida would his next priority. He knew he'd have to ship Sandy back to California before going any further, though he also knew that talking her into going back would not be easy. It had been like that from the start. Every time they planned some time together, it was cut short. He blamed himself for this. As Monica had told him so many times in the past, "No one can truly love you, Flint. You already have a love. Your damn, scary work."

Inwardly he feared that Sandy would soon grow tired of the interruptions. So far she went along with most of his unsettling and unpredictable assignments. But could it last? Would she continue to wait out the long days and nights not knowing if he was safe, or would ever return? He was weighing over the consequences of this while he phoned Harry in New York.

He heard it ring four times, then pause, and then ring again. He realized it was Harry's special transfer line, meaning he might be anywhere other than Central Headquarters at this time. Two more faint rings and Harry answered.

"Waite here."

Flint didn't say anything.

"I say Waite here."

Flint kept silent.

"Come on, Flint. I haven't time for these games."

"Just thought I'd keep you guessing," said Flint.

"No need to. I know your quirky mind likes to play tricks on me. It's no use, I've been there before. What's up?"

"Have a little address I'd like to you to check out in Catamount, New York. One Benjamin Lewis, alias Ben the Chem. Supposedly lives on a hill overlooking a ski complex by the same name near Hillsdale. Once worked for a chemical company, Sterling Winthrop in Rensselaer, New York, up near Albany. Has been biding his time since he retired in 1986 with killing horses and old ladies. A real nice fellow."

"Sounds like a goon," said Harry. "Pretty versatile too, killing horses and people. Sounds like he's really down on humanity."

"No," said Flint. "He loves people. Has three grandchildren. No secret to his motives, he just kills for money. Loses it as fast as it comes in. The tables in Atlantic City and on ponies at any track that will have him. The mob picked up on his talents when he owed them a big marker. Hell, he can fool just about any doctor around. Most of his victims, human or animal, generally die of natural causes, or what's perceived as natural. It's all neat and clean and wonderfully suited for collecting insurance money."

Harry let out a sigh. "Flint don't tell me he did in Claire Valova?"

"You're on the ball, Harry. Yeah, Ben the Chem slipped her cyanide in small doses. There's your mysterious poison you've been looking for."

"Christ sake," Harry shouted so that Flint's ear began ringing. "Don't know why he wasted time going through the motions. Could just have easily had her drink Hudson River water. It's full of toxins. Every fish from Montauk Point to Albany is full of the damn stuff."

"Well," said Flint. "I have to take care of the second half of the killing team in Florida. Then we'll package them both up for you. You know my friends in Saratoga are depending on me to wrap this up soon."

"Have it your way, Flint. When will you be coming in?"

"Maybe within a week, perhaps two."

He heard Harry scuffling some papers. "Just checking my schedule," Harry said. "That gives me plenty of time. We're on a big one this week in Manhattan. I'll have two of my best men track down this Lewis guy next week although my budget will damn near break. By the way, how's Sandy? She still with you?"

"Of course," Flint said. "But, I'm thinking of sending her back to California till this is over. Just can't get up the nerve to tell her. Any ideas?"

"Sure," laughed Harry. "If she doesn't mind spending a few days and nights with a slightly overweight, balding cop, let her come stay with me."

"I know your heart's in the right place Harry, but we'll pass on this one. I think a ticket back to California for Sandy at this time will be best. Nevertheless, we will have dinner with you in New York. Besides, it's your treat. At least the last time we met you offered to buy. Isn't that right?"

"No, I don't recall. I'll take you out anyway. I'll do it for Sandy's sake."

Flint's tone then turned serious. "Promise me you won't send two trigger- happy cops up to Catamount. I want this guy alive and I need to talk to him. We might even uncover some new mob people by talking to Lewis. He may even have a lead on others in Saratoga. My friends say funny things are taking shape up there. One insurance guy from Kentucky is missing and they're suspicious about a track employee who supposedly drowned in a nearby fishing stream. It's only late April, but the race course will be operating in July, so I expect I'll be back in Saratoga before it's all said and done."

"You need any help in Florida?" Harry offered.

"That depends," said Flint. "I'll be chasing a snake called Max Steiner. He's a horse hit man. Specializes in electrocuting his prey. Even uses rusty nails to infect the poor animals. Don't know if he's killed any people, but I wouldn't rule it out. We're being dropped in Fort Lauderdale. I have addresses for Steiner in West Palm Beach and Ft. Myers. Rich territory for a guy of his ilk, wouldn't you say?"

"Never know," said Harry. "Some of these low lifes run in elite company. The rich and famous are often attracted to them. They're a diversion from their boredom. Anyway, Charlie Torch, an old cop friend from the Bronx, is retired in West Palm. He's sixty-six, but as tough as a mountain lion. If you need help just call. Charlie's homesick for a good fight."

Flint was growing tired. "Must end this Harry. I haven't rested in a while. I'll check in with Torch. I'll contact you once I'm on land. And, take care. Remember I need Ben the Chem in one piece."

"Cheers, Flint," Harry said.

Flint, now feeling the fatigue of the past fifteen or so hours, hung up. He moved slowly back to his and Sandy's quarters, passing two crewmen on fire watch, two twenty-some-year-olds, with crew cuts and clean-shaven faces. For a moment it reminded him of his early service days. Days before the world had become complicated and mixed up. They were a mirror image of he and Ronnie Donato when they first went to Vietnam. Young without worry. Fearless beyond reason. Fun loving and carefree. But Nam hardened their youth in a hurry. The years that had passed since tempered that hardness like stainless steel. The business of war and murder was not a pleasant experience. You did what you had to do, but it never got easier. One never got used to it.

Flint walked the narrow halls back to his compartment. Sandy was sound asleep when he entered. He heard her soft breathing. He slid in beside her without turning on the light. Within thirty seconds he also was fast asleep.

Somewhere between a dream of being back in Vietnam and the tail end of another where he was sailing off Palos Verdes, Flint woke up. There was a commotion in the outer compartment. He heard someone run past the steel bulkhead door. The noise woke Sandy up. She reached for Flint and held his arm. "What is it?"

"Something's up. Sounds like an argument."

"My God," said Sandy in a frightened voice. "I hope we haven't struck bottom"

"You'd know it if we had," said Flint. "Must be some crew members having a dispute." He got out of the bunk and slipped into his T-shirt and pants. He opened the door and stepped out. Sandy stayed where she was. Down the hall he saw two ship's officers talking to the captain. Flew then saw Flint and motioned for him to come forward.

"What's going on?" Flint finally asked.

"You don't really want to know," Flew answered with a strained look. Flint came to him. "It's Donato, isn't it?"

"Yes," admitted Flew. "He hung himself with a belt."

It wasn't that he had expected anything like this, but he should have, he told himself. Yes. It was the way Donato would go. He cursed himself for not having taken the precaution to keep him under closer watch. But then again, that was Flew's responsibility, at least from an official view point. As an old war comrade of his, Flint felt he also carried part of the burden for Donato's death.

"Very strange," he told Flew, the sadness of the situation apparent in his voice. "I was dreaming of Vietnam when I woke up. Ron and I were on a beach tracking incoming landing craft. In the dream he fell on a personnel mine and died. I'm not one for believing in mental telepathy, but I'll bet that dream corresponded with the moment he hung himself. The thought of it spooks me."

"I'm sorry this happened," Flew said. "Sorry for you and for Donato. Wait till we inform the FBI in Florida. They'll be screaming incompetence."

Just then Putts appeared down the hall. He'd just come from Donato. The pinkness was gone from his face and was replaced with an ashen color that almost matched his beard.

"We blew this one, Flint," he muttered.

"No," said Flint. "It could happen to anyone."

"It shouldn't have happened on my watch," said Putts. "I completely misread the man. That he was despondent was natural. I didn't think he'd take it all the way. Did you?"

"None of us did," Flint assured him. "I'd like to spend a few minutes with him."

"I wouldn't recommend it," Said Putts. "It wasn't a pretty sight."

"I've witnessed hundreds of ugly sights,"

Putts looked at him. "Okay, Flint. They've taken him to the rear compartment." Putts motioned for one of the officers to accompany Flint. "We will meet you in the captain's quarters when you're finished. We will go ahead with our plans to drop you off in Lauderdale. One thing, though. The FBI has no idea you and Sandy are aboard *Big Fish*. I figured it's none of their business. You agree?"

"Thanks Putts. I'll repay the favor one day."

"No need to. Though, I know you'd do the same for any one of us."

Flint was guided to where Donato was laid out on a metal bunk, wrapped in a white sheet. He drew the sheet back to observe the face. The eyes were darkened, as if he'd been in a street brawl. The black hair matted on his head. The long, rough looking red mark on the neck where the belt had cut in had forced blood to Donato's head. It was swollen. Flint glanced then looked away. Putts was right. It wasn't worth seeing. Flint then got to thinking. Did Ron Donato have any living family or close relatives? He'd never heard him talk about family. It would be a shame to bury the lost soul, this war hero, without proper notification to relatives, if there were any. There would be no burial in Arlington National Cemetery, either. He'd wind up in a pauper's plot. Flint was really bothered by this reality.

After a time he returned to Sandy to explain what had happened. Then he went to Flew's quarters. Putts and Flew were drinking again. Actually sipping ice-chilled Russian vodka. They offered Flint a glass. He declined. His mood had changed since seeing Donato and Putts, realizing it, patted him on the shoulder and told him to relax.

"I was in hopes we'd have time to debrief Donato before hitting Lauderdale," said Putts. "Now we will be relegated to second guessing what his real involvement was. But that's of no concern to you, Flint. The two addresses you have will probably help to clean up your end of the murders and horse killings. As I said, we're cruising out here somewhere if you need us. Now let's all get some sleep if it's possible. We'll be dropping you off in the morning."

20. BEN THE CHEM

There was a freak late April snowfall in the Catskill Mountains, followed by two cold days that left an icy coating on the trees and farm pastures of the lower Hudson Valley. It was almost an isolated weather pattern, causing a temperature inversion and staying just in the valley region, never reaching further north than the town of Hudson, nor further south than Poughkeepsie. Saratoga and Albany never saw the snow. In fact, temperatures up that way were in the fifties and it was partly sunny.

Ralph Montague and George Fagan, two of Harry Waite's most trusted and experienced detectives, drove up the Taconic State Parkway right into the glittering winter setting in a 1995 Buick sedan. It was Montague's wife's car. A fortieth birthday gift from Ralph, who swore when he purchased it for her that she'd have it all to herself. He remembered telling her, "Ruth, this is yours and yours alone. You always wanted your own car, and now you have it. I won't even drive it. That's a promise."

Now, as Montague maneuvered the car precariously over the slick Taconic highway, he silently cursed Harry for having talked him into using Ruth's treasured auto.

"I'm low on budget again," Harry had pleaded with Montague. "I need a favor. I have an assignment, but can't spare a set of wheels. How about Ruth's car? She'll let you use it, won't she?"

So here he was, spattering the spotless underbody with slush and ice, streaking the sides and hood and windows with dirty snow while Fagan peered nervously through the windshield waiting for them to hit something.

"For God's sake, Ralph. Slow this thing down. What's the hurry?"

"I'm only doing sixty," Montague said.

"That's too fast in this slop."

"Hey," shouted Montague. "This baby weighs over three-thousand pounds. It's as solid as a Rolls Royce."

"Not on snow it isn't."

Montague let up on the gas pedal. "Where the hell is that turn anyway?"

"Harry said look for a silver diner. It's off to the right someplace."

Montague hit the electric window button and lowered the passenger-side window. Fagan drew his face back as a gust of wet air came inside. Then Montague saw the sign for Hillsdale. "That's it, we turn here. He spun a sharp right as he said it and the Buick's tail came skidding around. By the time Montague noticed the car drifting off the road the left front and rear wheels were digging into soft earth. He jerked the steering wheel hard left and the car leaped forward back onto the exit ramp. Immediately he saw the silver diner in front of them. Fagan was half down on the seat, his hands covering his face.

"You can come up now," Montague said. "We didn't crash."

"Not yet," said Fagan. "Just give us enough time."

Montague eased the car to a stop in front of the diner. "Go get some coffee, will you? I've got to inspect Ruth's car."

Fagan went inside and Montague, almost afraid to look, went around the car to search for damage. He knelt down and looked underneath. Mud, some grass strands, but no real damage. He was glad he didn't have to bring her any bad news. Fagan reappeared with two cups of coffee. He was also munching on a bagel. "Did you want one?" he asked, handing Montague his coffee.

"No, let's get over to Catamount and get this over with. I'll be damn disappointed if this Ben the Chem creep isn't around. If I had wrecked this car, I'd blame it all on him."

They drove on for another fifteen miles or so, passing through Hillsdale before they even noticed it. Then along the country road another four miles when they saw the sign for Catamount Ski Area. At the entrance road Montague pulled over to have a look.

"Not much to see in this soup," remarked Fagan.

"Yeah, it's real nasty."

Fagan opened his door and got out. "Harry says it's the second road past here. This Chem guy lives halfway up the mountain. Question is, how do we find his road?"

Montague spotted a truck moving out of the ski area. It was the only vehicle in sight. It crossed the large parking area and came directly up the hill to where they were parked.

"Catch that truck," he shouted to Fagan. "See if the driver can help us."

Fagan moved in front of the truck so that it had no choice but to stop. A young man in his mid twenties poked his head out of the driver's side. "What's the matter, fellows, you broke down?"

Montague got out. "No. We're looking for an address. Maybe you can help us?"

"Will if I can," said the driver.

"Supposed to be another road near this entrance that winds up the mountain. Man by name of Ben Lewis lives there. You know him?"

"Nope. But there is a road. Tough to drive on this time of year. I see you don't have snow tires. Never make it up there without them."

Montague thought for a moment, He pulled Fagan aside and whispered in his ear. "You think that kid will loan us his truck?"

"Probably take us there if you show him your badge," said Fagan.

Montague went to the truck. His street shoes began to leak and his socks were soaking up water. It was getting warmer, but the surroundings were still gray and the sky a blanket of thick clouds.

"Lewis is a friend. Understand he's sick. We came to see what we could do for him. We'll make it worth your while to drive us up there. Can you do it?"

"Oh, hell, jump in. I don't want your money. Besides, you wouldn't get ten feet with that car. Looks new, too."

"It is," admitted Montague. "Only two payments made on it so far. Can't get much newer."

Fagan squeezed in next to Montague who pushed against the driver so they could all fit. Fagan rested his feet on a tool box and Montague, feeling something pressing in his back, removed a flashlight that was wedged in the seat.

"My name's Jack Frost," said the driver. At which Fagan, observing the snow-covered ground, took it as a joke, as did Montague.

"For real?" asked Fagan.

"Yes. It's Jack Frost. I get my share of ribbing at the ski area when they hear my name mentioned. I'm in charge of lift operations. Ever ride a chairlift?"

"I get dizzy on escalators," admitted Montague. "Fagan can't climb a three-foot ladder. No. I'd be uncomfortable on a chairlift."

"You'll have to try it sometime. Maybe even ski. We have a seniors' program."

Montague's face twisted sideways with a surprised stare. "What age is that?"

"We consider anyone over sixty a senior skier."

"Beg your pardon," Montague snapped back. "I'm fifty-five. Fagan here is fifty-four. We don't qualify."

The driver smiled. "My mistake. Sorry."

He drove the truck down the road a half mile and turned into a small dirt road. It quickly started to climb up a steeper pitch and then leveled off for about two hundred yards, at which point it began climbing and

147

winding around a series of sharp bends. At a point in the ascent they passed a row of tall pines where they could look back down at the ski area. A little further on Frost pulled the truck to a stop.

"Over there. See it?" Frost pointed to a cabin twenty yards to their right. There was a Jeep parked near the cabin. "I don't know if your guy lives there or not. But it's the only home up here. There are no others on this road."

Montague studied the cabin for a while. "That Jeep's pretty well covered with snow. Must be he's home. Can you wait for us? We'll check in on him."

"Go on, I'm in no hurry. Besides, it's a long walk back."

Fagan got out first, with Montague right behind him. Both men instinctively felt for their revolvers, Fagan's in a shoulder holster and Montague's strapped to his belt. Frost was not aware the two men were armed. They proceeded cautiously toward the cabin. Fagan fanned out left and Montague went up the center of the slippery drive, his leather shoes sliding rather than gripping with each step. There was no sign of life at the cabin. Some thirty feet from the front door, Montague motioned with his right hand for Fagan to move in while he walked to the side of the dwelling. Fagan, with a leap that surprised Montague, bounded onto the front steps and positioned himself on the outer wall, his gun now drawn. Frost saw this action from his truck and looked on in shock. He was too terrified at the sight of Fagan's gun to drive away, though his better judgment told him this was no ordinary social call on the part of the two well-wishers.

Fagan reached across the door and tapped on the small pane of glass with his gun barrel. And just as quickly pulled back tight against the wall. There was no response. He tapped again. This time lowering to his knees just in case Ben the Chem was inside and decided to shoot through the door. Five minutes later the two were still trying to get a response. When he figured this wasn't going to work Montague, growing impatient, was prompted to walk up and kick in the door. Montague was startled when it literally flew open and he almost fell through the threshold on his face. Fagan was right on his heels, gun at the ready. Frost was dumbfounded by it all. It was a scene right out of a gangster movie, a bad one at that. The young man had visions that they were mob hit men. It sent chills up his spine. Then he started thinking that he'd be shot along with whoever they were going after. He reached for his truck keys. They were gone. He looked on the seat, then on the floor of the truck. No keys.

When he next looked in the direction of the cabin, both men were gone from sight. He thought about running away, but was too frightened. Then he heard Fagan calling. "Hey, kid, come over here."

He jumped from the truck and walked slowly to the cabin. He wasn't much on praying, but he began saying a prayer anyway. For all he knew, it might be his last. The only consolation he had was that no shots had been fired. Unless, he thought, they were using silencers. It was the scariest moment in his life. He stopped just short of the door. Montague, tucking his revolver back in his holster, came outside. He looked grim. The sick feeling in Frost's stomach became worse.

"Is there a workable phone around here?" Montague asked.

Frost looked around. "There's a phone line to the cabin." He pointed to a nearby pole with a wire stretched to the rear corner of the cabin.

"That's my point," said Montague. "It doesn't work."

Frost was hesitant to ask the next question, but felt he had to. "Is your friend Lewis inside?"

"Oh, yes. He's in there. But he's not talking. To be truthful, he's dead. Sitting in a chair with a book in his hands as if he were asleep. Must have died of a heart attack, or some other sudden illness. We got here too late to be of help."

Frost moved closer to the open door and peered inside. He observed Fagan moving about the room checking out its contents. It was a strange interior, filled with an assortment of religious pictures, small statues, what appeared to be prayer beads, and several rows of candles set up on long tables on the room's perimeter. On the far wall Frost saw what looked to be test tubes of various size. Fagan turned on a lamp and Frost's mouth dropped wide open as he saw Lewis. He was sitting in an over-sized chair, his head tipped slightly forward and, as Montague had said, his small white hands clutching a book. He was dressed in a dark double-breasted blue suit with a white shirt and tie. Thick clumps of gray hair shot out from the sides of his head, though he was bald on top. His lips were pursed tight, the jaws hollow looking, as if he'd been grinding his teeth in the moment of death.

"Well," said Montague, "is there a phone?"

"Back at the ski area."

"Take us there," Montague ordered, handing him the keys to the truck.

They waited a few minutes for Fagan who was jotting down notes on a pad. Fagan lifted a few pieces of paper from a small desk and just before leaving, also picked up a small leather binder from one of the tables.

149

Considering the circumstances, Frost deemed it a short visit. Though he wasn't about to question them further. He was happy to be alive and driving again. Down the steep road no one said anything. Fagan was reading the binder. Every so often he'd poke Montague in the ribs and have him read part of it. Not once on the ride to the ski area did either man mention Lewis' name nor refer to his death. Frost didn't know what to make of them. He fought back an anxiety attack and tried to calm his nerves. Only the noise of the engine drowned out the sound of his beating heart and his labored breathing.

At the ski mountain, Frost directed Montague to a pay phone on the corner of the main lodge. The gray afternoon was getting grayer, though it was still fairly warm and no snow was falling. The sudden April squall had come and gone. The ski area was deserted.

Montague called Harry Waite. It took a minute to transfer the call. Waite was with some investigators at the city morgue and had refused all calls for the afternoon. He made an exception when Montague's call came in.

"Ralph, what did you find up there?"

"A man that belongs where you are, Harry. Someone iced him."

Montague had to wait out the barrage of typical Harry Waite superlatives. Ending with the classic Waite remark, "Doesn't anything ever go right?"

"Guy lived in the middle of nowhere. Don't know how anyone could approach his place without being spotted. Only thing I can figure out is that he knew his assailant. Damn smooth job, whoever did it. It had us fooled when we first found him. Fagan thought he was sleeping. Guy was sitting in a chair reading a book, a mystery novel at that. Probably poison, but we can't determine how it was administered. No drinking glasses in sight nor signs of food in the room. Funny, his color wasn't all that bad."

"Flint will be raging," said Harry. "He wanted this guy in the worst way. What else did you find?"

"He left a binder full of code words. Could be some secret chemistry codes. You said he was a chemist. Then again, it could be addresses and phone numbers. The tech people should be able to decipher it. We kept it. Left everything else in place. One little problem though. We couldn't get up to his place with Ruth's car. It snowed in Catamount today, can you believe that? Some kid from the ski area drove us in his truck. He knows Lewis is dead, though he has no idea who he is. We're calling from the ski area now. The kid's in the truck. What do you suggest?"

Harry was swearing at the top of his voice. Montague held the receiver away from his ear. The verbal dressing down lasted at least two minutes. "You took a strange kid on this operation? Where the hell are your brains? Does he know who you are? This could ruin everything."

Montague tried to explain, but knew it was fruitless. "No names. No identification. The kid knows nothing of us, except that we came to aid a close, ailing friend. We're splitting out of here when I'm off this phone. By the time the local authorities respond to the call I'll have placed before we leave, the snow will be melted. Our involvement here will be melted as well."

"It better be," Harry sighed.

"We've got no other choice," repeated Montague. "See you in The City."

Back at the truck Montague, tongue in cheek, said he had called the state police to take care of his friend, Lewis. He then asked the kid to drive them back to their car. Montague slipped the kid twenty dollars saying, "Nothing any of us can do now. Maybe I'll be in touch if I come this way again."

He and Fagan drove off in the Buick, as the kid sat and watched in a state of utter bewilderment. They were gone ten minutes when it finally dawned on the kid that he didn't get their names. The whole episode was a wash. He couldn't even remember what they were driving, nor whether they had gone east toward Connecticut or west toward Hudson. He had been so damn scared for his life, everything else didn't matter. Not even the dead man in the cabin.

Montague did call the state police to report the death, but he and Fagan were halfway back to New York before he made the call. At that, it was done on an anonymous basis. The call Harry subsequently made to Flint about Ben the Chem while Flint was still in Florida only went to enforce Flint's hypothesis that the back track killings were being carried out in a very cleverly planned manner. This made Flint more anxious than ever to find Max Steiner in his Florida haunts because, if he didn't, there was good reason to believe Steiner would be the next victim. Without Steiner, the trail could get very cold indeed. Also, Ben the Chem's murder convinced Flint that Sandy, for her safety, would definitely have to go back to California until he could complete his investigation.

21. SUBMARINE SANDWICH

Captain Flew hosted a small farewell dinner for Flint and Sandy on *Big Fish*, before their departure for Fort Lauderdale. Those invited included two senior officers and six regular crew members who took part in the rescue on Anguilla, Flew's second in command, Lt. Jerry Hanson, Dusty Putts and, one surprise invitee, a lovely brunette, Sharon Spear, who Flint immediately recognized as the helpful receptionist from the Royal Tango on St. Martin.

Flew introduced everyone. When Spear was introduced, her eyes met Flint's, then turned to Sandy's, and she broke out a smile. "We meet again, Mr. Flint."

Sandy gave her a curious stare, wondering what she meant by the remark.

"So we do," said Flint.

She extended her hand to Sandy. "We haven't met, but I've been shadowing you since you arrived in the Caribbean. Dusty insisted on it. I'm with the CIA's special codes bureau. This has been a training run in field operations for me."

Sandy guessed Spear was a few years younger than she. The hair was combed straight back and she was wearing a one-piece jump suit that hugged her body. The face was narrow and slightly tanned. Her brown eyes, long black lashes and exquisitely shaped mouth and nose, belied a beauty not often found in military ranks. In a sense, she looked out of place on *Big Fish*. Flint pressed his hand in Sandy's and whispered, "The best looking cop I've ever seen." At which Sandy squeezed his hand, driving a sharp fingernail into his palm.

He laughed. "It was only an observation."

Flew drew everyone to one side. "The incident of yesterday has been disposed of, and Donato's body was removed last night to another ship when we were on the surface. I'm only mentioning it now because it's the last time I will speak of the matter. I also felt that individually we all were carrying too much guilt for his death. We go our separate ways once in Fort Lauderdale, but we take with us the experience of the last few days and the brief friendships we've established." He moved in front of Flint. You have a long road to hike before you put a lid on your end of the investigation. I want to wish you luck and a safe return. Same goes for Sandy. We're not at liberty to offer our services for any civilian endeavors, but unofficially we will be there for you, if it can be justified. Much like Putts did at Anguilla. There's always a gray line. It becomes even grayer when we're assisting a former comrade. We always have a soft spot in our hearts for navy veterans. The fact that you are former CIA doesn't go unnoticed, either. I believe Putts concurs with me on this. This now said, shall we have a few drinks and try to put an upbeat spin on this gathering? We expect to be in Lauderdale by mid day." Flew lifted a glass of wine and toasted Flint and Sandy.

"Here's to a time when you can both take an uninterrupted vacation." Everyone laughed. It wasn't the first time Flint attended a cocktail party, but it was the first he'd attended one on a multi-million dollar nuclear submarine. It was a unique experience he knew they would not soon forget.

When he and Sandy returned to their quarters to wait out departure time, he started writing down a chronological list of the events of the past few days, finishing it with a recording of the last phone call from Harry Waite telling him Ben the Chem was dead. Like he had done so many times in the past, he would sink these events into his memory and go over them several times so that every piece of relevant information would fall into place when he needed it. The notes on Claire Valova drew most of his interest. He surmised that she must be the key to the whole investigation. Not because she was the central figure, but more because her involvement didn't make any sense. Killing horses for insurance money for those who were desperate financially, he could comprehend. Valova didn't need money. Her late husbands had provided for her. So where did she exactly fit into the scene? It could boil down to two reasons as far as Flint was concerned. She either was being blackmailed, or manipulated. He was not content to go with the information he had at hand. What this required was a deeper investigation into Valova's background, including her earlier life in Russia. Might it have a bearing on recent events? Maybe not. But he knew he'd not be satisfied until he had looked into her past.

Then of course, he'd need a list of all her associates, business related and personal friends, even those associated with her husbands, if they could be found. This would all take time, of which he had precious little at this point. The domestic data he could have Harry and his contacts in the federal government obtain. Before leaving *Big Fish*, he'd ask Putts to have his CIA contacts in Europe check out Valova's Russian and other European associates, and present background. Much of it probably wouldn't tie into the investigation, but he couldn't rule out the possibility. Who knows, they could be framing the European insurance companies.

He'd learned from previous situations, nothing was impossible. Money and greed respected nothing. There was also the Bifford connection to be settled. How involved was she? Partly because of her close tie to Valova? Or more deeply? Word from Dr. Blake said that FBI agent White had mentioned that the bureau already had a half dozen veterinarians under investigation, though he wasn't sure Bifford was among them. Once he had set all this in motion, he'd get directly to finding Max Steiner, if, in fact, Steiner was still alive. The way people were disappearing and turning up dead, Steiner could very well be included. Flint knew time was not on his side. There were other things to check out, too. For one, the mysterious insurance man Wainwright. The one Dr. Blake said Chief Nealy received the plastic cylinders from. Strangely enough, given him by none other than the missing Stuart Clayborn Witt. Who the hell is Wainright? And what significance do the plastic cylinders have among the rest of the subverted data on this investigation? He wondered if the test results were back yet from those cylinders.

When he had completed his list, he sat back and reviewed it again. He was tired then, and decided to rest a bit before departing *Big Fish*. He leaned over and kissed Sandy, who was resting. After a time she woke up. It was then he informed her of his decision to send her back to Palos Verdes. She cried at first, he expected she would. When they had both settled down, he made the necessary phone calls to secure her safe passage once they reached Lauderdale. This parting, however painful for both of them, was a test of their love. Flint knew that. Sandy also knew it, though she did not express her feelings as she prepared to leave. He was not so reserved. He kissed her several times and told her how much he'd miss her. In the end, it only made the parting worse. She resigned herself to accepting the inevitable.

Big Fish was nearing Florida's coast and the crew was readying a motorized rubber boat to take Flint and Sandy ashore, keeping to the original plan to ferry them around the main beaches and deposit them safely at a designated rendezvous point on the Intracoastal Waterway.

Flint wasn't going to chance keeping Sandy in Lauderdale for more than a few hours. He wanted her on a plane back to California. Monica, as always, agreed to meet Sandy at L.A. International and put her up till Flint's work was done. As Monica told Flint on receiving his phone call, "You know something? The lyrics change, but the tune's still the same. You'll never quit, will you?"

He could not deny she was right.

22. HOT DIGS

Frank Duffy, working late at the paper, which he often did, was going over several files on Claire Valova's early days in Saratoga. So many wonderful happenings had come and gone since the sixties, Duffy was amazed at how much he had forgotten. The crowded parties at upper Broadway mansions, some within a stone's throw of Burke's funeral home where she was waked, and the carriage rides for charity all over town, even the grand ballroom dances at the Casino on so many other festive occasions, too numerous to recall unless you were rehashing them as Duffy was by reading the old social columns. She was a unique person, he remembered sadly. How gray and cold this spring season was without her presence. Was it just his age that provoked these nostalgic feelings, or was it truly a better time in his life, now so distant? Given it to do all over again, he knew he'd rather live in that period than in today's seemingly unsettled and unpredictable world.

Yes, the forties right through the sixties and seventies were pretty good years in Saratoga, the counter culture of the mid sixties and the protest and college marches against the Vietnam war notwithstanding. The eighties and early nineties didn't come off so well. The town lost some of its sparkle. Even the race course was losing some of its appeal. There was too much shifting in local and state politics. A notable absence of many money people, opting, Duffy believed, to spend their summers elsewhere. Yes, he had lived in the brighter days of Saratoga. He was sure of it. So it went, one story where she was interviewed at the race course when her horse, Shoe String, won the coveted Jim Dandy. She saying that only in Saratoga did she really feel at home, not that she could tolerate the bitter winters from January to March, but as a spring, summer and fall admirer of the Spa. Duffy, recalling how she had a special way with cub reporters, always giving them her attention, along with the seasoned writers. Claire Valova was a master at cultivating the press. She thrived on it.

Duffy was about to call it quits for the evening, when his eye caught the piece about the 1988 fire at Clearwater, Meredith Ostrander's estate. Though seven years had passed since the raging flames destroyed so many fine race horses, barns and outer buildings, it seemed like just yesterday. The horror of it was still finely etched in his memory, made fresh again by the feature story written by Harold Fink, a fledgling reporter. Fink didn't last long at the *Star,* Duffy recalled, but he did a yeoman's job writing about the big fire. The writing might have been a little stilted but the detailed account was superb. For the life of him, Duffy couldn't remember whatever happened to Fink. Probably wound up on a magazine someplace. His style was better suited for the mag market. Duffy read on.

Buried near the story's end was a brief mention of Carlos Mann. It drew Duffy's attention. Again, it was a point he'd forgotten, but had put in the back of his mind. Though he couldn't reason why he hadn't given Mann a thought in many months. How could he not think of this poor soul who was so central to the tragedy? In fact, the main suspect. Were it not for the leniency and big heart of Judge Lawrence Baker, Mann would have surely gone on trial for the fire and been convicted forthwith. But Baker would have no part of it. He felt Carlos was not involved in lighting the fire, and that he could not be tried until such time as the doctors could restore his lost memory. So Carlos for the past seven years was confined to a mental hospital and almost forgotten. Even tragedies with the magnitude of Clearwater's had a way of being usurped by other events. Time washed away much of the public's initial anger. If it didn't altogether forget, it became disinterested. Unless, of course, it was one of your Thoroughbreds that got destroyed that fateful night.

Duffy now concentrated on looking up more on Mann. There were enough follow-up stories and police reports to keep one reading for a week. There was a line or two among the stories that repeatedly said Mann, coming to right after the fire did mention a lady. It was a fragmented recall that lapsed when Mann finally couldn't even remember his name. Loss of memory yes, Duffy realized, but still there were little things he told those that found him. Like, "It was so hot," or "Where is my horse?" And a repeat statement of "Lady." Duffy felt all of this was relevant to the fire. The police took none of it seriously. Many thought Mann was faking it at the time. So many perceptions developed from the tragedy, revenge ruled the day.

Duffy decided he'd pass this along to Nealy and Blake. Maybe Blake would want to pass it along to "His Man" as he called him. It might aid the investigation. Though again, it probably had nothing to do with Valova's and Bifford's deaths, Duffy was suspect of every incident involving the loss of race horses. As agent White had said, the persons behind killing horses for insurance money have been at it since 1986, so the 1988 Clearwater fire just might have some bearing on recent events. A wild card at best. But worth considering.

Duffy was tired. He turned off his terminal and rubbed his eyes. Out of the back window he could see the lights of the Parting Glass. He was half tempted to go over and belt down a few stiff ones, but dropped the idea. No, he would go home to Martha.

He went to the parking lot and got in his car. He started the engine and let it warm for a minute. When he finally started rolling out of the lot, he heard someone call his name. He stopped and looked in the rearview mirror. It was was Billy Farrell, staggering his way over from Caroline Street to a mid point in the parking lot. Duffy didn't have to think twice as to where Farrell had spent the last few hours. Surely it was Sperry's, one of Farrell's favorite watering holes. He often went there to drink and eat Sperry's gourmet fare. Duffy guessed Farrell was sipping a rich, dark stout beer this day, simply because he tended to get snockered faster on heavy beer than he did on whiskey. In truth, even for his huge size, he was getting to a point where he could not handle either. He was too damn old, and Duffy realized he was in the same boat. Their ages were working against them.

Anyway, Farrell came to the car and asked for a ride to Saratoga Lake.

"I was going directly home," said Duffy. "Take a cab."

"They charge too much. I told Bob Stratton, the trainer, I'd meet him for a drink."

Duffy looked around. "You don't need another."

"Oh hell, who are you to tell me what I need or don't need? Take me to Smith's on the Lake. I told Stratton I'd be there."

"It's against my better judgment," remarked Duffy. "But I'll take you anyway. I'm not staying. Martha has a late dinner waiting."

They drove over Circular Street to Union and headed east past the Race Course. It wasn't quite 8:30 P.M. They caught a light at East Avenue and waited for it to change. There were a few cars in the parking lot of the Springwater Inn on the corner of Union and Nelson Avenues. Duffy spotted a handful of diners. The light turned green and they proceeded, passing the track's front entrance and then the darkened oval and grandstands. A drop of rain appeared on the windshield.

"Damn if it isn't raining," Duffy remarked. "Can't see a thing when it rains." He wasn't sure Farrell had heard him, for his head was tipped to one side and he was snoring lightly. "You'll not make Smith's tonight," Duffy said under his breath. "Stratton can wait. You've had your fill, friend."

Farrell's snoring grew louder. Duffy decided to turn around and take Farrell home. He could call Stratton from home and tell him Farrell wasn't coming. That is the smart thing to do.

157

By this time they had reached the gate to the backstretch where, with one sharp turn of the wheel, Duffy swung the car partially into the entrance, stopped and then prepared to back out on Union. The rain had increased, so he had to turn on the wipers. The right one worked fine, but the driver's side wiper was streaky. The wiper's malfunction, coupled with his limited night vision, made Duffy mad. Now he'd have to chance making it home safely with Farrell, whereas if he had gone directly home earlier, he'd be sitting comfortably at his dining room table eating some of Martha's roast duck and gravy.

Just then Duffy saw flames some fifty yards away, coming from the direction of the first row of backstretch barns. With the wipers continuing to streak across the windshield, the flames appeared to leap in all directions. Duffy poked Farrell. "My God, the place is on fire!" Farrell was fast asleep. He shifted once and went back to snoring. Duffy opened the door and got out. Now he could see the flames climbing into the sky. Three distinct orange and red tunnels going up some thirty feet. He jumped back inside and began honking the horn. At which point Farrell came to life.

"What the hell is it?" Farrell shouted. "Where are we?"

"The barns are burning!" Duffy informed him. "Look over there. Can't you see it?"

Farrell pressed his nose against the windshield. "Damn if you're right. We've got to call the fire department."

"There's no phone out here," said Duffy.

"Well, let's get to one. The Springs is the closest place."

As they were talking, a series of red lights appeared further down Union Avenue and then they heard sirens. Before Duffy could back away from the entrance, one fire engine was pulling in. They flashed lights and blasted their loud, ear-piercing truck horn at Duffy's car. He fumbled with the shift, his foot slipped off the brake and the car shot backward into the fire truck with a dull metallic thud. They both heard glass breaking and one of the truck's headlights went out.

What followed was a Keystone Kops comedy with firemen swearing and running around Duffy's car while others tugged and pulled at the bumper trying to disengage it where it had locked onto the truck's front bumper. Then Duffy and Farrell, standing in the glare of the truck's remaining headlight, in the rain, wet and cold, tried to explain what had happened. And all the time the flames continued on the backstretch and the firemen couldn't get to them, save for a few who grabbed portable fire extinguishers and went running in the direction of the fire. It was mass confusion for several anxious minutes. Finally, Jerry McFee, the fire chief came by in his car and settled everyone down. He looked at Duffy and Farrell and laughed. "You're the last two I'd expect to see out here."

"I was taking Farrell to. . . "

"No need to explain," said McFee. "What happened, happened. Now let us get to the fire."

So much commotion was going on at the backstretch, no one took notice of Sweetfeed driving the front loader to the burial plot. Every hand that could be mustered was racing to assist in putting out the fire which, as Sweetfeed had planned, was nothing more than barrels half full of hay dowsed in kerosene that were burning with such ferocity. And with the thick clouds and rain darkening the sky, Sweetfeed went about digging up Stuart Clayborn Witt. Using all his strength, he was able to pull away the metal plate that had stopped his earlier effort. He then positioned the machine so that in one deep dig he could scoop up Witt's rotting corpse. Sweetfeed wasn't prepared for the stench that came out of the thick dirt and clay soaked with Witt's remains. Luckily for Sweetfeed, Witt was still in one piece, except in the digging the loader's heavy metal forks severed Witt's right arm, so that it dangled off the end of the bucket. Shining a small pocket flashlight, Sweetfeed went and pushed the arm back into the bucket. All of this time holding his nose with one hand against the wretched smell. The flames at the far end of the backstretch were still leaping upward when he got back on the front loader and drove behind Barn 17 and headed for the drainage ditch undetected. He was elated that his temporary diversion was working. By the time they had trained their fire hoses on the burning barrels, Witt was deposited safely in the culvert pipe drain and Sweetfeed was driving the machine back to its normal parking spot. First he made a pass by the plot and pushed the large mound of earth back into the hole. He struggled to push the plate back in place and finished it with his shovel and quickly raked the site level.

Ten minutes later he was standing among the excited backstretch workers and fire personnel near the burned-out barrels. Five fire trucks had entered the grounds out of seven that had responded to the call. Red flashing lights and search lights lit up the area. Sweetfeed looked across and saw Jerry McFee shaking his head in disgust.

"This is the work of some damn sick kids," he heard McFee say to an aide.

"No doubt about it, Chief."

"They should be shot! Imagine if the fire had reached the barns?"

One hour later everything was back to normal. The fire trucks were gone and the only trace of the fire was a stale burned smell carried on the night's breeze that swept in and over the barns, disturbing the nervous horses and equally wary workers. Some trainers showed up later to check their stock. But aside from that, it was written off as just another prank, one among many that plagued the backstretch each season. Fortunately for Sweetfeed, Joe Hennesy was away. Otherwise he'd have turned the place upside-down looking for the rotten kids who did it.

In the morning, before there was light, Sweetfeed remembered he had to wash down the front loader. So he got up just after five and went and hosed the machine. In the process he found one of Witt's fingers and, wouldn't you know, it had a ring on it. A rather large diamond at that. He did away with the finger, but not before taking off the ring. Somewhere he knew he could pawn it for a good buck. But that somewhere wouldn't be in Saratoga. He was smart enough not to press his luck too far.

Sweetfeed went to breakfast, read a day-old newspaper and was back at Track Baron's stall by six-thirty. The backstretch was alive by then and the first one he saw was Water Man.

"Hey," called Water Man. "You had a phone call about five minutes ago. Man said he'd call back at noon. Wanted you to be standing near the pay phone at Scotty's bar on Union Avenue. Now that's a weird request. Why doesn't he just call you here?"

"Don't know," replied Sweetfeed. "Thanks for the message."

"Anytime," said Water Man. "Wonder if they caught those kids who started the fire?"

"Oh, they'll get 'em. You can count on it." Sweetfeed then got a thought.

"Hey, Water Man. Come to think of it I'll be busy at noon. Mind taking that call for me?"

"If you want me to, I will," said Water Man, always pleased to accommodate Sweetfeed. "What'll I say?"

"Nothing," replied Sweetfeed. "Just take the message. Tell him I'm busy."

"Will do, Sweetfeed. Just like you ask."

Sweetfeed felt the perspiration drip down his wool shirt. His knees began shaking slightly. The Voice. That's who it was, The Voice. He had to do something about that man. So much for the plan to confront him, he thought. Well, he had half the day to worry about it.

23. SUGARTIME

While still in Fort Lauderdale, Flint received a message to call Harry Waite in Boston, he was there visiting a retired detective, Johnny Bunno who had, among other things, once dealt with an investigation that involved horse killer Max Steiner. The case didn't involve horse killings, but it did involve insurance fraud. Steiner, according to Bunno, was sinking boats in Tampa and later claiming they were stolen. Bunno claims he got involved when Steiner sank the wrong boat one day. Steiner thought he was sinking a yacht belonging to a local real estate tycoon when, in fact, it was owned by Bunno's ex-New York Special Headquarters partner, Clarence Thompson. So they went after Steiner. Problems arose in the middle of the investigation because of a conflict with the local authorities. Bunno later discovered that Steiner had protection from certain principals in the Tampa police ranks. Bunno was actually surprised to hear that Steiner was into killing horses, which really was the basis for Harry's call to Flint.

"Bunno says Steiner is not considered the violent type. Not in the classical sense, anyway," Harry told Flint from Boston. "He's got a temper, but doesn't have the malice to kill humans. At least that's what Bunno says."

"I don't buy it," said Flint. "Anyone who can go around killing fifteen-hundred-pound animals certainly is capable of killing humans. They may not want to, but they would if paid enough. That's my opinion. Bunno can have his."

"Well you can rest on the Ben the Chem killing," Harry assured him. "It wasn't Steiner. We just got the report on Chem. He committed suicide. Drank a batch of cyanide with some vintage wine. Autopsy report says he was suffering from prostate cancer. Funny thing, Chem never used cyanide to kill horses. We almost got caught snooping around up there in Catamount. It's a long story I won't go into now, but worth telling sometime when we can sit over a cool drink. Ever remember when you had time to relax over a cool drink, Flint?"

"Yes, Harry. We had one relaxed day in the Caribbean. Then you called. It's been a hectic time ever since."

"Sorry, Flint."

"No. I'm sorry. Sorry I let myself get talked into these messes. There must be someone on the planet other than me who can handle it."

He could hear Harry munching on some food. "I'm not boring you, am I Harry?"

"No, no. Not at all. I was just finishing a peach when you called."

"Have two," said Flint. "They're healthy for you."

"Bunno says Steiner spends most of his time in Fort Myers and likes to float between two favorite restaurants. Weekends at Channel Mart on Hurricane Bay and some weeknights at Anthony's a bit further up the beach. He keeps a small yacht just south of Hurricane Bay. Calls it *Ocean's Over*. So take your pick. He'll probably show up at one or the other. Things generally are quieting down in April in Fort Myers, so he shouldn't be to hard to locate. Has a girlfriend over there, Lisa Lane, a former dancer in Miami. She's approaching her late seventies. He just turned sixty. Imagine, Flint, it's like dating your grandmother."

"Don't discount this slicker," said Flint. "He may teach me a few tricks."

"Understand Sandy's back safe in California?"

"I had to send her. This could get sticky. Besides, I'll be moving fast. It looks cut 'n dry on the surface, but you never know till you dive in. Right, Harry?"

There was a pause. Harry was munching down the rest of his peach. Then in a slurred tone, replied, "You're right on that point, Flint. Remember that case we had one time on Long Island when the mob moved in on that fancy beach club? Who'd have thought they'd get so upset when we arrested the Don who practically lived there. One guy got killed in that operation. Yes, an old friend, Sergeant Markey. We never did pin down the Don on that hit, but he did time anyway for extortion. Yeah, you never know when the heat will be turned up. Be careful with this Steiner fellow."

"I have to find him first. I'll go through West Palm and check out that address for Steiner and give your friend, Torch, a call. If nothing pans out there, I'll head for Fort Myers."

"Sounds like you have a long day ahead of you, better get some rest," Harry told him. "If you need a back up I have a couple of pretty good boys retired over in Naples. They'll come by if you want them."

"Won't hesitate to call you if things get out of hand."

Then Harry begged off. Flint sat back and pondered his next move. He'd stay in Fort Lauderdale this evening and leave for West Palm and Fort Myers early. Before retiring for the night, he put a phone call into Dr. Blake. He couldn't reach him in Saratoga. Blake's answering service suggested he call Lake George. Blake, he was told, went up to Castle Rock.

He reached Blake on the fourth ring. On answering, the doctor sounded short of breath.

"That you, Flint? Good to hear your voice."

"You sound bushed," said Flint.

"Oh, I just ran up the front lawn from the boat house. Heard the ringing when I was halfway up the porch landing. Afraid I'm out of shape."

"That's two of us. We should take up aerobics. That your place?"

"No, it belongs to my Uncle Charles. But I look after it. Flint, we met here the other day. Thought it would be a safer place to gather. I know you have the details of what's been going down up here, so I won't go into that again. But it's scary, wouldn't you say?"

"Certainly," Flint agreed. "It's a spider's web. You don't know whose going to get caught next. I'd advise caution at all times."

"Actually I came up to check on Uncle's neighbor. Elderly gent by the name of Robert Butcher. We saw him walking across the front lawn the other day during our meeting. Seldom ever see him up here this early in the season. He'll be eighty in July. Takes care of himself. No maids nor groundskeepers. Though he does employ some local guys to cut the grass. Always puttering in his summer garden. Well, I went over about an hour ago to look in on him. No signs of the life. Not sure if he's still here or went back to New York where he generally winters. The truth of it is, I've never really talked to him. No one does. He's a loner. Not sure he has any living relatives. Only heard Uncle mention him on one occasion. Said he was richer than most Lake George barons. Must be true, especially when my rich old Uncle says so. Found that quite strange. They've been neighbors for thirty-five years. Maybe I'll try and look in on him again before I leave for Saratoga."

Flint was listening and thinking at the same time. "Doc, given what's going on in Saratoga, and what I perceive to be maximum exposure at your uncle's place, I'd have that mansion wired. Scanners as well as motion lights on all exterior sections. Trip wires on porches and stairs if necessary. Installation is expensive, but they can rig that ark in two days. My Palos Verdes home is a fortress. If you're spending considerable time at Castle Rock, do as I say."

"On the contrary, I feel safest when I'm up here," Blake reassured him.

"That's my point," insisted Flint. "These type people always hit you on the soft side. Just when you're feeling secure. Think about it."

Blake was suddenly more aware of the rattling and creaking at Castle Rock. And the very fears he spent so much time counseling his patients about gripped his psyche for a moment.

"You know something, Flint? For a second I felt real fright. It's not a nice experience. But I will take your advice. Maybe I'll do the same at the office and at my home." Then he added, "Do you think this will end soon?"

"Let's hope so," said Flint. "Let's hope so."

"You take care, Flint."

"I always do, Doc. I'm a cat with more than nine lives. I'll be in touch."

In the morning, Flint hired a car and started out for Fort Myers. Within two hours he was getting bored with the flat terrain. He crossed over the shell of an alligator at one point and spotted several snakes slithering across the road at another. Worse than the California desert, he thought. There were some fine looking rows of trees along the route, but also many areas that had been blighted recently. Aside from the warm temperature, he decided Florida was not for him. He'd take California anytime.

During the long drive he had time to think, piecing everything together as best he could from the available data. So in his head he played it all back, beginning with Valova and Bifford's deaths. He passed a string of motor homes, a biking group and one old smoking truck. It was either badly in need of a ring job, or it was burning diesel. He couldn't tell. His right front wheel bumped over a dead carcass of some sort and he held the wheel firmly till the car straightened out again. Halfway to Fort Myers he pulled off the road for a cup of coffee. He went inside a small diner and sat at the counter. One waitress and one ruddy-faced guy with a big straw hat turned to look at him.

"Coffee, please," he said.

"Sugar and cream?"

"No. Make it black."

"Black it is. Care for something to eat?"

"No. Just coffee."

He spotted a pay phone on the back wall. He went over and dialed a special code number and waited. There were three beeps and a voice came on. Flint took out his pen and scribbled several notes on a small pad he had with him. There was a delay, then more information. He made further notes. He then went back to his coffee, which had cooled. The waitress noticed and gave him a fresh, hot cupful. He smiled at her.

"Where you going, stranger?" a voice under the straw hat asked. He couldn't see the face.

"Fort Myers. Little vacationing."

"A tad late, aren't you?"

"Maybe so," said Flint. "But the rates are cheaper."

"Well, you got another good two hours of driving. Make sure you've enough gas. Not many stations between here and there. Of course if you want, we can fill you up right outside."

"Thanks, but I'm fine. Half a tank left."

"Just thought I'd ask," said the man.

Flint glanced at his notes. He recognized the phrases as dictated to him. It was surely Dusty Putts relaying an international message on Valova.

Probably from Interpol out of Moscow, via *Big Fish*: "CV from peasant stock - Parents: farmers - Psychopathic tendencies as a child - Never institutionalized - More to follow. Good luck. Happy hunting." The report came as a shocker. Flint pressed the paper back into his pocket and went to his car. The sun was beating down between a spray of thin white clouds. He welcomed the air conditioner once he was underway. In his rearview mirror he saw the man with the straw hat leave after him and get into a black pickup truck. About five miles along the car started to buck. He gave it more gas, but it hesitated again, skipped a beat and went on. Flint looked at the gas gauge. Just under half full. Another mile or two and the motor cut completely out and he had to grab the wheel with both hands as the power steering quit. He managed to get it off the shoulder of the road before it quit altogether. He pushed the hood lever and got out. It was beastly hot and he was on a deserted stretch of road. It smelled of damp marshes. Checking the engine, he could detect nothing wrong with the wires nor hoses. The car wasn't over heated. He figured it must be in the gas line itself. When he went to check the gas cap he noticed some white granules stuck to the car's side. More inside the gas latch. Someone deliberately poured sugar in the tank.

Flint was pondering his next move when, out of the corner of one eye, he saw the pickup truck pull up behind him. The driver got out and came straight at Flint. He was wearing a big straw hat that shaded his face. Flint recognized him as the man from the diner. And he wasn't coming to help. He was wielding an ax handle in his right hand and it was aimed straight at Flint's head. Flint ducked and the wood nicked his left shoulder. Spinning around, Flint drove a fist directly into the attacker's sternum. He heard a sucking sound come forth and the gasping for air. The straw hat flew off revealing a bald head and a scarred face as ugly as Flint had ever seen. He had bulging eyes and thick, dark eyebrows. Flint figured he weighed over two hundred pounds. Just when it appeared the assailant was dropping to his knees, he grabbed Flint's left leg and leaned over and tried to bite him on the calf. Flint delivered a backhand to his neck, hearing the bone snap as it landed. The ugly face went into the red earth. There were teeth marks on Flint's pants, but they hadn't penetrated the skin. There was no other traffic in sight. Flint lifted the bulk into a sitting position next to the car. He was still unconscious and breathing heavily. Flint fumbled through the stranger's pockets. He lifted a small leather wallet from the hip pocket. Opening it, he discovered a deputy sheriff's badge. "What in hell's name is this?" he said aloud. He searched the truck's interior and found the registration. The vehicle was registered to a John Smith. Certainly a bogus name, Flint thought. So who was this guy working for?

He went back and tried to wake him up, but couldn't. Flint again checked the truck. He found a five-gallon can of gas and some hoses. Sugar granules were visible on the floor. Flint inserted the hose into the car's gas tank and began siphoning its content. He then poured in the can. With his attacker still propped against the car, he got in and turned the key. More sputtering and hissing from the engine, then it suddenly kicked over. Running rough for a minute, but at least running. Letting the car idle, Flint got out and dragged the hulk to the truck, and lifted him into the back, dropping the tail gate so he could shove him completely in. The car continued to run. Once again, seated behind the wheel, he put it in drive and drove off. He kept the badge. Just one more thing he'd have to check out when he had time. Then a thought struck him: was the straw hat character working for Max Steiner? Or was this just a coincidental road mugging, not unlike other rural scams that took place in Florida over the years? He hoped it was the latter. If there was a Steiner connection, Flint knew he'd have to devise a new plan before entering Steiner's domain of Fort Myers. More variables to be overcome.

24. VOICE LESSON

There were so many loose ends in the ongoing investigation, that one end didn't always know what the other end was doing. Duffy, assisted by Farrell, was trying to find out more about Carlos Mann's medical incarceration. Flint was dead set on tracking down Max Steiner in Fort Myers. Dusty Putts and Captain Flew, though geographically far removed from the scene, were making contact with their friendly domestic and international connections to see what else they could piece together to assist Flint. Dr. Blake, curious as to why Mr. Butcher was prowling Castle Rock's property, was checking him out. Chief Nealy and his crew were literally turning Saratoga upside-down in their search for Stuart Witt, and Harry Waite was sweating out whether the police in Catamount would find out it was his men up there looking for Ben the Chem and not some tough mob boys. Sweetfeed was trying to plan what he'd do pending his meeting with The Voice. That was, of course, if he could drum up enough nerve to rendezvous with the mysterious voice and depending on what the message to Water Man would entail.

One thing Sweetfeed had decided. He'd not agree to any daytime meeting with The Voice. No, this meeting would have to be at night and on his terms. So he called Water Man over to Track Baron's stall and told him that he was to tell the caller that Sweetfeed would meet him, but after work hours. And it would have to be on the track grounds. "Tell the man I don't really care where I meet him, as long as it's within the domain of the track. Tell him that."

Water Man was on time and took the expected phone call. The scary, strange voice started talking. Water Man interrupted.

"Sweetfeed wants to meet you at the track, at night. He told me to tell you that. Anywhere at the track."

He heard deep breathing. A chill went down Water Man's back. It was Halloween spooky.

"Tell Sweetfeed I will meet him as he prefers. Tonight at nine. Somewhere between Barns 33 and 27. Tell him I have a wonderful new mix for Track Baron. He'll understand. Tell him not to be late."

Water Man tried to say something, but the voice was gone before he could utter a word. He wondered to himself what this was all about. Who was the man behind this inky voice? Why was Sweetfeed so nervous when he mentioned him? As far as Water Man was concerned, Sweetfeed had been acting nervous and jerky all spring. It wasn't his way and it bothered Water Man. Others on the backstretch had noticed it, too. Later that day he sought out Sweetfeed at Track Baron's stall and told him about the call. Sweetfeed's reaction was one of a man caught between a choice of jumping off a cliff to avoid a rushing bull, or standing his ground in the face of certain danger. His eyebrows twisted up and his eyes grew narrow. Water Man knew something was wrong, but he dare not ask. Track Baron must have sensed Sweetfeed's nervousness for he kicked and butted his head against the wall.

"Man says he'll meet you at nine. Suppose he has a super secret new feed for Track Baron here. Well, it may be, but I don't like that voice. You talk to him often?" He looked at Sweetfeed.

"Once or twice. Don't know what he looks like. But don't you go worrying about it Water Man," Sweetfeed told him, putting an arm around his right shoulder. "Just business. You know how that is. Man knows Track Baron's going to be a good one. They all like to get close to winners. You've seen that before, I'm sure? No different here. I got my own mix. Raised me some good runners in my time. So I won't be interested in his mix. But if the man wants to come talk, I'll talk. Doesn't cost a dime to talk."

"That's right," agreed Water Man, feeling better. "Might even learn something." He hesitated and held his left ear. "Still can hear that strange voice, though. For myself, I think I'd rather do business with someone else."

It wasn't quite six yet, so after Water Man had left, Sweetfeed slipped a bridle over Track Baron's head and took him for a walk. He was doing it for two reasons. The horse hadn't gotten his proper exercise in two days and Sweetfeed, not certain that the poison had completely dissipated from the horse's body, wanted to see how he carried himself. Halfway in the mile or so walk, Sweetfeed became panicky inside. Fear that The Voice was coming to settle the score with him, that score being Track Baron. Yes, most certainly that was what he was up to. Track Baron should have been dead by now and the insurance claim should have been processed. The Voice was on to him, he was certain of it. He checked the time. It was almost seven. He walked swiftly back to the barn, pulling on the bridled Track Baron who apparently was in no hurry to follow him. It was the last of April and warmer than expected. The horse was enjoying the stroll under the tall, budding maple and oak trees. The barn smells filled the air. Sweetfeed's mind was racing ahead to the pending meeting. If The Voice was going to meet him between the barns Water Man had mentioned, then he only had two viable ways to get on the grounds. He'd either come in the backstretch gate where the fire engines had entered, or he'd come around from Clare's Court and the far barns. Barn 33 near the gate was always pretty well lighted, but Barn 27, the furthest one away, wasn't. Sweetfeed wanted to position himself so that in either case, he'd have the advantage of escape, if needed, and the most light in which to do it. He knew his way equally well in the dark, as he proved when he deposited Witt with the front loader. This, however, was different. Some backstretch workers would still be finishing up chores around that time, so it was unlikely The Voice could make any drastic moves, if that was his intention. Maybe, Sweetfeed then started thinking, The Voice wasn't coming for any of those dark reasons. Perhaps he was coming to tell Sweetfeed that the insurance game was up. That they had milked it as far as they profitably could. The Voice owed Sweetfeed several hundred dollars. He was rationalizing all these scenarios as he entered Track Baron's stall. He took off the bridle, went outside and filled up a bucket with water and came back inside and held it for the race horse to drink. Setting it on the floor, he then took a curry brush and started stroking the great horse, starting at the massive shoulders and finishing at his midsection. Dust from the short walk brushed out of Track Baron's coat. It was now dark and the lights came on.

"How's Track Baron?" a voice called from outside the barn. "You gonna run him in the Travers?" Sweetfeed recognized the voice as that of La Mar Bert, a hot walker he often worked with.

"Oh, there'd be no contest, La Mar. The Baron here wouldn't even have to work up a sweat." Then they both laughed.

"Well, you take good care of him," said La Mar. "He's the best on this backstretch. Everyone knows that."

"That he is," admitted Sweetfeed pushing the brush up behind Track Baron's ears. A cat came by and poked its nose inside the stall, dashing off when it saw Sweetfeed. The cat, an orange and white puffy giant Sweetfeed had seen many times, was made fat from eating sugar rolls and tossed-away hot dogs. No mice on his menu. After that it was quiet near the barn.

When it came near 8:30 P.M., Sweetfeed's adrenaline started flowing. He'd peek outside the stall every few minutes and look in both directions. No sign of The Voice. He must have brushed Track Baron over six times trying to keep busy. So he put the brush back and leaned against the stall wall. Track Baron munched on hay, and that's all Sweetfeed could hear at this point. The snap of the hay as Track Baron's sharp, powerful teeth cut it in half and then the grinding of the teeth themselves. One half hour to go and he knew he'd have to face The Voice. The tension was building. He did not relish the dreadful moment. Then a brilliant thought struck Sweetfeed. Why not move Track Baron to another stall? Yes. Move Track Baron down to the next barn where there were empty stalls. Then when The Voice came, he'd simply tell him the horse had died that same afternoon. This would serve two purposes. First of all, it would catch The Voice off balance if, in fact, he was coming because Track Baron was still alive. And secondly, it was unlikely he'd do harm to Sweetfeed until the insurance matter was settled. So without hesitation, Sweetfeed walked Track Baron to Barn 26 and secured him for the night. Then he went back to his regular stall and cleaned it thoroughly. By the time this was all done, it was five minutes before nine. He then waited outside once more. One worker passed by and said good evening to Sweetfeed. As 9 P.M. approached, Sweetfeed began pacing back and forth in front of the barn. No signs of The Voice. So he strolled further down toward Barn 29, taking the utmost care to stay away from the darker places and walking in the lighted areas. He'd made the round trip from Barn 24 to Barn 29 twice and still no sign of The Voice. He turned and was starting back again when, with the same strange piercing tone he recognized from his many phone calls with The Voice, it called to him.

"Sweetfeed, I'm over here."

Then it was apparent to Sweetfeed that the voice was coming from the track's direction. He looked out into the darkened area, but could only make out the lines of the track's railings. He moved ever so slowly toward the track. His mind was imprisoned by fear. Then he found the courage to move a few more feet.

"Finally we meet in person," The Voice said.

Sweetfeed looked straight ahead. A dark figure was posed up against the inner track railing. Sweetfeed estimated they were of equal height, though he couldn't see the face nor make out what The Voice was wearing.

"I can't see you," Sweetfeed said.

"Exactly," replied The Voice. "It's the way I want it."

Sweetfeed stopped short of the railing. "If we're going to deal with one another, I want to know who I'm talking to."

The Voice let out a sinister laugh. "I don't think you're in any position to demand anything, Sweetfeed."

"Not so. Not so. I have been a partner in this. . ."

The Voice interrupted him again. "Hush those words. I have no partners. I make deals and pay people good money for what they do.

You have been well paid over the years. That's where we draw the line on our partnership. It was where I drew the line with Claire Valova." The mention of her name sent renewed chills through Sweetfeed. The Voice went on. "I believe we have reached a juncture in our business dealings that calls for an immediate termination. Since Valova's and Anne Bifford's deaths the situation has changed. You know what I'm talking about. If you don't, then I'll spell it out for you."

"You don't have to," said Sweetfeed. "I know the heat is on."

"Good," replied The Voice. "Then you know where I'm coming from on this. But before we part there's the matter of our last transaction to settle." With his eyes now having adjusted to the dark, Sweetfeed could see The Voice's full silhouette, though still not the actual face. His shoulders were broad and he was wearing an Irish-style cap and what appeared in the darkness to be a shoulder cape. He carried something in his right hand that Sweetfeed couldn't exactly make out, but figured it was a walking cane of some sort. Or maybe an umbrella. He wasn't sure. He was certain he'd stand back a cautious distance just in case.

"Track Baron. You haven't kept me informed of Track Baron," The Voice insisted. "I take it everything has gone according to plan?"

Sweetfeed began to sweat. "You must have known," said Sweetfeed. "Known what?"

"Track Baron died today. Sad. Very sad. He died of acute colic. I had no way of reaching you since you cancelled the special number."

"Where is the carcass?"

"It's been removed to the holding barn to wait the official veterinary toxicologist's report. I feel we will have no problem, though it was much easier when Anne Bifford was doing the examinations."

"You say he's dead. That's fine. I will file the insurance claim just as soon as I have the doctor's report. When will you have it?"

Sweetfeed paused to answer, "Oh, probably tomorrow. Yes. Certainly by tomorrow. How can I reach you?"

"You don't reach me. I have made that clear. I will contact you."

Sweetfeed figured it was an opportune time to ask for his money. "I have several hundred dollars coming. Are you prepared to pay me?"

The Voice answered with a growl, "Have I ever not paid you in the past? Why do you insist on it now?"

"I have obligations," said Sweetfeed. "Money to pay daily bills has been slow in coming from Valova's Ballet Farms. I don't need it all, but I'd like some of it. Five hundred will cover me for now."

"I will pay you in full when you deliver Track Baron's death certificate. Tomorrow. I want it tomorrow. Then you'll get what I owe you, plus an additional fifteen hundred for Track Baron. That's my offer."

Sweetfeed was anxious to end the meeting. He agreed to accept The Voice's offer.

"Tomorrow it will be."

"Fine," said The Voice. "And, keep Water Man out of it."

"I have no problem with that, I was busy with Track Baron today. Well, they got a pay phone at Barn 22. I'll be near that phone by noon tomorrow. Call me then."

He waited for The Voice's reply. There was none. He peered at the railing and suddenly realized The Voice was gone. Sweetfeed gazed all around. No sign of him. Had he retreated across the oval in the direction of the grandstands? Or had The Voice walked away toward Union Avenue? He called out. "Are you still there? Can you hear me?" Then as quickly as he had disappeared, he was back again on the railing. The Voice was holding something in his right hand.

"I almost forgot to give you this, Sweetfeed. Something you lost, I believe."

The Voice tossed the object over the railing and it landed at Sweetfeed's feet.

"Be waiting for my call." Then he vanished in the track's darkness.

Sweetfeed reached down and picked up the object. His hands went cold as he touched it and his heart rhythm increased. His cold fingertips touched the damp, rough texture of Stuart Witt's straw hat.

25. CARLOS MANN

Frank Duffy, going on a tip from a close friend within the New York State Mental Health Department, discovered that Carlos Mann and other inmates in the special maximum security hospital Hillgate, located in the heart of the Adirondack Mountains near Jay, New York, had been undergoing treatment with a new experimental drug for restoring partial memory in extreme amnesia patients. The treatments had been going on for two months, though no word of them had leaked to the press. It wasn't exactly a hush-hush experimentation, but it was being carried out with utmost caution and strictly limited to a few patients at Hillgate.

Duffy, fresh from obtaining written permission from Mann's lawyer to speak to him, drove over the narrow road to Keene Valley, watching as he went, a flock of snow geese flying low over a thick clump of green pines. Beyond that he could faintly make out the ski trails on Whiteface Mountain's Olympic slopes. Thin twisting lines of white still hung on the mountain's face. Although skiing was done for the season, Duffy knew the packed, hard snow base probably wouldn't melt until sometime in mid-May. The Adirondacks, especially Whiteface Mountain, were the last areas in that region near Lake Placid to welcome summer. Though April's sun warmed up the days, evenings in the mountains could be very cold.

In center Keene, Duffy turned onto Route 9-N north in the direction of Jay. A rushing stream, which he assumed was part of the Au Sable, came almost to road level. As he passed over a series of small bridges he noticed the water was dirty and thick with floating debris, much of it washed down by the heavy spring rains and melting snow from dozens of smaller streams high in the mountains. He didn't see any rafters in his travels, but he expected they'd be challenging the roaring waters come the weekend. This was Thursday, bingo night for Martha and her women's group in Saratoga and, up to the time that he hurt his right elbow in a nasty winter fall, Duffy's bowling night with Billy Farrell and some other long-time cronies. Martha would get her night out in the smoked-filled bingo hall of St. Peter's but Duffy, feeling the persistent pain in his elbow as he gripped the car's wheel tightly, would have to be content with his visit with Carlos Mann. His editor's gut feeling was that Mann was the key to unraveling much of the mystery surrounding the proceedings of late in Saratoga. Notwithstanding the fact that he had been locked up since the fateful fire of 1988 at Clearwater. It was a bizarre hunch, but Duffy liked it.

A few miles above Jay proper, he spotted a small white sign, *Hillgate*. It was so small, he nearly drove right on by. He turned right between two stone gates and started up a steep, tree-lined gravel drive. It got steeper as he drove on. At one point the trees ended and the drive became very narrow. He stayed in the middle of the drive for fear of going off the soft shoulders. Then the drive began a series of loops. Round and round Duffy drove, as if meeting himself at each sharp turn. He realized it was the only way the car, or any vehicle for that matter, could manage to climb up this mountain road. He had it in low gear all the way and still the engine was straining. At times the rear wheels spun out long sprays of gravel. Then he'd slow down and ease forward until he could feel the tires gaining traction again. He wondered how anyone got up here in winter.

Finally, after spinning his way around one sharp bend, a square, two-story gray wooden structure appeared. It was a tasteless looking building with black trim and tall, narrow windows. Gray and drab in Duffy's estimation. As he pulled to within twenty yards of the front entrance, he noticed that the building was deceiving from a frontal view. It actually was longer, and eventually became four stories as it was tucked into the mountain slope on the back side.

He parked near several other vehicles to the right of Hillgate and made his way to the front door. There was no guard house or fenced-in area. He thought this strange for a mental hospital supposedly holding maximum security patients. It appeared more like an old age home. He announced himself by ringing the door bell, then waited. When the door finally opened, Duffy was greeted by a short, fat man wearing a pair of faded jeans and a red work shirt, holding a mop in one hand. He smiled at Duffy through thick, wire-rimmed glasses and welcomed him inside.

"How long have you been ringing?" said the greeter.

"Oh, just once," replied Duffy, trying to adjust his eyes to the rather dark interior of the building. "Just once. You were very prompt. I'm Frank Duffy, Doctor John Little is expecting me."

"Yes. He told me so."

"Your name?" Duffy said.

"They call me General Gates. You know, after the real English General Gates. Don't ask me why. Everyone in here has an alias attached. It goes with the unreality of the place. Dr. Little is called Blackbird. By the time you leave, they'll have you named. You can bet on it."

"Your real name?" Duffy persisted.

"Wallace. Wallace Tanner. I'm a local boy. Born in Lake Placid, but lived most of my life right here in Jay. Worked for a local lumber yard before I landed this state hospital custodian job. Now I'm much warmer in winter. Besides, I get my health plan and pension when I retire. Damn lumber companies work you to death and let you go home with practically nothing. Only good paying jobs with any security at all are these state jobs." He gave Duffy a puzzled look, then added. "You work for the state?"

Duffy shook his head no.

"You got a relative up here?"

"An acquaintance."

"What's the name?"

"Mann. Carlos Mann."

Tanner grinned at Duffy and winked. "Firefly. You're here to see Firefly."

Duffy's face tightened. "I don't think that's appropriate or called for. Do you?"

"Just telling you what they call him. I said everyone's got a nickname here. They call him Firefly. That's all."

"I fully understand that you have your own jargon at Hillgate. That doesn't mean we have to disrespect other human beings. Regardless of what they have done, or reportedly have done. It's a matter of dignity. Do you agree?"

Tanner didn't answer. They had reached Dr. Little's office. Tanner rapped once on the closed office door and then went down the hall, leaving Duffy to wait on his own.

Presently, Dr. Little opened it.

Duffy was taken back by Dr. Little's appearance. No starched, white uniform. No suit or tie. Not the slightest professional demeanor of a doctor. Duffy was shocked to see Little clad in blue sweat pants, a Buffalo Bill's pullover shirt and ratty looking sneakers. The only thing that gave Duffy the faintest hint he was addressing a doctor were the bright, blue, intelligent eyes, youthful face and soft voice. That, and the sign on the office door reading, "Dr. John Little, M.D. PhD." And at that it was half scraped off and difficult to read.

"Come in, Mr. Duffy. I don't have much time, but we can talk some about Carlos before you go to see him."

Duffy seated himself in a sagging leather chair opposite Dr. Little, who was seated in solid oak chair behind a large round desk that was covered with yellow notebooks of some sort. There seemed to be no order for these books. Untidy and very unprofessional in Duffy's mind. It reminded him of his office at the *Saratoga Star* before they installed all the terminals. A large picture window gave the office a clear view of the mountains. From this high-up point, Duffy figured he could see forty miles. It was still sunny and clear outside. A wall clock read 3:30 P.M.

Little put his feet on the desk top and wrapped his hands behind his head. He had thick, black hair and full, dark eyebrows. On the walls of his office hung pictures of several professional football players, all from pro teams. Judging from his pullover, Duffy pegged him as a staunch Buffalo Bills fan.

"You like football, I see," said Duffy.

"Live and breathe it," remarked Little.

"I generally go with the New York Giants," Duffy told him.

"Well, we're not far off from one another," said Little. "At least we cheer on teams in the same state. As you can see, I champion Buffalo. Used to practice up in Buffalo before coming to Hillgate. Great city. Great in summer, too. Of course, as many in Buffalo do, I made regular visits to Canada. Now there's a country where people have heart. Wonderful, those Canadians."

Duffy played with the end of his soup-stained red tie and smiled at Little. "Well, Doctor, you know my game. I'm too old to learn new tricks and trying hard not to forget the ones I did learn over the years. Editors are prone to sticking their noses into subjects many others would just as soon forget. That's why I'm here to see Carlos Mann. I'm one of the few in Saratoga who never bought all that bull about Carlos burning up Meredith Ostrander's estate. One of very few, I might add."

"So I understand," said Little.

"It made no sense to me at the time, and it makes even less sense to me now," Duffy continued. "A man has to have a powerful motive to do something so drastic. Nothing in all the reports I have read since the fire shows me that Carlos ever came close to having such motive. The fact is, he loved his job and he loved the Ostranders. No, I believe that fire was set by someone with a very sick and devious mind. I don't perceive Carlos as that type of person. I'd like your opinion on this."

The sneakers came off the desk and Little stood up and paced the office floor a few times. He was built like a fire plug, Duffy noticed. Perhaps not an inch over five foot eight, but heavy to the tune of 220 pounds, with square, powerful shoulders. Yet he walked lightly, almost as if every step was on the tips of his toes. Duffy, never a good judge of a person's age, guessed he was in his mid-forties, maybe a tad older, but still very young for a man in his position, plus the responsibility under his keep.

"You know, Mr. Duffy," Little suddenly said, "you're right. I'd have to go along with you. Carlos Mann, by his very nature probably didn't do it. What I'm giving you is a personal, non-professional opinion. I look at him the way you do. The way most laymen might view him. Based on that observation, he's a simple guy suffering from amnesia and maligned for the past seven years by his peers and the citizenry of Saratoga, probably falsely. Now, from a professional point, all that appears black and white about Carlos from a layman's view takes on a different tint. Take motive out of the equation. Just observe the man as we professionals do. It's then that Carlos Mann becomes many persons. We may be dealing with multiple personalities here. Then again, we just may be dealing with a crafty person, capable of acting out the parts he wants to play on a given day. I don't know at this juncture where he's coming from. We may never know until he comes around from the amnesia. So this is what you will find. The man you come to see is not exactly what you see. Get my point?"

Duffy thought for a moment. "If you're right, Doctor, I've driven a long ways for nothing. And I assume you're correct. It is your business to know these things. But as long as I'm here, I'd like to speak to Carlos. It will at least ease my curiosity. Also that of those few who feel he was wronged from the start. Is this a reasonable request?"

Little tilted his head forward and smiled. "Most certainly, Mr. Duffy. I think you should have your talk with Carlos."

Ten minutes later Duffy was seated on a bench in the rear courtyard of Hillgate waiting for an orderly to bring Carlos Mann along. Dr. Little thought it best that they talk outdoors where Carlos would be more relaxed. Little alerted Duffy to be watchful of off-the-cuff statements Carlos Mann might make about the hospital's ill treatment of patients. Most of the patients reacted in the same manner following months of confinement, according to Little.

When Carlos was brought to him, Duffy tried to be friendly, not knowing what to expect in these first moments. At the orderly's request, Duffy said nothing and Carlos sat down next to him. It was like that for several minutes. The two just sitting and staring off at the purple mountains in silence. The orderly, a tall muscular man with a crew cut and a protruding, boxer-type chin, backed off and waited by the building out of earshot. It was then Duffy was taken by surprise when Carlos spoke first.

"You're the editor at the *Saratoga Star,* aren't you?" he asked in soft voice, one that had been trained over the last seven years of confinement to speak so that others could not hear.

"Yes," admitted Duffy, further surprised at the frankness of the question.

"Then you were the man in charge at the paper at the time of the fire? Is that right?"

Duffy moved uneasily on the bench. "I'm surprised you have any recall of that time," he said.

"I don't," said Mann. "I'm suffering from amnesia, I can't recall details of the incident. Haven't they told you that?"

It was a weird way of putting it, Duffy thought. Was this the multiple personality Dr. Little talked about? Or was Mann in full command of his faculties and speaking to Duffy as he had not dared to speak to anyone in Hillgate. Very baffling, Duffy further thought. Mann pressed on.

"Through all those investigations. Through all the news stories, not once did I hear or see the name Claire Valova mentioned. Did you ever ask yourself why?"

Duffy didn't know what to say. He was both baffled and leery at Mann's remarks, though he kept quiet, letting Mann go on.

"So here we sit on a mountain top in view of the great Adirondacks. You're free to come and go as you please, while I'm a prisoner of my lost memory. Saratoga hates me. Society hates me. They blame me for burning down the only place I ever really called home. I'm the one. Well, I tell you Mr. Duffy, they can keep thinking that way for the rest of their lives. I'm content at Hillgate. Meals are not bad. I have a certain amount of freedom and, strange as it may seem, the other patients don't bother me. My only gripe is with the doctors who like to experiment with drugs. They've been using one on me for several months now. Supposed to bring back my memory. So far they haven't succeeded. For my part, I hope they never do." Mann crossed his legs and rested his chin in one hand. "The orderly can't hear us from that distance. But he can see us. I'm going to cross my left leg over my right. I have something in my left sock I want you to have. Turn your back so the orderly's line of sight is blocked."

Duffy didn't know what to make of all this. He was beginning to get nervous. What if Mann were hiding a knife, or some such similar object? Duffy actually felt threatened. However, he went along with Mann. When Mann had crossed the leg, he pulled up his pant leg slightly and there was something in his sock, as he had said. Duffy reached down and got it. Before shoving it into his coat pocket, he glanced at the object. It was a shining gold and silver cigarette lighter with the initials CV clearly etched on one side. Duffy's hand shook as he shoved it into his pocket.

"That's your real Firefly," said Mann.

"Where did you get this?" Duffy asked.

"It doesn't matter," said Mann. "What is done is done. No weeping on our part will restore Clearwater. Like my memory, it's lost and gone forever. Just ask the doctors. As I said, I like it here. There's really no place else for me to spend my remaining days. I'm a dead man in Saratoga. People will believe what they want to believe. That includes the cops. Now you know differently. That's all that matters to me. It must never go any further then this bench. Since I have now learned that Claire Valova is dead, revealing this to the public would appear even less important. Let the dead sleep." He looked up at the clear blue sky.

"Somewhere in the heavens justice will be handed down." With that Mann ended their meeting. They walked back with the orderly and stopped just short of Hillgate's rear entrance.

"Carlos," Duffy counseled him, "you don't have to spend the rest of your days here. You know that. With your memory now intact I'm sure we can clear your name within weeks. The whole damn sordid case should be reopened. And Claire Valova, for all her philanthropic goodness, should have her past laundry washed and dried in public. It's the American way. You did no wrong. You must have your name cleared."

"Forget it, Mr. Duffy. If you persist on pushing this, I won't cooperate. After all, I'm a lost mind wandering in the Adirondack wilderness. I want it that way."

On the way out down the long, drab, depressing hallway of Hillgate, Dr. Little came out to say good-bye to Duffy.

"How did your visit go?"

"I'm not sure," replied Duffy. "Not sure if it was good or bad for me to speak to Mann. One thing I can verify. He has many sides, as you say. I hope I got on one of the good sides. I'd appreciate it if you'd keep me posted as to his progress, especially with the new drugs. You have a wonderful facility, Doctor. Keep up the good work."

It was almost 5:30 P.M. and the sun was hanging low in the far mountain ridge when Duffy started up his car and began the steep descent toward Route 9-N. He looked in the rearview mirror as he pulled out and saw Carlos Mann standing on the building's right, his hands on hips. Then just before Duffy steered around a sharp bend, Mann raised his hand and waved. Duffy felt a sadness he hadn't felt since Claire had died. This time it was different. He was driving away with the terrible guilt and knowledge that an innocent man was in Hillgate. It went against Duffy's grain and he vowed to do something about it, regardless of Mann's wishes. Maybe not right away, but somewhere down the line. He felt it his personal and civic duty to rectify the wrong that had been dealt Mann. It was growing dark and Duffy was inching his way down cautiously, braking at every turn and pitch. At one turn he stepped on the brake pedal and felt the car slide over the gravel base. He repeated the braking at another turn, and then another. Then the road straightened out as he approached the steepest and final pitch. His foot touched the brake. Suddenly the pedal went right to the floor and the car bounded forward. "God, no!" Duffy shouted. "I've lost my brakes!"

The car swerved wildly from side to side, narrowly missing going off the road's shoulders, and it was picking up more speed every second. Duffy was terrified. His hands glued to the steering wheel that slipped beneath his moist fingers. All he could see was trees flashing by and ahead the junction on Route 9-N, coming at him. Beyond was the Au Sable River, its swift waters near overflowing.

It was over in seconds. Duffy's car crossing Route 9-N, tearing a wire fence down as it headed toward the river. It spun around twice, tossing hunks of cow pasture in the air before it plunged into the cold, dirty brown river water.

The call to Chief Nealy's office came in just after 8 P.M. from the State Police barracks in Keene, New York. Duffy's car had been found a half mile downriver caught up on a fallen tree. Divers had been on the scene since 7:30 P.M. There was no sign of Duffy. State Police at the crash sight feel he was either thrown from car as it went into the water or he was washed out of the automobile by the raging river at the hang-up point.

Nealy, notified at home of the accident, immediately called all parties about the tragic incident. Billy Farrell was sitting in the Fire House Restaurant having a few drinks when the call came.

By 9:30 P.M., Farrell and his wife, accompanied by a weeping Martha, were being driven in a state police van to Jay. It was one of the longest and most dejected drives Farrell could ever remember making. All three were praying. They could think of nothing better to do.

Nealy, Sergeant Galea and a group of volunteer cops from Saratoga, weren't far behind.

26. FADED MEMORIES

Mike Flint's odyssey across Florida, as bizarre as it was from the start, finally settled into a smooth uneventful ride for the last few miles. He was glad to see Fort Myers just ahead. The first thing he did upon entering Naples was to phone Dr. Blake. He got no answer. He tried again. Flint expected the answering signal after a fourth or fifth ring, but it just rang on. He gave it a few more minutes and tried once more. Still no answer. Becoming frustrated with not being able to reach Blake, and assuming he might later reach him at his office, he dialed Harry in New York City. The phone had barely rung and Harry was on the line.

"You must be psychic, Harry. Waiting to pick up my call so fast."

"Who in hell is this?" Harry's rough cigar choked voice blurted.

"It's your favorite beach bum calling from Fort Myers. You should be here. The sun and sand is just fabulous."

"Watch out for gators," said Harry. "They'll bite your nose off."

"I wrestle them for fun, don't you know that?"

"Well, I got bad news," Harry informed him. "Bad and sad. Editor Frank Duffy, Blake's close friend, got dunked in some nasty river up in the Adirondack Mountains. They can't find him. Every available cop in that area is searching for his body. They believe he got washed downstream. They say the streams and rivers in the mountains are roaring over their banks from the strong spring rains. Mud slides at Whiteface Ski Center have been reported. What we're trying to figure out is why Duffy was up there in the first place. He told his wife he was going to visit someone up north, but didn't say who. I don't know how long you'll be tied up in Fort Myers, Flint, but I think you had better get to Saratoga as quick as possible when you're finished down there.

"Between Witt's disappearance and now Duffy's accident, if in fact it were an accident, added to Valova and Bifford's murders, Saratoga looks like the focal point right now. The person or persons you're after are obviously covering their tracks. I'm warning the rest of the Saratoga group to take utmost caution, and that includes Chief Nealy. This bunch of snakes would kill a senior police officer if they thought it would sidetrack the investigation. We've all dealt with these types before. They'll stop at nothing."

"I agree, Harry. If I can catch up with this Max Steiner, I should be able to wrap things in the next day or two. I couldn't reach Blake on my last phone call. So if you make contact with him, perhaps at his office, say I'll head north by no later than week's end."

"Be careful, Flint," said Harry.

"No fun in that, Harry. Taking risk is the only true fun in life."

"Well," added Harry, "You now have Sandy to think about."

"Glad you reminded me," replied Flint. "I have to call her soon. Must run for now."

A light rain was falling when he reached the address he had been given for Steiner. It was a condo building a short distance from a popular beach restaurant called Anthony's on the Gulf. He was hungry, so he went into Anthony's and sat at a table facing the beach. The rain had stopped and streaks of sunlight broke through a mixture of gray and white overhanging clouds. Some wind surfers were gliding on a fairly high surf, but the beach wasn't crowded. He ordered a tuna sandwich and iced tea. The blonde, college-aged waitress who took his order smiled at Flint and asked if he were here on vacation.

"Yes. With a little business mixed in." He then asked her if she were familiar with the condo he was looking for? She gave him a funny look when he inquired.

"It is nearby, isn't it?" Flint asked again.

"Yes. We're at 3040 Estero Boulevard. It's a good two hundred yards down from here." Then she smiled again and her wide blue eyes lit up. "That's the high-rent area as they say around here."

"Expect it would be," said Flint, further asking, "Do you know a man by the name of Max Steiner?"

She tossed her head to one side. "No. Never heard that name. Of course we have so many patrons, it's hard to know them all."

"How about a Lisa Lane?"

The waitress' face broke out in a wide smile. "Yes, I know her. You mean the actress? The double for Veronica Lake in the old movies?"

Flint went along with her. "Yes, the actress. Does she live at the condo?"

"Not quite sure where her place is. But she comes in here. Generally on weekends. Likes to drink rum Cokes. Come to think of it, she comes in with a younger guy. When I say younger, I mean he's in his sixties. He doesn't drink. Always has tea. Hot tea. Uses a lot of Equal. Never touches sugar. But I haven't seen him lately. She's been coming in by herself."

"Thanks for the information," said Flint.

After lunch, Flint went out near the beach and walked a bit. He was thinking that if Max Steiner were at the condo, his best approach would be from the beach. It was unlikely Steiner would be alert to this, because so many swimmers and sun worshippers passed in that direction.

After viewing the landscape, Flint went back to his car and put on a sweat suit and sneakers. He strapped on a small shoulder holster with his Smith & Wesson revolver, moving it back beneath his left arm so that it didn't bulge under his sweat outfit.

Once again on the beach he walked the two hundred yards to the condo. He observed that each condo had its own beachfront patio. Max Steiner's condo on the end, was located at beach level. After watching the condo for a time, Flint went further down the beach where a hot dog vendor was set up. Two men in their twenties were operating the square metal cart on wheels with a large, red canvas umbrella over it.

"Can I help you?" asked one of them.

"Yes. I'll take a dog," said Flint.

"Everything on it?"

"Why not?"

As they prepared the dog, Flint kept an eye on Steiner's condo. "The end unit over there, do you know the number?" Flint asked.

The first boy answered. "That's probably 10-A. Yeah. It's got to be 10-A. Guy two doors down is 8-A. He's a big dog lover. Practically keeps us in business. You interested in buying that unit?"

"No," said Flint. "Someone said Lisa Lane lives there. She's pretty well known on Fort Myers Beach I'm told." Then the second boy spoke up.

"She's a living legend here, man. Movie queen at one time or something. Big stuff in the forties. Still carries that celebrity status. Once Hollywood, always Hollywood."

Flint came closer. "Is she married?"

They both laughed.

"Not married?" Flint said.

The first boy spoke. "Heard she was married five times. No husbands now. She had this guy for a long time. He'd come and go. Haven't seen him in several days. Creepy kind of character. Older, but he died his hair. Sometimes dark black, then he'd be blonde. It would run when he spent too much time in the sun. They were always fighting. She'd come on the beach and he'd trail after her, just like a puppy. Word is that she's the one with the money. No one knows what he does for a living, probably nothing meaningful. We heard she ditched him."

Flint reached in the zipper pocket of his sweat pants and took out a hundred dollar bill. "Tell you what. Do me a favor and go see if she's alone. If she has company, or if that creepy character happens to be around, let me know. This is for your assistance." He handed them the hundred.

"That's a lot of money for a small request."

"Think nothing of it," Flint assured them. "I'm an agent, I can afford it."

"Real talent agent? Movies and the like?"

"Along those lines."

Then the first boy flexed his muscles. "Well, here we are, just waiting to be discovered."

"Sorry, this time, boys," Flint kidded. "I'm interested in casting an older female in an upcoming part. But I don't want her to know that. Understand?"

"Hey, it's your call," said the second boy.

The first boy went up to the condo and knocked on the sliding glass door. Flint really couldn't see anything from where he was standing, but it was obvious the boy had made contact with someone. He came back down the beach. "She's all alone today. Not looking any too good, either. I'd say she's been crying. Sad to see someone with her illustrious past so down."

Flint thanked them and went to the door of the condo. Like the boy, he rapped and waited. Through the thin curtain he saw Lisa Lane making her way across the room. When the door slipped open and she was fully in front of him, he couldn't believe what he was seeing. It was, as they had told him, the sultry persona of the late movie star legend, Veronica Lake. The long blonde hair falling over one eye. The figure in a tight, black satin, full-length dress, and the long delicate arms and pointed fingers. Her face, however, was a tanned, streaked road map. Yesterday's beauty was gone, yet the Hollywood presence remained. This was a lady who carried herself well, despite the faded looks. He guessed she was in her eighties. It was hard to tell.

"Who might you be?" she asked, her hair cut right down the center of her face.

"Jerome Roth. I'm a talent agent," Flint found himself answering.

"Come inside then. It's not often I get calls from the industry."

Her condo walls were covered with large black and white pictures of various Hollywood luminaries. Several silver and gold frames held pictures of Veronica Lake. In fact, the pictorial collage was strung throughout the condo, some sitting on a small piano in the living room and others on dressers and tables. Even the little kitchen area had pictures. No color shots. All black and white. Flint marveled at them.

"You like the pictures?" she remarked.

"Magnificent."

"They should be. They were taken by the best Hollywood had to offer. You won't find photographers like that these days. They don't have the patience nor the caring with their subjects." She pointed to a picture on the far wall, wherein she was standing next to the original Veronica, and they were posing in dark pantsuits and both wearing men's fedoras. "I remember that shot. Looks simple, doesn't it? Well, it took us the better part of two hours to get it right. We were on the back lot at MGM and it was hot and dusty, but you'd never know it by that masterpiece. Jake Ruth took that shot. You probably never heard of him. Most haven't. Jake was a Rembrandt with a box camera. I was in love with his talent." Then she perked up her lips and blew a kiss at the picture. "He gets a kiss from me everyday. Sweet Jake."

"Wonderful shots," Flint agreed, walking slowly about the room, admiring each distinctive photo. It reminded him of a picture art show he had once seen in England. Everywhere in the condo, on every wall where there was space to hang one, were pictures. Sitting, standing, stretching out in a sexy pose. Bathing suit shots, full dress shots. It was like a shrine. Lisa even had little candles placed about the rooms, not lighted, but still giving that special touch that illuminated the pictures. She went and drew back the curtains of the side windows. "Now you can see them for real . . . Mr. . . . Mr. . . . I forgot your name."

"Jerome. Jerome Roth."

"Yes. Well, Jerome, I don't suppose you came here to gape at my old photos. What's on your mind.?"

He was sizing up her true character as he talked. He knew he could not continue with his charade, so he came right out with it. "I'm really looking for Max Steiner."

She flipped back her head as he mentioned Steiner and her bleached blonde hair went over both shoulders and the tanned hard face went taught.

"How dare you bring up his name," she said, her voice rising in anger. "He's not welcome here anymore. I haven't seen him in weeks. We've parted ways and good riddance."

Flint could feel the rage within her. "I'm sorry. I didn't know."

She relaxed. "No, you wouldn't know. Who would? A rat's a rat, but you don't always know one till they've bitten you. That's what Steiner is. A rat."

He figured she was telling the truth because he saw no trace of a man's belongings in the condo. He could even see into the bathroom. One tooth brush. No shaving cans. No razors. She was being truthful.

Sweetfeed

He also knew she was hurt, lonely and perceptively foolish in her dealings with men. The trustful type that gets stepped on easily. The softhearted, gullible movie blonde of the forties and fifties, conned by the best of the con men. This would be Max Steiner's beat. Flint was glad that Lisa had held her ground with Steiner. He could see she was a trained survivor. She reminded him of a much older version of Monica. Hollywood was the great survival training ground of the world. It bred hard men and tough women. He was curious as to why she had finally settled in Florida. But he didn't ask.

"Any idea where he headed?"

"No, and I don't care."

"Would be very helpful if I knew his whereabouts," Flint pressed her.

She went to a mahogany cabinet and took out a bottle of Jamaican rum.

"Care to join me, Mr. Roth," she offered, holding the bottle for him to see.

"Be happy to."

"Cokes in the fridge. I have to drink it with Coke."

"Same for me," said Flint.

"Grab some ice while you're at it," she called.

She was holding two glasses when he came from the kitchen.

"Let's sit on the patio. Rum always tastes better when drunk in the sun."

Before going outside, she put on a large straw hat and covered her head with a silk scarf which she tied in such a way that it covered most of her face and neck. Hidden behind the silk veil she could have passed for a lady of fifty, Flint observed. Her aging figure was still tuned.

Seated on the patio, Flint could see the hot dog cart and the boys watching him and Lisa Lane rum-and-Coke it. He imagined they were having a good laugh over it. Lisa went on about her days in Hollywood and her early budding relationships with this and that actor, with most of whom Flint was not a bit familiar. It was like talking to someone just out of a time capsule. A rerun of an old movie, except it was in person. After three strong rum drinks, Lisa became even more talkative. Flint had been waiting for her to loosen up. She started maligning Max Steiner in earnest now.

"Max was mixed up when I first met him. Didn't even have a job. I put him on the right path, but he always got sidetracked. Couldn't hold a job. Didn't want to work. Not real work. Then he started hanging around with a bad bunch up in Ocala. Can't understand why he went

186

way up there when we had this beautiful beach place. Told me he loved horses, and Ocala was horse country, so I believed him. Then he'd be gone for days on end. No phone calls. I'd stay awake all night waiting for his call. It went like that for months. When he was here, things went pretty well. He was good to me in many respects. Real good. That's the shame of the whole thing. We could have been happy. After five husbands I thought I'd latched on to a man who really cared. You know what I'm trying to say?"

Flint tipped his empty glass and nodded. "Yeah, I do understand. We spend our whole lives searching for Mister and Miss Right. Few of us find them. And the older we get the more importance we put on achieving that dream. Yes, Miss Lane, I fully appreciate what you're trying to tell me."

She began to cry softly. Tears ran down her face. She pulled her scarf close to hide them from Flint. "Christ, there I go again. Getting mushy and sentimental on rum. Forgive me."

"Nothing to forgive. We all have to have a good cry now and them. It's good for the soul, so they say."

They poured one more round of drinks and the rum bottle was finished. "I've got more," she said.

"No. I've had my quota," Flint assured her. "Besides, I have to be going shortly."

"Now don't go running off just because I got weepy."

"I'm not running. In fact I'll stay a few more minutes. But no more drinks."

She let out a sigh and slumped in her lounge chair. She watched him for a time and then sat up. "I have been on the level about Steiner. I really don't know where he is. However, he left a box behind and I have been toying with getting rid of it. If you want, you can take a look inside it. I don't feel any further obligation to protect his personal stuff. It's just a bunch of knickknacks anyway." It then dawned on Flint that Lisa Lane had virtually no idea of Steiner's real background. She couldn't hide anything about him, simply because she didn't have a clue as to his makeup. As far as she was concerned, this was a late-life love affair gone sour. And that was that. She would tuck it away with hundreds of previous disappointing stages in her long career. Time would bury it, as it had done in the past. Yes, Lisa Lane was a true survivor.

She went into the bedroom and came out with a cardboard box. It was taped shut. Flint tore off the tape and started taking out its contents.

What he found was an assortment of wires, outlet plugs, ping pong balls, and several little plastic cylinders. Lisa looked on as he carefully inspected each piece.

"Told you," she finally said. "Junk. Little pieces of useless junk. Now why in hell's name would a man keep that trash?"

Flint picked up one of the plastic cylinders. "Really can't say, Miss Lane. Doesn't look like they're much use."

"Ping pong balls," she said. "I never saw him play ping pong." Then she thought a moment. "He did fool with wires, though. Used to string them around here for a time. I told him to stop it. He was trying to connect the wires to a black box he once had. Never said what he was doing it for. But I told him I didn't like playing with electricity and live wires. I saw a backlot electrician at Paramount Studios get fried one time. No. I told Steiner to get them out of here."

"Can I take this box with me?" Flint said.

"By all means. It's one less thing that will remind me of Max."

Flint was amused at the box. All the tools of a horse killer's trade were there. Just like Ronnie Donato had explained the night Flint grilled him on *Big Fish*. Seems funny he left them behind. Probably figured she wouldn't have a clue and would toss them. Or, maybe he forgot where he put and was planning to come back and get it. They talked for another twenty minutes and then Flint said he had to leave. She tried to extend the conversation, but he begged off. Just as he was leaving, Lisa Lane handed him a small address book.

"What's this for?" Flint asked.

"Oh, another little something Max Steiner forgot when he left me. I never opened it. I was afraid. I know he was playing around on me. He always had an eye for the girls on the beach. Mind you, even at sixty-five he could be a charmer. That's what I miss the most. I was used to being charmed. Hollywood excelled in charming us when we were young. The press and fans pampered us. You're too young to appreciate what I'm saying. But you know something, Mr. Roth, you have that charming way. You should have been around when I was going strong. We'd have made a great duo. She stepped up and planted a big kiss on Flint's forehead. Come back anytime. It was fun talking to you."

She remained standing on the patio when he left. The wind was up and the surf was tossing wildly on Fort Myers Beach. Her hair was blowing about her face and Flint, though not being able to see her face, knew that she was crying again. He waved at the two hot dog boys as he walked back up the beach to his car. The boys were both laughing and wondering what it was he had come away with from Lisa Lane's place. He clutched the little address book in his left hand and carried the box in his right.

Back in his car, Flint opened the address book. A whole series of coded names and telephone numbers were listed. There was no sophistication to the coding. Actually it was nothing more than inverted letters and numbers. Written gobbledygook for a layman, but easy for Flint's trained eyes. On one page he discovered several Saratoga names and numbers. Also one in Lake George. The others were mostly in Florida, several in Ocala. On the last page Flint found Ben Lewis' name and number in Catamount. It all tied in very nicely. The question now was where did Max Steiner go? Flint, realizing he couldn't accomplish much more in Florida, made up his mind to make his next stop Saratoga.

27. DINNER BELL

Harry Waite was waiting for Mike Flint at the USAir terminal at JFK Airport when Flint flew in from Florida. It had been their first meeting in a year and Flint was dead set on taking Harry up on the long promised dinner offer. Waite had been out of town on assignment when Flint and Sandy had come through on their way to the Caribbean. Harry had one of his men drive him to Kennedy in an unmarked car and the car sat just outside the entrance with its motor running. Harry was in the back seat going over the up-to-date information on Valova, some of it developed by his own staff and some he'd received from Interpol and other sources. Like Flint, Harry had received the same preliminary reports on Valova's early life in Russia. That she was considered psychopathic as a teenager surprised Harry, as it had Flint. He'd run up against all types of criminals in his career, but certainly this revelation was unexpected. It just didn't fit with him that a world-renowned prima ballerina like Valova could be pegged a psychopath. How did she ever make it this far without being detected? Harry wondered. Aside from that point, there was nothing in her background, child or adult, that appeared out of place.

"Who would have believed it," he thought aloud.

To which his driver, Tommy Black, turned and said, "You want something boss?"

"No. It's nothing. Just talking to myself."

Just then Black spotted Flint coming out of the terminal. He was wearing dark slacks, a short coat and carrying two travel bags, one swinging off each shoulder.

"Here's Flint," Black told Harry.

Harry pushed open the rear door and Flint slid in beside him, lugging his bags.

"Why Harry, you've changed. You're half the size you used to be. I'm impressed."

"Living right. That's all it takes." He smiled. "Flint, you look like you're still dressed for the tropics."

"Never found time to change," said Flint. "I'll have to dress warmer for Saratoga, that's for sure."

"Oh, it's practically summer up there now," Harry assured him.

"I know Saratoga, Harry, remember. It's only May in Toga Town. May in that neck of the woods still spells winter to me. I'm a California man these days."

Harry patted him on the shoulder. "Don't fret. We've got a north country wardrobe for you. You can use my favorite tailor for any alterations. Let's swing by my place and have a drink and we can discuss this mess."

Flint pushed one bag on the floor and positioned the other between them.

"I'd rather not, Harry. I don't have a lot of time. I only made this stop off to collect that dinner you owe me."

"Dinner. I owe you a dinner?"

"You bet."

Harry lifted a cigar from his inner pocket and wet it with his tongue. Putting it in his mouth without lighting it, he frowned at Flint. "Okay, you name the place."

"I'm leaving it to you," said Flint, smiling.

"Fine," replied Harry. "Then I can pick a cheapo joint."

"No. First class or no dinner."

As Black moved the car out of the terminal and onto the main exit ramp, they sparred back and forth on a suitable dining spot. Halfway to Manhattan the pseudo argument had not yet been settled. So Black, feeling they weren't going to agree, suggested a little known but excellent Italian restaurant near Penn Station.

"That's fine with me," said Harry.

Flint leaned over the seat while they continued to swerve through a maze of oncoming headlights.

"I know the mayor eats there. Some Broadway types, too. Best home made pasta in New York. Guaranteed. You don't like, I'll pay." And he looked back at Harry, adding. "Even on a measly sergeant's salary."

"Just drive, Black," Harry ordered.

They were seated at a rear table at the City Bistro, the only table available this evening. A single candle burned in a blue glass, reflecting on their faces as if they were partaking in a seance. The Bistro was Black's choice, so he selected the meals. He ordered shrimp diavolo for all. They began with a Sicilian appetizer, caponata, mesquite grilled vegetables with tomatoes. Harry, claiming he hadn't gone off his strict diet in five months, decided he'd relent this one time in honor of Flint's visit.

"I'll have some wine tonight," Harry informed the waiter. "White and red. White first." Two bottles of wine consumed and the meal finished within an hour's time, Harry treated them to a nightcap of Chivas Regal over ice.

"Just like the old days," remarked Flint.

"I'll drink to that," agreed Harry. "The old and younger days when we could dine and drink like this every night and never feel the worse for it in the morning."

They sat and drank in silence for a time. Harry finished his remaining Scotch and turned to Flint. "What do you make of all this, Mike?"

"The meal? It was superb."

"No," Harry said. "This horse thing."

It was an open question that Flint wasn't able to clearly answer. "A big mess to begin with. Actually a dirty mess if you will. Not very different than other cases we've tackled in the past, but I'm more taken aback by the players. Who'd have thought horse killing would attract such a cast of characters? Veterinarians, horse trainers, lawyers, stable owners, socialites, insurance executives. You name it. Greed and money. What else can I tell you, Harry? I know Blake and that group are devastated by what happened to Valova and Bifford. Now with the possibility of their complicity in these schemes, there'll be no consoling them."

Harry took out the same cigar he had in the car and wet it again. "The FBI has a list a mile long," Harry noted. "What we have to do now . . . or you have to do, is find out who's behind the shenanigans in Saratoga. Right now it's a turkey shoot up there. All your friends are scared to death. According to Blake, whom I finally caught up with, this Witt guy is still missing. Now the editor is missing. I'll see if I can get the New York State Police report on Duffy's car. Ten to one, someone tampered with his brakes. We did find out what Duffy was doing in the Adirondacks, though. He made a call on one Carlos Mann, the main suspect in a big horse farm fire near Saratoga in 1988. Mann's in a mental hospital called Hillgate. The guy known as Ben the Chem is gone. By the way, lab reports now say he was killed by one big lethal dose of sodium cyanide. We first thought he did himself in, but it now looks otherwise. Maybe your Max Steiner got to him. Or someone else. I don't know what to tell you, Flint. It's gotten so bad, the American Horse Shows Association is requesting help. Seems our fiendish little killers have gone after all equestrian types. Wouldn't be surprised if they're not the ones responsible for sudden animal deaths with that traveling circus troupe. Just last month two lions died of unknown causes. Three guys in Ocala were caught on federal fraud charges for falsifying test results. Another for the 1993 electrocution of a Derby runner-up, called Fleet Foot. Now that I've started a file on this racket, there's no end to the list."

Flint, sipping his Scotch, was half listening to Harry and half pondering his next course of action. Where to stay in Saratoga? Whether or not to expose himself to all of Blake's friends, or keep his distance and work strictly through Blake? He knew his biggest enemy now was time. He peered over at Harry nonchalantly, then at Black, and said, "I don't know why I got hooked on this case. But as long as I'm on the line, I might just as well go all the way." Then addressing Harry. "You still got that safe house in the mansion?"

"No," replied Harry. "We lost our lease. To tell the truth, we dropped all our options in Saratoga right after your last sortie up there. In fact, I got a call from internal affairs to get my butt out of Toga. They weren't a bit happy about our little sortie up north last summer. Even they're calling it 'The Ninth Race Caper.' They cut my budget, too. No budget, no Saratoga. It's the reason I'm calling it quits in September."

He saw Flint raise his eyebrows.

"I mean it, Mike. I'm all done in September. Black here knows where I stand, don't you?"

"Only what you've told me, Chief. You sound serious."

"I am serious, damn it. Though few believe I'm serious. It's all getting too political. Now that they've changed governors in Albany it's not only political, it's confusing. They tell us to get tough on crime. Fine. Then they whack off the money to operate. You tell me I'm not serious."

The waiter came and took the check. Flint gave Harry a grin as he took it. "Have you ever noticed how much better food tastes when someone else is paying the bill?"

"Very amusing," Harry remarked.

They didn't go directly to the car when dinner was over. Instead, Flint and Harry walked around the block and compared notes on the investigation while Black waited at the City Bistro having a coffee.

Flint filled Harry in on his visit with Lisa Lane. As expected, Harry found the story amusing. Flint then handed him one of the small plastic cylinders from Steiner's belongings.

"What are these?" said Harry.

"Really don't know."

Harry paused beneath a street light and inspected them. "Some sort of test tube, I'd guess."

"Really don't know," Flint repeated himself. "But I'd suspect they held that cyanide Ben the Chem used to kill his victims. Makes it

193

quite clear to me that Steiner and The Chem collaborated on some killings."

"By the way, the lab report the Saratoga cops got on those tubes from that Wainwright fellow showed poison, too," Waite said.

Flint nodded, not surprised. "So from the start, trying to piece it all together, I believe the following scenario. Claire Valova had mental problems. We've established this fact. To accept this, we have to draw a blank on her adult dancing career and concentrate on her earlier childhood problems. I only read a skimpy report from Russia on this, so I can't say how these early negatives were suppressed for so long. I do think, however, they never really were suppressed and that Valova's connection to the horse killings was nothing more than an extension of her self-destructive nature taken out on her Thoroughbreds. Dr. Blake can analyze this better than I can, of course. Blake also sent along some data on some of Valova's close associates. One in particular is a guy called Sweetfeed who ran her stables and trained many of her horses. He's a old coot, but he was very close to her and her operations. So I have to put him into the equation. Anyway, we will probably get a full, meticulous report on Valova's life soon. The book is closed on Ann Bifford's death, thanks to Donato's confession. But though we know it was a contract killing, we still don't know who ordered her dead. As for Witt's disappearance, I wouldn't look any further than the track. Mind me, Harry, these are only thoughts. I always try going the logical route on these things. If an investigation becomes more complicated I'm not averse to calling the technical folks for help. My gut feeling is that Witt went to the track and for reasons I can't explain, nor do I expect anyone can, was done in." In the dim glow of the street light, he could see Harry's face wrinkle up. Flint went on. "Sweetfeed. He's got to be the key to finding Witt. All my instincts tell me this. Just trace the lines of thought here. Sweetfeed worked for Valova. He also dealt with Bifford. If he's not involved in the horse nonsense, then who is? Follow my reasoning?"

Harry leaned against the street light and shook his head. "Makes sense so far."

"Well," Flint said quickly, "If Sweetfeed is involved, it makes even further sense that Duffy's crash was no accident. Wonder if they've found his body?"

"Last I heard only the car was found," Harry said. "Come to think of it, you'll have to check Hillgate while you're in Saratoga. Could be there's a tie-in with Carlos Mann we don't know anything about. The editor must have thought so. That wasn't a social call."

"Right, Harry." Flint laughed. "You took the thought right out of my head. See if you can get the file on Mann before I leave tomorrow. But, if they've penned him up for seven years in a loony bin, I can't see where he fits into the recent scene. Though stranger things have happened in our profession, haven't they?"

"The cop business gets more bizarre everyday. Remember, I told you I'm splitting from this rot in September."

They were now talking again and Flint was saying he'd probably stay right in downtown Saratoga. "Might just as well put up where I can be close to the restaurants," he told Harry. "I will need a car, though. Can you have one driven to Saratoga?"

"On my budget? Yeah, one will be at the airport somehow."

"One link that hasn't come together is Wainright, the plastic cylinder guy. I suppose he's in Kentucky. He's in the loop somewhere. You can bet on it. I'd appreciate you having someone look into his background. He may be bogus, but I want to make sure." Black was out of the City Bistro and sitting in the car when they came around the block.

"One thing more, Harry. I'd lay dollars to donuts the cylinders in your pocket and the ones Nealy received are identical. Could it be that Wainwright is a good guy trying to alert everyone to what's going on? Or is he a bad boy trying for a little diversion? Makes you wonder, doesn't it?"

"That's for you to find out in Saratoga, Flint. Good luck."

28. IF, IF, IF...

Saratoga was in that traditional springtime crossover from winter to summer-like weather. The maple trees along historic Broadway were sprouting green leaves and the shops, hotels and restaurants were sprucing up their exteriors, all in anticipation of another tourist season. The outdoor patios of many eating places were being readied for patrons who delighted in dining on Saratoga's grand promenade.

It was to this very setting that Flint, for the second time in two years, arrived in Saratoga to begin again a search for a killer. There was no doubt in his mind that the key to the investigation was right here. Why Saratoga? Who could say? The little town with the nationally known race course seemed the most unlikely place in the world for such intrigue and mayhem.

As promised, Harry had placed a car at Flint's disposal at Albany Airport. An Albany cop met his plane and took him to the unmarked car. After considering several hotel and motel options, he chose to stay in the renovated Adelphi on Broadway, with its period rooms and 1800s decorative lounge, bar and dining areas replicating Saratoga's former opulent era Flint also made this selection based on its central downtown location.

His room was on the second floor and faced Broadway. It had a balcony the width of the building with comfortable sitting chairs—one of few such balconies left in a town that once boasted fifty miles of veranda. Flint placed a call to Dr. Blake at his office. The secretary said he wasn't in and wasn't expected all day. It was Monday. "Maybe his day off," Flint theorized, though the secretary didn't say so. Flint then called Castle Rock at Lake George. Blake answered on the third ring.

"Good to hear your voice, Flint. I feel better knowing you're nearby. I just returned from Jay where they're still searching for Duffy. The car has been removed from the river and the New York State Police have lab people going over it. Nealy wasn't any too happy about this. He's afraid they'll find Duffy's notes or something and it will go blowing the lid off our own investigation. Duffy, as you would expect, always kept copious notes. God knows what he had in that car that they might read. Nealy said Duffy was definitely visiting with Carlos Mann at Hillgate. But Nealy says the doctors at Hillgate say Mann still has memory loss and actually has developed multiple personalities. From my experience, he'll be there for some time to come. Why and how the car suddenly lost control and ditched in the Au Sable River has us all worried and scared. What do you think?"

"You're probably not far off the mark," Flint agreed. "I'd say some-one deliberately got to Duffy's car while he was making his visit. I'm sug-gesting we all meet and go over this thing from top to bottom. I have wheels, so I can move around at will. Where's the best place."

"Right here," said Blake. "Some are still in Jay. I'll call and see if we can meet tomorrow. I'll leave word for you. Where are you staying?"

"I'm at the Adelphi. Leave word with the desk."

"I'll do that."

"Tell me a bit more about Duffy's accident," said Flint.

Blake's voice drifted off and then returned. "Sorry if you get a weak signal. I've been having trouble with this phone. Must be a tree limb or something. Every spring one or two branches fall and damage the wires. Anyway, you could not imagine how far the car slid across the cow pas-ture before it landed in the Au Sable. He must have been going over eighty or ninety. The police say it spun and dug up mounds of earth before hitting the water. They think Duffy was tossed out when the car was spinning. The road leading down from Hillgate is very steep."

Flint interrupted. "Do you think there's any possibility that the car never initially made it to the water? That Duffy may have been taken out of the car by some assailant and then the car pushed into the river? Any inkling that might have occurred?"

Blake gave it some thought. "No, a trucker actually saw the car go across the field and into the cold water. He had a CB radio. That's the reason the state police responded so quickly. The trucker said Duffy's car damn near hit another car crossing Route 9. It all happened so fast the trucker didn't have time to react. Neither did he see Duffy being ejected from the vehicle."

"Well," added Flint, "it doesn't solve the matter, but at least we know Duffy was not dragged off by the killers we're tracking. I assume police divers are still on the scene?"

"Yes. They've been all over the river. Troopers, volunteers and offi-cers from the state conservation department have combed every inch of the terrain. The waters are wild. One local told me that the river is so heavy that several new tributaries have been formed. So the divers have to search in uncharted shootoffs, too. Then there's every conceivable type of debris floating and hampering diving operations. It's near flood stage at this juncture. Martha refuses to leave the scene until Duffy's body is found. With her age and recurring ailments, her state of health at this point is very precarious. I have a physician friend from Lake Placid watching over her."

197

"No need for me to go up to Jay, then" said Flint. "But I do want that meeting. Let's say we gather at 7 P.M. at Castle Rock. That gives them the daytime to work. I'd like to include Nealy, Galea and Farrell. In the meantime, I'm personally going to call on Sweetfeed. Witt's disappearance is just too fishy for my blood. We may have other difficulties in the person of Max Steiner before it's all over. I couldn't locate him in Florida. He may well be our tracker. I'm not certain. These next days will be critical. Take some extra caution, Doc. Alert the others. You all should be savvy enough at this point. Whoever is behind this now knows that we know the game is coming to an end. They've got everything to lose. They'll stop at nothing in their desperation to cover their tracks."

"I'm with you all the way with that thinking," said Blake.

"Fine," said Flint. "Give me directions to Castle Rock now, then leave word by noon tomorrow that everything is in order." Flint copied down the directions and hung up. He went to the window and looked down at Saratoga's Broadway. He observed little traffic and only a few pedestrians. The afternoon sun, like a giant solar mirror, was glaring off storefront display windows. It was 1995, but it might just as well have been 1895, for the restored decor and rich period tapestry of the Adelphi held time in place.

His thoughts then focused on Sweetfeed. Was he telling the truth about Witt? If not, why not? But if so, where was Witt? So many ifs. And so little time to filter out all the ifs. Flint also glanced at the apartment house across Broadway. Sandy had lived there. This started his emotions rolling in another direction altogether. He was tempted to call her, but didn't. He wanted to keep his thoughts and energies directed on the investigation. Calling Sandy would distract him and he knew it. He could feel her love in this moment. Her thoughts could reach him over the miles, like a magic mental telephone line. He missed her very much.

29. CLUBHOUSE LAMENT

At shortly past 6 P.M. that evening Water Man, heading for his rooming house on Saratoga's west side, stopped at Slim's Bar for a quick beer. It wasn't his habit to stop at Slim's, but he'd put in a long day forking hay and lifting feed bags on the backstretch and he craved a cold one. The small bar was almost empty this Monday night as Water Man climbed onto a stool and ordered his drink.

"Water Man, where have you been?" asked the bartender, slapping the beer glass on the bar in front of him. "We thought you'd gone back to Kentucky."

"Hell no," shouted Water Man. "I've been here since early April. You know we've got some pretty fancy horses to care for at the track. Too busy to play, that's all. Besides we're working more hours than we used to. Money's tight and we don't have the help we once did." He picked up his beer and downed half of it in one gulp. "But this beer tastes great tonight, I can tell you that."

"Well, I'm glad to see you back," remarked the bartender, putting a head on Water Man's beer.

"Oh, hold it there," Water Man insisted. "I only have time for one." He paused. "Maybe two. Yeah, fill it up. I owe it to myself."

When he finished, he said good-bye to the bartender and started for home. A cool May wind was whipping at his face as he walked briskly over Congress Street, feeling the sting of his second beer. As he was about to cross the street, a dark car raced down on him, forcing him to jump to the curb to avoid being hit. The car stopped and the passenger side window went down. Water Man couldn't see the driver. Yet he froze in place when he heard The Voice call his name.

"Water Man. Water Man. Where is Sweetfeed?" The Voice asked.
Water Man did a slow backward shuffle, moving a few inches at a time. As he moved the car moved with him. "You didn't answer me, Water Man. That's not polite."

"Don't know where Sweetfeed is. Haven't seen him all day. Why you asking me?"

"You're one of his closest friends, aren't you?"

Water Man knew it was useless to keep moving. He was trapped and there was little he could do about it. "You can say we work close by. Never thought of myself as Sweetfeed's best friend. He ain't exactly the friendly type on all occasions. Sometimes he can be mean. No. I'm not his best friend. So whatever it is that you want, you had better go ask someone else. Someone who knows him real good. Why not go ask Joe Hennesy?"

"Are you trying to be smart with me?"

The Voice had a particularly unpleasant tone to it now, and Water Man suddenly feared for his life. But he held his ground.

"Tell Sweetfeed to meet me tonight at the race course near the club-house entrance. Tell him ten sharp."

The car darted away as quickly as it had come. Water Man watched as it headed toward Broadway past the First Baptist Church. Then he thought to himself. "Did that man mean tonight? How am I ever going to get in touch with Sweetfeed at this hour? Why it's almost seven now. He'll shoot me if I call the barn phone and disturb the horses." After pondering this for a few minutes, Water Man decided he might just as well walk the two miles or so to the track and give Sweetfeed the message in person. He was kicking himself for having had that second beer at Slim's. It made him tipsy. He reversed his direction and headed back eastward on Congress, crossed Broadway and walked through the park to Union Avenue, having to pass by the Canfield Casino in the park's center as he did so. On Union he went right by John Roohan's Real Estate offices and continued till he reached the backstretch entrance. By now his legs were ready to give out. He found Sweetfeed at Barn 26. He practically stumbled into the stall where Sweetfeed was tending to a horse. Water Man was wheezing from the cool night air and the exhausting trek. Sweetfeed looked startled as Water Man entered.

"What on earth are you doing here?"

Water Man was having a problem catching his breath. He slumped to the stall floor and leaned back against a partial bundle of hay.

"Don't know what's going on, Sweetfeed," he said in a wavering voice. "But that awful voice stopped me on Congress Street earlier and demanded that I tell you to meet him at the clubhouse entrance at ten this very evening. That man gives me the creeps. Who is he?" Sweetfeed straightened, rubbed his head without answering. When he did finally glance down at Water Man his face had the look of a frightened man. Sweetfeed's stark, fearful look sent renewed fear through Water Man. He knew from Sweetfeed's face that his question didn't require a reply. Always superstitious, Water Man was thinking the worst. He'd been haunted by visions of The Voice ever since he first heard the man. Though he had never seen his face, he visualized a wicked monster behind the voice. The cruelest anyone could devise. He could clearly see that Sweetfeed was shaken by the mere mention of The Voice.

Following several moments of suspended silence, save for the horse's breathing, Sweetfeed spoke.

"How ridiculous. Meet him at the clubhouse entrance at ten? The man is crazy. Would he expect me to go there in the dark? Does he think I'm that much of a fool?"

He was talking as much to himself as to Water Man. He was trembling inside and his troubled mind was trying to figure exactly what to do. Certainly The Voice was coming to settle the score concerning Track Baron. There was only one reason The Voice was coming. He wanted to tell Water Man all about it, to get this great burden of guilt off his mind once and for all. But he couldn't. There was no one he could tell, and fewer yet who would believe him if he did. It was all too preposterous. How would he begin to explain the killings to his fellow backstretchers? Would they believe him if he said he went along with the deadly scheme out of devotion to Claire Valova? Would they, could they, understand that? No. This was a disgrace he'd have to shoulder alone. As for The Voice, Sweetfeed realized he had no other choice but to meet him at the clubhouse. However, he wasn't about to just walk over and expose himself. No. He decided he'd make the meeting with The Voice, but he'd have a little surprise of his own when they met.

He glanced at his watch. It was 8:45 P.M. That gave him over an hour to put his plan into action. First of all, he asked Water Man to finish grooming the gray mare he had been working on. Then he moved swiftly down a few units to where Track Baron was stabled. Thinking all the time to himself that if The Voice was hell bent on seeing Track Baron dead, he'd give The Voice his wish. He bridled the big horse and led him out of the barn and walked him all the way around the darkened oval to the rail just off the clubhouse paddock entrance. He tied the rope to the rail and walked back again to the barns. The round trip took him twenty minutes. After making sure Water Man was performing, he went to Track Baron's old stall and, reaching up behind a wooden shelf, took down a foot-long round canister. He opened the canister and pulled out a cylinder of Mace and the shoved it into his inner coat pocket. Yes, he mused, he'd meet and talk with The Voice. He'd get so close that he'd be able to stare him directly in the eye. Then he'd Mace the SOB right then. And when The Voice couldn't see and cried out, as he surely would, Sweetfeed would beat him to a bloody pulp, the same way he had beaten Witt. He'd rid himself once and for all of this faceless ghost. But before he killed The Voice, he'd force him to tell where all the insurance money was stashed. After all, with The Voice out of the way, there was no one left to split this money with. The more he thought how easy it would be, the more he relished getting on with it. So somewhere near 9:30 P.M., with the Mace tucked securely in his pocket and ready to squirt on a moment's notice, Sweetfeed trekked off to keep his rendezvous.

Coincidentally, Flint, in his quest to talk to Sweetfeed before the next day's meeting at Castle Rock, arrived at the backstretch at precisely 9:30 P.M. He parked on Union Avenue and walked through the backstretch gate. Somewhere in the dark, Flint passed unnoticed by Sweetfeed heading to the clubhouse. Seeing a light on in one of the stalls, Flint went over. He found a backstretch worker asleep in the hay near the gray mare and woke him up. The track groom came out of his sleep in near panic, curling up in a ball and then putting his back to the stable wall as if Flint meant to attack him. Flint was immediately conscious of the man's reactions. "Hold on there. I'm only here to see Sweetfeed. Do you know him?"

The man's arms came to the front of his chest and he held his right hand over his heart. "Shouldn't go waking up Water Man in such a hurry as that. My heart is still pumping two-forty. I thought . . . I thought you were The Voice," he exclaimed in a frightened voice.

"What Voice?"

And then Water Man, knowing he had said something he shouldn't have, tried to change the conversation. "Oh, this here is Mary Jane. She'll give the boys a run for their money when she's trained right. Yes, sir. Mary Jane is one fine filly."

Flint knelt down next to him. "I'm not interested in horses at the moment. Who's this voice you mentioned?"

Water Man was beside himself now. Should he, or shouldn't he tell this stranger where Sweetfeed was? He was all mixed up and starting to shiver.

"I haven't got all night," said Flint, his own voice taking on a command tone which sent further shivers into Water Man. "I want an answer."

The right arm came up and pointed toward the door. "Over there. He's gone over there."

"Where?"

"The other side of the track."

"At this time of night?"

Water Man was shaking all over. Flint realized something was drastically wrong.

"The Voice is meeting him. I'm scared for Sweetfeed," Water Man finally managed to say.

"What's the meeting about?" said Flint.

Water Man sat up. "That's the problem. I don't know. I just know that the man with the strange voice is scary. As scary as I have ever heard. I see nothing but bad happening to Sweetfeed if he keeps that meeting. Are you a friend of Sweetfeed's?"

"I could be," admitted Flint.

"Then you had better go and find him," Water Man begged. "They're meeting at the clubhouse entrance at ten. But don't tell him Water Man sent you. Sweetfeed would be very mad at me."

"That's in twelve minutes," Flint shouted. "You stay right here. Don't tell anyone else about this meeting. You understand?"

Water Man nodded his head, adding. "Ain't no one here to tell except Mary Jane. I'm sure she doesn't care."

Flint was amused with Water Man's humor.

Flint, on a dead run around the world famous oval, where hundreds of champion Thoroughbreds had raced since 1893, knew he had little time to spare. Here was sure of one thing: Sweetfeed was in danger. It would certainly fit the pattern of recent weeks pertaining to anyone connected with Claire Valova. The irony of this singular sprint around the track made the whole investigation even more bazaar. He thought, if Harry could only see him now he'd probably have an odds-on bet that Flint couldn't make it around without falling down. Right now he needed the speed and stamina of Kelso to reach the clubhouse by ten. A thick mass of dark clouds covered the track. It couldn't have been darker.

His lungs were straining for air when he finally came near the towering grandstands on the clubhouse end. He slowed to a fast walk and moved silently near the inner rail, slipped beneath it at one point and stopping just short of the paddock area. Like a prowling cat, he had to adjust his eyes to the night. There was a small light at the gate leading to the paddock. It was not bright enough for him to see anything plainly, but sprayed just enough glow so that Flint could see if anyone was moving in or about the clubhouse's first level. He waited a spell and nothing moved. Pressing a button on his watch, the hands lit up and he saw that it was one minute before ten. At ten on the nose, Flint, looking directly at the clubhouse, detected movement. In the pale light he could see a figure inch toward the main building. Then, to the right, he picked up someone else coming at the first in slow motion. It was obvious neither party could see the other, though Flint figured they would, once both had reached the open clubhouse entrance. What happened next, happened in a split second. One moment it was dark, then the figure to the right flashed a bright light on the first figure, and from a distance of fifteen yards, Flint could see the first figure hold up hands to protect his eyes from the blinding light. It was an older man dressed in a nondescript dark jacket, overalls and knee-high rubber boots. Must be Sweetfeed, he thought. The second person was hidden behind the bright light.

"Voice," The first man screamed. "Voice. I'm coming for you."

With that the old man ran with surprising speed directly at the light. Flint sprang from his position as the two figures clashed in a fury of shouts and physical struggle. The light went out and Flint couldn't see anything. He could hear Sweetfeed and The Voice's labored breathing as the two fought in the darkness. One man screamed and the other grunted. Then Flint heard the dull snap of a silencer. One shot, then two. He ran to the sound and upon reaching the first clubhouse level, tripped over a body. He fell sideways against a railing and then righted himself. He had his own gun out at the ready. The second figure was gone. Flint reached down and rolled the body over. He shined a pencil light into its face. He'd never seen Sweetfeed, but from the description he'd been given, this was most certainly the old backstretch sage. He felt his pulse. Sweetfeed was dead. Near Sweetfeed's right hand Flint found a can of Mace. It had not been sprayed. The safety lid was sealed tight. The bullet, from what Flint could make out, went in Sweetfeed's neck on the right side and came out the other. A stream of blood was making a round pool beneath his gray-haired head. It was all-too-familiar for Flint. He listened in the darkness for any sound of The Voice's movement. Without a light, Flint figured The Voice could not move any faster than he could through the clubhouse labyrinth without making some noise. Several seconds later he heard footsteps on the second floor. The level where he was located was right near the Paddock Rail Bar and there were stairs leading to the second floor and tiers.

Flint figured The Voice had slipped up those stairs and was probably trying to make his way though the box section to the general grandstand section, where eventually he'd try to escape down the far end and go out on Union. Flint backtracked and moved hurriedly along the perimeter of the building where he could take advantage of some small, red fire lights that were placed every few yards. He then climbed the center stairs and came out about midway between the clubhouse and grandstands. He sat in a grandstand seat right near where the walkway passed. A noise to his right brought him to his feet. The earlier dark cloud cover was splitting apart and a partial moon shown some light over the track. In that faint opening, Flint made out the silhouette of The Voice working his way along the walkway. Just as The Voice reached Flint's position, Flint jumped from his seat and grabbed for his arm. The Voice bolted to one side and Flint locked one hand on his belt and pulled. But as Flint tried to come forward, his pant leg caught on the edge of the grandstand seat and he couldn't move. In that split second, The Voice twisted himself free of Flint and started running. Flint yanked at his trapped pant leg and lifted his body. The pant leg ripped open as he came free, so he found himself chasing The Voice with one pant leg. At the Carousel Restaurant area, The Voice reversed his direction and headed back toward the clubhouse. Flint then saw him go up the stairs near the main elevator. Flint pursued him. The Voice went up one more level to the dining section and then climbed ahead of Flint to the roof area, where Flint heard him moving on the hard, slippery slate roof.

As Flint darted through the opening at the roof level, a bullet splintered the wood next to his head, sending a sliver into his face. He felt blood begin to flow, though he knew it was only a surface wound. Ahead of him he could see The Voice. He was trying to walk where the roof's configuration now became a series of flat areas, then pitched angles and finally, several spires.

Flint called out, "You can't go any further. Drop the gun and we'll make a deal."

The Voice paid no attention. Flint inched his way along the roof. The moon went behind the clouds again and the roof became hideously dark. Flint felt a raindrop on his face. A west to east wind now began to whip across the race course.

"Don't be a fool. There's no place to go. Come in now," Flint's voice carried over the building. No reply. Though hidden in the darkness, Flint still heard him clinking on the slate, though the frequency of his steps seemed to have slowed to a crawl. Flint knew The Voice was running out of space. When five minutes or so went by without a reply, Flint grew fearful that The Voice might work his way to the back of the roof and somehow be able to shimmy down one of the pipes. He didn't relish this prospect. Not when he was so close to catching him. So Flint made one last effort to get as far along the roof as was safe and without sliding off. The light rain was making it more difficult.

Besides, he had dirt and racetrack clay on his shoes from his dash around the oval. He had no traction. His only hope was that The Voice had the same problem. He swung around one of the spires and was about to move further when another bullet whizzed over his head, striking the slate of the spire. It threw him off balance and he lost his footing. As he did, he cupped one hand onto a metal lightning rod and this prevented him from tumbling off the roof. In that instant, he heard The Voice coming in his direction. He probably thinks he hit me with that last shot, Flint thought. His reaction time was hampered by the fact that he had to hold on to the rod to keep from falling. So as The Voice came head-on at him, Flint put the free arm out and struck him in the groin. The Voice let out a painful cry and spun to Flint's left. Flint reached for him. It was too late. The Voice, sucking in a desperate breath, dug his finger tips into the hard, wet slate roof and gradually began slipping backward to the front side of the clubhouse. Flint could only listen to a man gasping and fighting to grip anything that would keep him from going over the edge. Just then a streak of lightning flashed from an angry blackened sky and a loud thunder bolt echoed over Saratoga Race Course. It was followed by The Voice's death cry as he slid down the remaining ten feet of slick, slate roof and fell screaming to the pavement right below the famous Whitney Clubhouse box.

When Flint finally made his way to The Voice, the intermittent rain had stopped. The gun was a late model .38 caliber with a silencer. It was on the ground three feet away. Flint could barely make out the dead man's face. It was blackened and red on one side where apparently it struck the building on the way down. He wondered if this was The Voice. The man was dressed in black pants, sneakers, a tight knit shirt and short leather jacket. Flint went through all the man's pockets, but found no identification.

Reaching inside the jacket, however, Flint felt a money belt. He lifted the shirt and examined the belt. Inside he found several one-hundred-dollar bills and a card. He moved over to a red fire light and squinted. "Oh, now there's a surprise," he said aloud. "Here's Lisa Lane's address and her telephone number." He figured the assailant was none other than the elusive Max Steiner. It was simple to figure out. The Voice had contracted Max to get rid of Sweetfeed. The big question Flint had to ponder now was who else was ear-marked for assassination in Saratoga?

He was stunned. The whole Claire Valova, Bifford thing wasn't over by a long shot. Flint then had genuine concern for Dr. Blake and his gang. Flint's gut feeling told him The Voice would be going after the others pronto.

Flint crossed back over the race course to Water Man, this time skipping the all-out sprint. He wanted to make a quick phone call to Dr. Blake. The light was still on in the stall. Flint went in. Water Man was gone. So was the filly. Back outside, Flint looked for any signs of life. He noticed a light from a barn some fifty yards away. There he found a worker sleeping in a chair, a wool blanket wrapped about his body and his feet propped up on a wooden box. He woke the man up.

"You know Water Man?" Flint asked.

"Ya. He works over there. The other barn."

"He was there earlier," said Flint. "He's not there now. Nor is the filly he was caring for."

The worker rubbed his sheepish eyes. "Oh, I know. He sometimes goes and takes care of Sweetfeed's Track Baron. Used to be in that barn next to ours. But Water Man said Sweetfeed moved the Baron last week to another barn. I think it's Barn 26. Yeah. Try Barn 26."

He tugged at the blanket and went back to sleep before Flint could depart.

Flint now saw the light coming from the third stall of Barn 26. He went directly over. As he entered, he stopped dead in his tracks. Track Baron was laying on his side in the center of the floor. Water Man under him. His eyes were two bulging sockets of purplish and red blood and his head, with blood seeping from both ears, was swollen to the size of a ripe melon. The full weight of the dead horse lay on Water Man's chest.

At the barn pay phone, Flint called Dr. Blake.

"Our meeting still on for tomorrow?"

"Yes," Blake assured him.

"Well, be damn careful," Flint warned him. "I'm at the track. Things are not going too well tonight."

"What's happened?" Blake inquired.

"I can't go into that now. In fact, I want to split out of here. Nasty business. Three dead men and one new dead horse. As bad as you can imagine. We can discuss it all at the Castle Rock meeting. See you there."

"Fine Flint," Blake said.

A deepening dark covered the race course as Flint departed the grounds. He felt a cold sweat on his neck and decided he needed a drink. A very stiff double Scotch on the rocks. It had been just that type of night.

30. FLICKER OF HOPE

Noah "Raindeer" Rondee, 82, one of the Adirondack's most acclaimed hermits, stuck his head out of his Au Sable riverbank hut to investigate a weird noise he heard coming from down river. Raindeer first thought it was a bobcat crying. He was used to animal cries in the night, for he'd been a hermit for over 50 years and he spent more time among wild creatures than he did with humans. If a blackbird called, he'd know it right off. Same for a hawk or a swooping blue heron. Deer calls or bear grunts. He'd recognize just about any call but the one he was now hearing. He listened over the rush of the Au Sable. Between the river's noise and a howling damp wind, he picked up bits and pieces of the cry. Then it would fade and begin again.

"Be damned if there ain't someone out there in trouble," he said to himself. He went back in the hut and put on a heavier coat, one made of wool with a canvas waterproof shell. It was the only decent garment he owned. All his other clothing was a mixture of baggy jeans, tattered shirts and smelly moth-eaten sweaters, acquired from mountain dump sites or left for him by hikers on their way through his Adirondack domain. This night, even though it was May, he needed the heavy garment. Noah started down the west side of the river making his way through a tangle of fallen trees and slippery, matted weeds and grass. He'd stop every so often to listen for the cry. When it came, he'd take another bead on its direction, repeating the stop-and-go process several times. At a fork in the river where the main body of water went left and a smaller stream continued right, he halted to get his bearings. At this very moment the cry came loud and clear down along the river bank. He couldn't see anything in the dark, but he moved slowly along the west bank and came out on a gravel bed.

"Who is it?" he called out. "Can you hear me?"

"Is that you Blake?" a voice shouted back.

"No," Noah replied. "It's me, Noah Rondee."

So it was, on one of the darkest spring nights in memory that Frank Duffy, his body severely bruised, wet and on the brink of hypothermia, was found alive. Noah's age kept him from lifting Duffy, but he was able to pull him to higher, dryer ground. Duffy at this point was near convulsions. Noah knew he had to light a fire immediately, yet he had no matches.

"We gotta get you dry, mister. You'll die of cold if we don't."

Duffy tugged at his arm.

"I'll have to go back and get matches. I hope you can last that long."

Duffy could hardly talk at this point. "My pocket. Look in my pocket."

Noah fumbled through Duffy's soggy suit pockets. In the right inner pocket he pulled out a cigarette lighter, barely able to make out what it was he was holding. He pressed the top and nothing happened. He pressed again and this time a flame shot six inches in the air. He jumped back.

Within minutes Noah had a bonfire going. He stripped Duffy and wrapped his canvas coat around him. He then made two other fires so that they could sit in the middle of the burning triangle, heated and protected from the chilled air.

Duffy's suit was eventually dried and he slowly and painfully dressed. It was a struggle guiding him back to Noah's hut, but he made it. A heated cup of elderberry wine and honey did wonders for Duffy's dispirited soul. He later was able to eat some smoked venison and sourdough bread. Noah watched over him as he then slept the deep sleep of an elderly man who had survived against all odds.

The next day, assisted by Noah, they walked five miles to the nearest gas station phone. Duffy called Martha at home. He got no answer. He then called Dr. Blake's office and was told that Martha was in Jay helping with the search. He then called the state police in Jay and told them who he was. The officer on duty transferred the call to a field truck at the search area. When Martha finally came on the line and heard Duffy's voice, she fainted in the truck.

In Saratoga, word of Duffy's rescue brought tears of joy and rejuvenated the gloomy *Saratoga Star* news room staff. Billy Farrell was astonished by the good news. Duffy would be ever grateful to Noah Rondee, but before he could thank him, Noah had slipped away and returned to his solitude. It reminded Duffy of a quote he had once read. "Real reward is in knowing that you helped a human being."

Then he remembered that Noah "Raindeer" Rondee had possession of Claire Valova's engraved lighter, the one Carlos Mann had given Duffy at Hillgate. It was remarkable, he thought, that the propane would still work having not been used since the great fire at Clearwater in 1988. How ironic he thought, that the lighter that had caused so much destruction and grief that fateful night in Schuylerville should in the end, save his life. Was the ghost of Claire Valova trying to redeem itself?

31. STAR BRIGHT, GAS LIGHT

There was a high cloud hanging over Lake George as Dr. Blake entered the long driveway and flipped on the electric switch that activated the lights to the sprawling grounds. The light beams made eerie streaks through the thin spring night air. It had rained not an hour earlier and the grass about the mansion was still wet and glistening. It was shortly before seven and already pitch dark out on the lake. Only a faint gray horizon gave off enough distant light so that Blake could make out the rim of the mountains to the east.

Further down the lake he could also see the reflection of the village lights off the night sky. Had it been July, he'd probably have seen running lights of boats on the lake. But it was too early in the season for this activity, warmer than expected, yet still too cool for night cruising. For Blake it was a night of high expectations. Perhaps, just perhaps they could put the lid on these tragedies. Certainly he was counting on Flint to come across with enough information to tie up the several loose ends of the past few days. Flint's expertise and current knowledge of things seemed like the last hope they all had to unravel this diverse plot and bring it to a head. Blake, like the rest, was growing physically weary of the daily grind and intricacies of the puzzling investigation and the way it had affected so many lives. Duffy's miraculous rescue by Noah Rondee certainly cheered everyone up, but the balance of the investigation bordered on the ridiculous.

The rumor mill was rampant about town during the day, Blake reflected. Sweetfeed, Water Man and the mysterious Steiner's gory deaths dominated the headlines and TV news. Hours after their bodies were discovered at the track, the old town became one big media parade. Hotels, motels, rooming houses and every available bed & breakfast in Saratoga were filling up with news people. Chief Nealy had to sneak out of headquarters to make the meeting. Nealy and several police officers had spent the better part of the day combing the race course area and talking with Joe Hennesy. There was much concern from horse owners and trainers from across the country. Special phones were installed to answer all the calls. Saratoga Chamber of Commerce director, John Ralton, was a wreck from all the pressure on his office.

So much was going on, there was little time to mourn the recent dead. Though the backstretch crowd, with funds donated by several rich owners, did make arrangements to give Water Man and Sweetfeed surprisingly decent funerals. Neither had any immediate family, so it was decided to bury them quickly following a memorial service at the First Baptist Church on Washington St. Of course this could not occur until autopsies had been performed on both men. For that they had been taken to Albany Medical Center Hospital. The backstretch put Hennesy in charge of the funerals mainly because he was, as one worker put it, "their closest friend."

Needless to say, workers on the backstretch were jittery since the murders took place. Hennesy had a particular problem with some of the help, many of whom viewed the killings as a bad omen for the coming race season. Some workers were so shaken by the murders, they quit altogether. No one wanted to work at the barn where Water Man was found dead, so they roped it off and moved the horses to other stalls. In spring they could do this. No incident in recent memory had such an impact on the backstretch. Worst of all, there was no other strong, can-tankerous personality like Sweetfeed to lead them. No father figure to guide this band of horse nomads. His death had put a serious void in the general goodwill and demeanor of the backstretch. Water Man's parting took away the subtle humor needed to maintain a sense of balance among the workers. Dr. Blake had offered to come and counsel the grieving workers in the next few days.

Chief Nealy and Sargeant Galea arrived at Castle Rock ten minutes behind Blake. Billy Farrell, as promised, drove a game yet feeble look-ing Duffy to the meeting. He'd made a fairly good recovery from his Au Sable tribulation, though he wasn't himself by any means. Farrell noticed more than others that Duffy's former spunkiness was gone. His generally quick walk was now slow. He was unsteady on his feet. As Duffy got out of the car Blake came down to assist him. Duffy held up his hands and informed everyone within hearing distance, "I'm perfect-ly capable of walking up those stairs on my own." Though about midway up the stone steps he faltered and Farrell, cupping one arm under Duffy's arm, lifted his friend to the veranda landing. Shortly after, FBI special agent Ken White showed up. Blake then invited them all into Castle Rock's living room.

"Well, gentlemen, we're all here except Flint. I expect he'll be along soon."

All were seated, save for Nealy who paced back and forth near the front window, its drapes drawn shut. It was the first time Blake had seen Nealy dressed in civilian clothes. Out of his chief's uniform he appeared shorter and fatter. The authoritative manner Blake always associated with Nealy was measurably diminished with this mode of dress.

Blake thought he'd relax everyone by offering drinks. As usual, they served themselves. He then toasted Duffy.

"Here's to a fighter. Our friend and close associate. And, I might add, the world's best editor."

"The pen is mightier than the Au Sable," added Nealy, patting Duffy on the shoulder. Blake then opened up the general conversation.

"Again we give thanks for Duffy's rescue," Blake said. "I'm certain Flint will have a lot to add to this gathering when he arrives. The main point is that we all have something to say. Let's not hold back. We can't consider anything too insignificant. Actually we've pieced the bulk of it together," He looked at Nealy. "Wouldn't you say so, Chief?"

"All but a few loose ends," said Nealy. "Witt's still missing. That bothers me. But after the deaths of Sweetfeed, Water Man and Steiner, I don't put out any hope of finding Witt alive. Then, of course, there's Wainwright. I have nothing more to go on but what Stuart Witt said at our meeting, though I have people trying to locate Wainwright. Aside from that, we still have a killer still on the prowl in Saratoga. I guess that's the main reason we're meeting here. Isn't that so, Doc?"

"Yes. Flint is worried for our safety."

"More than ounce of precaution is in order here," Nealy continued. "Till we've solved this case, I've taken the liberty of having Farrell, Duffy and you, Doctor, guarded day and night by some of my officers. They've all volunteered to do it without extra pay. I hope you don't mind. My men are close by. I want everyone on max alert when we leave Castle Rock tonight. I want you to stay that way till we catch the killer. Blake's man Flint warned him we'd all be targets till this is over. The cop in me says he's right. I don't think this killer will stop at anything right now, including me."

"I have some further sad and disturbing news," Agent White said, addressing Nealy. He glanced around the room. "The bureau informs me Wainwright is dead. He was, as Witt told Nealy, an insurance man. All on the up and up. His underwriters paid out some pretty big bucks on some of the dead horses. Turns out Wainwright did some of his own investigation, working through Arlo Spiker, a private investigator in Ocala. Subsequently, however, Spiker had been placed under indictment on insurance fraud. He went to Wainwright and told him what was going on. Spiker thought he'd be able to cut a deal with federal and state prosecutors. We think he told Wainwright about the poisoning aspects and also gave him the plastic cylinders. Why he sent them to

212

you, Tom, is anybody's guess. We may never know. Spiker's ace in the hole, then, was that an indictment doesn't constitute evidence of guilt. The whole case was later thrown out by a friendly Ocala judge. Spiker turned up dead two weeks later in a swamp outside of Ocala. So this leaves us with Witt's disappearance, Fisher's supposed drowning and the three recent deaths at the track unsolved. Still not a very nice situation. Unless, as you say, Blake, Flint has further input on it."

Duffy, who had been sitting with a long face and barely touching his Scotch and water, got to his feet and started to say something. Just then a car came up the drive and parked near the side portico.

"Sorry to cut you short, Duffy," Blake said. "That's probably Flint."

"Oh, I can wait," Duffy managed to say. "God knows we've waited long enough to meet your elusive friend."

Flint's entrance was not what they had expected. Even Blake did a double take as Flint came into the room. To begin with, he was shorter than Nealy had envisioned him. Older than Galea had expected. Surprisingly ruddy appearing in White's opinion and, owing to all the buildup Blake had given him as the personification of an elite investigator, he was dressed in unbecoming sweat pants and matching shirt with red and white Reebok jogging shoes.

Duffy, taking one look at Flint's tanned, roadmap-lined face, sat back down, remarking, "Well, you're no Sherlock Holmes, that's for sure."

"Give me two drinks and I'll talk like him though," Flint replied.

Blake stepped in. "Meet Mike Flint. And no, he's not the local high school coach."

This was just the right touch to break the mixed mood in the room. For what Blake knew and Flint felt upon entering, was that his small group of men, Nealy included, were caught in an unhappy situation that not only affected their personal lives, but the very bedrock of their foundation: Saratoga. The old town was their heart and soul. The murders, and those involved in them, had presented an unseen future for Saratoga as a prime tourist attraction and none of them wanted to face the terrible repercussions associated with this disclosure. If the public really knew Valova and Bifford were part of the horse murders, there would be no end to its collective indignation. Surely the fact that Claire Valova and Anne Bifford were murdered was public knowledge. But aside from those now gathered at Castle Rock, no one else alive, except Harry Waite in New York City and The Voice, knew of their true implications in the insurance schemes. All of these thoughts were weighing very heavily on their minds as Flint faced them.

Flint filled up a glass with straight Scotch and sat down next to Farrell on a couch. "I guess I had better fill you in on my sojourns of the past two weeks." Then he thought about it. "Better yet, I'll begin with the most recent incident." He looked over at Nealy, then at White. "I'll save you some time trying to figure out what really happened last night. Max Steiner was sent in to kill Sweetfeed, which he did before I could stop him. I had no idea he was tracking the old gent. I surmise the fellow they called Water Man was nothing more than a pawn who got killed just because he was in the wrong place at the wrong time. And to take the guess work out of it, I witnessed Steiner's death. He slid off the clubhouse roof on his own. He could have surrendered to me, but he elected not to. It began to rain. The slate roof got slippery. I was flabbergasted when I discovered it was Steiner. I beg your pardon for not staying around when your men finally came to the track, Chief, but I'm sure you can appreciate how precarious my position was at the time. That's why I left his wallet there. I tried to be helpful."

Nealy smiled, as the others sat transfixed by Flint's revelations. "As for Sweetfeed, he played it stupid. From what I can gather I'd guess he was baited to his fateful meeting with Max Steiner, thinking all the time he was on his way to meet the real mastermind, the person Water Man referred to as The Voice. While this meeting was taking place, The Voice apparently went back to the barn and killed Track Baron and Water Man. That's the latest in Saratoga. One week ago I was in Fort Myers, Florida. Steiner's old girlfriend, and I mean old, Lisa Lane, gave me some of his belongings. Suffice it to say he had all the tools required for electrocuting horses. Also ping pong balls and other objects used to suffocate the animals. I even have his private address book. While in the Caribbean before visiting Florida, I obtained a confession from an old war comrade, Ronnie Donato. He's now dead, but he put me on to Steiner.

"Donato. Donato," White broke in. "We've been investigating that guy for over three years. How did you come by him?"

"Oh," replied Flint really not wanting to reveal that Dusty Putts had assisted him, "I had help from a former navy man. Can't recall his name at the moment. I can tell you it was Donato's men who drowned Anne Bifford." White didn't press him further.

"Most of the killers operated in and around Ocala in the early days," Flint informed them. "The stakes got so high later on, and the insurance payoffs so profitable, they expanded out across the country. Eventually,

Saratoga was a natural hunting ground." Flint paused to let everyone refill their drinks. Duffy, propped sideways in his chair, eyed Flint with a quizzical expression. Flint wondered what was going through Duffy's inquisitive newsman's mind. He then went on.

"There was another hired killer, but he's now dead as well. A rather sleazy character known as Ben the Chem. Sleazy but highly educated. A chemist who went down the wrong path and had no other way of paying off his gambling debts. He duped his victims into ingesting cyanide. Ben the Chem was responsible for Claire Valova's prolonged, agonizing death." On this point, Duffy dropped his drink on the thick red and blue oriental rug while letting out a long exacerbated breath. "You tell me she was poisoned by a chemist?"

"Yes," said Flint. "So were many fine horses. Steiner drew no lines between people and horses."

"Well, there's not much more to say. My preoccupation now is figuring out who The Voice is." He then eyeballed each one in the room and added, "For all I know, it could be one of you. If that hypothesis sounds far out, just consider how strange this whole thing is. Better yet, ask Agent White how far the FBI has taken the insurance fraud investigations. What's it now, Mr. White, fifty-eight or sixty people facing indictments?"

"Pretty close," admitted White.

"It'll probably double in a few months," Flint assured them. "Logic tells me it's not all connected. It may have originated in Ocala, but once it got going, many other devious minds decided to ride the insurance train. No, it's very big, very widespread and extremely complex. Knowing this doesn't help us at the moment, though. We still have our problems to figure out in Saratoga. The Voice is out there waiting and watching. I'd dare say he has better eyes then we do at this point. And that's a simple deduction. He knows what he's looking for and we don't. He can pick you off one at a time, and do it at his own pace. You're all very easy targets, I'm afraid. This also applies to me. He knew I was involved somehow, or else I wouldn't have been attacked in Florida. What we have to do here and now is some serious brainstorming. Let's begin by playing the name game. Names. Single names. Male or female, it doesn't matter."

"Damn silly," Duffy mumbled.

"Perhaps," said Blake. "Except for one thing. It helps us eliminate a lot of names in the process. You may even kick in a name not previously considered as a possible suspect. Just start spitting out names. Coworkers. Insurance brokers. Horse owners. Trainers. Hot walkers. Backstretch hands. Get the drift? Real interesting when you name names. I'll begin with you, Chief."

Nealy stood up and stretched his arms above his head. "Christ, if I have to name everyone I know at the race course officially or unofficially sanctioned by the NYRA, it'll take a week."

Flint persisted. "If you can think of just one, then maybe we can determine if there is ample motive for that person or persons to be a suspect. Get my meaning?"

"Why there's hundreds of such people," Nealy insisted. "This is an exercise in futility. I see no sense in this."

"You're taking me too literally," Flint shot back. "Be realistic. I'm not asking you to name the parish priest or rabbi. I want names that may fit. For example, who may have access to the key Thoroughbreds. Who, for example, might be privy to the insurance records? Who is processing the claims for the carriers? Maybe they're in cahoots with The Voice. That's what I'm striving for. So let's start tossing out some names."

Blake opened a desk drawer and took out some of his uncle's monogrammed stationery. "Might just as well write them down," he said. "There's extra pens if you need one."

"I've got some names, but I'll be damned if I can spell all of 'em," Galea noted.

"No problem," said Blake. "Relate them to the good editor here. Duffy's our human dictionary. Aren't you, Duffy?"

"If you insist," Duffy said.

So it began. Duffy's left hand scribbling down names as fast as they could deliver them. No one was left out. Galea even came up with Antoni Ballo, the clubhouse captain. Nealy added Larry Wentworth, the chief steward. As Flint had said, there was a litany of names popping up that had either not been considered before or completely forgotten over time. Duffy would pause every so often to remark, "Oh, yes, I remember that name," or "Wasn't that person related to this or that family?" It became a sort of contest to see who could come up with the most names. All found themselves scrambling to better the list. Blake and Flint were mildly amused by it.

******

As the small group in Castle Rock proceeded with this exercise, four of Nealy's volunteer officers were gathered in the Algonquin Restaurant just down the hill, waiting for Nealy to signal them when the meeting was concluded.

They consisted of Detectives John McLaughlin, Steve Harris, Olan Blazer and Sergeant Tim Block. All were seasoned members of Saratoga's police force, boasting forty years of combined service. McLaughlin was the senior officer, having just one week earlier celebrated his fifteenth year on the job. If they hadn't volunteered, Nealy would most likely have asked them. He wanted the best men possible for this zigzag game. Besides, for the first time in his long police career, he felt personally threatened.

The four had arrived at the Algonquin in two unmarked police cars which were parked near the main entrance. Each officer had something to eat and then relaxed over coffee. Out in the Algonquin parking lot, moving slowly toward the two cars, a figure hesitated and then came forward. Within seconds of his appearance, the tires of the two vehicles were slashed, the rush of escaping air drowned out by the blare of the Algonquin's TV. Satisfied that the tires were fully deflated, the lone figure slipped away.

At Castle Rock, the listing of names continued. Part way through the list, Carlos Mann's name came up. All eyes turned on Duffy.

"What about Mann?" asked Nealy. "Frank, you damn near lost your life following your visit with Mann. What do you make of it?"

Duffy looked thoughtfully down at the paper he was writing on. Nealy's question posed two dilemmas for Duffy. First of all, he was sworn to keep Mann's trust. Secondly, by keeping that trust, he was compromising his personal and journalistic ethics. He decided to fend off Nealy's question in the only way he knew how. "Nothing of substance, Chief. I thought by now you would have touched base with the state police who investigated Hillgate after my accident. Any word on who might have tampered with my car?"

"I thought you had received that report?" Nealy said.

"Not a word," Duffy snorted.

"Well, I'll get you one. Your brake lines were cut. At least that's what they reported."

"Funny that I should be the last to know about it," Duffy blurted out.

"Let's not get personal here," said Flint. "We haven't all night to do this."

To draw Nealy's attention away from Carlos Mann, Duffy threw in Doctor Little's name.

"John Little runs Hillgate. It doesn't seem sensible to include him, but for the sake of this exercise, I'm including Little. Is that fine by everyone?"

"Anyone's name, regardless of their position," Flint assured him.

An hour later they had compiled some one hundred and eighty names. Duffy was getting writer's cramp.

Flint and Blake reviewed the list. "OK," said Flint. "We'll read the names and you fill in missing parts. What I'm striving for here is clarity. If you think individually or collectively that the name called out really doesn't belong, we'll eliminate it. Once we've narrowed it down to a reasonable number, we can break up in teams and try to refine our reasons for keeping a particular name on the list. Nealy can work with Galea. I'll review it with Blake. After all, most of these names mean nothing to me. Farrell, Duffy and White can work together." Flint checked his watch. "Let's try and do this in the next hour."

Duffy found the whole thing repulsive. He got more disturbed when Joe Hennesy was considered as a suspect. Under his breath he was saying to himself, "Why don't we dig up my great grandfather and implicate him?" And he almost laughed when someone proposed Molly Fullmont's name. After all, Duffy reasoned, how likely would it be that an NYRA trusted accountant turn out to be The Voice? He went along with it, however, hastily writing away as the teams filtered through the names. Eventually, they had whittled the list to 25 names and were laboring to refine it even further. Flint then suggested they take a ten-minute break to which Duffy, rubbing a numbing left arm, wholeheartedly agreed.

Blake and Flint went out on the veranda for fresh air. Duffy mixed another drink and sat down. Nealy, Galea and White went in search of the bathrooms.

On the veranda Blake mentioned the Butcher mansion to Flint, relating how he had seen Mr. Butcher earlier in the season. Further telling Flint that he had gone to see his uncle's neighbor but found the place still shut tight. In fact, he hadn't seen any signs that Butcher had been there, though there's no denying he walked across Castle Rock's lawn the day in question.

"Could be it wasn't Butcher," Flint said.

"No. I'm sure it was Butcher. He walked with his cane and that limping gate he's always had. It had to be him."

"How old is he?" Flint inquired. "Does he have family up here?"

"He's pushing mid-eighties," Blake guessed. "Reclusive by nature. Fond of cult religions and very much into spiritualism, much like the former owner of Castle Rock. I once saw his mansion full of burning candles. The smoke was so thick you couldn't breathe inside, but you couldn't open a door or window because one big draft would sweep fire through the place. I know Uncle fooled with it for a time. Not so much that he believed like Butcher does, but merely to placate a neighbor. Still, I run across many modern-day spiritualists in my counseling sessions in Saratoga. I'm surprised at how many I encounter that come from traditional religions. At the root of much of it is simply mind control. Once they're hooked, they're hooked."

Flint suddenly had a wild thought. "Doc, I think you've hit it."

"Hit on what?"

"The Voice, that's what. Ben the Chem was found dead with dozens of candles in his home. Not lit, mind you, but still candles. Harry Waite's men couldn't understand it at the time either. Valova was prone to following weird paths. Troubles stemming from her childhood. It all begins to fit. I don't know if Sweetfeed was into cults, but I'd dare say it's a fair guess. Your theory of mind control. How else could The Voice involve so many prominent people in the insurance scams? There had to be more to it than money. On the other hand, a dedicated follower would go along with anything. Do you agree?"

"Well, let's say I don't disagree. But even at that, it's stretching a point."

Flint became excited. "Ever hear of Eric Hoffer? He wrote *True Believer,* a marvelous book. His main theme was that true believers will follow any cause blindly. It's conceivable Valova and the others were true believers in an unjust but believable cause."

Blake weighed Flint's words, saying, "Insurance fraud isn't exactly a cause. People can be swayed, I grant you. Greed sounds more normal in this case. Maybe fear had something to do with it. Yet, that's not to say they weren't caught up in cult activity of some sort. Was Butcher a part of it? Unlikely. Most unlikely."

Once again inside Castle Rock everyone sat down and Duffy, reading from all his notes, began highlighting the pros and cons of the list. He was just about to hand out some of the notes to Blake when Castle Rock went completely dark. Flint's instincts immediately told him a crisis was at hand.

The darkened room suddenly filled with a sour odor and a hissing sound which both Flint and Agent White immediately recognized as gas being let out of a pressurized cylinder.

"Who the hell dowsed the lights?" Duffy shouted.

"Keep quiet," Flint ordered. "Get on the floor and lay on your stomach. We're being gassed." While he spoke, Flint was sliding toward the kitchen door. Nealy, however, had another plan of action. He rose, grabbed the first solid object he could find in the dark and tossed it at the picture window. The glass shattered in one loud burst, and the rush of Lake George cold night air that invaded Castle Rock pushed the gas all about the room. Blake had by this time managed to reach the front door which he flung open. Instead of providing immediate relief from the eye and throat burning fumes, the air blowing in the front door neutralized the air coming in from the window, so that the fumes remained penetrating and suffocating. Billy Farrell, rising to get out of the area, was the first to collapse. He hit the floor with a thud right next to Duffy. Galea passed out when he tried to sit up. Nealy was going fast. White covered his head and stayed face down on the rug, breathing as little as possible. Only Blake at the front door and Flint, now already in the kitchen, were conscious. Flint, crawling and feeling his way in the dark, reached the stove and tried to turn on the exhaust fan. No power. All electricity was out. Flint then rolled over and was making his way back to the living room when the side kitchen door opened and a silhouetted form appeared. A flashlight beam went over Flint's head, and the stranger came forward unaware of Flint beneath his feet. It was then Flint struck with his right foot, hitting the intruder solidly between the legs. The flashlight dropped and the stranger went flying backward. Flint picked up the light and shined it at the door. He was just in time to see a dark form going over the porch railing, followed by a loud scream. Flint's lungs were still fighting the fumes, but he managed to make it to the porch and direct the light down on the ground. The intruder was gone. It was a matter of pursuing the stranger or returning to rescue those in the living room. He heard one of them coughing and wheezing. He had no choice. By the time he was back in the living room, Blake had pulled Nealy safely to the veranda and was trying to remove Farrell's hulk. Together they dragged him out. White recovered from the initial gas attack and assisted Duffy outside. Galea, who had taken in a good amount of gas, struggled, and crawled out on his own. Nealy staggered to his car and called for backup. John McLaughlin was the first to respond.

"Get your tail up here quick," Nealy barked. "We've been gassed. No sirens. But come fast."

The scramble to the cars at the Algonquin left a shocked waitress holding a tray of refilled coffee cups and a stunned look on patrons' faces. Only to become baffling when the four officers came running back inside demanding the use of anyone's vehicle. Quickly they showed their badges.

McLaughlin and his men settle for a ride in the Algonquin busboy's pickup truck, a breezy and perilous trip down a narrow, two-lane road to Castle Rock. McLaughlin, was grinding gears everytime he shifted the four-speed vehicle. Harris, Blazer and Block sat on a clump of soggy pine bark chips that smelled rancid. Every bump in the winding road sent tremors through their bodies. Halfway to Castle Rock McLaughlin saw a red light flashing. He gunned it but the red light kept after him. Then there were two red lights flashing and eventually a third. When they finally pulled into Castle Rock's drive, there were four sheriff's patrol cars and two trooper cars in pursuit of the pickup. Nealy, witnessing the flashing noisy caravan from his perch on the veranda, cursed McLaughlin at the top of his voice.

What had really taken place at Castle Rock and what was the leak in the mansion. Blake, Galea and Duffy went along with Nealy's story that there was apparently carbon monoxide built up in the mansion. Flint and Agent White had departed the premises in separate directions minutes earlier. Neither man wanted to be identified at Castle Rock. White's position was very sensitive. There'd be no forgiveness on the bureau's part should his part in this investigation be exposed. Flint had no badge to lose. He did, however, have a killer to catch. His best hunch was that the killer was holed up in Butcher's mansion. It was just a gut feeling, which was often Flint's most trusted barometer in these matters. As he made his way through the tangle of shrubs and maze of hedges between the two estates, Flint could hear all the commotion coming from Castle Rock.

On the far side of the Castle Rock property, the landscape dropped off so that he had to cross over a small bridge spanning a stream that flowed to the lake. Butcher's mansion was all dark when Flint came up the hill on the other side. He moved cautiously till he came within twenty yards of the darkened stone building. He made his way to the south side where the drive turned to face the lake and a broad set of stairs climbed to a roofed porch. No signs of any movement. He went up on the porch and backed along the outer wall till he came to a set of large, double lake-view windows. He took a look inside. The curtains and drapes were closed but he could make out flickering light. The light would come and go, casting shadows on the curtains. Nearer to the front door, Flint lifted himself up so he could get a better look through a side panel window. His eyes were drawn to dozens of burning candles. They were set all about the entrance hall and into the far room, which he took for the main sitting room. If only Blake were here

221

to see this, he thought. Paranormal activity was alive and thriving on Lake George, Flint mused. He could feel The Voice's presence in that moment. Every fiber in Flint's body told him The Voice was inside. How to flush him out without losing him was the secret. He could just go charging in, or he could spook him by making noises at several locations around the mansion. Flint then had a better idea. He decided he'd do the very thing The Voice would not be prepared for. He'd ring the door bell. If The Voice thought for a moment he was secure in Butcher's house, he'd have to think twice if someone rang the door bell at this hour of night.

So without hesitation, Flint pressed the bell. A series of chimes immediately began ringing. In the split second it took to ring the bell, Flint heard someone run across the room. Moments later, Flint heard a door slam. Then, out of the corner of his right eye, he caught a glimpse of someone dashing by the side of the mansion, headed toward the lake. In one big jump, Flint cleared the entire length of steps and was in pursuit. He was running down a steep lawn in the direction of Butcher's boathouse. As he approached the dock area, a motor started up. Flint ran to the end of the dock and was just in time to catch a speedboat pulling out of the boathouse. He leaped at the person behind the wheel, forcing them both to fall backward as the craft spun wildly about twenty yards off shore. Flint struck the first blow, a sharp closed fist into his opponent's midsection, followed by an equally solid blow to the right shoulder. It was then he realized he'd hit a rock-hard body. This reality became more evident as the stranger sprang to his feet and drove an elbow into Flint's face. Flint went down from the force of the blow and the slipperiness under foot. When he went to regain his footing, the dark figure came at him again. As he was about to strike Flint, the boat turned sharply to the right and he went over the side into the frigid lake water. Flint fumbled till he found the ignition key and turned the engine off.

The stranger surfaced near the boat but backed off as Flint reached out his hand. Then he began swimming back toward the boathouse. Flint had no intention of going into the freezing water after him, so he tried starting the engine. The engine sputtered once or twice but wouldn't start. He pulled on the choke lever and tried again. More sputtering. Again and again Flint tried. He could hear the stranger nearing the boathouse, amazed that he made it that far without succumbing to the cold water. "God, I'm losing him," Flint muttered in frustration. Suddenly the engine kicked over. Flint shoved the throttle forward and headed for the boathouse. He didn't waste any time docking the craft. Instead he jumped to the wooden deck and left the engine running in neutral.

Flint was dry and had recovered from the initial blows. With his opponent thoroughly wet and no doubt chilled to the bone, Flint felt he had the advantage in the chase. Though still dark, Flint heard his attacker's heavy breathing as he apparently made his way toward the mansion. Flint also felt it wasn't likely he'd try to go into the mansion, so Flint cut on a bias to the mansion's west side where the driveway ended at a large parking area. Whoever it was, they'd be going for their vehicle, Flint guessed. As Flint cleared the corner he made out the outline of a vehicle. He went straight for it. It turned out to be a van and it was locked. He saw no other cars in the vicinity.

As he prepared to go back around to the east side, the undeniable roar of a motorcycle engine broke the silence of the night. A single headlight shown in Flint's face blinding him. It bore down on him, its exhaust pipes spitting sparks three feet long, illuminating the driveway, its engine screeching. Flint did the only thing he could do. He kicked out as high as he could at the passing cycle and his foot caught the driver's face square in the nose and eyes. Flint was thrown to one side, landing on his left shoulder in a soft grassy area. The bike, however, with its rider still on it, careened to one side, spun madly and went crashing over a hedge row. Flint heard it strike something metallic, and then all went silent.

It had not been one of his better chases, he conceded to himself, as he slowly got up and went to investigate. He approached the hedge and walked around it. As he was about to search the darkened area, a bright light suddenly lit up the area. Flint jumped for cover. Then the familiar voice of Dr. Blake shouted. "You out there, Flint?"

It was followed by Nealy calling, "What the hell happened here?"

Flint remained hidden near the hedgerow till they came forward. Then he stepped clear so they could see him. "Never know who you're going to meet on a dark night," Flint quipped. "But God A'mighty, I'm glad it's you two."

"Heard that awful crash," said Nealy. "Thought for a moment Butcher's mansion had collapsed."

"Not a chance of that," said Flint. "It'll be standing long after we've all departed this world. No, what you heard was someone trying to run me over with a motorcycle. Fortunately, it missed me. Shine those lights over in that direction and you'll find whoever it was."

Blake drew a beam on a section near the hedgerow where a wrought iron fence wrapped around a stone wall and ended at an exit gate. Nealy's light found the motorcycle. It was wedged between the iron struts, its handle bars crushed in a pretzel shape and its front and rear tires tangled together. Blake moved in closer and ran his light down the fence. Just at the entrance, impaled on the spiked fence, was a body. The spikes were driven clear through the rider's chest and protruded from just below the shoulder blades. His clothing was wet. Flint went over and took a look.

"Well, he said, "it's a man. This must be The Voice. Who'd ever think we'd end it this way?" Anyone you know, gentlemen?"

Nealy went up for a closer look. "Oh, no," he said in disgust. "It's Randy Scott."

"Who?" asked Blake.

"Scott. Randy Scott. The landscaper."

"Funny," Flint added. "He ended up where he belongs. In a landscaper's paradise. Now figure that one out."

Nealy and Blake took a further look, but avoided touching Scott. Flint sat down on the lawn.

"How did you handle the holy hell at Castle Rock earlier?"

Blake answered. "Nealy told them it was a carbon monoxide leak that had built up. You know something, they all bought the story. For a time I thought Duffy might be principled enough to tell them the truth, but he didn't. He hasn't been acting himself since his trip north. There was a time when Duffy wouldn't think of lying. I guess old age does that to people."

"True," said Nealy, still standing near Scott and shaking his head in disbelief. "My boys blew it. I was embarrassed to no end when the sheriff and the troopers tailed McLaughlin and the rest from the Algonquin. McLaughlin claims his tires were slashed, so he borrows this damn truck and next thing he knows, every cop in Warren County shows up. Damn foolishness if you ask me. Oh, I didn't fool Sheriff Baker for one minute. But he figured I was covering for good reasons, so he backed off the questioning. I told them all to stay at the house and we'll be back. I assume White made it out of there in time, though we haven't heard a word from him. Not often you get an FBI agent to play along with you. I expect they'll be back when things settle down. That is, of course, if they think others are still involved in Saratoga."

Sargeant Galea came running up and they caught him up quickly. He instantly remembered questioning Scott and not being satisfied.

"Damn," he snapped, too loudly.

"Let's get into the mansion," Flint said. He ran out so fast he didn't exactly have time to lock the door." Nealy told Galea to stay with the body.

As they entered, the stifling, choking scent of burning candles made their eyes water. Throughout each room it was the same. Red, blue and yellow candles of all sizes. In the outer drawing room Flint discovered a small chest sitting on a round oak table. Around the chest were several cards. Each had a devil face drawn on it. He flipped one over and saw Claire Valova's name.

"Come see this. I believe these cards tell us all we need to know."

Blake and Nealy turned more cards over. All the names were there: Ben Lewis, Max Steiner, Ann Bifford and Ronnie Donato. Flint opened the chest. It contained a gold plate with the initials RS. There were also two more devil cards, but neither had names attached.

"It's my bet RS was recruiting two others. Wonder who they could have been?"

Nealy observed the gold plate. "What I'm trying to figure out is how Randy Scott got access to this place?"

"That's easy, replied Blake. "He's been the landscaper here for over five years. In fact, he's done landscaping for every prominent family in Saratoga and Lake George. Only logical that Butcher would trust him implicitly. Christ, he had keys to most estates he landscaped for."

Flint picked up the chest and dumped all the cards into it. "See no reason to leave this around now, do you?"

"No reason at all," agreed Blake.

"Likewise," said Nealy.

"I'll do my uncle's friend a favor and douse all the candles," Blake offered. "Then I'm all for locking the place up and going back to Castle Rock to clean up a little. Are we all in agreement on this?"

"As for Randy Scott, I'll leave that in your hands, Chief. You're the expert at the well-placed phone call. Maybe it would be a feather in Sheriff Baker's cap if he were the one to solve this case. This will help keep Saratoga slightly more sheltered from the fallout when the media gets hold of it. And while I'm at it, I see no reason to drag Claire Valova and Ann Bifford's names any further into this mess. It would serve no purpose now and I'm damn sure it would be very harmful to Saratoga on the whole. Besides the names we've just seen on those cards, there is no real proof that they were guilty of anything. If Randy Scott had used mind control on them, they'd be less guilty. I believe you see my point?"

"I'm done with my investigation," said Flint. "It's your town, you know what's best for it." Nealy pressed his hands together and pondered the doctor's statement. "The community comes first, Doc. I go along with that."

They went back to get Sheriff Baker. Everyone, except Flint, returned to Castle Rock. He held back for a few minutes and decided he'd take a look upstairs in Butcher's mansion. His investigators curiosity and a inner gnawing told him that the landscaper thing just didn't fit. So he went up the long, wide carpeted stairs and started going from room to room. On the far end of the hallway, just past the bedrooms, he entered a narrow room that wrapped around to a double glass door that lead out to a balcony. From the door he could see down into the garden where Scott's lifeless body was impaled. Even for a man of Flint's experience, it was an eerie sight. The Sheriff hadn't gotten to the mansion yet. Flint was about to leave the room when he suddenly heard a floor squeaking above him. Then he noticed another door. He opened it and found a pair of stairs leading to the attic area. He had a small flashlight in his pocket, which he took out. Slowly and cautiously he went up the stairs. As he reached the attic he heard something drop to his right. Flint turned off the flashlight. He heard a moaning sound, followed by heavy breathing. He flicked on the light. A man's body, completely wrapped in plastic, except for his head, lay on the attic floor. His eyes were swollen and his mouth was covered with silver duct tape. Blood was caked on his thick black hair. Flint moved quickly to remove the tape, rolling the man on his back as he did so. He started to remove the plastic.

"God, man. What's happened here?" Flint said.

He got no response. The man moaned again.

"Can you hear me?" Flint said.

One eye opened and the man managed to whisper. "Are you Father Doyle? Have you come to save my soul? Thank the Lord I can be saved before I die. Thank the Lord."

Flint realized in that instant he was listening to a dying man. A man in mortal fear of meeting his maker, wanting badly to confess. So Flint went along with the man's wishes.

"Yes, I'm Father Doyle. Confess your sins. I'll pray for your soul."

In words Flint could barely hear, the man wheezed, his breathing became faint, as he revealed his identity during his last moments.

"Bless Joe Hennesy, Father. Bless and forgive all my dark deeds of these past few years. I never wanted to kill horses nor any person. You must believe me. I was not myself. I was a victim of Butcher's spiritualism and his mystic world. We all were, all that took part in it. I do hope you understand. It was not for the money. We were powerless under the cult's influence. The money people are all evil. Butcher taught us that. Claire Valova and the rest. They were prisoners of their own wealth. Someone had to put an end to it all. Bless me Father for I have sinned. I have sinned gravely."

The fat face turned upward to look at Flint with the one open eye. Hennesy's color was a pale gray. Flint lifted one hand and felt it grow cold.

"Go on. Tell me more," Flint insisted.

His voice began to fade. He struggled. Somehow he found the strength to continue. He would not be denied this confession. The voice was filled with guilt and remorse.

"I know what I have done. I'm willing to accept the Lord's judgment. I denounce all my involvement in Butcher's spiritualism. Ask the Lord to keep me out of the fire of Hell. Please intercede on my behalf." Hennesy let out a long sigh, then went on. "I will pay for my sins. I know that. I hope the person who did this to me will do the same. I want you to pray for Randy Scott. A young man who hasn't yet seen the error of his murderous way. May he find the truth before it's too late. The killing must stop. It must stop for good. I recruited Randy and he recruited others. I never thought he'd turn on me. But then I should have expected it. We all turned on each other in the end. Bless his soul, anyway. And, yes, Father, I was The Voice they were so scared of."

Flint watched helplessly as Hennesy took one more rattling breath and died. The fingers of his right hand closing tightly on Flint's wrist as he went to meet his Maker.

Flint left the attic and the mansion and walked slowly back to Castle Rock.

Dr. Blake and Chief Nealy were flabbergasted when Flint filled them in on Hennesy. Nealy listened in disbelief to Flint's account of Hennesy's confession. How they would eventually explain all this to Duffy was anybody's guess. Of all people, they all agreed that Hennesy was the last one Duffy would ever suspect. They weren't sure he could take this shock. It was decided, however, that Dr. Blake would break the news to him. At least Saratoga could begin its racing season by shedding the dark cloud and fear that had hung so ominously above its historic city for all these uncertain months.

Sheriff Baker came in to say goodbye to Nealy and the rest.

"Ready for this?" Baker asked. "We just got a message to relay to you that the NYRA people at the track found your missing man, Stuart Clayborn Witt this afternoon."

"Where?" Nealy asked. " Some place on the track grounds?"

"Right on the money," Baker said. " One of the backstretch people discovered Witt's remains when dogs were barking at the end of the giant culvert pipe that serves as a drain for the track. Don't know yet how he died, but it was a pretty gruesome discovery. The boys say it smelled like hell down there."

"My men searched that very area and found nothing," Nealy assured him. "You never know."

"One more thing," said Baker. "A large gold ring with Witt's initials was found in Sweetfeed's barn area. They think Sweetfeed most likely killed Witt. What do you think?"

"I'd believe anything at this juncture," said Nealy. "Thanks for your help, Sheriff."

He turned to Blake and Flint. "I won't soon forget this day. I guess none of us will."

At Castle Rock, Flint placed a call to Sandy in California. She was speechless when she heard his voice. "You're alive and breathing," she said. "We had our doubts. I couldn't sleep at night. I'd walk Palos Verdes cove from one end to the other wondering about you. It is really you, isn't it? Oh, speak to me again. I have to know it's your voice."

"Yes, It's me. I'm OK. We're done here. I want you to meet me in New York City. Then we're going to finish that vacation in the Caribbean."

"You're kidding?"

"Not kidding. I mean to finish it in style. But we'll go a bit further down this time, perhaps to Aruba. Yes, Aruba. I'll have Harry make the call. He's got a friend in Aruba."

Sandy stopped talking.

"Are you there?" asked Flint, switching the phone from ear to ear.

"I never want to go to any place that Harry Waite knows about. That's out. I'll make the arrangements. Is it a deal?"

"Love," Flint laughed, "you can do anything you want."

"Remember," she warned him, "no conversations with Harry. Promise?"

"I promise."

"Good. Then I'll make flight plans tonight. We'll meet in South Carolina, not New York. See you love."

EPILOGUE

There was a joyous reunion of sorts off the Caribbean island of Aruba aboard *Big Fish*, shortly after Flint and Sandy arrived to complete their previously interrupted vacation. It was hosted by Dusty Putts who, in putting the special event together, decided he'd make a double celebration by announcing his own retirement from the service.

Midway through the evening, Putts came over to Flint and Sandy and made a further startling announcement.

"I'm getting married. Imagine that. An old salt like me tying the knot."

Flint held Sandy's hand and he felt her fingers tighten around his as Putts said it. "That's great news, Dusty. I assume you've rekindled a former relationship?"

"No," said Putts. "I'm starting a new one. New and young. Like you and Sandy, I'm cradle robbing a bit. I find it flattering."

Sandy blushed and looked away.

"I'd like to introduce you to the future Mrs. Putts." Out of the midst of some gathered white uniforms came Sharon Spear, the pretty CIA agent. Sandy shook her hand and Flint bent over and kissed her lightly on the forehead. Putts was beaming.

"Old guys are in these days," Flint teased her.

"Age is a relative thing," she countered.

"Experience triumphs over youth," Sandy observed.

"No," said Sharon. "Youth recognizes maturity. This could go on all night."

"Much success and happiness," Flint added. "We want to be at that wedding."

"You're already on the guest list," said Putts. "We might get married in California, so you won't have far to travel." He turned to face Sandy. "This can be contagious. Better yet, we could even make it a double wedding. That is if he's ready to make it a permanent thing between you two."

Flint's eyebrows raised up. "Let us know the date and we'll see if we can work it into our schedule."

"Is that a proposal?" asked Sandy.

"I don't know. I've never proposed before. Would you call that a proposal, Dusty?"

Putts didn't hear him. He was holding Sharon and looking out at the rolling ocean. Sandy put both arms around Flint's shoulders and whispered in one ear. "Married or not, you'll always be mine."

The party ended as the sun was beginning to set off Aruba. Putts saw to it that Flint and Sandy were given transportation back to the island. Before departing *Big Fish*, Putts handed Flint a newspaper wrapped in plastic.

"Thought you'd enjoy reading the editorial page. Remember that date in California is open for one more couple at the altar of St. John the Divine Church in Palo Alto. September 5th is the date. If you're not Catholic, bring your friendly preacher, we're very liberal Christians."

On the ride to Aruba, Flint took out the newspaper. He showed it to Sandy. "Wouldn't you know, it's the Saratoga Star. I can guess. Frank Duffy's magic words are inside."

Editorial:
Opening Day Jitters
By Frank Duffy, Senior Editor

No one dreads opening day at the race course more than I do. I dread it for one good reason. I get no meaningful work done when the Chic Chic's are running. They occupy all my time. As the kids like to put it, I'm a Saratoga Race Course junkie. Win or lose, I'm addicted to the track. Much like I'm addicted to Saratoga as a place. For it was in this magical kingdom seventy-odd years ago I was born. I remember when track-goers had all they could do to keep from spending their hard earned dollars at the gambling parlors on their way to the big oval on Union Avenue. Many say we should return to those days. I'm not so sure it's a good idea anymore.

Things being what they are, enough surplus dollars are spent in the few days the track is open. If you have gambling all the time, common sense tells me the average bettor won't have much left come race time. No, I'd rather save my greenbacks for the track. Besides, it's more exciting watching Thoroughbreds than slot machines and roulette tables. So much for casino gambling.

Every year has its seasons. This spring in Saratoga was a bad one. It seemed as if we were being put to the ultimate test of will. It began with the untimely deaths of Claire Valova and Ann Bifford, and came crashing down with the eventual deaths of Sweetfeed and Water Man. I have purposely omitted the last two proper names because if you don't know them by their nicknames, this piece will have no relevance for you. As the workers on the backstretch often say, "It's something only among us." Meaning, if you will, among Saratogians. The old Spa was crying out in spring for justice. Wrongs had been done. Murders were committed. There was treachery and mayhem in sufficient quantity. Its ugly tentacles reached far beyond Saratoga, but we felt it most severely because we had thought of ourselves as above such deceitfulness. Greed renders some powerless against reason. The cowardly act of murder took those near and dear to our hearts. We grieved, as we should. Like it or not, we ran scared. My personal misfortune has taught me a good lesson. I now view life with a more passionate intensity. More respect. You should too.

So as the track season begins, let us all pull together to make Saratoga stronger. Whether it is in dealing with your elected officials or the man, woman and child you meet on the street. And let us remember that the good of the community is in all of us every day of our lives. Saratoga is our past and future. One nasty spring doesn't unsaddle such a treasured heritage.

Finally, to a man I know named Mike Flint, wherever you are. We salute you. Don't be a stranger to our town.

The End